The PENDRAGON™ fiction line presents the best of modern Arthurian literature, from reprints of long-unavailable classics of the early twentieth century to new works by today's most exciting and inventive fantasists. The titles in the series are selected for their value to both the casual reader and the devoted scholar of the rich, varied story cycle known as the Matter of Britain.

More Titles From Green Knight

Percival and the Presence of God
by Jim Hunter

Arthur, The Bear of Britain
by Edward Frankland

To the Chapel Perilous
by Naomi Mitchison

Kinsmen of the Grail
by Dorothy James Roberts

The Life of Sir Aglovale de Galis
by Clemence Housman

The Doom of Camelot
edited by James Lowder

Forthcoming

The Arthurian Companion, Second Edition
by Phyllis Ann Karr
[January 2001]

The Pagan King
by Edison Marshall
[March 2001]

**The Merriest Knight:
The Collected Arthurian Tales of
Theodore Goodridge Roberts**
edited by Mike Ashley
[May 2001]

Legends of the Pendragon
edited by James Lowder
[August 2001]

PENDRAGON™ Fiction

EXILED FROM CAMELOT

Cherith Baldry

GREEN KNIGHT PUBLISHING

Exiled From Camelot is published by Green Knight Publishing.

Exiled From Camelot © 2001 by Cherith Baldry; all rights reserved.

Cover art © 2001 by Richard Pace; all rights reserved.

Similarities between characters in this book and persons living or dead are entirely coincidental.

PENDRAGON is a trademark owned by Green Knight Publishing.

Reproduction of material from within this book for purposes of personal or corporate profit, by photographic, digital, or other methods of electronic storage and retrieval, is prohibited.

Please address questions and comments concerning this book, as well as requests for notices of new publications, by mail to Green Knight Publishing, 900 Murmansk Street, Suite 5, Oakland, CA 94607.

Green Knight Publishing
Publisher: Peter Corless
Executive Editor: James Lowder
Consulting Editor: Raymond H. Thompson

Visit our web page at: http://www.greenknight.com

FIRST PAPERBACK EDITION

10 9 8 7 6 5 4 3 2 1

Green Knight publication GK6207, January 2001.

ISBN 1-928999-16-6

Printed in the United States.

Acknowledgements

I should like to thank my agent, Bill Neill-Hall;
my editor, Jim Lowder;
my sons, Will and Adam, for asking the right questions;
members of the Brighton and Bromley writers' groups,
for comment and criticism;
and especially Phyllis Ann Karr, for unfailing encouragement.

IN MEMORY OF

PETER BALDRY

1947 - 1999

'…Gawayn, with his olde curteisye,
Though he were comen ayeyn out of Fairye,
Ne coude hym nat amende with a word.'
                Chaucer, *The Squire's Tale*, 95-7

Chapter One

Sir Kay, High Seneschal of Britain, placed his elbows on the edge of the Round Table, rested his chin on his hands, and suppressed a faint sigh. Somewhere across the golden reaches of the Table, Sir Colgrevaunce was maundering on about the need to hold out the hand of friendship to King Claudas of Brittany. Colgrevaunce was a great one for holding out the hand of friendship, especially if the recipient was a safe distance away.

Kay wondered whether it was worth noting that King Claudas had been a pestilential nuisance for more than twenty years, since before Arthur pulled the sword out of the stone. Undoubtedly Claudas would go on being a pestilential nuisance for twenty years more, if the Lord in His infinite wisdom saw fit to spare him.

Only the knowledge that any argument he sparked would prolong an already tedious council kept Kay silent. He had a thousand things to do between now and supper; exchanging insults with Colgrevaunce was one he could well do without. Irritably his eyes flicked round the Table, meeting first of all the profile of Sir Gawain of Orkney. Gawain was seated beside him, his face evoking the eager austerity of a carved angel. Even looking at Gawain communicated to Kay something of the younger man's repose.

Beyond Gawain was the king himself, Arthur, his tawny hair glowing in a shaft of sunlight. Kay wondered whether his sleepy demeanour rose out of boredom, or was the habitual veiling of his power, the lion at rest.

On the king's far side, Sir Lancelot's seat was vacant, as it so often was; a few places farther round the Table sat Sir Gareth, Gawain's brother. Gareth was stretched out in his chair, his eyes bright under tousled chestnut hair. Catching Kay's eye, he gave him the ghost of a grin. In reply the seneschal intensified his glance into a repressive stare.

Sir Gareth's grin broadened, and Kay hastily looked away, lifting his eyes to examine the ceiling of the council chamber. You might almost think, he reflected, that the vaulting was specially built to echo the segmenting of the Round Table beneath it. But that was rubbish. The castle, and therefore the ceiling, had been built long before the Table . . . certainly before the Table had been placed there. Yet there they were: Table and vaulting, voice and echo, mirror and image, like the two halves of a shell. For all his pride in his own logic and common sense, Kay had found it was never safe to rely on them when dealing with the Table.

He had given up on Sir Colgrevaunce's peroration and was in the midst of mentally composing a scathing letter intended for the merchant who had provided the court's last consignment of wine when he gradually became aware of a disturbance in the anteroom. He could hear a voice, high and petulantly protesting, the words themselves indistinguishable, and an answering bass rumble from one of the guards. Intrigued, Kay banished the wine merchant's iniquities from his mind, and gave his attention to the guard who stood in the council chamber doorway.

"I beg your pardon, my lord. There's a young man here who says—"

A second, slighter figure appeared in the doorway and tried to push past him. The guard grabbed his arm.

"Get out of my way!" The stranger spat the words. "How dare you try to—"

"All right," Arthur interrupted, nodding to the guard. An amused look brightened his face. "You can let him go. I think we'll manage to defend ourselves."

The guard withdrew, and the newcomer straightened himself, clutching at tattered dignity. Kay studied the stranger: He was young, no more than fourteen or fifteen, not tall, but slender, with golden hair that had been elaborately curled but now looked dishevelled. He wore a blue cloak, heavy with gold embroidery. His head was arrogantly raised.

"Do you ask your servants, my lord, to keep out your guests from Camelot?"

"No," Arthur said mildly. "Though my guards have orders to prevent strangers from entering a confidential council. How may I help you?"

The boy drew himself up and took breath for an announcement. "I have come to help you. I have come to be made a Knight of the Round Table, and one of your advisers."

A murmur of voices broke out around the Table. Kay saw Gareth wince and momentarily close his eyes. Like the other knights, the seneschal had heard fledgling warriors use this approach before; it had never worked, and Kay was about to make certain it did not work now.

He leant forward, chin resting on one hand. "Goodness," he said sweetly, "an untested knight and adviser is just what we've all been waiting for. How have we ever managed until now without one?"

There was some appreciative laughter, but the king shot Kay a warning glance. To the stranger, Arthur said, "A place at the Table is not to be had just for the asking, but you're welcome to stay and be trained. What's your name, boy? Who is your father?"

The youth had been flushing uncomfortably, casting sidelong, hostile looks at Kay. Now his embarrassed flush became one of triumph. "My name is Loholt," he announced boldly, turning his full attention back to Arthur. "And you, my lord, are my father."

Kay felt an unpleasant jolt of something that was part surprise, part foreboding, as if he caught the first flicker of lightning on the hills. He thrust the fanciful thought impatiently away. He remained immobile, eyes fixed on the boy, while clamour broke out around the Table, protest and challenge. A few men rose to leave their seats. Even Arthur was briefly taken aback, though he retained enough self-control to sign for silence. The boy Loholt stood in the midst of the confusion, wearing a faint, satisfied smile.

When Kay could make himself heard without shouting, he inquired, "You have proof of this?"

Loholt's smile was wiped off his face, leaving a pinched, venomous look. "Are you calling me a liar?" His voice shook with anger. "How dare you speak like that to your king's son? Who are you?"

His hand was on his sword; Kay would not have been surprised if he had drawn it.

Kay rose, and bowed ironically. "Sir Kay, the king's high seneschal." He reseated himself. "As to what I call you, few of us remember the hour of our birth, much less the time of our parents' coming together. More than one young man has grown up in ignorance of his true identity."

Kay dared a glance at Arthur, but the king's attention was fixed on Loholt, and he paid no heed to Kay's reminder of his own upbringing, when they had believed that they were brothers. Kay wondered if the king ever thought of that time, or whether it meant nothing to him any more. He had never had any answer to that question, and never expected that he would.

More sharply than he had intended, he said to Loholt, "I ask you again, have you proof of your claim?"

Gracelessly, Loholt fumbled in the front of his tunic and took out a letter, which he slapped on to the Table in front of the king. "A letter from my mother, the lady Lisanor."

In silence Arthur broke the seal and read the letter, then pushed it along the Table so that Kay and Gawain could read it in their turn. It was no more than a formal reminder to Arthur of his meeting with the lady Lisanor, commending their son to him. There was nothing of the living woman behind it, but Kay could call her to mind very easily. She had come to Arthur after Bedegraine, the battle that had truly established Arthur's claim to the kingship. She had been all beauty, all compliance, and her act of homage had ended in Arthur's bed, there in the camp. Kay chiefly remembered the occasion because it was the first time that Arthur had taken a step into new experience and left Kay himself behind.

Finishing the letter, Kay studied the young man again and found that he could well believe the claim. Loholt looked very like the king—not so tall or so broad-shouldered, but that would come with maturity. He had the same golden hair and, most compelling of all, the same amber eyes, but all were paler, colder, as if some enchanter had tried to fabricate a copy of the king, yet failed to instil in it the living warmth.

"It is possible," Arthur said, "that the young man you say you are exists." Loholt opened his mouth to protest, but something about the king's manner kept him silent. "Though I knew nothing of him until today. It is even possible that you are he." Suddenly Arthur relaxed, smiling, and held out a hand. "You're welcome, and more than welcome, if you can make me proud of you."

Loholt came forward and clasped his hand. He was smiling, but Kay thought there was no warmth in the smile, as if the welcome was less than he had expected. Well, he would not have been the first young man to walk in thinking that he was God's gift to chivalry, only to learn very quickly that there was more to it than that. Sharp irritation stabbed at Kay. Did Loholt think it was so easy? Did he not understand what he asked, or value it no more highly?

"My lord," Kay said to Arthur, "do you not mean to confirm this story? Or test the boy further? Are we now to accept every young puppy, still wet behind the ears, who walks in here with a tale to tell? Have you—"

"Kay!" The king did not often speak like that, softly, but with a gathered power. "You're too grudging. We have a duty of hospitality at least."

Kay took a breath to say more, but he felt Gawain's hand touch his arm, and saw his friend very slightly shake his head. He subsided into silence.

Meanwhile, the king spoke the formal words that brought the council to an end. To Loholt, he added, "Now you'll need some time to settle in. We'll talk again later. Kay, find him somewhere to sleep, and then bring him along to supper. And remember that the welcome we give him reflects my honour, not his own—or yours."

Arthur clasped the boy's shoulder for a moment before he left the council chamber. Loholt stood motionless, his hand still on the hilt of his sword, his face sullen now, in spite of the king's welcome, while the knights filed out around him. Gawain stopped, smiled, said something friendly, as he always would, but Loholt scarcely responded. Kay guessed he had not expected to be dismissed. The seneschal's anger increased. Did Loholt not understand the change his presence had brought? Could he be so stupid as not to understand how difficult it was for Arthur? Faced with a son he had not known existed—and in the presence of a full council, faced with the need to make provision for that son's future—Arthur needed time to think. Time, too, to make his peace with the queen.

Kay remained in his seat. When the others had gone, he rose and spoke. His tone was brusque but groping towards a friendliness he could not feel. "Come on, boy, let's find a room for you." He made for the door, not looking to see if Loholt followed him.

"Sir Kay!" Loholt called.

Kay, impatient, swung round, saw the gleaming arc of Loholt's sword as it scythed towards him, and could not stop himself in time. He stepped straight into the blade as it lashed across his chest. He stared, an unformed sound came from the back of his throat, and he sagged to the floor.

For a moment, mist swirled around him. As if at a distance, he heard a shout, and rapid footsteps, but he did not ask himself what they meant. His hands were fumbling at his tunic; though he felt no pain, he was prepared for a gush of blood. But all that he could feel was a long slit in the fabric, from one shoulder diagonally almost to the waist. As his vision cleared he could see that there was no injury; the flat of the weapon must have carried most of the force of the blow.

He felt himself shaking as he realised the blade had not touched him. Looking up, he saw Loholt pinioned between the two guards from the anteroom; his sword lay on the floor at his feet. He was white, his eyes hot with anger. As Kay watched, he writhed in the guards' grip as if he wanted to throw them off and spring at Kay, but the men were rock solid, far beyond Loholt's strength.

"Are you hurt, sir?" one of them asked. "Shall I send for help?"

Kay looked from the guard to Loholt, and back again. He was recovering, but still felt shaken. At last he said, quietly, "No, thank you. I shall do very well."

He forced himself to his knees, and then to his feet. The room tilted again; he hoped he was going to stay upright.

"What shall we do with him, sir?" the guard asked.

Kay considered. For what Loholt had just done, he could have been thrown into a cell, or out of the gates, and Kay would have been delighted to give the order—if the boy had been anyone but Arthur's son. "Let him go," he said.

The guards looked doubtful, but they obeyed. Loholt, released, shook himself and twitched his tunic straight. He was still furious.

"Thank you," Kay said to the guards. "You can go back to your posts." As they started to move off even more doubtfully, Kay added, "Don't gossip about this."

As well command the rain not to fall, he thought. Of course they would gossip, but perhaps by the time the story got out he could have dealt with Loholt.

When the guards had withdrawn to the anteroom Kay took a step towards Loholt. "Lesson one of knighthood," he said. "Never draw sword on an unarmed man. Lesson two: Never attack without warning. You have just done both. If those are the standards of wherever you come from, you had better learn right away that they won't do for Camelot."

Loholt shrugged, sulky and defensive. "You're not hurt."

"That's no thanks to you!" Kay retorted. "You didn't know how that blow was going to fall—and you didn't care. A knight could be challenged for less than that."

"You're too much of a coward," Loholt sneered. "Look at you—you're white, trembling. Everyone knows Sir Kay will do anything to avoid a fight."

Kay set his mouth, struggled to hold on to his own temper, and achieved a precarious silence.

After a moment, when he thought he could keep his voice steady, he said, "I cannot challenge you, for you are no knight. I might put you over a bench at supper, and beat you with the flat of my sword."

Loholt's head jerked up. "You wouldn't dare!"

Kay held his eyes. He soon saw, though it was a barren satisfaction, that Loholt was uncertain. He believed that Kay might carry out his threat.

"Pick up your sword," Kay said.

Loholt obeyed him, stooping without taking his eyes off Kay. Kay was quite prepared for him to lunge again, and tensed himself. Loholt simply straightened up, the blade dangling from one hand.

"Put it away."

Warily, still with that fixed stare, Loholt fitted his sword into its sheath.

"Now," Kay went on, "I'm going to show you a room where you can sleep, and by the time you've unpacked, they'll be serving supper. When we go into the hall, you're going to remember that you're Arthur's son. Try to exercise your limited imagination on how Arthur's son ought to behave."

Loholt muttered something under his breath, and Kay was half prepared for another attack, if only in words, but the boy merely shrugged and turned away from him, towards the Round Table. He began to walk round it, his fingers fluttering above the silky, golden surface, inspecting the names engraved in gold at every place. The afternoon sun was dying, and the room grew shadowed.

Watching the drifting, circling figure, Kay grew uneasy. "It's time we—"

"Where will I sit?" Loholt interrupted.

Kay supposed that by now nothing should surprise him. "Not here, to begin with," he said. "Not every knight has a place at the Table. I waited a good while for mine."

"But I'm the king's son," Loholt said. "One day, I'll be king."

The calm assumption left Kay speechless, while Loholt progressed round the Table until he came to the king's own seat. Kay half expected him to sit in it.

"Listen," Kay said, "you may be the king's son, but you aren't the son of his wife, the queen. . . ."

"Guenevere is barren," Loholt said.

Kay stiffened at the insolent tone, but decided to ignore it. "You're Arthur's illegitimate son. As such, you have no automatic right to inherit." He had the feeling that Loholt had stopped listening, but he ploughed on. "Arthur will find a good position for you, but unless he has a son of his own by the queen, Sir Gawain of Orkney—you met him just now—who is Arthur's nephew, will be king after him."

Loholt looked up at him, across the Table. "I shall be king," he said.

He stretched out a hand, poised it over the Table as if he meant to stroke the silky surface, almost as if he intended to take possession of Arthur's place, then seemed to freeze. For a moment Kay thought that the descending hand had met an invisible barrier.

"Loholt?" he said uncertainly.

Loholt still stared at him, but Kay had the odd feeling that the eyes were blank, seeing nothing. His spine crawled. The seneschal thought that the shadows were making him too imaginative. He began to move round the Table towards the boy, and as he did so, Loholt snapped into movement again, withdrew the extended hand, and turned to meet Kay as he approached. To Kay's utter astonishment he fell to his knees before him.

"Oh, sir, forgive me!" he said. "I've begun so badly. I didn't mean—I was afraid, and I thought you wouldn't accept me. I thought you might turn my father against me. . . ."

Kay stifled a bitter retort. If Arthur had ever listened to his advice, those days were long gone. He looked down at Loholt, who had clasped his hands as if in prayer. The boy was gazing up at him, his face twisted with anguish.

"Sir, forgive me, please."

For a few moments, Kay left him where he was and moved over to the window; its pointed arches framed the city below, where lights were springing up as the night gathered. Kay rested one hand on the sill; with the other he fingered the ravelled edges of his ruined tunic. A wave of nausea swept over him as he thought that with only a slight change in the angle of Loholt's sword his chest would have been slashed open just as easily.

"You're Arthur's son," he said. "But just remember, boy, Camelot is crawling with kings' sons. You won't be judged by who your father is. What matters is how well you serve."

"I know that," Loholt said submissively. "That's what I want."

"Then show it." Kay moved back until he stood over the kneeling boy. An unexpected spurt of passion touched his voice. "Be Arthur's son. Do as he asked you, and make him proud of you."

"Yes, sir!"

Loholt's voice was exalted. He gazed up at Kay, the amber eyes shining. He was the picture of sincerity and earnest resolve. Kay knew that he would never trust him for two minutes together.

"Get up, boy," he said curtly. "Come with me. I'll take you to your room."

Chapter Two

The city of Camelot was rousing. Lamplit windows grew paler as the dawn light strengthened. A cold breeze whispered along the stones, bringing to Sir Gawain's ears the sound of a rhythmic creaking that mingled with the hollow echo of the horses' hooves on the cobbles.

Gawain shivered in the dawn chill, and drew his cloak tightly around him. "When you speak of an early morning ride . . ." he complained.

Kay, who had drawn slightly ahead of him, glanced back over his shoulder, a bright, mocking look. "Blow the cobwebs out of your head," he said unsympathetically. "Maybe I should ask what you were doing last night when you should have been in your bed?"

Gawain forbore replying, in no mood for a match of wits with Kay. He followed the seneschal around the next corner, where the source of the creaking was revealed: a young lad bearing down vigorously on the windlass of a well.

Kay drew rein and bent over towards him. "How is your mistress? Is she delivered yet?"

The lad paused, panting, arms thrust down at the bottom of his swing. "Yes, sir," he said. "Two days ago. A daughter. Both well, sir, though the baby do squall at night."

Kay laughed, and tossed a coin on to the stones at the boy's feet. "My compliments to her, and to your master. Good day to you."

The boy grinned and saluted; the creaking gathered momentum behind the two horsemen as they moved away.

"Do you know everyone?" Gawain asked.

Kay looked startled. "His master is a silversmith." His tone suggested an explanation should not be necessary. "A fine craftsman. He's done work for the court. Married a pretty wife last year—you would think no woman had ever been with child before!" Reflectively he added, "I must make sure the king sends a token to the christening."

Unexpectedly touched, Gawain smiled but said nothing. He was well aware of the complexity of Kay's job, but he was continually being surprised by the seneschal's care for tiny detail. Nothing was beneath his notice, and nothing was ever forgotten. Gawain asked himself if Arthur would be so well-loved if it were not for Kay.

At the end of the next street, the guards were dragging open the city gates. They halted, standing to attention as Kay and Gawain rode through and dropped into single file to skirt the line of loaded carts already waiting to be admitted. Gawain, in the lead, found himself waiting for Kay at the end of the line, since his friend had become entangled in conversations with the various carters and invitations to inspect the produce.

When Kay finally joined him, he had acquired from somewhere a large red apple. It nested in one hand while he controlled the reins with the other. He looked faintly embarrassed.

"Surely not a love-token?" Gawain teased.

Kay's eyes glinted. "There I bow to your experience, Sir Gawain, and since I know your fondness for fruit . . ."

Without warning, he tossed the apple to Gawain. Startled into the reflex, Gawain caught it. Meanwhile Kay was gone, bending low over the horse's neck, urging it to a rapid, thundering gallop over the smooth turf. Gawain stifled an exclamation, thrust the apple into his tunic, and took off after him.

He did not expect to catch Kay, who was undoubtedly the finest horseman in the court, and who chose his mounts with skill and dedication. Yet Gawain managed to keep him in sight, across the swell of ground that rose gently to the dark line of the forest, and came up with him at last, waiting on a track that wound among the outlying trees.

Kay wore an expression of elaborate patience. His horse, a fiery little black—and were ever horse and man more alike, Gawain wondered—was still restive. Even after the gallop, it sidestepped with a quick dancer's grace.

"What kept you?" Kay inquired.

"I could kill you," Gawain said amiably.

He caught Kay's answering smile. Together they walked the horses under the overhang of the trees.

"Are we going anywhere in particular?" Gawain asked.

"There's a stud farm," Kay said, "just over the shoulder of the hill—you know it, surely? I've a colt there I'd like you to see. He'll be ready for the king, next year." He gave Gawain a sidelong look, with a touch of shyness. "I—I had thought, a New Year's gift. You won't tell him?"

"No, of course not."

They rode on. In the east, the sun was rising, a smoky orange glow behind cloud. Frost starred the grass, melting to dew where the light touched it, crystalline still in the long shadows of the trees. The air was cold and crisp.

Contented, Gawain asked idly, "How is young Loholt settling in?"

Kay shrugged. "Well enough. Surprisingly well, considering how badly he began. Arthur is pleased with him."

In contrast with his words, Kay's expression had settled into disdain, as if a thin film of ice had formed over him. He had become the public Kay, distant and reserved. For all their friendship, Gawain knew that it took little for Kay to retreat from him.

"What's the matter?" he asked.

Kay's smile was forced, almost as if he were trying to break through the barriers he had instinctively raised.

"Arthur . . . wants a son." The words at first were slow, difficult, as if he could scarcely bring himself to confide in Gawain, and then grew more rapid, as he dared to go on. "You and I can't imagine it, perhaps, how it must feel to be a king and have no true-born son. Arthur is still young, but old enough to look to the future and feel the next generation pressing hard on him. Queen Guenevere—"

He broke off, constraint overtaking him again. Gawain edged his horse up beside him, wishing they were having this conversation somewhere else, somewhere he could be closer to Kay.

"Queen Guenevere cannot conceive," he said quietly.

Kay hesitated, as if he wanted to protest, and then nodded, acquiescent. "It seems so."

Gawain had never dared to ask Kay about his feelings towards the queen, but he was not stupid, and he could guess. Kay had no lady of his own, and in a court where gossip had been raised to high art, his name had never been linked with anyone. His rigid celibacy had itself become a ribald joke for those who had never tried to understand him. Yet for the queen he felt a warmth that he could offer to no other woman.

There was nothing of lust about it—Gawain was sure of that—but a true impulse of service, that showed itself in Kay's autocratic management of the young men who had been chosen as the Queen's Knights; in the care he lavished on the furnishings, the clothes and jewels that he provided for Guenevere to choose; in the way that visiting harpers and storytellers were directed first to her apartments; and in the way Kay himself, who found it too easy to hide from anyone else behind his duties, was always free for a game of chess with the queen. Gawain was terrified at the thought of discussing Guenevere with Kay.

Kay had brought his horse to a standstill again, absently patting its neck as he stared out across the brightening land, the forest a sombre mass at his back. "I know little of women," he said, almost as if he had divined something of what Gawain was thinking. "But it seems to me hard for a woman who can never hold her child in her arms, especially if she is a queen."

His voice grew suddenly tight. "She plays with other women's babies, and chooses gifts for them, and stands as godmother. . . . I have never seen her weep." He drew a long breath. "I have never heard Arthur reproach her. But he longs for a son."

All the while Kay had been talking he had never looked at Gawain directly. Now he met his friend's eyes, the look almost apologetic, reminding Gawain how difficult the seneschal found it to reveal himself.

"Tell me," Gawain said gently.

Kay looked away again, down at his hands twisting the reins. "I know the king has named you as his heir, my lord Gawain." He spoke stiffly, the formal title setting Gawain at a distance. "God forbid I should ever quarrel with his choice, or say that I think you are not worthy. But—"

"Kay, I know."

Kay's words had opened up a prospect that Gawain preferred not to think about. When he tried to visualise himself in Arthur's place—sitting in his high seat, wearing his crown, with all the trappings of kingship about him—his mind refused to call up the pictures. Gawain was well aware that other men would call him a fool for having no more ambition, but he tried to know himself, and he knew he was no king.

"I'm too old," he said. "Too near in age to Arthur. Don't worry about it. I don't want to rule."

Kay gave him another flickering look. He was still not at ease. "I'm older than Arthur. If I outlive him, it would not be for long, and I thank God for it. I shall never see what comes after. But we have built, Gawain, we have built order and justice and grace out of nothing. I would not think that after Arthur's death it will all decay and become nothing again, for want of an heir to guard it." His mouth set grimly. "I do not think that the kingdom will be safe in Loholt's hands."

Gawain could see all his knotted anxiety, all the buried passion that Kay could scarcely ever acknowledge.

"Kay, you worry too much," he said. "Aren't you being too hard on the boy? He's young, and he serves willingly enough. Gareth tells me he's a good swordsman. I know he attacked you and insulted you, but—"

"Is that what you think?" Kay snapped. "That I bear him a grudge? That I can't see his worth because of what he did to me? Very well. Think so if it pleases you. It's no more than anyone would expect of Kay!"

"Kay, don't—"

Gawain tried to reach out to him, but Kay urged his horse into motion again. His friend was half prepared for another wild gallop, as if he could escape pain by flight, but the seneschal kept to a brisk trot, drawing close to the shoulder of the hill and the farm beyond.

After a moment, he flung words across to Gawain, almost as if they were torn out of him. "How does she feel, do you think, to see another woman's son in his heart?"

Kay pushed on towards the ridge where he halted, silhouetted against the sky. Gawain came up beside him. Just below them, the path looped around a bramble thicket, struck out from the forest edge, and then crisscrossed the side of the hill, leading to the comfortable huddle of farm buildings in the valley, all before winding away towards the distant gleam of a river.

"Kay, I meant no offence," Gawain said.

Kay shrugged awkwardly, started to speak, and then broke off. Gawain saw the movement on the road at the same time: a single horseman, riding fast. His immediate thought was to get down from the skyline. He urged his horse crabwise down the first, steep stretch of the track, and manoeuvred into the cover of the brambles, where he could watch and not be seen.

Kay followed more sedately. "You think, trouble?"

"One man alone? No. But bearing trouble, perhaps."

They waited, eyes following the progress of the rider, who seemed at that distance no more than a scurrying insect, his pace painfully slow. Instead, Gawain knew, he rode a powerful horse, not galloping at full stretch, but moving in a tireless canter that devoured the miles.

The rider had not yet reached the spur of road that led off to the farm, when a suspicion sprang up in Gawain, rapidly hardening to a certainty. Sudden joy pierced him. "Lancelot!"

Smiling, he turned to Kay, only to see his friend all ice again.

"So," Kay said, a biting edge to his words, "he deigns to honour us with his presence at court."

Gawain had to admit that Kay was justified. Lancelot had been away for over three months, through all the summer's heat, while news of him had arrived at the court in travellers' tales and songs on the lips of harpers, and in the steady stream of prisoners coming to yield themselves to the queen. Kay thought it a ramshackle way of serving, yet he knew, as Gawain knew and all the court with them, why Lancelot did not stay.

"Kay," Gawain said, "behave yourself."

Kay turned on him a look that quivered on the edge of fury. Something like that, Gawain thought, might be the last thing the sparrow sees as the falcon strikes. He waited for a scathing retort; instead, Kay suddenly relaxed, the fury fading, replaced by a deep-seated uncertainty.

"Do you want to go on ahead and meet him?" Kay suggested. "I'll wait for you here."

Regretfully, Gawain could do nothing but agree. He set off down the hill. By this time, Lancelot had passed the farm and begun the climb. Seeing Gawain, he raised an arm in greeting and slowed his horse to a walk; Gawain wheeled and fell in beside him.

"A good journey?" he said. "What brings you back?"

Lancelot paused before replying. He was always guarded, Gawain knew, thinking before he spoke. While he waited, Gawain studied him. He had not changed, as if he had been away days instead of months. Tall, dark, loose-limbed to the point of looking clumsy, though anyone who had ever fought with him knew better than to be deceived. The ugly, ascetic face would be more appropriate for a priest or a holy man—one of the crazier ones, Gawain thought affectionately, who squat on poles or wall themselves up in caves in the desert. His tunic and cloak were threadbare—they had been just as shabby on the day he left—though his mail, now rolled up in a burlap sack and slung behind him, would be flawless, and his sword blade honed to a hair.

He replied now to Gawain's question, not a word wasted. "News for the king."

"Am I allowed to share it?"

This time, before Lancelot could reply, they came up to Kay, still mounted but motionless in the shadow of the bramble thicket. Gawain saw a change flicker through Lancelot; he scarcely moved, but suddenly he was the fighting man poised to meet trouble. Then he saw who the waiting horseman was, and relaxed. He nodded. "Kay."

"You're welcome, Lancelot. Quite a stranger at court."

There was a barbed edge to Kay's greeting, but for him it might count as courtesy. Lancelot in any case seemed unaware of the sharpness; he was already saying to Gawain, "Share it if you will, but you won't like it. Briant des Isles is in Britain."

Gawain was acutely conscious of his next indrawn breath. Kay flung up his head, his hawk's face vivid with disgust.

"And what is he doing in Britain?" Gawain heard himself asking. "Paying us a friendly visit? On his way to give homage to Arthur?"

Lancelot snorted. "If I didn't know you better, Gawain, I'd think your wits had gone birds'-nesting. Briant landed on the south coast, not far from Pevensey. Raided a village, burnt a farm or two. I led the men from the garrison there, and we beat him off, but he'll be back."

"Raiding? Burning?" Gawain said. "This is something new. Has he turned pirate?"

Lancelot shrugged, unwilling to commit himself. Glancing at Kay, Gawain had to stifle laughter at the seneschal's affronted expression. "Kay disapproves," he said.

"Briant des Isles is an uncivilised lout," Kay said acidly. "He built himself a fortress on the Breton coast, and dared to call it Castle Pendragon. By what right a Breton lord claims sovereignty in Britain I do not know and never will. Piracy is just about his level."

He jerked his horse's reins, setting it at the slope, breasting

Exiled From Camelot

the shoulder of the hill as he led the way back to the city. Lancelot followed. Gawain brought up the rear, with a single, regretful glance behind him—regret for the peaceful morning ride, for the visit to the farm that had never taken place, regret for the gentler side of Kay that had been driven back under the surface by Lancelot's arrival and his news. Gawain knew that in the same way, all that he valued might be broken.

The track that skirted the forest was too narrow for more than two horsemen to ride side by side. Kay had drawn a little way ahead, leaving Lancelot and Gawain together.

"We'll send men to strengthen the coastal garrisons." Lancelot was almost thinking aloud. "I'll lead them myself. If this is the start of an invasion—"

"Invasion?" Gawain echoed. "Has Briant declared war?"

"Declared war?" Kay tossed the words over his shoulder. "You don't expect the courtesies from Briant des Isles? Strengthen the Cornish garrisons, too," he advised Lancelot. "Briant and King Mark should just suit each other, like two fleas in a pelt."

Lancelot made a noncommittal noise; Gawain guessed that he did not appreciate being given advice about strategy by Kay, though the advice was sensible enough. Gawain half smiled. Kay always treated the existence of men like King Mark of Cornwall and Briant des Isles as a personal insult. On the one occasion Gawain could remember when Kay and Briant had met, the seneschal had gone around as if he had a perpetual bad smell under his nose.

They reached the point on the track where Kay had waited for Gawain on the outward ride, and paused again without a word being exchanged. By now the sun was up and the morning mists had cleared away. Across the valley the city rose: the strong retaining wall, the houses tumbled almost haphazardly on the slopes of the hill, and above it all, the white walls of the citadel, crisp against an ice-blue sky.

This was the centre, Gawain thought. Everything flowed from here and returned in a perpetual cycle of strength and justice and love. The very word *Camelot* conjured up an ordered splendour, an aspiration, that the world had never seen before. How long could it last? A thousand years? A hundred? Or only until war or sickness or old age ended Arthur's life? Gawain felt almost overwhelmed by the gust of fear that swept over him when he realised that everything he loved was threatened.

Lancelot was still gazing across the valley, paying no attention to anyone else, but Kay was giving Gawain an odd, perceptive look, almost as if he had guessed the thoughts that were running through his mind. Gawain took a long, calming breath. The notion slid into his mind that if Briant des Isles had wanted to weaken Arthur, he could have placed an archer in these trees and destroyed the three men who bore most of the weight of the kingdom.

Lancelot, Arthur's war leader and the finest fighting man of his generation, was still more than that—someone with the intangible spirit that inspired others to follow him. Kay, for all his impatience, was a brilliant administrator. And Gawain himself; he smiled ruefully. Compared to the others, he was unimportant, frivolous even. But he was the king's heir, for want of a better, and he thought he understood, at least a little, what Arthur wanted his kingdom to be. If nothing else he was, without ostentation, willing to die for that dream.

Shrugging, almost laughing at his own pretensions, Gawain followed Lancelot down the hill towards the city.

Chapter Three

Sir Kay, using the castle gardens as a short cut between one pressing duty and the next, was brought up short by the sound of laughter. Across the grass he could see Queen Guenevere with some of her ladies, picking apricots from the tree growing against the sun-warmed wall.

Hesitating, half reluctant, he was moving on, when he heard the queen's voice calling him back.

"Kay! Kay, don't go!"

She had left the tree and was advancing over the grass to meet him, a hand held out to him. In the other hand she held a shallow basket, piled with fruit that glowed golden as a dragon's hoard. "Look," she said, holding out the basket. "The very last, this year."

She was as tall as he; her eyes laughed into his. Her skin glowed with the gold of the apricots, her hair the darker gold of honey. Kay could not imagine a woman more beautiful. Not for the first time he wished he had Gawain's charmed tongue; Gawain would have been able to say something witty and graceful, and, Kay believed, such things were pleasing to ladies. He was painfully conscious of how inarticulate he was himself. "Lady, if I can serve you . . ."

"You can," Guenevere said. She took his hand and led him across the grass to a bench in the sun. "You can stay and listen to us gossip and try to make us all a little more serious-minded. There."

She sat him down on the bench and put the basket down beside him. Her fingers poised over the pile of apricots, and then chose one, which she held out to him. "Now, tell me if this old tree hasn't the sweetest fruit of all?"

"It must be sweet, from your hand," Kay said, surprising himself.

Guenevere laughed. "Kay, you're turning courtier!" Something changed in her laughter, bringing a sudden ache to his throat. "Don't," she whispered. "We have many courtiers, but only one Kay."

She went back to her women, leaving him utterly astonished. He sat turning the fruit in his fingers, content to admire the bloom on the skin, and the warm, musky smell. Quick movement distracted him, as the lady Lionors came and sat herself on the grass at his feet. Sir Gareth's lady, barefoot and wearing an unbleached linen gown that might have been cast off by her own serving maid, pushed back her fleece of dark curls with both hands and smiled up at him from her triangular, cat's face.

Kay held out the basket to her; she waved it away.

"The smell turns me sick. I'm with child," she confessed happily.

Kay's delight in her news was tempered by the memory of another child, small, perfectly formed, the daughter who had lived three hours. Lionors laid a hand at her waist, though as yet there was no swelling to betray the life kindling in her.

Almost as if she guessed what Kay had been thinking, she said, "This one will be strong."

Confronted by her blazing happiness, Kay felt awkward, as if by saying the wrong thing he might spoil it. "Lady, if you want anything—anything at all that I could get you . . ."

Lionors laughed up at him, shaking back her hair. "Yes, of course, Kay, I know I can ask you. I will, I promise. I think if I wanted strawberries at New Year, you would find them!"

She was teasing him, but gently, and once again Kay wished he had Gawain's facility, and could answer her in the same light-hearted way. He would always be a plodder, he thought, the quicksilver thread of words slipping away from him. Happily embarrassed, he was still trying to frame a reply when Lionors twisted away from him, looking out across the garden.

"Truly, this garden must be Paradise," she said acidly, "for here comes the snake."

A servant approached down the path, carrying a jug of wine. He was followed by Loholt, bearing a tray with cups.

A little startled, Kay leant forward and spoke softly to Lionors. "Your servant displeases you, lady? Do you wish me to have him soundly beaten?"

Lionors looked up at him through her lashes, an exaggeratedly demure expression. "Sir Kay, you're infecting me," she said. "A very bad influence. It was Loholt I meant, and you know it. Poisonous little brat."

Kay watched Loholt and the servant as they set down what they were carrying on another bench a few yards away. The seneschal was surprised by the strength of feeling Lionors had betrayed; he had given up expecting that anyone would share his dislike of Loholt. In the short time he had been at court, the boy seemed to have won approval from everyone. From the knights, Kay corrected himself; he did not suppose that anyone had asked their ladies. "He's young," he said. "He'll learn."

"If someone doesn't kill him first," Lionors said. "I heard what he did to you."

"That's all over." Kay moved a hand dismissively. "What has he done to make you angry, lady?"

The laughter died out of Lionors' face. "To me, nothing. I'm nowhere near important enough to interest His Highness. It's my lady . . ."

"Yes?"

"When he has duties near her, he says things . . . oh, little things. Nothing anybody could repeat, or blame him for. But he never lets her forget that he is the king's son and she has no child. Lately, whenever he comes into the room where she is, I can see her change."

Kay felt anger rising in himself, and firmly forced it down. "Do you want me to speak to him?"

"And say what? I told you, there's nothing anyone could blame him for. He's too clever for that."

Clever. Kay considered the word. He had never thought of Loholt as clever. And yet he had never been able to shake off his first distrust of the boy, while to everyone else he was the paragon of aspiring young manhood. *Clever*—yes, that might well be the right word.

"I'll find something else to keep him occupied," he promised.

There was no teasing now in the look Lionors gave him. "Kay, if you would—oh, I'd be so thankful! So would the queen. But she can't ask you—you know that she could never ask."

Kay nodded. Across the stretch of turf, beside the other bench, Loholt was bending over, pouring the wine; the servant had withdrawn and left him to it. He was ungraceful, Kay thought critically, sticking out his rump as if he expected to lay an egg.

With a murmured excuse to Lionors, Kay rose and went to him. "No," he said, taking the wine jug away from Loholt. "Hold it like this. You can pour without splashing, and you present a more pleasing appearance."

With a curt nod, he handed the jug back. Quick venom flashed in Loholt's eyes; Kay expected the wine to be dashed into his face, but within a second Loholt had recovered himself, bowed in acknowledgement, and went on with his pouring.

Kay took one of the filled cups. "I will take this to the queen. You may serve the other ladies."

He withdrew, deliberately stately, feeling eyes boring into his back. Guenevere, with most of her other women, still searched among the clustering leaves of the fruit tree. As Kay approached and gave her the cup, he saw her gaze go past him, fixing on Loholt, saw the lines of strain set in her face, and understood what Lionors had meant. Then her face changed again, no less tense, but with a different quality. She was looking beyond Loholt, to where, through the trees, the king had appeared, talking with Lancelot, and close behind them, Gawain and Gareth.

An instant later, Guenevere was the great lady again, advancing to welcome her guests, offering her basket of apricots, as if she had nothing more momentous on her mind than finding everyone a seat in the sun.

Kay joined Loholt in serving the wine. The boy had gone straight to Arthur, kneeling to present the cup with a formality that might have been appropriate for the feast at one of the great courts, but in this impromptu gathering was, in Kay's view, decidedly overdone. But Kay saw Arthur's smile and heard his word of thanks, and bit back a stinging rebuke. Loholt, he saw, had the king's favour.

He had risen to his feet again, and stood in front of his father, his smile all boyish eagerness. "I don't know who to serve next," he confessed. "Is Sir Lancelot or Sir Gawain the greatest of your knights?"

The question was no more than tactless, perhaps, and yet Kay could not forget what Lionors had said. Clever. Little things . . . nothing anyone could blame him for. This time, king's favour or not, Kay was drawing breath to suggest that a page's duty was to stop chattering and get on with the job, when Gawain laughed, blunting the edge of Loholt's words. "Oh, I yield to Lancelot! No question of it."

Gareth interposed a second later, from where he sat on the grass beside Lionors. "Loholt, we have no 'greatest knight,' nor least. That's why the Table is round."

Kay was not sure whether Gawain or Gareth had meant to rebuke Loholt. Both the brothers had spoken amiably, but Gawain at least was subtle enough to convey a reproof with a smile. Whatever had been intended, Loholt sensed no disapproval. Forgetting his duties, he folded himself up on the grass at his father's feet, hugging his knees and gazing brightly into the faces of the knights around him.

As Kay turned aside to pour more wine, he heard Loholt say, "But that's—well, that's just for show, isn't it? Everyone knows who are the best knights . . . and the worst."

No need to guess who he has in mind as the worst, Kay thought.

"Everyone?" Gareth countered swiftly. "Who are they?"

"Whatever gossip says," Gawain added, "the knights of the Table are equal. We all strive for the ideal. We all fail."

"None of us is worthy." That was Lancelot's deeper voice, adding his measured contribution to the debate. Kay turned to see him leaning forward, scrutinising Loholt with unconcealed interest. This might be the first time Lancelot had met him since his return to court on the previous day; Kay could not help wondering about his opinion of the king's newly acquired son.

"The Table was made," Lancelot went on, directly to Loholt now, "in memory of the table where our Lord sat with His followers. As none of them could claim to be the greatest, nor do we."

"Even at our Lord's table, there was a traitor," Loholt said.

His voice was grave now, as if in respect for the holy mysteries of theology, but Kay could not help wondering if the words were meant for him. He began to distribute cups; an unexpected misery had crept up on him, and in the sunlight he stood in darkness. They were together; they belonged; none of them, not even Gawain, could see the taint in Loholt. The boy would be one of them, while Kay stood apart, always, his service disregarded.

"Because they were fallible human beings," Gawain was replying to what Loholt had said, "just as we are. We have no wish to be first, but only to give the best we can. Which is why," he added, smiling up at Kay and taking the cup of wine which Kay offered to him, "the High Seneschal of Britain can serve the wine without losing his dignity."

The bitter bands of loneliness clamped around Kay began to ease a little. He remained standing beside Gawain, as if by keeping within the circle of his friend's warmth he could melt the ice in his own heart and stifle his growing uneasiness. He wondered if Guenevere was listening, and what she thought, but when he turned to look for her it was to see that she had withdrawn, her women around her, and seemed to be paying no attention to the group of men around the king.

Meanwhile Arthur was laughing, and saying, "Lancelot, you saw the boy at practice this morning. What did you think of him?"

Lancelot gave Loholt another long look. At last he smiled faintly. "Promising."

Loholt's eyes shone. Of course, he knew of Lancelot's reputation. His joy in hearing praise from him might even be real. Most of the lads in the court would have slaved for years to earn the word "promising" from Lancelot, with that particular smile. Kay was not wholly immune to it himself.

Arthur's pride in his son blazed out of him; he too knew the value of Lancelot's praise. He gripped his friend's shoulder. "Perhaps you can give him some lessons? Show him a trick or two?"

Lancelot nodded. "When we've settled Briant des Isles."

Kay took a step forward. "My lord, I had thought—" the idea had been in his mind for all of thirty seconds "—that you might let Loholt ride with Lancelot when he goes south. It would give him some experience of campaigning."

The warmth of the look Arthur turned on him almost brought Kay to his knees. He knew he did not deserve it, hated his own deviousness, almost wished that he had meant the suggestion for Loholt's good and not just as a way to remove him from the court.

"Of course, Kay," the king said. "I should have thought of it myself. Lancelot, what do you say?"

Lancelot did not have any reason to disagree, but Loholt suddenly looked less than pleased. Kay could not understand it. Even on the previous evening, with news of the expedition just getting out, he had watched the pages and esquires vying for Lancelot's attention, trying to manoeuvre themselves into a place among his men.

"My lord, I would rather stay with you," Loholt said.

Into Arthur's face there came a faintly puzzled look. "Loholt, my men go where they're ordered."

Impulsively Loholt came to his knees and reached for his father's hand. "But it's such a short time since I found you, Father." His voice held a fervent sincerity. "I want to serve you, I want to do everything I can to be worthy of you, but—"

As he began to speak Arthur's face softened into an expression of indulgence that thoroughly disturbed Kay. Only momentarily; then he was alert again, and Loholt, seeing the change in his face, broke off and turned to see what the interruption was.

Through the trees rushed a servant, an agitated look on his face. Kay felt a different kind of disturbance. Thoughts of a possible attack fled through his mind. He stepped forward, but the servant was beyond caring about correct behaviour, and spoke directly to the king. "My lord, a herald has arrived—"

"From Briant?" Kay asked, unable to stop himself.

The servant seemed not to have heard him; he went on hurriedly: "—from the lady Elaine of Corbenic. She is on her way here, and will arrive before nightfall."

If he had known that his death would follow, Kay could not have avoided looking at the queen. She had heard the gasped out message. The sounds of talk among her women had died, and Guenevere herself, white, frozen, stared at the messenger.

A second later, she had risen, and came to stand by Arthur's side. "The lady Elaine has some urgent errand?" she inquired evenly.

"Lady, I don't know."

"It must be urgent, if she neither waits for an invitation nor gives us notice of her coming."

No one made any comment on that, least of all Lancelot, who sat looking at his clasped hands. Loholt, curled up again at the king's feet, had an alert air; had he picked up that item of gossip in such a short time? If so, Kay thought, he worked fast. As he must do himself.

Kay bowed to Arthur. "With your leave, my lord, I'll go and arrange lodgings for the lady Elaine." He had a good, remote tower in mind. "Send the herald to me," he said to the servant. "I must know the size of his lady's retinue, and—"

"No, Kay," the king interrupted. "There's something I want to talk to you about. Something that won't wait. My dear—" he reached out a hand to the queen "—will you give the orders? Arrange for the lady Elaine to be suitably entertained?"

Down in the dungeons, among the racks and thumbscrews, Kay speculated. Guenevere did no more than drop an icy little curtsey, and moved away, gathering her women around her. Lionors made an eloquent face at Gareth, scrambled to her feet, and followed.

Arthur waited until the queen was out of earshot, and almost out of sight, among the trees of the garden, before he spoke again. "If the rest of you will excuse me, I have something to discuss with Kay."

Kay was mildly surprised. Arthur never bothered to give him directions about the day-to-day running of the court. The only break in their routine, apart from the unexpected arrival of Elaine of Corbenic, was the campaign against Briant des Isles. And Arthur would discuss that with Lancelot. As he watched the others withdraw—Loholt with clear reluctance—Kay's uneasiness returned.

He was not used to being alone with Arthur. Desperate for something to do, he began collecting up the scattered wine cups and returning them to the tray, until he heard Arthur's voice behind him. "Kay, leave that. Come and sit here."

Kay turned to him. The sun was setting, slipping below the towers that stood out dark against a rosy sky barred with cloud. A swathe of shadow had crept over the garden, and the only sunlight that still remained was gathered in the distant corner where the queen and the other knights had disappeared. The tops of the trees rippled silver in a breeze that as yet did not disturb the stillness below. Kay shivered.

The bench where Arthur sat was in shadow now, and yet it seemed as if a gleam of sunlight still clung to his tawny hair, or lurked in the amber eyes. He patted the bench beside him. "Kay."

Hesitantly, Kay approached. He felt himself closing up, growing colder and more remote. The ease he had once felt with Arthur, long ago when they were boys together, was as distant now as the vanishing sunlight. He could not even talk to him, except formally, as high seneschal. Never as Kay, never any more.

He sat and clasped his hands tightly together. "How may I serve you, my lord?"

Arthur's reply was the last thing Kay had expected. "What do you think of Loholt?"

The king smiled a little, his gaze distant, the sort of look Kay had seen on the face of a very young man who has just set eyes on the only possible lady. . . . Seeing Arthur look like that, with Loholt's name on his lips, disturbed Kay profoundly.

It was impossible to give voice to his uneasiness. Awkwardly, he said, "He is young, and I believe he makes progress. . . ."

"Lancelot called him 'promising.'" Arthur had only half listened to Kay's hesitant reply. Eagerly, he leant towards Kay, laying a hand on his arm. "He's my son, Kay—worthy of the name, don't you think?"

The eagerness, the touch, made Kay stiffen. Feeling still more awkward, looking for words that did not come easily, he said, "My lord, I scarcely know. I—I'm not the best person to ask. Gawain, or Lancelot, know better what—"

"But it's you I'm asking, Kay." Arthur's sudden impatience showed at least that not all his wits were wandering. "I've a reason for asking." He paused, but Kay said nothing. "Kay, I want to acknowledge him. I want him legitimated."

"No!" Kay was on his feet, appalled, the rejection bursting out of him. At once he saw Arthur's sudden withdrawal, the hardening of his features.

"Kay," the king said, "I never thought you were the man to hold a grudge."

Kay struggled for self-control. He wanted to face Arthur and ask him a single question: *Don't you care that he almost killed me?* He dared not. He was afraid of what the answer might be.

"My lord," he managed to say, "Loholt's attack on me is over, and—"

"You still condemn him."

"No, not—not condemn. . . ."

Once, as a young man, Kay had fought a speech impediment, and now he felt almost as if the old hesitancy might be returning to plague him, it was so hard to force out the words, under Arthur's cold look.

"My lord, it is too soon. He has been here so short a time. What you suggest should be a—a prize, that he could work for, and deserve in the end, not a gift tossed for the asking. . . ."

"He has not asked."

"I didn't mean . . ."

He sank down on the bench again, and put his head in his hands. A moment later he felt Arthur's touch on his shoulder, and ventured to look up at him. Arthur's expression had softened.

"Kay, you're too harsh. With him, and with yourself. I know it comes from your loyalty. Listen."

A little, Kay could let himself relax. Seeing it, Arthur smiled again. "Kay, I need a son," he said. "I need an heir."

Thoroughly alarmed again, Kay forced himself to remain calm. "My lord Gawain is your heir."

"Yes, I know. And if I died in battle tomorrow he would succeed me. But if I live my life out—Kay, you know very well that Gawain is only four years younger than I am. He could die before me. I need a younger man—a son. Besides . . . I've asked myself before now, if Gawain is the right man to be king."

Kay stared at him, not sure if he understood what he was hearing. "My lord, Gawain is the noblest of your knights."

Arthur gave him a half-smile. "I thought we had no order of precedence? No, Kay, I don't doubt Gawain's nobility, or his loyalty. I don't speak to dishonour him. But still I ask myself, has he the steel to be a king?"

Kay still did not think he understood, or at least could not see Gawain as Arthur saw him. He had lived so long with Gawain's brilliance, his warmth, the light to his own shadow. Gawain would not be a king after Arthur's stamp, but even in his commitment to Arthur, Kay was able to ask himself if there was no other way.

"My lord, he is—"

"Your friend, I know," Arthur interrupted, not saying what Kay had wanted to say. "It's right you should defend him. I love Gawain, and I trust him. But we have to put personal feelings aside, and think of what's best for Britain. How many of the lesser kings who pay me homage think of Gawain as no more than a courtier? How many of them would follow him?" He balled one hand into a fist and brought it down hard on the bench beside him. "Kay, I need a son," he repeated.

"There is still time," Kay said; every word was painful. "The queen may still—"

Arthur shook his head. "Guenevere will not bear a child. There are men who would have put her away before now, and taken another, but that I cannot do. If I have a son, it must be by another woman, not my wife." His voice grew impatient again. "Kay, I don't see why you're making difficulties. What reason is there for not declaring Loholt my heir?"

Reasons, Kay thought. A look in the eyes. Words that could be weighed two ways. A pricking on the skin. And that moment in the council chamber, when Loholt had reached out. . . . What was he to say, Kay asked himself, that the boy did not touch the Table? Or perhaps, he *could not* touch the Table? It was all superstition, all shadows. Nothing that he could set against Arthur's overmastering need, a man's need for a son, a king's need for an heir to keep safe the kingdom he had built from nothing. Kay sighed, and kept silence.

"Besides," Arthur said, "there is the other. Mordred."

Their eyes met in a haunted awareness of that other, Mordred, son of Arthur by his half-sister Morgause, growing up now in the North. Mordred had never visited the court; Kay hoped he never would.

"I must leave no loophole for Mordred to inherit," Arthur said.

As if the shared memory had released him, Kay reached out to the king, clutching at his hands. "My lord, if only I—"

"Kay, don't torment yourself. We'll meet that difficulty when it arises. Loholt is a different matter, praise God." He hesitated; Kay was acutely conscious of the warm clasp of his hands. "Kay, you'll back me in this? It's your legal expertise I want. You'll know how to draw up the declaration. I want it watertight—so that if I do die in battle tomorrow, no one can contest Loholt's claim."

Hardly knowing where he found the strength, Kay drew away. He knew what his face must be revealing, and he saw with a kind of despair Arthur's warmth dying away, lost to him. He braced himself for what he had to say.

"My lord, you spoke of Gawain's unfitness. Yet Gawain is a seasoned knight, King Lot's eldest son, and he has a reputation for wisdom as well as courage. If the lesser kings don't accept Gawain, what are they likely to think of Loholt? Not take him for their king. Not yet," he added hastily, with a jolt of fear at the anger growing in Arthur's eyes. "My lord, why not wait? Let him gain experience, be made knight. Give him tasks to do that will win allegiance for him. Give him time to show what he is made of."

"'Time to show what he's made of'?" Arthur repeated the words; he rose and looked down at Kay, who felt himself shrinking. "Time to condemn himself, do you mean? Because of one mistake, when he was new here?" His mouth grew hard. "No, not even that. There's a mean spirit in you, Kay. Your first words to him were an attack."

Stung by the accusation, Kay sprang to his feet and faced him. "Should I neglect my duty, then? And fill the court with self-seekers, and fools, and traitors?" His anger lifted him like a wave; his fears were swamped by it.

"You call Loholt 'self-seeker,' or—"

"No. But if I did, how could you tell me that I lie? You have never tried to find out what he is!"

Arthur's hand went to his belt knife. Sudden agony tore at Kay's throat, and he raised a hand as if he needed to loosen his shirt fastenings and gasp for air. He stood his ground.

"I can see what he is," Arthur said levelly. "But you are blind to it, as you're always blind to excellence."

"Excellence!" Kay flung back at him. "Try asking the queen what she thinks of Loholt's excellence!"

Before he had finished Kay knew he had said the unforgivable thing. He wanted to claw the words back, to change the world so they had never been spoken. The king's impulsive anger, that might have driven him to attack, died away, leaving only ice. Kay would a thousand times rather have felt the rending of the knife than faced that implacable look. He wanted to fling himself on his knees and beg forgiveness, but he could not.

"You have your orders," Arthur said. "You'll draw up a deed, Kay, declaring Loholt my legitimate son, and my heir. Legally, so no man can challenge it. On your loyalty to me as a knight, you will do this."

"And if I do," Kay retorted, "you can prepare for war. Your subject kings will tear Britain apart. Is that what you want?"

"War? Kay is suddenly an expert in war?" Before Kay could retaliate, Arthur turned away, and spoke the last words over his shoulder. "I raised you, Kay and I can throw you down. Remember that. You will obey me."

He strode away, leaving Kay alone in the darkening garden.

Chapter Four

Gawain stared down into his wine cup, disregarding the music and talk of the hall washing around him, and wished he was somewhere else. Supper that evening had seemed interminable; it really was longer because Kay at short notice had managed to produce a more elaborate meal, and suitable entertainment in honour of the lady Elaine, but Gawain knew the time would have passed more quickly if he had not been waiting for disaster to strike.

Someone ought to have told Elaine about discretion. A lady of her rank did not spend the whole of the meal gazing devotedly at one particular knight, even if the knight were Lancelot, even if he happened to be the father of her son. Seated beside the king, she paid Arthur so little attention as to be downright rude, while Lancelot, on her other side, looked more embarrassed than pleased.

At least the queen showed more sense. As soon as it was decently possible, she decided that it was time to go; she rose and gathered the other ladies with her, escorting Elaine from the hall with a gracious courtesy Gawain could not help admiring. He allowed himself a sigh of relief. He would wait a little, discourage any gossip that might come to his ears, and then take his own leave.

Lancelot had moved into the empty place beside the king; from what Gawain could hear, they were discussing the campaign against Briant. He left them to it, only noticing that Loholt, who had been pouring the king's wine, stood close by, eagerly listening. Arthur had seen him there, nodded and smiled, and let him stay. Perhaps Loholt would go with Lancelot; that had been an excellent suggestion of Kay's. It would give the boy experience of campaigning that he badly needed, and Gawain knew he could not have a better commander than Lancelot.

The tables were emptying rapidly now, and servants came into the hall to clear away the remains of the meal. With them, Gawain saw Kay. The seneschal had not taken his place in the hall at supper, had not even changed from the shabby black tunic he had been wearing earlier in the garden; Gawain guessed that he had been too busy.

Kay stood near the doors of the hall, questioning a serving man who held a wine ewer. He held himself erect, the elegant dark head tilted, his face severe. Gawain hoped the serving man could give a good account of himself. Then Kay moved, his swift, transforming smile flickering briefly as he dismissed the man.

He came further into the hall. Half rising, Gawain beckoned him over. "Kay, where have you been? Have you eaten?"

Kay shrugged. "I'll get something later, in the kitchen."

"You'll have something now."

He grasped Kay's arm, and pulled him into the vacant place at his side. Kay looked tired, on edge, Gawain thought. He called to a page and asked him to bring food, poured a fresh cup of wine and set it at Kay's elbow.

"You've managed quite splendidly. I hope Elaine is suitably grateful."

"I doubt it," Kay said.

"Have you found out what she's doing here?"

Kay's brows went up. "Gawain, asking *me* what goes through a woman's mind? No, I don't know what she's doing here. I don't want to know. I mind my own business." He murmured a word of thanks to the page who came and set food in front of him, and waited until the boy had gone. "I spoke to the knight who leads the lady's escort. She returns to Corbenic—" he positioned a discarded wine cup "—after making her pilgrimage to the Holy Isle." Another wine cup was set into place. "So of course she takes us in on her journey—here." Kay set down a dish of salt to represent Camelot, and surveyed the resulting triangle. "All I can say is, the lady has a very strange sense of direction."

Gawain smiled at his severely repressive tones. "Kay, all you're saying is that she takes any chance that offers to visit us and to see Lancelot. Which we knew already." His smile faded. "She loves him too much for her peace, or her reputation."

Kay made no response. He sat in silence, no more than playing with the food that had been brought for him. He looked weary, as if he had something more on his mind than the vagaries of the lady Elaine. Gawain began to wonder what it was that Arthur had said to him when he kept him alone in the garden, but he knew that he could never ask.

He half hoped that Kay might confide in him, but when the seneschal spoke again, it was to say, "Lancelot should marry her."

"Marry Elaine?" Gawain shook his head gently. "Kay, you know why Lancelot will never marry."

Quick impatience flared in Kay's eyes. "Then it would become him better to stay out of the lady's bed!"

"Kay—"

"She is high born, and virtuous—or was, until she looked on Lancelot. And beautiful, or so I'm led to believe. And she is the mother of his son. He should marry her." Kay frowned, with a faint, exasperated noise. "This way is untidy. I detest untidiness."

Gawain was unable to suppress his laughter by the time Kay had finished speaking. Kay watched him, hawk's face filled with hauteur, incapable of understanding what he had said that could be remotely amusing.

"Forgive me, my lord Gawain," he said sarcastically. "I forget that I speak to an expert in these matters."

He turned the same look of severe disapproval onto the food in front of him, and pushed the plate away.

"Meanwhile, down in the kitchens they're taking bets on where Lancelot will sleep tonight." Kay made another, stronger sound of exasperation, and took a gulp of his wine. "Is that any sort of behaviour for Arthur's court?"

"I am surprised they dare, in your hearing," Gawain said mischievously.

"They don't. There are times when I'm surprisingly deaf. A convenient affliction."

The seneschal sat swirling the wine slowly around the cup, his expression still disapproving. At the head of the table, Lancelot rose to his feet, bowed to Arthur, and went out. Arthur watched him go, and then beckoned to Loholt and said something to him in a low voice, before getting up and leaving by the door to his own apartments.

Loholt approached Gawain and Kay. "My lord Kay," he said. He bowed formally. "My father sent me to ask you if you have any more orders for me tonight."

Kay ignored the attempt at courtesy. "No, lad, you can go to bed. And remember," he said tartly, "in public, you say 'the king,' or 'King Arthur,' not 'my father.' In private, as he gives you leave."

Gawain thought Kay snapped unnecessarily; it was only because he was tired, and the sharp tone did not seem to bother Loholt. Instead of leaving, the boy edged a little closer to Kay.

"Is it true, my lord? What they say about Lancelot and the lady Elaine?"

Kay banged the wine cup down on the table. "Shall I send someone to cry it through the city streets? It could hardly be less secret. Yes, lad, it's true, and if I find you gossiping about it, I'll have your ears."

"Oh, no. I don't mean that. Everyone knows that." Loholt took another step towards Kay, so that they were almost touching, and bent his head confidingly. His expression was tense, almost frightened, with an undercurrent of excitement that disturbed Gawain. "I mean the other story."

"Other story?" Kay grew more impatient. "What other story?"

"The other story," Loholt said quietly, with a glance from side to side, "about the time Lancelot first visited Corbenic, the time he first looked on Elaine." Kay's brows lifted, but he said nothing. "You haven't heard?"

"Loholt, I think—" Gawain had an idea now of what the boy meant to say, and hoped to stop him.

Kay gestured him to silence. "No, Gawain. Let him say what he wants to say."

"I heard . . ." Loholt was almost whispering now. "I heard that he was tricked into Elaine's bed. He only went to her because—because he thought it was the queen."

Alarm flared in Kay's eyes, and he half stood, only to sink back into his seat as he realised that no one was close enough to have heard Loholt's soft-voiced remark.

"Merciful God!" Kay began. "Do you know what you said? Do you know the damage that—"

Gawain leant forward and put a hand on his. "Kay, listen," he said urgently. "What he says is true. Lancelot told me himself."

Kay stared at him. "Does the whole court know?"

"No, praise God. I think Gareth knows, but no one else, unless the queen—"

He broke off, aware that Loholt still stood there listening. As he hesitated, Kay swung round again on the boy. "And who told you, lad? Where did you pick up this other story? Here in the court?"

Loholt shrugged. "No, before I came here. Some traveller . . . maybe a harper. I don't remember."

Gawain grew anxious. If stories about Lancelot and the queen were circulating around Britain in the mouths of harpers, then sooner or later Arthur would have to take notice. And if this particular story was circulating, it must have come from Corbenic. But would Elaine want the story spread, would she even admit there was any truth in it? Gawain frowned, puzzled.

Meanwhile, Kay continued: "If I hear one more breath of this," he told Loholt, "I shall hold you personally responsible. Is that clear?"

"Oh, yes, sir." The excitement had died away now; Loholt looked only worried. "But I thought you ought to know."

"Then take yourself off."

Loholt turned away at Kay's nod of dismissal. As soon as he was out of earshot, Gawain said, "Don't be hard on the boy, Kay. He tries his best."

"I'll thank you, Sir Gawain, not to interfere with my management of the pages," Kay snapped back at him.

Gawain said nothing, and almost at once Kay's affronted expression faded, replaced by a look that was an apology in itself.

"Forgive me," Kay said quietly. "Will you tell me what you know of this?"

Gawain smiled at him, aware once again that something had shaken Kay badly off balance.

"Lancelot spoke to me when he came back from Corbenic," he

said. "He was bewildered, sick, disgusted with himself. He had to tell someone. Think of it, Kay. How could any man confuse two ladies so utterly unlike? Only if he were drunk or . . . enchanted. And Lancelot would not be drunk."

Kay listened in silence, his face shuttered now, giving nothing away. "Enchanted?" he repeated, when Gawain had finished.

"Lancelot told me that while he was preparing for bed, Elaine's waiting woman came to him. She said that the queen had arrived unexpectedly, and was asking for him. He went to her. The next morning . . . it was Elaine. She admitted the enchantment. She pleaded with him to stay. She even told him that she had conceived his child. How would she know that, so soon, without enchantment?"

Kay's expression was still unreadable. "You believe all this?" Although he asked the question, he did not sound really sceptical. Kay was no friend of Lancelot, but he would not accuse him of lying.

"Oh, yes," Gawain said, "Corbenic is a strange place. Uncanny. Things have been seen there. I've even heard it said that Elaine's father holds the Grail—or knows where it might be found."

"You won't find the Grail in any king's treasury. Not in this world." Kay shook off the momentary abstraction. "Gawain, if it was anyone but you telling me this, I would say he was drunk, or mad, or a superstitious fool. As it is . . . yes, there are strange tales about Corbenic."

Kay sighed. There was a wary look about him. He met Gawain's eyes at last. "And tonight?"

"I don't know. Dear God, Kay, I don't know. Would Elaine dare, here, in Camelot?" Anxiously, he said, "Whatever happens, you won't repeat this story?"

"Story?" Kay was sharp again. "What story? I told you, sometimes I'm very conveniently deaf. Elaine may conjure all the devils out of hell for all I care. There's enough gossip in this place without my adding to it."

He got up, wished Gawain a curt goodnight, and stalked out of the hall.

Kay had no heart for sleep that night. After he took leave of Gawain, he supervised the final clearing up in the kitchens and the preparations for the next morning. He went to his workroom and wrote letters for an hour. By the time he had finished, he was exhausted, an ache in his head and between his shoulder blades, and yet his mind went on circling the same well-worn track like a mule turning a spit.

He dropped wax on the last of the letters and pressed his seal ring on it. When the impression was made he sat looking at it, the vivid falcon's face, and its reverse, engraved in miraculous detail on the carnelian set in gold that the king had given him.

Kay sighed. He remembered that day very well. Arthur had just been crowned king, but he was very far from being accepted by the whole of Britain. There were still battles ahead, but the danger seemed remote from the more pressing problems of what Arthur's kingship would mean. Kay had begun with very little idea of what it meant to be high seneschal, yet he could not doubt that it was what he had been born to do.

Arthur had called him into his private room. He held the ring, turning it in a shaft of sunlight so that the stone flashed fire.

"Look, Kay," he said. "He's exactly like you: small and fierce and damnably arrogant. My falcon."

He had slipped the ring on to Kay's hand, and embraced him, and Kay had thought that no one in the whole world could ever have known such happiness.

The letters finished, Kay put the ring on again. The glow of the lamp woke a little of the fire of that long-ago sunlight. Kay sat thinking, drew a fresh piece of paper towards him, and dipped his pen, but he wrote nothing. He knew the law; most of it he had made himself, back in those early days. He could draw up a document that would declare Loholt legitimate, that would be accepted without question by men like Gawain and Gareth and Lancelot, men who put the king's interests before their own.

But what about the others? The like of Briant des Isles or Mark of Cornwall, who would take the slightest excuse to claim rights in Arthur's lands, once Arthur was dead. Kay gave a sardonic little smile. He might cut his document on stone tablets and they would still take no notice of it. It was, in the end, quite worthless, because the only men who would uphold it were the ones who would be faithful without it.

Still, Arthur had commanded, and the document must be drawn up—but not tonight, Kay thought wearily. He put aside pen and paper, and thrust back his chair. Remembering that by now the torches in the passages would have burnt out, he lit a taper before he blew out the lamp and then, carrying it carefully, let himself out of the workroom.

He shielded the tiny flame with one cupped hand as he went quietly down the stairs and along the passage past the entrance to the great hall and towards the living quarters. He scarcely needed the fragile sphere of light; he knew every stone of this castle. If anyone had accused Kay of loving the place, he would have told him sharply not to be so absurd, but he would have found it hard to counter the accusation. The walls fitted him like a second skin.

As he climbed another stairway and reached the upper corridor that led to his apartments, he heard, ahead of him but still distant, a woman's scream. Kay stopped abruptly; the scream came again, and rapid footsteps swept towards him out of the darkness. At the head of the stairs the running man was upon him, thrusting him back against the wall. Kay dropped the taper, but in the instant before the flame was quenched he saw the face, frozen and terrible: Lancelot.

Recovering his balance, Kay called his name, but Lancelot ignored him. Kay thought perhaps he did not even realise that anyone was there. In the darkness he heard sounds that suggested Lancelot had fallen down the last few steps, scrambled to his feet, and continued his flight until his footsteps died away. All the while the screaming continued, ripping the night.

Kay groped his way forward. As soon as his eyes grew accustomed to the darkness, he began to make out a faint light ahead. As he turned the next corner he could see lamplight angling out of an open door, and in the doorway the lady Elaine. Her hair was in disorder, she had a bedgown dragged around her, and she was screaming. A little way beyond her stood Guenevere, staring at her, white-faced and silent.

For a second, no one moved. Then Kay strode rapidly down the passage until he came up to the lady Elaine, and slapped her across the face. Her scream was cut off. She drew in a breath of pure shock, her eyes disbelieving, before she collapsed into noisy sobbing.

Kay did not want her collapsing all over him. Distastefully he fended her off and to his relief caught sight of one of her waiting women, hovering in the doorway. He took Elaine by the shoulders, spun her round, and propelled her into the woman's arms.

"Your lady is ill," he said. "See to her. I will send her a restorative draught."

The woman—a dumpy little creature, with brown hair neatly braided—shot him one look, saying nothing, and drew her lady inside the room. Kay closed the door behind them and turned towards the queen.

Guenevere came to meet him, her frozen calm shattering as Elaine disappeared. She clutched at Kay's arm; her hands were shaking.

"Kay, he was with her," she whispered faintly. "I heard them together. I heard her—"

Kay closed his hand over hers. He could not be unaware of her, of her warmth, her nearness, the honey-gold hair spilling over her shoulders, the scent of it reaching him on an indrawn breath. He could not be unaware, but he forced himself not to react.

"Lady, don't distress yourself." He spoke clearly, not just for Guenevere's ears. By now doors were opening all down the passage. "The lady Elaine has been disturbed. By evil dreams, no doubt. Her women will take care of her."

To his profound relief, Guenevere took the hint he gave her. Understanding flooded into her staring eyes. He felt her hand tighten on his arm and then release him.

"Thank you, Sir Kay," she said evenly. "I'm glad it is no worse."

She turned; Kay would have escorted her back to her own rooms if he had not seen, farther down the passage with a lamp in his hand, Arthur himself approaching. Kay waited until the king and queen had withdrawn, thankful that Guenevere by now was in command of herself. He then raked the remaining watchers with an icy glance suggesting without words that the hour was late and gossip unprofitable, and went back to the kitchens.

His first task was to rout out a kitchen maid and set her to brewing a herbal posset for the lady Elaine. He refrained from making one or two creative suggestions about what she might put in it. Then, following a suspicion, he let himself out of the door that led to the stable yard.

One of the grooms was still up, blundering around in the dark and cursing. He was only too ready to share his story with Kay. Lancelot had come down, banging on the doors and demanding to have his horse saddled, ". . . as if all the devils in hell were on his heels, sir, and his eyes rolling as if he was mad. Foaming at the mouth he was, sir," the groom added with relish.

Kay doubted it. The facts were no more than that Lancelot had called for his horse and fled from the court. Remembering what he had learnt earlier from Loholt and Gawain, Kay could deduce a little more. Surely the same thing had happened again; Lancelot had been tricked into Elaine's bed, only to leave her, screaming, when he discovered she was not the queen.

Kay reached this conclusion rapidly. It was not until he had said goodnight to the groom and was making belatedly for his own bed, that he thought to ask himself: How was it that Guenevere, distanced from Elaine's apartment by a staircase, a passage, and several closed doors, had been able to hear Lancelot and Elaine at their lovemaking?

The following morning, Elaine and her retinue left Camelot. Not far behind them went the troops of men to reinforce the south coast garrison against the raids of Briant des Isles. They were led by Gawain's brother Gaheris. Loholt remained with his father. There was nothing to tell anyone where Lancelot had gone.

Ten days later, a courier arrived at Camelot, almost falling from his exhausted horse. Briant des Isles and his men had taken Arthur's castle of Roche Dure, on the northwest coast. From there, Briant was preparing to lay siege to Carlisle.

Chapter Five

Gareth of Orkney moved reluctantly away from the warm curve of his wife's body, and raised himself on one elbow, looking down at her. Lionors slept curled around the life within her as if she protected it.

One more night, Gareth thought, before he rode with Arthur to face Briant in the North. One more night, and then he might never see his wife again. He might not see his unborn child at all. Better to be a farmer, perhaps, and live from season to season, and have nothing to do with knights and kings. Gareth half smiled. If Lionors had been awake, and he had spoken his thoughts to her, she would have told him not to be such a fool.

He bent his head and kissed her bare shoulder under straying dark hair. Carefully, so as not to wake her, he slid out of bed and stretched. Light seeped pale through the chinks of the window shutters and already Gareth could hear, faint from the courtyard below, the trundling of a cart.

Even though it was so early, Gareth's servant had left hot water for him to wash. As he dressed, his natural, buoyant optimism reasserted itself. He whistled softly as he let himself out of his apartments.

He meant to go to the stables and make sure that his horse was ready for the journey tomorrow, but as he passed a door halfway down the passage, he checked, hesitated, and tapped. A voice told him to come in.

His brother Gawain sat at the table in the outer room. He wore a bedgown; his hair was ruffled and he had not shaved. Gareth wondered if he had been to bed at all. Spread out on the table in front of him was a litter of packets spilling herbs, jars and boxes of salves and ointments. The aromatic smell caught Gareth at the back of the throat.

Gawain smiled as his brother came in and gestured towards the table. "I'm running low. I must speak to the healers." He picked up one of the pots and sniffed critically. "Tansy. Last season's gathering. The healers will have fresh."

He sat looking up at Gareth, still with the same faint smile, not questioning why he was there. Gareth could not have answered the question, except that if he had to ride into danger the next day, he was glad that Gawain would be with him.

He wondered whether anyone who saw the public Gawain—the polished courtier, wise councillor, the greatest knight of all except perhaps for Lancelot—would have recognised this self-effacing man, weary, a touch uncertain, with the herbs of healing in his hand instead of the sword. Arthur, perhaps, but Gareth was not sure of that. Or Kay, who was uncomfortably perceptive under his brusque mannerisms. Certainly not Lancelot, seeing life as he did in splendid gold and purple. And no woman, any longer, who came closer to Gawain than the courtly exterior.

"You're looking thoughtful, Brother," Gawain said, breaking in on his thoughts. "Is Lionors well?"

"Yes. I left her sleeping."

"She'll have the best of care here."

The brothers' eyes met, neither speaking his full thoughts, both of them aware that last time all the care that the whole of Camelot could lavish on Lionors had not saved her child alive.

"We'll not be long away, please God," Gawain said. "But it's hard to ride out when those you love are left behind."

His lips closed in a faintly bitter line that Gareth did not often see there. Gareth guessed what he was thinking, though he knew he would never really understand. Gawain had married while Gareth was still a boy, at home in Orkney, and Gareth had never met his wife. Ragnell, the beautiful, the fey, had walked into Gawain's life and out of it, leaving behind her an incomparable story and a hurt that might be hidden but never healed.

"I'm going to the stables," Gareth said. "Shall I look over your horse for you?"

Gawain's expression lightened. "Yes, if you please. My squire will do it, no doubt, but I'd as soon not trust my life to him. He's a good boy, but scatterbrained."

He was smiling again, a rather twisted, humorous look that made Gareth suddenly want to embrace his brother, and not at all sure of how he would explain himself if he did. Forcing a grin, he said, "Go and top up your tansy," and went on his way to the stables.

He was passing the stairs that led to the great hall when quick footsteps sounded behind him and Loholt caught him up. There was a bright, breathless air about the boy, and his eyes were shining.

"You look pleased with life," Gareth said.

Loholt drew himself up, pride in the tilt of his head. "Yes, sir. I ride with you tomorrow."

Gareth was mildly surprised. As far as he knew, all the squires and pages had been ordered to remain at Camelot, to help in its defence if Briant carried war up to its gates. The force that rode north tomorrow would be made up of seasoned fighting men.

"You're honoured," he said.

"Yes, sir. I'll try to be worthy."

Gareth hid amusement at the fervent tones. He had been like that himself not all that long ago, seeing every new campaign as an adventure.

"I'm to go to the armourer," Loholt said. "My father—no, my lord the king—" he corrected himself, "told me to ask for a mail coat. I hope there's one that fits," he added anxiously. "There's no time to have one made."

"The armourer will find you something," Gareth said. "Or if there's a problem, ask Sir Kay."

Loholt gave him a nervous look. "Sir Kay doesn't like me."

Gareth grinned. "I sometimes think Kay doesn't like anyone. Including Kay. Don't let it worry you."

"I suppose he has cause," Loholt said. "I drew sword on him. But I hoped for his forgiveness. . . ." Biting his lip, he let his voice trail off.

Gareth stopped and put a hand on his shoulder. "Listen. Kay has a sharp tongue, true. God knows, I've felt it often enough! And he can be harsh with the young men. But he is . . ." Gareth paused, wondering what he wanted to say, or how much he could say, to Loholt. He certainly could not try to unravel for the boy the perverse complexity that was Kay. He was not sure he understood himself the man who had once been his master. "Kay is a true knight," he said, "and Arthur's faithful servant." He laughed at Loholt's look of wide-eyed uncertainty. "Loholt, Kay is rude to everyone, from King Arthur down to the kitchen cat. Don't think you're singled out for special treatment."

He clapped the boy on the shoulder, and led the way out into the stable yard. He was not sure if he had convinced Loholt, or even whether it mattered. Gareth watched as Loholt trotted off obediently towards the armoury, and then turned in the direction of the stables.

Before he reached them, he could not help noticing a knot of men standing in the entrance to the barn where the horses' fodder was stored. Bors and Ector, Lancelot's kinsmen, his own brother Agravaine, and Kay. Kay was speaking; although Gareth could not hear the words at first, he could see vehement defiance in every line of Kay's body. Gareth was reminded of a cat spitting at a pack of hounds. Quietly he drew closer.

". . . since Briant deceived us and drew off all our strength to the South," Kay was saying scathingly. "What else could he wish for, but that Lancelot leaves us, too?"

Sir Ector put his hand on the hilt of his sword. Lancelot's half-brother, he had Lancelot's tall, loose-limbed figure without the poise and balance that made Lancelot so formidable.

"Are you accusing Lancelot of treason?"

Kay ignored the implied threat. His dark eyes were snapping fury. "Treason? That's your word, not mine. All I say is that now, when Arthur's need is greatest, his chief warrior is not here." The last three words were spat out as if Kay tasted poison. "And if you, my lords, have had no word from him and do not know where he might be found, then no one knows and we cannot send for him." He let out a snort of disgust. "All because of some piece of foolishness over a woman."

"They say Lancelot was ensorcelled," Bors said.

He was one of the most reserved men Gareth had ever met, and he spoke now with a complete lack of emotion; there was no telling what he thought of Lancelot's defection. Gareth knew that the loss of Lancelot could not have come at a worse time. He was needed at Carlisle, not just for his own formidable fighting skills, but because he knew how to kindle the flame in others. No one, perhaps not even the king himself, could take Lancelot's place. No wonder that Kay should try to get word to him.

"Perhaps you think that was Briant's doing?" Ector said to Kay. "You seem to fear him enough."

A spot of red flared in Kay's cheeks. He wore no sword, but he took a step towards Ector. "I do not fear Briant. But I fear what he may do to Britain, before Arthur drives him out."

All this while Agravaine had been standing propped against the barn wall, his thumbs stuck in his belt, listening with a slack-mouthed grin to Kay and the others. Gareth knew very well that trouble seemed to attract Agravaine, whether it was any concern of his or not.

Now Agravaine shifted his shoulders against the wall, and said, "No need to fear, Kay, when we have your sword to defend us."

Kay spun round to face him. Gareth thought that his shoulders began to droop, his taut defiance fading, but he jerked up his head. "I do not ride tomorrow."

"No?" Ector said, a sudden malice in his face.

Kay shook his head; his mouth was set. "My duties keep me here."

Gareth could see a sick longing in his eyes. He knew himself how it felt to ride out into battle and leave someone you loved behind, and he had wondered if it was even harder for Gawain, who had no one to wait for his return, but he had never considered before how it must feel to be left behind when all your friends were facing danger. Perhaps Lionors could have told him, yet no one expected a woman to ride to war.

Agravaine gave a sneering laugh. "It's a good enough excuse, for someone whose sword grows rusty—if you even remember what you've done with it."

The jibe went home because Kay was unarmed; if he had been wearing a weapon, he would have drawn it. As it was, Gareth was ready for him to spring at Agravaine's throat. Agravaine was ready too, waiting with open amusement, for there was a bitter seed of truth in what he said. Kay was no fighter. If he lost his temper now, he would be humiliated in the end.

Gareth thrust himself between them, and gripped Kay by the shoulders, though it was to Agravaine he spoke. "What do you think you're doing? Starting a quarrel when there's trouble enough without it? Kay, don't listen to him."

"Sir Gareth, I wonder you defend Kay," Bors said, "when he insults Sir Lancelot, who made you knight."

Gareth swallowed anger at Bors' sanctimonious air. "I heard no insult," he said. "Kay must respect Lancelot, to want him here, as we should—"

His grip on Kay's shoulders tightened as he felt Kay gather himself to interrupt, but the seneschal was beyond taking the hint.

"Who made you Sir Gareth's conscience?" Kay asked Bors. "Or mine?"

To Gareth's surprise, Bors was silent for a moment, and then bowed his head stiffly. "True. I ask your pardon. Ector, come."

He laid a hand on Ector's arm and drew him away. Ector went reluctantly, glancing back over his shoulder. "If Lancelot were here, you would be shamed."

That left only Agravaine, who lolled back against the wall again with an insolent half-smile.

"Gareth, let be," Kay said. He shook off Gareth's hands. "I've better things to do than start a brawl with Agravaine."

Gareth began to relax, but he might have known that Agravaine had not finished.

"If you're too much of a coward to face me, no wonder you don't want to ride out against Briant. Do you think he knows? Or is he shaking in his boots, thinking that the terrible Sir Kay will come looking for him?"

Kay had turned away towards the barn, where workmen were cording bundles for the pack horses. Now his fury flared up again.

"At least, Sir Agravaine," he said caustically, "I would be sober enough to find the road north. And perhaps of more worth than a swordsman who is drunk as a drowned mouse every night."

Agravaine started to draw his sword, only to sheathe it again with a grin of pure satisfaction. Gareth followed the direction of his gaze, and saw that Arthur himself had just come into the stable yard, beside Loholt, who carried his mail coat bundled up in his arms.

"All right," Agravaine said. "Prove your courage, Kay. Go and ask Arthur now if you can ride with us."

Kay's head snapped round towards him. His eyes lit. Without

a word, he strode off across the yard. Gareth said, "Kay—" and followed, a few paces behind.

When he came up to Arthur, who had stopped for a word with one of the grooms, Kay knelt in front of him. Arthur looked astonished; Loholt stared. Gareth found that he wanted to smile; he would not have thought it possible for anyone to look so supremely arrogant while on his knees in the muck of the stable yard.

"Kay, what is this?" Arthur said.

"My lord, please grant me a favour."

His voice had recovered its imperious tone; he sounded the very reverse of a humble petitioner.

"I want to know what it is first." Once recovered from his surprise, Arthur sounded wary, and not entirely pleased with Kay. He frowned a little.

"My lord, take me with you when you ride tomorrow."

Arthur's frown deepened. Gareth saw that under the king's gaze, Kay's initial confidence began to waver.

"And who will hold Camelot for me while I am gone?" Arthur asked.

"The queen, my lord, is more than capable."

Gareth guessed that Kay had rehearsed this conversation in his mind many times, but perhaps would never have had the courage to speak if he had not been goaded by Agravaine.

"Sir Kay thinks a woman could fill his place."

Agravaine, just behind Gareth, spoke apparently to the empty air, but his voice carried. Gareth saw Kay's hands clench. His voice desperate, he said, "My lord, do not dishonour me!"

Arthur went on looking down at him in silence for a moment. Slowly, the king began to smile—a smile of such tenderness and understanding that Gareth did not dare contemplate what Kay must be feeling.

"Very well. Have your own difficult way, if you must." Arthur held out a hand. "Come, get up. Can you be ready in time?"

For a moment Kay remained kneeling, clinging to Arthur's hand. "Yes, my lord!"

Gareth caught a glimpse of Kay's face—exalted, and somehow young and vulnerable, the competence and experience of his seneschal's office momentarily stripped away. He bent over Arthur's hand, raising it to his forehead, and then rose, bowed, and hurried away.

Gareth wondered whether to follow him, and decided that his presence—or anyone else's—would be the last thing Kay would want. Instead he turned to Agravaine. "Satisfied?"

Agravaine lounged away, grinning. Arthur, shaking his head as he looked after Kay, beckoned to Gareth. As Gareth moved to join him, he noticed Loholt. There was an alertness in the boy's face. Gareth knew very well how nervous he was of Kay, but he could not explain his expression now. Loholt might be dismayed at the thought of having Kay as a companion on the road north, but why should he look calculating?

Gareth woke, wondered why he felt so stiff and cold, and remembered with a groan. He pushed himself up on one elbow and, blinking to clear his vision, peered out across the camp and the sweep of moorland that looked just like all the other inhospitable hillsides where they had camped on their journey north. Behind him, a grey dawn light outlined the crest of the fell.

Around him men blundered into wakefulness, gathering in little knots around campfires, making ready for the day's journey. Gareth could not repress a lurch of uneasiness in his stomach when he saw how few they were, all the men Arthur had been able to gather in that frantic day of preparation after word came that Briant had taken Roche Dure. He had written to Gaheris, recalling him with his troops, but Gareth knew his brother must be some days behind.

Arthur's force had travelled fast, and now they were only three days from Carlisle—three days, Gareth reflected, before they would find out whether they had only to raise the siege there, or whether they would find Briant des Isles already walled up inside. Three days before they would know whether they had come in time.

Beside Gareth, his brother Gawain still slept, nothing visible outside his blanket but a few honey-gold curls. Beyond him, Kay was already awake, hunched over the previous night's campfire, raking the embers together with a half-burnt branch. A few pale flames flickered in the breeze.

"What did you do, glare at it?" Gareth asked, crouching down beside him.

Kay gave him an acid look, and settled a small pot of water on the fire. "If you've nothing better to do, go and fill the water skins. Spring's up there, between those rocks." He pointed, stretched, and sighed. "Dear God, I'm stiff," he complained. "Too much soft living."

Hiding a grin, Gareth went to do as he said. He would never have referred to Kay's gruelling schedule at Camelot as "soft living," but he understood what Kay meant. It was years now since Kay had ridden out on campaign. Gareth had never known him except as seneschal, tied to the court by his duties. He had wondered, when they first left Camelot, whether Kay would regret his decision, whether, perhaps, he would need help on the road. Like everyone else, Gareth tended to forget that Kay had campaigned across the face of Britain when Arthur was first made king, fighting at Arthur's side when few others had given their allegiance.

Now Gareth could only be thankful that he had kept his wondering to himself.

By the time Gareth returned with the filled water skins, Gawain was awake. Kay stirred oatmeal in the pot on the fire. Around them, in the strengthening light, the camp was rousing, making ready to ride. Gareth caught sight of Arthur, moving from campfire to campfire, with a smaller, slighter figure—Loholt—dogging his footsteps. Gareth watched the two of them as they drew nearer, pausing to talk to each separate knot of men, until at last they approached, just as Kay was sharing out the breakfast.

"Don't get up," Arthur said. He squatted down on the turf and held out his hands to the fire; Loholt remained standing a pace or two away, as if he was uneasy with all this informality. "All well?" the king asked.

"No," Kay said tartly. "These lodgings are far too draughty, and the beds are hard."

Arthur laughed. "You asked for this, Kay; don't blame me now." The laughter died out of his face. "Listen. Later today we'll ford the river a few miles upstream from Roche Dure. After that, we have to be prepared to meet Briant."

"But has he enough men?" Gareth asked. "To hold Roche Dure, and to lay siege to Carlisle, and have troops out in the countryside?"

"Are you saying he's waiting for us?" Kay said sharply.

"I hope not." It was a reply to both questions. Arthur rubbed his hands over his face. He looked tired and strained; Gareth knew that by now they all were. "But we can't be certain. I've men-at-arms who know these hills well, and they'll lead us by hidden ways to Carlisle. But if Briant can cut us off, he will."

"He can't know where we are," Gawain said. "Or what road we'll take."

"No," Arthur agreed. "So from now on we go as quietly and as carefully as we can. No unnecessary noise. No more fires at night—I'm sorry, Kay," he added, as the seneschal made a disgusted noise. "And all the time, keep a lookout. We've made good time from Camelot. I don't believe Briant can be expecting us yet. I want to give him the shock of his life when we ride down on him at Carlisle."

The troop of horsemen reached the river in the middle of that afternoon. By that time, a fine, drizzling rain had set in, a rain that soaked everything, turned the hillside to a treacherous glissade, and hung in the air like mist, obscuring everything beyond the river.

The horses picked their way carefully down the final slope, through light woodland. The trees' autumn colours had faded to a neutral brown; rain dripped from every twig. Every man already obeyed the king's orders for quiet, and there was no sound but for the movement of the horses and the occasional jingle from a bridle.

The river ran fast and deep, with brown peaty water off the high fells. The leading horsemen reined in on the bank. Gareth, riding a little way behind with Kay, saw Arthur lean over and speak briefly to Gawain, and then dismount and begin leading his horse out into the river. By the time he reached the midpoint, water swirled around his chest. Gawain and Loholt and the first of the others followed, some of them trying to swim their horses across and being carried downstream by the fierce current.

"They call this a ford?" Kay said disdainfully.

Gareth laughed. "Come on. You can't get any wetter than you are already."

He dismounted in his turn and took the first steps out into the current; the force of it almost took his breath away. The bottom was shale, shifting under his feet. Leading his horse, Gareth ventured farther out, then glanced back over his shoulder to make sure that Kay followed safely. The seneschal had stayed mounted; his black, Morial—after throwing up its head once or twice as if it shared its owner's disapproval of the whole exercise—quietly obeyed his urging.

Arthur and the leading horsemen were already climbing the bank on the far side. Turning once more to look back, Gareth saw Gawain. Then out of the silence and the mist ahead of them, he heard a sound like ripping cloth, and saw a horseman just ahead of him throw up his hands and topple from his mount to disappear into the rushing water. Behind, someone cried out, and other voices joined the first in a growing clamour. Farther downstream, a horse thrashed around, out of control. Gareth, his mind seeming to work very slowly against the sudden rapid movement all around him, realised that what he had first heard had been the flight of an arrow. At the same moment, he felt a violent blow on his shoulder. He lost his grip on the bridle and his footing on the shifting river bed. Water surged over his head.

The current drove Gareth against the flank of his horse. He got his head out, tried to find his feet again, and reached up to grab the mane. But somehow his body was not obeying him. He went under again, rolling and scraping along the bottom, was flung up against something that moved—man or horse, he never knew—and carried out into deeper water. Desperate for air, Gareth fought to reach the surface, but his senses were growing dim and he was not sure which was the right direction.

Then he felt a hand fasten in his hair. His head broke surface. He coughed water, managed to get a breath. Kay was in the river beside him, yelling curses at him. Suddenly Gareth felt better; at least Kay was himself in this suddenly bewildering world.

He seemed to want Gareth to swim for the far bank, and Gareth tried to obey, if only because obedience to Kay came naturally to him, but his limbs felt heavy. His left arm was no use at all; his riding boots were filled with water and dragged him down. He could make out the bank now, but it drew no nearer.

Kay had a hand under his arm, trying to help him along. He was still spitting fury, so that Gareth felt it would be a personal insult if he gave in now. But he was very tired. Everything was growing grey, shrouded in mist, and the grey grew darker every second. Out of it Gareth caught a swift, vivid glimpse of Kay's white face, black hair streaking his forehead, and then even that seemed to dissolve. He tried to say, "I'm sorry," but dark water lapped against his face and a soft surge of darkness engulfed him as he sank once again beneath the surface of the river.

Chapter Six

Gawain stumbled along beside the river. Behind him he could hear men and horses crashing about in the woodland as Arthur's scattered band drew together again. Ahead of him were the mist-shrouded trees, and no sound at all except for the surging of the water.

Gawain had his hand on his sword hilt, but he thought that for the moment the danger was over. Briant had hidden his archers in the trees, and when Arthur and his men were exposed at the ford, they had opened fire. Gawain wanted to shut out of his mind what had happened next—the screaming, the men and horses struggling in the river. Most of all he wanted to forget following Arthur up the slope, and the hand-to-hand fighting among the trees. He relived the sensation of his own sword biting through flesh; the rush of blood; the look of disbelief on his dying opponent's face. Shuddering, he tried to force his mind away from it, before he had to stop somewhere and be sick.

At last, Briant's men had been beaten off. Somehow, Gawain had come out of it unscathed. Somehow, he had found the strength to go back to the river and start directing the rest of the troop to the crest of the hill where Arthur was pitching camp and organising a defence in case the attack was renewed.

At the riverbank there was still turmoil, horses trampling about riderless, men dead and wounded, scarcely anyone who understood yet what had happened or what to do next. Gawain was not sure that he himself understood. Briant had ambushed them, that much was clear, but how had he known where they meant to cross the river?

Since the attack started, Gawain had not seen Gareth or Kay. He had found their horses, Kay's black plunging about on the bank in a fury, Gareth's chestnut heaving itself out of the water farther downstream, but of their riders was no sign. No one he asked knew any more. When he was sure that the rest of the troops were withdrawing to the hilltop, Gawain set off downstream to look for them.

The river flowed on, revealing nothing. Gawain had already found one man, drowned and washed up on a spit of land that projected into the current, beyond any help that he could give. He was terrified that he would find another who would be his brother or his friend.

As the noise died away behind him, Gawain slowed and

finally stopped. Would the river have carried them so far? How long should he go on? He knew that he risked walking into a nest of Briant's men. Perhaps Gareth and Kay were prisoners; from all he had heard of Briant, they might be better off dead.

He gazed around him, but the trees, the river, gave him no help. Already daylight began to fail; Gawain knew that his search would be hopeless in the dark.

"Gareth!" he called. His voice cracked on the edge of panic. "Gareth! Kay!"

From some way ahead he thought he heard a faint answering cry. He could still see nothing. Uncertainly, he took a step forward. "Gareth?"

The cry was repeated, seeming to come from the river. Gawain flung himself down on the edge, and leaned over. Along this stretch of the river, the water ran deep, scouring out a channel for itself so that it undercut the bank. Beneath the overhang Kay was clinging to a projecting scrap of root, his white face gazing upwards.

"Gawain!" he gasped out.

Gawain reached down to him. "Give me your hand."

"No—it's Gareth. I can't . . . I think he's dead."

Between the mist and the gathering twilight Gawain had not seen at first that Kay was supporting someone else in the water. Now he could make out a tangle of drenched hair, the line of one shoulder, a hand floating, tugged by the current. Fear lurched into his throat. "Hold on," he said. By stretching over the edge, he managed to get a grip on Gareth's shoulders, relieving Kay of his weight, but he feared that his strength was not enough to haul his brother to dry land. As he struggled, Kay heaved himself up until he was able to grab hold of Gareth, helping Gawain to drag the inert mass of his body over the lip of the bank and to safety.

Gawain crouched over his brother's body, hand trembling as he reached towards his lips, and sobbed out, "Thank God!" as he felt the faint but unmistakable exhalation of breath. Rapidly examining him, he found the blunt feathers of a crossbow bolt, the shaft buried deep in Gareth's shoulder. By some miracle it seemed to have missed anything vital. Gareth's face was pallid; he must have lost a lot of blood, but he still lived.

"He's not dead?" Kay asked, his voice shaken.

"No. Thanks to you, Kay."

Kay shook his head. "I couldn't get him out."

The seneschal plunged his head into his hands and slicked back his hair, water streaming from it. Clumsily he tried to wring water out of his cloak.

"Are you hurt?" Gawain said. "Can you help me with Gareth? We should get back to camp, if we can."

"I'm all right."

Kay struggled to his feet, stood unsteadily for a moment, and then stooped to help Gawain lift his brother's body. "What's happening?" he asked. "Briant's men?"

"We've driven them off," Gawain said. "For the time being." He manoeuvred along the water's edge, trying to guide Kay along the easiest path with their awkward burden. "Arthur is setting sentries on the hilltop. We should be safe for the night, at least."

Darkness was falling as they reached the top of the hill. A challenge rang out; Gawain answered it, and one of the men-at-arms stepped forward, with Loholt peering suspiciously around him. Gawain sent the boy to find his pack, and Loholt, with a startled look at Gareth, sped off obediently. Then, to Gawain's infinite relief, they were able to set Gareth down in the lee of a rock. He pondered what to do for the arrow wound.

A yard or two away lay the body of another man, huddled ominously still. Kay stooped and turned him over; it was no one they knew. His dead hand still clutched a crossbow, and a red dragon sprawled across his surcoat. Kay muttered something inaudible and with the sentry's help dragged the body into a clump of bracken.

"Is Briant claiming the dragon as his device?" Gawain asked.

"No doubt, since he calls himself Pendragon." Kay sounded as crisp and pedantic as he ever did at Camelot. "And he uses crossbows, unlike any decent man. . . ." By the last few words his voice was wavering again, and he swayed, a hand to his head.

"Sit down before you fall down," Gawain said. "I don't want you on my hands as well as Gareth."

He had already set to work with his belt knife, cutting away Gareth's surcoat, unfastening the mail and laying back the padded undershirt to expose the wound beneath.

"Will Gareth be all right?" Kay asked.

"Yes, of course."

Kay seemed to accept the reassurance, and lowered himself to the ground nearby. He leaned back against the rock, his eyes closing, only to rouse a few minutes later as Loholt appeared and tossed Gawain's saddlebags down beside him. Gawain pounced on them with a word of thanks; while he sorted out bandages and salve, Loholt watched him in silence, then asked, "Can I help you, sir?"

Gawain managed a quick smile for him. "No, thank you. But if the king has no orders for you, you could find the surgeons and see if they need you."

Loholt nodded and disappeared into the shadows.

"At least he's making himself useful," Kay said, a weak trace of acid returning to his voice.

"He did well today," Gawain said. "He followed Arthur up the hill, to attack Briant's archers. It could have been his first fight, but he wasn't afraid."

Kay made a noncommittal noise. Gawain guessed that it would take more than one skirmish to make Kay approve of Loholt, but at least it was a start.

Gawain worked swiftly on Gareth's shoulder, cutting out the crossbow bolt and dressing the wound, thanking God as he did so that his salves and bandages had stayed dry. Kay watched his every move with the intensity of a cat at a mousehole.

"Can you sit with him for a while?" Gawain asked when he had finished. "I ought to look at the other wounded. He should sleep, but if he wakes you can give him a drink—water, not wine."

With Kay's assent, he took his pack and went to see where his help was needed. To his relief, only two of the men who still lived were wounded at all seriously, and the two camp surgeons, with their helpers—including Loholt—had everything well in hand. Gawain spent an hour doing what he could, patching up various lesser hurts. His patients included Agravaine, who had a deep scrape along one arm—and a lot of superficial scratches that suggested he had dived into the undergrowth when the attack began, and stayed there until it was over.

Gawain's task became more difficult as the darkness thickened. Arthur took back his order about not building fires, since Briant undoubtedly knew where they were, but in the persistent drizzling rain everything was too wet to burn. It proved impossible to get even a taper to light.

At last there was no more to be done, and Gawain was free to return to Kay and Gareth. Gareth had not moved. Kay sat beside him, holding his hand; at Gawain's approach he looked faintly awkward, but he did not relinquish the clasp. "Gawain, he's so cold," he said.

"Look," Gawain said, "Gareth is young, and strong, and tough as boot leather. He's not going to die. I promise you."

Kay looked up at him, still uncertain. "It's this damnable rain," he said shakily. "He needs shelter, and fire, and a warm bed."

Gawain knew that at Camelot, Kay could have summoned all those things with a flick of the fingers. "Why don't you go to sleep?" he suggested. "You've had as much as you can take for one night. I'll keep watch for a while."

For a few seconds Kay still stared at him, then averted his face with a helpless, inarticulate sound of anger. He lay down beside Gareth, his head buried in the crook of one arm. Gawain laid a hand gently on his shoulder before settling down against the rock, pulling the saturated folds of his cloak around him, and gazing out over the dark camp.

By the following morning the rain had given way to white

mist that coiled sluggishly up from the river. Gareth was awake, sitting up and asserting that he was ravenously hungry, only to complain loudly about the sodden bread and strips of salt meat that were all Gawain could offer him. Kay, sitting at his side, made a poor job of disguising his relief.

"Can you ride?" Gawain asked. "We're making horse litters for the other two. We can't leave anyone behind."

"I can ride." Gareth gave Kay a look of impish amusement. "Kay will make sure I do, just as he got me across the river yesterday. He has a very wide vocabulary."

Kay looked embarrassed. "I was hoping you had forgotten that."

Gareth's tone was teasing, affectionate. "No one who is sworn at by Sir Kay forgets it in a hurry."

Gawain laughed and, leaving them to it, went to find the king. Arthur stood at the centre of the camp, with Loholt beside him as he always was now, as well as Bors, Bedivere, and a few of the others.

Arthur broke off what he was saying as Gawain came up to him. "Gawain. I was going to send for you. How is Gareth?"

"Arguing with Kay, my lord. Much as usual."

Arthur seemed to relax. "That's good news. Now . . ." He gazed around into the swirling mist. "Yesterday, Briant found us. I don't know how."

Somebody in the group around him muttered, "Sorcery." Arthur flicked a swift look in the direction of the voice, a rebuke without words.

"I hope it was no more than a lucky guess," he said. "We may have beaten him off, or—or he may be out there now, waiting for us to make a move."

Bedivere spat out a curse.

"Our first duty is what it always has been," Arthur went on. "To bring help to Carlisle. If Briant is watching us, we may be able to lose him. We have good guides, and the mist may help." He nodded curtly. "Get everyone ready to move off. And remember—speed and silence."

The column formed up and moved off. Their guides led them along a winding track at the foot of dark hills, their tops lost in a blanket of cloud, their lower slopes thrusting out like the paws of huge animals. Mist shrouded everything, thinning now and then to reveal a line of forest or an open valley, only to close in again. Every sound, even the plash of the horses' hooves on the wet ground, was muffled by it.

Gawain, riding towards the head of the column, was uneasy. His shoulder blades pricked. He could not believe that all Briant's men had been killed at the fight by the ford, or that the survivors could not have called up reinforcements. Their enemies could

Exiled From Camelot

well be keeping track of them now. The mention of sorcery came back into his mind.

He said nothing of his fears to Gareth or Kay; there was no need. Gareth's cheerfulness was quenched by pain and apprehension; Kay was on edge, every nerve end twitching. None of them wanted to talk.

In the featureless mist it was hard to judge time, but they had ridden for some hours when a shout broke the stifling silence. Hoofbeats sounded as a man-at-arms spurred up from the rear of the column. Gawain caught a glimpse of a set, terrified face. He was close enough to hear as the man gasped out his tale to Arthur. His friend, riding beside him, had dropped back a pace or two. Suddenly, he was no longer there. The man had shouted; no one had replied.

Arthur raised a hand for the column to halt. He had begun to issue orders, choosing a small group to go back and look, when a horse came careering out of the mist. Bors thrust his mount into its path and grabbed the bridle. Its rider slumped over its neck; there was an arrow in his throat.

The mist billowed, rolled back. Through the remaining strands of it Gawain could make out dark figures, crouching, running, a spear raised. Three horsemen broke away from the column and rode in pursuit. The mist flowed back, hiding them and their adversaries. In response to Arthur's shouted order, only two of them returned.

The column closed up after that. They moved on; there was nothing else to do. The mist was a white wall, hiding death. Gawain had to stop himself from looking around and trying to penetrate that featureless curtain, instead stoically watching the back of the rider ahead of him. When white began to fade to grey, they made camp. Nothing more had happened, but no one was stupid enough to think that they had shaken off their enemies. They camped in a tight circle, shielded by rocks, and posted sentries. No one expected to sleep.

Gawain went to look at the two badly wounded men. One of them was recovering and would be able to ride the next day; the other was dead. Sick and shivering, Gawain went back to his brother. For the first time he began to face the fact that they might not reach Carlisle.

Gareth leaned against a rock, his cloak wrapped around him, his eyes closed. He looked exhausted.

Gawain sat down at his side. "Where is Kay?"

"Seeing to the horses," Gareth said.

Anxiously, Gawain glanced round. The horses were tethered a short way down the hill from the main camp, on a flatter stretch of turf too close for his liking to the darkening wall of mist. He was about to go and look, when Kay appeared, head down and stumbling as if he were on the edge of collapse. When he reached Gawain's side, he sank down and put his head in his hands.

"Kay, what is it?" Gawain asked.

Kay's voice was stifled. "Morial has gone lame. He must have picked up a stone at the ford yesterday. I was looking at him with one of the grooms. He was getting the stone out, and suddenly the man fell forward. There was an arrow in his back."

Gawain started up, but Kay put out a hand to stop him. "There's nothing you can do. He's dead."

Kay hid his face again. He was shaking. Unevenly he went on, "His name was Madoc. He was a good man. He knew horses. He has a wife, and a child, in Camelot." He let out a sound between a sob and a curse.

Gawain reached forward and touched his arm. "You can see they're cared for."

Kay looked up, hawk's face wild. "If we ever get home. Briant's men—they don't mean to let us reach Carlisle. They'll pick us off like this, one by one, until we're too weak to make a stand, and then finish us."

Gawain gripped his shoulder. "Kay, stop it."

For a moment longer Kay stared at him, and then relaxed. Gareth, who had roused to listen, moved closer to his side. Kay gave him a flickering, apologetic look.

"I prefer to face an enemy I can see." The seneschal let out a long sigh and brushed a hand across his eyes. "I'm sorry. I won't go to pieces, I promise you."

Gawain smiled at him. "Of course not."

He had turned aside to see what food remained in his pack when there was a movement from across the camp. Arthur approached, with Loholt, as usual, at his heels.

Gawain and Kay both got to their feet. Arthur nodded an acknowledgement. He looked anxious, while Gawain thought that Loholt had an almost rebellious air about him.

"They have us pinned down," Arthur said. "If we can't shake them off, things look bad."

He paused, but no one spoke. The king had not come just to tell them that.

"I want to get a small group out," Arthur went on. "In the dark and the mist, a few men should be able to slip away."

That was true enough, Gawain thought, and a way of saving a few lives, but what was the point of it? Their main force would be weakened, and there was no help within reach, not if Carlisle was already under siege.

Then Loholt said, "I don't want to go, Father. I want to stay with you."

"You'll do as you're told, boy," Arthur snapped. "This is no place for you."

Exiled From Camelot

Gawain understood. Of course Arthur would want to save his son's life, and he was right that this was no place for a half-trained boy.

"I'm sending Loholt away," Arthur said, "with one of the guides and a couple of men-at-arms. And Kay, I want you to go."

Kay stiffened, and drew himself together as if someone had just raised a sword at him. "No, my lord!"

Arthur frowned. "Kay, that was an order."

Kay drew breath for another protest, but before he could speak, Loholt broke in. There was a sparkle of satisfaction in his face. "Don't worry, sir. We'll get through safely."

Gawain could hardly believe what he had heard. Loholt could not have said more without accusing Kay outright of cowardice. Kay's head jerked round towards the boy; the look in his eyes made Gawain put a restraining hand on his arm.

Kay shook him off. To Arthur he said, "You dishonour me. Do you think I lack the courage to stand with you to the end?"

Arthur took a moment before he replied. Gawain could see that the strain was telling on him, too, and his patience was growing ragged.

"I said nothing about your courage, Kay. I gave you a task to do, and I expect obedience."

"Because you think I'm no use to you here?"

All Kay's pent-up tension was finding release in anger. He might have lost control completely if Arthur had not kept a grip on his own temper. The king stood still for a moment, confronting Kay, and then took a step forward and rested his hands on Kay's shoulders. "I must send someone. I'm trusting you with Loholt's life."

All the fury drained out of Kay; Gawain saw his expression change to an open, vulnerable look. He could guess what Kay was feeling. He was a man who hid his deeper feelings so successfully that almost everyone believed he had none. Now he was exposed, every nerve quivering. Gawain could only be thankful that there were very few people to see it.

"My lord," Kay said hesitantly, "please send someone else. I want—I want to stay with you."

They were the same words Loholt had used, but it was not the same plea. Arthur understood, but he would not give in.

"Kay, I'll be easier in my mind if I know the two of you are safe."

Kay flung up his head. He took a step back, away from the clasp of Arthur's hands. "You *do* call me coward! You think I'm useless here. Have I done so little that I deserve to be put to shame?"

Arthur's face hardened. "You'll obey your orders." The words were curt, pitiless. "Get your baggage and saddle your horse."

The king swung away, beckoning to Loholt, and strode off towards the horses. Loholt followed, casting one look over his shoulder at Kay. Kay stood rigid, staring after them.

Quietly, Gawain began repacking Kay's saddlebags. He exchanged a look with Gareth, but there was nothing either of them could say. When the bags were ready, he went to give them to Kay, who had not moved. At Gawain's touch he seemed to start out of a kind of stupor.

"What? Oh—thank you, Gawain. I—I must go." He hesitated, glancing at Gareth; roughly, he said, "If I'm going to be slaughtered, I'd rather choose my company."

"We'll meet in Carlisle," Gareth said.

"I wish I believed you."

Kay's voice revealed all his helpless frustration. For a few seconds Gawain thought that he would give way. But before he could think what to do, Kay stepped back. His eyes were wide, dark; he had no more words. Abruptly he seized his bags, and fled, almost running, towards the horses.

Gawain let out the breath he had not been aware of holding, and sank down beside Gareth.

"Cruel," Gareth murmured. He looked white and sick, and relapsed into a brooding silence.

After a moment, Gawain said, "Loholt isn't afraid."

"Then he's mad," Gareth said sourly. "Or ignorant."

"I thought he did well yesterday," Gawain went on. "But just now . . . he was almost baiting Kay. I can't help wondering . . ."

He let his voice die away. He did not say what he had been wondering, and Gareth did not ask.

Chapter Seven

By the time Kay reached the horses, Loholt and the men who were to accompany them were already there. Arthur stood a pace or two away, watching as they saddled up. He nodded, acknowledging Kay's arrival, but did not speak.

Somewhere above the mist and cloud, the moon was rising. It was only natural, Kay thought, that on this damnable journey they should have light when they least wanted it, but for the time being it was no more than a faint drift of silver, enough to see by but still leaving them with the hope of slipping away undetected.

He found the saddle and slung it across Morial's back. His hands shook too much for him to fasten the straps with his customary deftness, and he felt clumsier than ever when he realised that Loholt's eyes were on him. Kay avoided looking at him. He could not bear the boy's self-possession, or dare to risk another of his reassurances.

He felt sick with humiliation. Since leaving Camelot, he had felt more at ease with himself than he had for years. Gawain and Gareth had accepted him as their companion on the journey. He had even dared to believe, just for a little while, that he might win Arthur's approval. Mentally, Kay lashed himself. How could he have been such a fool? He would never be any different—a responsibility that Arthur had to shoulder because of the accident that they were brought up as brothers. If Kay had ever doubted that, it was clear enough now. Arthur did not even respect him enough to let him die at his side.

Kay finished tightening the straps, heaved the saddlebags into place, and stood for a moment resting his forehead against Morial's sleek neck. A hand gripped his shoulder; he started, and turned to see Arthur.

"Not in anger, Kay," the king said.

Kay averted his face. He felt as if his heart had slammed into his throat, and the pain would not let him speak. He managed to shake his head.

"We may meet in Carlisle," Arthur said.

Kay still could not look at him, even though a voice inside his head was screaming, *The last time*! He wanted to hold Arthur in a last embrace, but he knew that if he tried he would give way completely, under Loholt's interested gaze.

"Perhaps." He forced out the single word.

Kay managed to raise his eyes to Arthur's face at last. The king met his gaze with a steady, appraising look, a look that searched Kay to his depths. Kay wanted to cry out: *How was it that Arthur could see so much and understand so little*? But there were no words for what he wanted to say, and if there had been, he would not have dared to say them.

Arthur's grasp on his shoulder tightened. "Kay—"

Whatever he would have said was lost as shouting came from the other side of the camp—shouting and the clash of weapons. Briefly, Kay thought that the enemy had begun its attack.

Then Arthur said, "That's for you. Bedivere's making a diversion. Hurry."

He left Kay, went over to Loholt, and spoke rapidly. Kay did not try to hear what he said. The seneschal swung himself into Morial's saddle and brought his horse into position behind their guide. He could not avoid seeing Arthur embrace Loholt in farewell, and said nothing as Loholt in his turn mounted and came to join him. Staring rigidly between his horse's ears, Kay followed the guide down the hill, over stone and rough turf. The sounds of the camp slipped away behind them.

The first few minutes of their escape were the most dangerous. If Briant's men were watching, Loholt's party would die. Kay felt none of the revulsion he had known when the arrow came slicing out of the night to kill Madoc. He did not even try to listen or look for their enemies. He did not care.

Nothing interrupted the silence of their passing. After a few minutes, they came to a narrow track leading between boulders; their guide turned into it. Kay began, very slightly, to relax. They were well away from the camp by now; surely they must have passed through the ring of their enemies. But the boulders would offer good cover to a waiting archer, and Kay grew more alert for danger.

The track gradually became wider, and as soon as he could Loholt manoeuvred his horse so that he could ride beside Kay. "Father said we might turn back and try to meet Gaheris at the river. His troops can't be many days behind us."

So, Arthur made plans with Loholt and had not seen fit to tell his seneschal, Kay thought bitterly. He let none of the bitterness surface, contenting himself with saying, in a furious undertone, "If you can't keep quiet, lad, all you'll be meeting is an arrow."

Loholt smiled. "We're out of danger now, sir, surely?"

Kay heard an unspoken charge of cowardice in the silken tones. His mouth tightened on a scathing retort. No one else ever seemed to see the subtle insult behind Loholt's respect; perhaps it was not there for anyone else. He might be the only target for Loholt's baiting, but at least he would not rise to it. He

Exiled From Camelot

shook out the folds of his cloak as if he could shake Loholt off like a troublesome insect, and concentrated on the road ahead.

The track wound downwards, becoming wetter underfoot. The boulders gave way to scrub and the occasional twisted tree. A breeze sprang up and teased the mist until it was torn away in ragged strips, leaving them in the midst of a clear night with a moon nearing the full. The sounds of their movement, previously deadened by the mist, were magnified now. Kay could not repress the idea that someone or something watched and listened. He shook off the thought as stupidly fanciful—he would certainly never have shared it with Loholt—but he could not help growing more vigilant, and straining for any sounds other than their own.

They dropped down into a valley with a stream, shallow and stony, in its bottom. Trees clothed the opposite hillside. At the far end, Kay caught sight of the flat shimmer of a lake. The air seemed warmer. Below them, trees massed in a dark band, and before long they were riding beneath the outermost branches.

The slope grew gentler, and the track widened to a forest ride carpeted by pine needles. Moonlight barred the path with silver. Clots of shadow seemed to move under the trees. Kay's edgy feeling grew more intense; unobtrusively, he loosened his sword in its sheath. He was scarcely surprised when, a few paces ahead of them, horsemen thrust into their path and stood waiting.

Kay glanced back. Behind them, more horsemen had appeared. On their shields he caught the red-gold gleam of Briant's dragon. He drew his sword.

"Keep together," he snapped. "We'll try to break through ahead. If we're separated, regroup at the river."

Not waiting to see if Loholt would question his order, Kay set spurs to Morial and drove straight at the cluster of horsemen. He thanked God for Morial, the warhorse trained to perfection, responsive to every slight movement and as dangerous as another fighter.

All the same, they were too badly outnumbered. Kay knew with cold clarity that he was going to die. He had recovered from his bleak mood when he left the camp; he wanted to live, even if living meant the continuing struggle to prove himself.

All these thoughts fled through his mind in the few seconds before his sword engaged his enemy. He glimpsed the young leader's face—wild with a fierce delight, Kay thought, at the speed of the attack. The man flung his sword up in time to parry Kay's first blow; Kay felt the shock of the clash run up his arm, and almost lost his grip on the hilt of his own weapon. A skilful fighter might have finished his opponent then, but Kay's adversary was erratic, not pressing his advantage, giving him the chance to wheel Morial away.

All around Kay the fight surged, the silence broken now by

trampling horses, and the clatter of weapons, and the shouts of men as they struck and struck again. Briant's remaining men had come up by now; Kay's little group was surrounded. Kay saw blood spurt from the chest of one of Arthur's men-at-arms as a sword slashed across it. The man toppled from his horse and went down among the thrashing hooves.

Kay defended himself now, his opponent taller and with a longer reach; only Morial's speed kept him away from the darting blade. There was another man at his back; Kay steeled himself for a stroke from behind, but he instead felt a hand grab at his sword arm. In that instant he understood. These men were not trying to kill—or at least, not trying to kill him, and perhaps Loholt. They wanted prisoners.

He gripped hard with his knees, willing a response from Morial, and the horse reared, hooves lashing out. Briant's men gave back. As Morial came down lightly, gathering himself to spring forward, Kay could see a clear road ahead, and the hope of escape. Nothing these men had could catch Morial.

He glanced back and saw Loholt struggling in the midst of three of Briant's men, trying to win enough space to use his sword.

At that moment Loholt cried out, "Kay! Don't leave! Help me!"

Cursing furiously, Kay dragged on Morial's rein, wheeling back into the melee. Almost at once an arm clamped round him from behind. Fighting to free himself, he dropped his sword. Even as his enemy dragged him backwards, Kay strained to reach his dagger, but as his fingers closed over the hilt he fell. His head struck the ground, and he went down into a vortex of whirling darkness.

When Kay opened his eyes, he could see nothing but a greyish blur. At first he thought that he had woken in the camp, surrounded by thick fog. He felt ice cold. When he tried to pull his blanket more closely around himself, he discovered that he could not move his limbs.

He fought a surge of panic. This was a nightmare; he must wake from it as soon as possible. He lay still, breathing deeply. As he did so, his senses crept back. He became aware of pain in his wrists and ankles, and in his head. He had a ravening thirst.

Gradually his sight cleared. He lay on his back. Above his head he could see a beamed ceiling, shrouded in dust and swags of cobweb. The walls were bare stone. There was a single shuttered window in the wall to his right, from which grey light leaked into the room. He could not see a door.

Still trying to believe that he was locked in an evil dream, Kay tried to sit up. Pain wrenched at his wrists. Turning his head from side to side, he saw at last and understood.

He lay, naked, on a mattress, stretched out with his wrists and ankles pinioned to the bed frame. Thin cords bit into him whenever he tried to move. When he lifted his head, taking the strain on his shoulders, he saw that the room was empty except for the bed. The door, in the wall at the far end, was closed.

Kay lay back, forcing himself to lie still and calm the mill-race of his thoughts. He was a prisoner, then. Briant's prisoner. And Loholt, too, would be a prisoner, or dead.

Kay wondered whether Briant's men knew who they were. They had clearly recognised them as Arthur's men, and important enough to capture instead of killing. And they had known him, or at least distinguished him from the men-at-arms whom they were quite ready to kill. Did they know who Loholt was? Had the boy been stupid enough to tell them, perhaps in the hope of frightening them into setting him free? The king's son would be a useful hostage, the most powerful piece on Briant's board.

Growing steadier as the first shock ebbed, Kay found that there was more to consider. The meeting in the wood had the air of an ambush. And there was the other ambush when they forded the river. Yet in both cases there was no way an enemy could have known where to find them, unless there was a traitor in Arthur's camp.

And even that did not explain properly. Before the river crossing, Kay was almost certain that no one had slipped away and taken word to Briant. Before their own departure, he was quite certain. Besides, very few people, apart from the guides and Arthur himself, had known the route they meant to take. There could not be a traitor, unless he was one of the guides.

Kay examined the idea. He did not like it. There had been three guides experienced in these northern lands, all of them men Kay had known for years. They were comfortable in Arthur's service. They had wives and families they would not put at risk, certainly not for the dubious rewards of throwing in their lot with Briant. So, Kay decided, there could have been no treachery. And yet they had been ambushed twice.

His thoughts came up against a blank wall. He could make no further progress with the problem, and once his mind stopped working, there was room for fear to seep back. He wondered what Briant would do with him. Loholt would be of more value to bargain with, but his own value was his knowledge. As seneschal, he could give Briant more information about Arthur's strengths and weaknesses, his fortifications and supply lines and the disposition of his troops, than any other man in the kingdom. When Kay considered what Briant would be prepared to do to get that information, his terror rose up and almost choked him.

He forced his mind into motion again, this time to plan escape. The window shutters looked flimsy enough, if he could break his bonds and get off the bed. Twisting his hands in the cords produced only pain. His fingers could reach the mattress, a thin pad of horsehair, and the smooth wood of the frame beneath—nothing made of metal that he might loosen and use to cut the cords. By straining, his fingertips could just touch the rough stone of the wall behind the bed, but he could not press the cords against it to rub them away.

As each attempt failed, Kay began to lose control of himself. Panic battered at him. His breathing grew shallow and uneven. He choked back a scream. This was Briant's place, wherever it was, and there would be no one to hear him if he called for help. Giving way to frenzied screaming would only take strength that he needed for other things. He lay still until he had managed to steady his breathing and his frantic heartbeat grew quieter.

Patiently, he turned his left wrist back and forth in the cords, setting his teeth against the stabs of pain, ignoring the blood when it began to flow. After a few minutes he found it was possible to watch the writhing hand as if it did not belong to him. But the cords did not give way.

Kay did not know how long he went on striving before he heard the sound he had dreaded, the key turning in the door. Instantly he lay still. They would see that he had been conscious and tried to escape, but they might believe, for a while at least, that he had fainted again.

He heard the door open and close, and light footsteps cross the room. He was aware by the change of light behind his eyes that someone was standing beside him. He imagined eyes looking down. A voice said, "Kay."

Kay's eyes flew open. Loholt was standing at the bedside. He looked as trim and self-possessed as he ever had in Arthur's court. In his hand he held a knife.

Kay started up, disregarding the pain that lanced through him. "Loholt!" he exclaimed. "Well done, lad. Cut me free quickly, and—"

The words died in his throat. Loholt sat down on the edge of the bed and bent over him. His amber eyes were bright, his lips parted. Kay felt warm breath on his face.

"Oh, no," Loholt said. "You don't think we're going to let you go, after all the trouble we went to, getting you here?"

The boy smiled, and laid the point of his knife in the hollow of Kay's throat.

Chapter Eight

Shock kept Kay silent. Loholt drew back and sat on the edge of the bed, twirling the knife in his fingers, watching light ripple down the blade.

Kay said, "You . . . serve Briant."

Loholt's eyes flicked back to him, narrowed and venomous. "No! Briant serves me."

"If you believe that, boy, you'll believe anything."

The knife danced in front of his face. "Don't call me 'boy.' I don't like it. Call me 'lord.'"

Kay was silent.

"Say it!" He leant over Kay again and held the knife poised just over Kay's eye.

The seneschal tried to focus on the glittering point. Dear God, not blindness, he said in his heart. A sweat broke out all over his body.

But Loholt was smiling again. "You will say it, Kay, before we're done," he promised.

Kay tried to moisten parched lips, tried to think, tried to form words that would reach Loholt and bring him to his senses. "What are you going to do?" he asked.

Loholt's smile grew pitying. "You know that, don't you? I've sent a messenger to Briant at Carlisle. He'll be here by tomorrow night, and when he comes, he'll question you. And when you've told us all you know, Briant will defeat Arthur and make me king."

Loholt sat back. Satisfaction radiated out of him; he obviously thought he was being very clever.

Struggling to keep hold of common sense in the midst of insanity, Kay said, "Do you really believe that Briant des Isles will wage war to make you king? Briant fights for Briant. He always has."

"Not any longer." Loholt gave him a sideways, secretive look. "He knows I am the rightful heir. I am the Pendragon. I will bear the dragon on my shield. Briant will be the first to kiss my hand and pay me homage." He giggled. "He will be seneschal. The post will be vacant."

As the boy spoke, Kay wondered if he dealt with genuine madness, not just arrogance and misplaced ambition. "Loholt," he said, "you don't need Briant. You don't need to rebel. Arthur loves you. He will make you his heir."

Loholt's eyes fixed sharply on him; madness—if he was mad—had not swallowed up all intelligence. "I don't believe you," the boy said.

"I was drawing up the documents before we left Camelot." Kay sensed a hesitation and pushed home his advantage. "Listen to me. Cut me free and come with me. We'll get away from here and find Arthur. If you'll honestly turn back and serve him, I won't tell him about this. We'll train you to be king. We can—"

"I don't believe you." The voice was scornful, the hesitation vanished. "You're saying that because you're a coward. You're afraid of what we're going to do to you. You would tell any lie to get away from here, but you won't. You won't ever leave here, and you won't see Arthur again. So don't expect me to believe you. Besides, I don't want to wait for twenty or thirty years until Arthur dies. I want to be king now."

Kay let out a long sigh and closed his eyes. He would not go on pleading, though he knew that before long he might plead, say anything, promise anything, so that the questioning would stop. He had made Loholt an honest offer, but perhaps it was his cowardice that had prompted it. He would never trust Loholt again; keeping his treachery from Arthur would be another betrayal. He tensed as he felt the point of the knife digging into his shoulder.

"Look at me when I'm talking to you," Loholt said.

"I'm sorry, boy." Kay forced an edge of sarcasm into his voice. "I thought you'd finished."

"I told you not to call me that."

He stroked the tip of the knife down the length of Kay's arm. Turning his head, Kay saw a thin red hairline, beaded with blood. He felt no pain.

Loholt kept the knife hovering over the cords that bound Kay's wrist. "Wouldn't you like me to cut them?" he sniggered.

Kay said nothing; there was nothing to say except pleading or meaningless bravado, and there was no use in either. Almost thoughtfully, like a craftsman at his work, Loholt made another hairline cut beside the first.

"We could do this for a long time," he said. "It might be fun. Where would you like me to start? Your sword hand? You don't really have much use for it, do you?"

He laid the knife across the fingers of Kay's right hand. Until then, Kay had tried to remain calm, to talk rationally, but now his body betrayed him into a desperate spasm of struggling. Loholt laughed as Kay wrenched vainly at the cords, only to collapse in the end, shaking, his chest heaving.

"I might be kind," Loholt whispered. Kay could feel the knife, the cold blade across his palm. "I might not do it. Not yet. If you ask me properly. Call me 'lord.'"

Thoughts fled through Kay's mind. To lose any chance of

escape, and if beyond hope he did get away from this foul place—never to hold a sword, or a pen, never any more to be useful to Arthur.

He turned his face away. "Please . . . lord," he gasped out.

He felt Loholt's hand fasten in his hair, dragging his head round to face him. "That's better. Don't forget that, Kay. We'll have other things to talk about later."

He stood up and slid the knife into a sheath at his belt. Kay watched him as he bowed with exaggerated courtesy and went out. The door closed behind him, and the key scraped in the lock.

Kay lay still. Humiliation washed over him. He wished he had not given in. Loholt's threat could well have been an empty one. He would not do anything irrevocable until Briant arrived to begin his questioning. But to his shame Kay knew that he had not dared to take the risk.

He shivered. His arm throbbed with pain. The knife cuts bled, his wrists, too, where he had struggled against the cords. On his right hand, the hand Loholt had threatened to mutilate, he still wore Arthur's ring, gold and carnelian, the one spark of warmth in this waste of terror. Kay felt a dull surprise that Loholt had not taken it, but then, Loholt did not know what it meant.

"Arthur," Kay whispered.

But Arthur could not hear him. He had danger enough of his own to cope with, and he could not possibly know that Kay needed him. Even if Arthur escaped his enemies and came to Carlisle, even when Kay and Loholt failed to join him, he would have no idea where to start looking. Kay knew he could expect no help from anyone.

When Briant came, on the next night, he would be questioned. Bleakly Kay admitted to himself that once his questioning began, he would, sooner or later, betray his king. Very well, Kay thought. I have until then. Almost two days to escape. Bracing himself against the pain, he returned to his patient striving against the cords that bound his left wrist.

Nothing in the grey room marked the passage of time. Nothing but the gradual ebbing of Kay's strength. He lay still at last, his body awash with pain. He had sweated in his struggles, and now the drying sweat chilled him, but his head felt hot. He could not stop shivering. He became aware of the sharp reek of his own body.

Later still, he heard the protesting sound of the key in the lock. He grew rigid. It was too soon for Briant to have come; this must be Loholt again, hungry for more amusement. And Kay was already weakened. He tensed his whole body into one spasm of straining against his bonds, an effort that left him limp and gasping. He turned his head away and closed his eyes.

He heard the door open, and footsteps approach the bed as

before. He waited for the sound of Loholt's voice, or his high-pitched laughter, or the gentle caress of the knife.

Instead it was a different voice that spoke. "Good day, sir. You're very welcome."

Kay's head whipped round, eyes staring. The speaker was a girl. His first thoughts, of relief and hope of help, were overwhelmed by shame that she was seeing him naked. Only then did he realise the strangeness of what she had said to him.

When she saw that he was looking at her, she swept him a formal curtsey, and then stood by the bed looking down at him. "I believe you have travelled far, sir," she said. "Are you tired from your journey?"

Kay thought his mind was becoming unhinged. Or he had fainted, and this was some demented dream. He gazed at the girl in helpless silence. She was young and tall, with pale hair in tangles, woven with a chaplet of leaves that were already withering. Her dress had once been fine—very fine, more suited to a great court occasion than this filthy room—but now the gold thread was tarnished, part of the trimmings pulled away and hanging in shreds, the fabric itself stained and crumpled.

Reprovingly, she said, "I had thought, sir, to find more courtesy from one of Arthur's knights."

The repetition of such a familiar accusation almost had Kay lapsing into hysterical laughter. He fought for self-control.

"Forgive me, lady," he said, trying to match her formal tones. "I had not expected to find so noble a lady in this place. May I know your name?"

Again she swept the low curtsey, her head held high in pride. "I am the lady Alienor. And you, sir?"

"I am Sir Kay, High Seneschal—"

He broke off. For a moment he had almost started playing her game, or slipping into the world she had created for herself, as if he could forget that he was a prisoner, bound and naked. With the recollection, shame returned in full force.

"Lady," the seneschal stammered, "you should not be here. It is not fitting."

Alienor's brows arched, her head went up, a perfect autocratic air. "I am chatelaine, sir, in my brother's absence. Should I not welcome a guest?"

"I fear, lady, I am no guest."

A frown settled on Alienor's face. She looked puzzled, as if she was considering for the first time that something was wrong. She bent to examine his bonds, touching his wrist; her fingertips came away smeared with blood and she rubbed them energetically on the front of her gown. The intelligence that had seemed for a moment to be struggling to the surface vanished in a renewed look of polite incomprehension. She could not see his injuries, the cords that bound him, his shameful nakedness, or, seeing, she could not interpret.

"I have often wished to see the court at Camelot," she said. "Is it very splendid?"

Kay wanted to scream at her, to beg her to release him, but he forced himself to remain calm. She was mad, but she was not, as far as he could see, his enemy. Probably Loholt did not know that she had found her way to his room, and while she stayed, there was a thread of hope.

"Very splendid, lady," he said. "And you would be graciously received, if you should come there."

Alienor shook her head. "A lady must have a knight, to come to Camelot. And I have no knight of my own." She paused, and her eyes travelled over him thoughtfully. "Will you be my knight, Sir Kay?"

The question left him gaping. "I—I cannot, lady."

This time the swift look she gave him was full of intelligence, and even humour. "Not even if I cut you free?"

Before he could react, or adapt his mind to this new aspect of her, Alienor sat beside him on the bed, where Loholt had been not long before. She reached out and laid a hand lightly on his shoulder. In most women, it would have been a sensual gesture; in most situations, it would have been an invitation. Here, from her, it was pure innocence. Whatever she was, Kay realised, she had no idea what she was asking or suggesting. He found that he could not lie to her, not even when the reward might be his freedom.

"If you free me, I will bring you to Camelot. The queen will welcome you. But I cannot make you my lady."

Alienor moved away from him, her face showing an almost childlike disappointment. "You already have a lady?"

"No. But I—I cannot . . ."

She smiled, understanding what he was trying to say, at least to her own satisfaction. "Ah, you have taken a vow. It is often so, I believe. But if it were not so, you would love me, for am I not beautiful?" She turned her head this way and that, displaying herself, the vanity once more totally innocent.

"Yes, lady," Kay said, "you are very beautiful."

Smiling still, a look of pure happiness, she rose from the bed and curtseyed to him yet again. It was, he realised, a farewell.

"No!" Kay exclaimed, his panic breaking through the courtly game they had played together. "Don't go. Don't leave me here."

"I may not stay, sir," Alienor said reproachfully, "for it ill suits a maiden's modesty to talk too long with a man alone. Perhaps later we will talk again."

"Please—"

He tried to sit up, struggling to reach out to her. She did not even look at him again as she crossed the room and went out. As the door closed, Kay sank back on the bed. Silently, he wept.

The hours stretched out until the grey light of day faded into darkness. No one came to Kay's room. He went on trying to free himself, but between pain and thirst and the gradual loss of blood, his struggles grew weaker. At last he slipped into an uneasy state between sleeping and waking. When he came unwillingly back to full consciousness, daylight once more angled through the shutters. The second day of his captivity. The day Briant would come.

Kay's body was failing him. Mist swirled in front of his eyes. He had given up hope of escape, unless Lady Alienor came back. He was half inclined to think he had imagined her. When the door opened, it was all he could do to hold back a whimper of terror.

This time it was Loholt again. He carried a cup, and held it out where Kay could see it.

"Water, Kay. Do you want it?"

"Yes."

"You know how to ask for it, then."

The edge of yesterday's humiliation was dulled, but Kay could still hesitate. Loholt shrugged, and tipped the cup so that water trickled out of it and splashed in the dust of the floor. "No!" Kay gasped. "Please—please, lord."

Loholt smiled. "Good. You remembered."

He sat down on the bed and held the cup so that Kay could drink from it, but tilting it so that more than half of it spilt over the mattress. The mouthful was hardly enough, almost seeming to make the torments of thirst increase, but it helped Kay to collect his scattered senses.

When the cup was empty, Loholt tossed it aside. "Now we can talk again," he said.

"Talk?"

"Just talk." He touched the knife, in its sheath at his belt. "For now. Briant comes today. I thought you might like to talk about that."

"There's nothing I want to say, to you or Briant," Kay responded, knowing how empty the words were.

Loholt knew it, too. The complacent smile settled on his face again. "Don't worry," he said. "I'll make sure that Briant is very careful when he questions you. I don't want you to die. I want to keep you alive for a long, long time."

Kay spat at him. Loholt's smile vanished; his expression grew ugly.

"Don't do that again," he said. "You should be trying to please me. When Briant has finished, I could leave you lying here in your own filth, but if you really pleased me, I might find some service you could do for me."

"I'll never serve you."

"You will—if I want you to. You're a coward, Kay. I knew how it would be on the moor, with Briant's men in the mist. It was easy to make Arthur choose you to go with me, because he knows you're a coward, too."

Sudden understanding dawned on Kay. "You betrayed Arthur."

Loholt's eyes widened, but Kay thought that the surprise was pretended. "Betrayed Arthur? What do you mean?"

"You sent word to Briant, to tell him where Arthur meant to ford the river."

"And how am I supposed to have done that?" Loholt said. "I sent no messenger."

The words were not a denial: a genuine question, rather, as if he were a teacher testing the aptitude of a not-too-bright pupil.

"I don't know how," Kay admitted. "But I know that you did. And you told his men where to find us when we left Arthur's company."

"But Kay," Loholt protested patiently, "no one knew which route we would take, except the guide."

Restlessly, Kay turned his head from side to side. The problem entrapped his mind as the cords pinioned his body; he knew he was right but he could not understand it.

Beside him he heard Loholt's snickering, and then a voice. "Kay."

It was not Loholt's voice. The single word even had a music about it, but it was a music that froze Kay's heart. Slowly he turned his head. Loholt stood beside the bed, but it was not Loholt. The figure seemed taller. The flesh of its face had shrunk back to the bone beneath. From the eye sockets looked out something cold, ancient, and irredeemably evil.

Kay whimpered and closed his eyes, as if that could drive the thing away. He heard laughter again, air bubbles escaping from a bone flute. At the base of his throat a hand was laid lightly, a five-fold touch, talons.

"Don't!" Kay sobbed out. "Dear God, help me!"

The talons scored across his chest. Kay screamed. His whole body convulsed. He expected the ripping claws to tear into him again, but there was nothing more. Only his own sobbing breath broke the silence.

At last he dared to open his eyes again. Loholt stood beside him; it was Loholt again. His eyes were heavy, his lips parted, a face sated with pleasure. "Now do you understand?" His voice was soft, almost caressing. "It was the Lady."

"The Lady?" Kay did not understand. He could not mean the sad, innocent Alienor. "Who is the Lady?"

"She comes." Loholt shuddered in ecstasy. "She comes and

sees through my eyes. She speaks through my voice. Her body moves through mine."

"Boy," Kay said urgently, "get down on your knees and pray to God to release you from that foul thing. Now—I'll pray with you. It isn't too late."

For an instant he thought he saw a flicker of uncertainty cross Loholt's face. Along with the uncertainty there might have been a flash of terrified understanding, but the surge of remembered delight rose up and swamped it.

"Pray?" Loholt said dreamily. "What's there to pray for? I shall be king." He sat down beside Kay and took out the knife. "See if prayer will help you now," he said.

Chapter Nine

At last there was nothing Kay could do except lock himself in the tiny, impregnable fortress of his own mind, where he had nothing to do with the writhing, screaming thing on the bed. The mercy of unconsciousness was long in coming.

He woke to feel someone shaking him. The room was dark, except for a wavering, golden light pouring upwards from somewhere at floor level. As Kay's vision cleared, he made out the features of the lady Alienor.

She bent over him, hands on his shoulders, her hair sweeping across his face. Realising he was awake, she let out a sound of satisfaction, and darted away into the shadows, to reappear a moment later with a knife in her hand. Kay flinched, but this time the blade bit through the cords that bound him, and he recognised his own dagger.

"Lady, I thank you—"

She signed to him to be silent. He tried to sit up, but every sinew of his abused body protested, and he sank back, setting his teeth against a groan. His head swam. At the second attempt he managed to sit up, but his hands and feet were numb, hanging useless as if they did not belong to him. Alienor pounced on him, chafing his feet to bring back the circulation, while he tried to work some feeling into his hands.

"Sir, you must be gone quickly," she said in a rapid undertone. "My lord Briant des Isles is come, and sits now at supper. When he has eaten and drunk his fill, he will speak with you."

Kay realised that she had a very clear understanding of what was going on. And he had thought her mad! There was a subtle difference about her now; she was no longer the drifting waif of the day before. He could not understand the change, but he thanked God for it.

Alienor picked up the taper stand she had placed on the floor and held it close, critically studying his injuries. His wrists and ankles were lacerated by his struggle with the cords, and still bleeding sluggishly. The wounds from Loholt's knife were less severe, but around the claw marks of the thing Loholt had called the Lady, the flesh was puffed up and reddened; blood and a clear ooze crept out of them.

"I have no healing salves," Alienor said anxiously, "and no time to use them. Will you be able to travel, sir?"

"I must," Kay said.

At the foot of the bed was a bundle of his own clothes, his boots and sword belt. When Kay thought he would be able to manage, he began to dress. He pulled on hose and undershirt, but he knew he would never be able to bear the weight of the mail; he simply fastened on the sword belt, and drew his cloak over all. Dragging on the riding boots was agony, but he had to bear it; he would never ride barefoot to Carlisle.

"Lady, is my sword here?" he asked.

Alienor shook her head. Now that Kay thought, he remembered dropping it, in the fight in the forest. Briefly, he grieved over it; it was a good sword. He took the dagger Alienor held out to him, and kept it in his hand as he got up from the bed.

At first he thought it would be no use. The pain of standing was too great; he would faint again, and they would find him. He swayed, and Alienor flung an arm around him. Still holding the taper high in her other hand, she guided him, step by step, to the door and out into the passage.

Kay began to fear what would happen if anyone saw them. He could not defend himself, or her; the dagger in his hand was an empty gesture.

"Lady, you should leave me," he whispered. "If they find you with me . . ."

A shudder went through him as he remembered Loholt's Lady and what she might do to this gentle girl. And yet, he thought, there was a resilience about Alienor; just now, at least, she was more capable than he.

"I am a poor, mad thing, sir," she said. "I don't know what it is I do."

Kay stopped and stared at her. Between pain, exhaustion, and fear, he wondered if he had imagined the sardonic edge to her tone, or the gleam of humour in her expression as she looked at him now. "You are . . . wise, and beautiful," he said.

"And you have a courtier's tongue, sir. Come—and quietly."

As they moved on, Kay began to find it easier to walk, so that he could manage without Alienor's support. She led him along a passage and then down a spiral stairway, where Kay had to steady himself by clinging to the rope looped along the inner wall. The stairway led into a wide hall. Alienor's taper could not reach from end to end of it, or up into the shrouding darkness of the rafters. The flame fluttered in unexplained draughts, and torn hangings on the walls flapped back and forth. A shutter rattled, driving Kay's heart into his throat.

Not far along the wall was a half-open doorway, and from it came the yellow glow of torchlight. As Kay and Alienor drew closer, there was a burst of raucous laughter, and what sounded like a beer pot being pounded on a table.

"Briant is still at supper." Alienor's voice was an almost

soundless murmur at Kay's ear as she guided him past the door and down the length of the hall. In the centre of it was a humped shape of darkness; as they drew close to it, Alienor paused and held up the taper so that Kay could see. The shape was a bier, and lying on it a mailed knight. His hands were clasped on the hilt of a tarnished sword. His cloak hung in dust-filled folds. A few rags of skin clung to his skull, and the empty eye sockets stared up into the dark.

"Lady?" Kay asked uncertainly, hiding revulsion.

"He is my father," Alienor said. The light from the taper fell on her pale hair, turning it to silver. Her eyes were shadowed, secret. "Sir Lancelot killed him in a tournament. My brother has sworn that my father will not be buried until he has taken his revenge."

Kay was searching for something to say to her when she beckoned him on, dismissing the matter of her father as if it were of little importance. She puzzled Kay even more; he felt this belonged to her earlier madness, and wondered where in all the nightmare was the real Alienor.

They approached the bottom end of the hall. Alienor hauled open one of a pair of double doors just enough to let both of them slip through it, and then dragged it shut after her. They stood in another passage. Kay felt cool air on his face. Ahead, a door stood ajar, giving out into the night.

"Guards, lady?" he murmured.

Alienor shook her head. "What would they guard? But the stables are at the back of the house, and there are men there. You cannot fetch your horse."

Kay knew a moment of panic. He did not think his strength would hold out to reach Carlisle on foot; he did not want to abandon Morial. But he had no choice; it was that or be recaptured. He nodded to show that he had understood, and followed Alienor to the door.

Outside the air was keen; Kay drank it in great gulps. He stood in a courtyard; opposite were the gates. Crossing the dark, open space, praying that no one happened to be looking out of a window, Kay saw by the light of Alienor's flickering taper that the main gates were closed by a heavy bar resting in iron hasps at shoulder height. He was not at all sure that he had the strength to shift it, and saw with relief that the wicket gate was loose, sagging on a single hinge and creaking softly in the night breeze. Kay tugged it open and stepped through.

Surprised, he found himself looking out across a stretch of water, the surface fluttered by the breeze. A causeway led into darkness; waves lapped gently at the edges. Kay could only make out the further shore as a mass of darkness, trees and undergrowth, against a sky silvered by the rising moon.

Alienor drew his attention with a hand on his arm. "The manor is built on a lake," she said. "This is the only way, unless you swim. Go quickly, before Briant's men come. The road leads north; that way lies Carlisle."

Kay turned to her, realising that this was where they must say farewell. But not forever, he vowed to himself. When he was safe again, when Arthur had swept Briant des Isles off the soil of Britain, he would come back, and he would keep the promise he had made. He made it again, now.

"Farewell, lady. And thank you—thank you more than words can say. When I can, I will come again, and I will bring you to Camelot."

He raised her hand to his lips, and for the last time she swept him the formal curtsey, as if she stood already in Arthur's great hall. Then, cautiously, he moved out on to the causeway, straining to hear any sound ahead of him that might tell him his enemies waited for him. After a few paces he glanced back, to see Alienor standing with her taper raised, the other hand shielding it. Kay lifted his hand to her, and she withdrew, swinging the wicket gate shut behind her.

Breathing a little more easily, Kay went on, but as he reached the midpoint of the causeway a figure seemed to rise up out of the shadows and stood in front of him, barring his way.

"Good evening, Kay," said Loholt.

Kay was still holding his dagger. "Stand back," he said.

Loholt did not move. "You've lost," he said. "Did you really think I wouldn't keep watch on you? Did you think you could walk away from here so easily?"

Kay weighed him up. He was young, inexperienced, and seemed to be unarmed. But Kay was weakened from his injuries, and one cry from Loholt would bring Briant's men from the manor.

"I wouldn't try," Loholt said, half laughing, as if he guessed easily what Kay was thinking. "There are men within call. You won't escape."

"But I could kill you first," Kay said desperately. "Do you want that? Stand aside and let me pass."

Loholt remained where he was, rocking on the balls of his feet, hands clasped loosely behind his back, relaxed as if all he had to do was enjoy the freshness of the night.

"I don't want to kill you," Kay said. "For Arthur's sake. He loved you. Stand aside."

When Loholt still did not move, Kay took a step forward. He held the dagger levelled. For the first time, Loholt looked uncertain. His arrogance, his contempt for Kay, had betrayed him. He had exposed himself; he could bring help from the manor to recapture Kay, but they would not come in time to save him, if

Kay was determined. Knowing that his enemy had underestimated him gave Kay an edge of courage that he badly needed.

As Kay advanced, Loholt retreated step by step towards the edge of the causeway, leaving a clear space for the seneschal to pass. His self-possession was broken up, his face surprised by fear. If he had expected the Lady to come and overwhelm his adversary, there was no sign of her presence. He did nothing to stop Kay.

As Kay went on, he expected an outcry behind him, and he was ready to make a run for the forest. Instead, he heard a voice sobbing, "Kay! Kay, don't leave me!"

He turned. Loholt was kneeling at the water's edge, hugging himself as an agony of terror coursed through him.

"Kay, take me with you! Please!"

Uncertainly, Kay took a step or two back towards him. He still held the dagger, but it hung loose in his hand.

"I'll tell it all to my father," Loholt was babbling, the words almost incoherent. "I'll beg his forgiveness, and yours. I want to go back. I want to be his son. Kay, don't let her take me!"

Kay drew closer. Almost without willing it, he stretched out a hand to raise Loholt from his knees. Loholt grasped it, and with a yell of triumph dragged Kay to the ground beside him. Kay, struggling to free himself, caught the mad gleam of the boy's eyes, before Loholt fastened himself on him, wrapping his arms around him as they rolled over together at the edge of the causeway. Kay heard the laughter of the Lady, a wind blowing across dried bones.

Talons tore at Kay's throat and ripped through his cloak between his shoulder blades. Revulsion gave him strength to free his sword arm; he gripped the dagger and thrust it upwards into the creature's entrails. He felt the body convulse; the clutching arms tightened and then gave way.

Retching, Kay forced himself to his knees. Beside him, Loholt was twitching, hands fumbling feebly at the hilt of the dagger. His eyes, anguished, were fixed on Kay. He tried to speak, and a gush of blood came from his mouth. The eyes glazed, and he was still.

From the manor gateway a shout rang out. Kay saw figures jostling in the entrance. One of them held a flaring torch. He thrust himself upright and ran.

Kay dared not stay on the road, where Briant's men would outpace him easily. As soon as he had crossed the causeway, he veered off into the trees. They were losing their leaves; enough moonlight slanted between the branches for Kay to see his way, but it was enough, too, for his pursuers to see him. As he fled he looked around wildly for a place to hide.

There were bramble thickets, clumps of dead bracken arching above the forest floor, but no shelter he could reach without leaving a trail that would betray him. He pushed his way through a hazel brake, the thin branches whipping into his face. He stumbled into unseen hollows in the ground. Brambles tore at his cloak. He tripped on a twisting root and fell, the breath driven out of him as he was flung against the tree.

Kay had not shaken off the pursuit. As he hesitated, head reeling, searching for the strength to go on, he heard trampling footsteps and voices not many yards behind. He struggled to his feet, clawing his way upright by clinging to the ivy growing on the tree trunk. The first branch was just above his head; driven by panic, scrabbling among the ivy stems that gave way under his weight, he managed to haul himself on to it, and then to clamber a little higher into a space between two forking branches.

He crouched there, panting, and looked down. A tracery of branches, a scattering of leaves still clinging to them, concealed him from below. He could still hear Briant's men, but he could see nothing.

Loholt's blood still stained his hands. Kay shuddered. He did not know exactly what had happened in those last few minutes. He did not know if Loholt's pleading had been a real repentance, or a trick to trap him. Had Loholt died serving the Lady, or had her strength overwhelmed his in the end?

Kay had struck out with his dagger to save himself from the Lady's claws. If he had not struck, he would be a prisoner again, or dead. But it was Loholt who had died, still trying to speak to him. To curse him, or ask for help? Either way, he was dead now.

"Arthur's son," Kay said to himself. "I killed Arthur's son."

He leant back against the trunk of the tree and let the silent tears come. Beneath him, among the trees, Briant des Isles' men crashed and shouted, trying to hunt him down.

Chapter Ten

Gawain slept uneasily that night. Although there was good hope that Kay and his party had got off safely, although Gareth's strength was returning, they were still a small company, on unfamiliar territory, and surrounded by their enemies. When Gawain tried to think ahead to the next day, or the day after that, fear rose and swirled around him like the moorland mist.

He sank into a deeper sleep towards dawn, and woke to find a grey light diffusing into the camp. The mist seemed lighter; he could see farther, though nothing was in sight except the sweep of the hillside, broken only by rocks and clumps of dried bracken the colour of rust.

Every stone and blade of grass was furred with dew. Gawain wet his hands in it and passed them over his face, the cold shock driving off sleep. He felt the rasp of several days' growth of beard, and combed his fingers through his hair. He thought longingly of a hot bath and clean clothes.

Stiffly he got to his feet, shivering in the raw morning air. Around him, the camp was breaking up. He looked for Gareth, and saw him already down with the horses. Forcing himself into movement, Gawain went to join him, sliding on the tussocks of wet grass under his feet.

Gareth had just finished saddling his horse. Looking bright-eyed and optimistic, he turned to welcome Gawain; it was as if he was throwing off the effects of his wound and the strain of their journey. Gawain wished he could feel the same. Hurriedly he flung the saddle over his own mount, trying not to think about the death of Madoc the night before, or of what might still be stalking around them under cover of the mist.

"A quiet night?" he asked Gareth.

"As far as I know," Gareth said. "At least, no one has told me different. There's been no trouble since Kay left."

"That doesn't mean there won't be."

The column of knights and men-at-arms was already forming. Gawain mounted and drew into the line not far behind Arthur, who led the way with Bedivere and the guide. At first they tracked diagonally across the slope of the hill, which soon furrowed into a deep, steep-sided coomb with a shallow stream at the bottom. The horses had to pick their way along its stony bed.

The mist was thin enough now for Gawain to see both sides of the coomb; they were broken rock, a dreary and uninviting landscape, but one which gave very little cover for an enemy. If Briant's men were still hunting them they must be ahead, or behind, or pacing them along the top of the coomb. They could not get close to the column without exposing themselves. Gawain began to feel a very little safer.

As they continued, trees appeared along the sides of the coomb: dark, bushy conifers, too sparse and stunted to give much cover to their enemies. The slope itself grew wider and shallower. Gradually, the plashing of the stream and the clatter of the horses' hooves was joined by another sound, a muffled roaring that grew louder until at last the column drew to a halt at the edge of a cliff where the stream plunged down over rocks in a spectacular burst of white foam.

Briefly Gawain wondered if their guides had led them into a trap. He glanced round sharply, but saw nothing except their own column of horsemen winding away behind. Arthur and the guide conferred, then the guide set out along a track that led off among the trees on the left of the stream. As he followed cautiously, Gawain saw that instead of petering out at the cliff's edge, the track doubled sharply back on itself, then continued in a series of tight loops until finally it reached the floor of the valley below and vanished into thicker forest.

Gawain swallowed, momentarily closed his eyes, and wondered whether he would rather die of a broken neck or an arrow in the back. They had to dismount and lead the horses in single file; the descent was agonisingly slow, but it was possible. Arthur had stationed archers at the top of the falls, for covering fire, but there was no movement at all from the trees below.

At last all the company were down, and formed up again for the next stage of their journey. Instead of continuing along the path, the guide led them into the forest at an angle. Within ten minutes, Gawain would have been completely lost, but the guide went on confidently, seeming always to choose an upward slope. That night they made camp in a clearing. All day, there had been no sign of Briant's men, no arrow piercing the mist. Gawain began to hope that they had shaken off the pursuit, and Gareth was frankly cheerful, whistling as he unsaddled his horse and unrolled his bedding for the night.

When they woke the next morning the mist had cleared. Within an hour or two the forest thinned out and they found themselves once again on the high fells. Gawain stretched thankfully and breathed in the cold air. Over his head, the sky arched pale blue and quivering with light; a hawk hung motionless high above. Anyone who followed them would have been exposed; there was no movement but their own and, in the distance, a scatter of grazing sheep.

Now the guide led them downwards. Before long they struck

another track that followed at first the contours of the hill, and then crossed another stream and plunged alongside it until it reached the valley bottom. With a flat, hard surface for riding, their pace increased. Suddenly Gawain knew, without understanding why, that they had shaken off their enemies. They would reach Carlisle.

Eventually their path came to an abrupt end where two great shoulders of the fell jostled together. Arthur, riding at the column's head, reined in his horse. Gawain, impelled by a sudden urgency, moved up closer to him. Looking over the king's shoulder, he could see, across a mile or more of open country, the grey walls of Carlisle. He drew a breath of relief. Arthur's banners still fluttered from the towers.

Hardly more than a bowshot from the walls was an untidy scatter of tents. There was no sign of movement. At this distance Gawain could not make out much detail, though he could see one siege tower, with its top half burnt away.

"Carlisle still stands," Arthur said.

"And where's Briant?" Bedivere, on the king's other side, spoke impatiently. "Can't see anything going on down there at all."

"Before the main gate," Arthur said. "As we must be." He drew Excalibur and raised it; the blade flashed diamond clear in the cold light. There was an eager stir from the horsemen behind him. "Forward!" he cried.

He set spurs to his horse and galloped down into the shallow valley, towards the castle walls beyond. Gawain followed, and Bedivere, and all the rest of the company streaming behind them. Out of the mists and shadows, out of the snares where death waited, Arthur led his men to the deliverance of Carlisle.

After a battle, Gawain never remembered clearly what had happened. A muddle of trampling horses and men screaming; blood and filth and fear and a clanging darkness. Before, or afterwards, he might listen to Lancelot and the king discussing strategy, pinpointing what made this battle unique from all the others. For Gawain, all battles were the same, and nearer to hell than he ever wished to be.

When he came to himself after the attack outside Carlisle, he was kneeling on the turf not far from the walls. He had been sick, and his stomach was still vainly heaving. An icy sweat bathed his body; he shivered.

Footsteps sounded beside him; he looked up to see Gareth. "Is it over?" Gawain asked. "Did we break through?"

Gareth looked anxious, but as Gawain spoke, he half smiled. "Yes, and yes," he said. "Are you hurt?"

Gawain shuddered again and shook his head vaguely. "I don't know."

Gareth bent and examined him more closely. "A lot of blood," he said. "None of it yours, as far as I can see. Come on."

He held out a hand, but Gawain did not reach out to take it. "Is the king safe?" he asked.

"Yes. And everyone else, more or less. Briant's men scattered. You've never seen such a rabble! And there was no sign of Briant himself."

Something stirred in Gawain's stupefied brain. "No? Then where is he?"

Gareth shrugged cheerfully. "I don't know. Or care. All I want is to get inside and clean up. So come on."

Gawain tore up a handful of grass and wiped his face, and then let his brother help him to his feet. "I'm sorry," he said.

"So you should be. There's everybody talking about the deeds of Gawain of Orkney, wanting to sing your praises to your face, and here you are, throwing up." He hugged Gawain affectionately. "Look, your horse is here. You can mount and ride in."

As Gawain rode slowly around the walls to the main gate, with Gareth walking at the horse's head, he began to recover. He was calm enough to exchange greetings with the excited crowd thronging the main courtyard, and steady enough to stay on his feet when he dismounted.

After that, it was as if Arthur had arrived at Carlisle in the course of a peaceful progress. Gawain was escorted to the suite of rooms he always occupied when he visited. There was an obsequious servant, with hot water for him to bathe, and fresh clothes to put on. Later there was supper in the great hall, where Gawain must sit, and smile, and make pleasant conversation, as if he had not killed that day, as if his duty might not force him to kill again tomorrow.

Two days later, Gareth came looking for Gawain in the castle infirmary, where he was consulting with the healers about the men wounded in the attack. Gareth's face was alight.

"Gawain," he said, drawing his brother out into the passage. "You're to come at once to the king. Gaheris is here!"

Gawain stood still for a moment, in spite of his brother's urging, overcome briefly by a mixture of relief and speculation. The arrival of reinforcements meant that the threat from Briant des Isles had almost vanished, but more than that . . .

He caught at Gareth's arm. "Are Kay and Loholt with him?"

"I don't know," Gareth said. "I'm just a messenger. I haven't spoken to Gaheris yet. But the king has sent for us both."

Gawain followed him through the network of passages and stairways that led to the king's private rooms. Arthur was seated in a chair by the fire; he held a cup of wine which he turned automatically between his fingers as if he had forgotten it was there. Gawain's second brother, Gaheris, stood in front of him; he broke off what he was saying as the door opened.

Gawain thought that Gaheris looked troubled, but he scarcely had time to wonder why before he noticed a third man, standing in the shadows by the window embrasure at the other side of the room. "Lancelot!" he exclaimed.

Gareth echoed his greeting, and went over to shake Lancelot enthusiastically by the hand. Lancelot murmured a greeting, but said no more. He had a subdued air that was not natural for him; although he was a quiet man, there was always a self-confidence about him that was missing now. Gawain, thinking about his recent departure from Camelot, could not be surprised.

"Gawain, Gareth," the king said. "Sit down; listen. I need your advice. Gaheris tells me he has seen nothing of Loholt and Kay."

Now Gawain understood Gaheris' troubled look, and could see the anxiety that Arthur tried to mask. He watched the king as he took the seat beside him, and accepted a cup of wine from Gareth. He knew that the same disquiet must be reflected in his own face.

"I told Loholt to make for the road," Arthur continued, "and to wait for Gaheris, unless he had to go into hiding. But Gaheris knows nothing of him."

Gaheris, his open features distressed, shook his head. "I had scouts out, looking for Briant's men. They would never have missed—how many? Five men? Never."

"Then someone else found them," Gareth said.

"Briant," Arthur said evenly.

Very carefully, he set the wine cup down on the table at his side. Gawain could see that only a determined self-control stopped him from hurling it across the room.

"I should have kept Loholt with me, but I thought I sent him by a safer road." Arthur interlaced his fingers into a tight clasp. "If Briant des Isles has my son, then we can expect a ransom demand. And God alone knows what that demand will be."

"If Briant knows who he is," Gawain said.

Arthur's level tones masked desperation. "If he does not, then what is there to keep Loholt alive?"

Gawain did not know what to say. Whether Briant had yet heard that Arthur had a son, whether he was able to recognise Loholt or not, the danger was very great. Gawain could not find it in him to believe that Kay and Loholt and their men were still wandering in the hills. They must be prisoners, or dead.

"And then what of Kay?" Arthur continued. "Briant will recognise him. And Kay can tell him too much about my defences."

"Kay isn't a traitor!" Gareth protested hotly.

The king gave him a bleak look. "Gareth, when it comes to extracting information, Briant des Isles is an expert. I wouldn't trust myself with him. I speak no dishonour of Kay."

Gareth subsided. Gawain could feel the tension singing in the room. It was not only the loss of Kay and Loholt; their capture might give Briant knowledge, and power, that would turn Arthur's recent victory into a defeat.

"Someone might look for them," Gawain suggested. "If they're prisoners, perhaps even release them. And if they're not . . ." At least we would know, he completed his own thought silently.

"I'll go," Gareth said immediately. "I'll collect some men and go right away. We can be miles away from here by nightfall."

He was all eagerness, already on his feet, waiting only for a word of permission from the king. A smile broke through Arthur's anxiety, and he gestured for Gareth to sit down again.

"Not so fast. I don't want to lose more men. What if you run into Briant?"

Gareth bared his teeth in a delighted grin. "Oh, I wish we could."

"There isn't much movement in the countryside," Gaheris said, supporting him. "A well-armed band shouldn't have any trouble."

Arthur frowned, considering.

"Please, Uncle?" Gareth prompted him. He had not taken his seat again, and he was quivering with impatience.

"Where will you go?" Gawain said. "And what about your shoulder? That arrow wound—"

"That's old history. As to where I'll go—" Gareth turned to Arthur again, stepping forward eagerly. "I'll take one of the guides who brought us here. We'll go back to where Kay and Loholt left us, and try to follow their trail. There might be some sign, or someone who saw them."

Arthur was still thinking, his face giving nothing away. His amber eyes were half closed, but Gawain knew the mind behind them was anything but sleepy. Alert, yes; but was he rational? The king loved Loholt immoderately, more than was wise. Such things, Gawain knew, were not in mortal control, and he knew too—none better—Arthur's urgent need for a son. But now, with Loholt missing, was it right to risk more lives in seeking him? Gawain suppressed a sigh. For Arthur, for himself if he had been in Arthur's place, there could be only one answer.

"Very well," Arthur said. "You may go. Take what men and equipment you need. Return, or send word, within seven days."

Gareth was across the room to the door before Arthur had finished speaking. Snatching at tattered courtesy, he bowed with his hand on the door latch, gave a brisk assent to Arthur's last

Exiled From Camelot

order, and was gone. Arthur looked after him, shaking his head a little, in silence.

When Arthur had dismissed them, Gawain found himself walking with Lancelot while Gaheris hurried off to make sure his troops were properly lodged. In silent agreement they climbed a stair, and let themselves out on to the battlements.

A stiff, cold breeze blew. Gawain leant against the parapet and looked out. He could see the road that stretched away to the south, through a wilderness of moor and rock and water, not the twisting path that he had taken through the hills with Arthur, but the high road along which Gaheris had ridden with his men only a short time before.

"It's good to have you back," he said.

Lancelot, standing at his side with his hands clasped behind him, did not respond at first. His features were shuttered, even the eyes impenetrable.

At last he said, "What tales are they telling in Camelot?"

"Tales? About the night you left?" Gawain laughed, though amusement was the last thing he felt. "Any tale you choose. Elaine bewitched you. You bewitched Elaine. It was a plot to discredit the queen. It was a plot to discredit you. You fled, naked and howling. . . ."

He let his voice die away as Lancelot let out an inarticulate sound of disgust. "It was . . . vile," he managed to say.

"It was unworthy of you," Gawain agreed gently.

Lancelot rested his elbows on the parapet and sank his face into his hands, rubbing them over it as if he were washing. They were large, bony hands, scarred from sword cuts. After a while, still with his face hidden, he began to speak. Gawain listened to the rough, quiet voice as if silent attention alone could heal the pain that vibrated through it.

"A woman came to me and told me that the queen had need of me. God, I was a fool! It was the same tale they told me that other time, at Corbenic. But I had to go with her. If it had truly been her command—Guenevere's—how could I have refused? And I thought the girl took me to the queen's apartments, to her—Gawain, you know what I'm trying to say—to her bed. And then, later—it was Elaine. Just as it was at Corbenic."

He groaned, and dug his fingers into his hair.

"And you left," Gawain prompted.

"All I could think of was getting away from her. Her lips, hands. . . . She tried to cling to me. I felt filthy. I had to get away." A shudder of revulsion went through him. "I couldn't face the court the next day. I couldn't face the sniggering. Most of all, I knew I could never face the queen. So I took a horse and rode away." He sighed, his voice steadying. "Perhaps I was mad for a while. I rode for days, and never knew where. But at last I came to the southern garrison, and found Gaheris packing up to leave because he'd had word that Briant had taken Roche Dure. At last there was something I could do! Gaheris offered me command, but I wouldn't take it. And I haven't needed to draw my sword, not yet. But at least there's clean service I can do for Arthur—and not at Camelot."

Lancelot relaxed finally, leaning against the parapet, staring out to where the hills grew blue and indistinct against the distant sky. Gawain silently rested a hand on his shoulder. From somewhere below, the clatter of hoofbeats rose, and a moment later a small group of horsemen appeared, trim and well-disciplined, heading at a fast trot down the south road.

"Gareth," Gawain said. He lifted his hand in farewell, though his brother, at the head of his little band, had no idea he was there.

"We'll pray he finds Loholt," Lancelot said.

"And Kay," Gawain reminded him. Lancelot nodded absently. "From all I hear," Gawain went on, "you have Kay to thank for smoothing over the trouble you left behind you in Camelot. Elaine and Guenevere might well have ended by scratching each other's eyes out, without him."

Lancelot turned and looked at him; Gawain still could not read the dark eyes. After a while Lancelot said, "I'm sorry."

"Sometimes," Gawain suggested mildly, "I think you underestimate Kay."

Lancelot spread his hands; Gawain could see the calluses that come from holding a sword. "Kay should keep to what he does well. As seneschal, he's second to none. As a diplomat—perhaps, when he guards his tongue. But he's no warrior, and never will be."

"He should attend to his books and accounts and letters?" Gawain said. "And forget about honour?"

He felt a tiny spark of anger kindling within himself at the thought that this man, whom he loved and respected so much, could sometimes be so obtuse. His eyes met Lancelot's; in its way, the look was a challenge. Lancelot did not take it up; instead, he bent his head in agreement.

"You're right. We give no honour to Kay's talents. Small wonder that he keeps on striving." A faint smile broke up the sombre countenance, and he clasped Gawain's hand. "I give you my word, that when Kay comes back I will speak with him about what he did for me in Camelot, and try to thank him. But truly he is a hard man to thank."

Gawain tried to echo his smile, knowing how affronted Kay might be by any attempt of Lancelot's to offer him gratitude. He would try to pave the way for that encounter, when Kay came back. He stiffened; unconsciously he had repeated in his mind the words Lancelot had just used: "when Kay comes back." And yet there was no certainty that he ever would. Gawain gazed down at the road, but Gareth's party had long since vanished into the distance.

Chapter Eleven

For the rest of that day, and the next, there was no word from Briant. Arthur sent out scouts to see if there was any sign that he was massing an army for another attack. He also sent an embassy, led by Bedivere, with his terms for Briant's surrender. The answer to that should show whether Briant was holding Loholt and Kay as his prisoners.

Towards the evening of their fourth day in Carlisle, Arthur went round the sentries. "They think it's all over," he said to Gawain, who accompanied him. "As far as I'm concerned, we're still at war, and will be until I have Loholt safe home."

Gawain made a noncommittal murmur. It was still too early to hope for word from Gareth, but every day that passed made it less likely that Kay and Loholt would return alive. Gawain tried to hold grief at bay by refusing to talk about the possibility; he knew that Arthur was doing the same.

As they reached the main courtyard, Gawain could hear a shouted conversation going on between the porter and someone outside; he could not make out the words. He exchanged a glance with Arthur; the king began to stride across the courtyard, and as he did so one of the guards unbolted and pulled open the wicket gate. A single man stepped through, took a pace or two forward, and stumbled to his knees. He was filthy and dressed in rags, but Gawain recognised him. It was Kay.

After an instant when he stood in frozen astonishment, Gawain snapped into movement to join the king, and came up beside him where he stood in front of Kay. Arthur had already begun to question him.

"What happened to Loholt?" Gawain heard, the words rapped out.

Kay was gazing up at the king. His face was haggard, exhausted, filled with pain, and yet joy was struggling to break through. "My lord—you're safe. . . ."

Arthur bent over, grasped Kay's shoulders, and shook him. "Loholt. Where is he?"

Gawain saw all the joy drain out of Kay's face. He could hardly bear to go on looking at the horror in his eyes.

"My lord, Loholt is . . . dead."

Arthur still held him by the shoulders. Now he thrust him away roughly so that Kay fell sideways on to the stones of the courtyard.

Exiled From Camelot

"Dead? Kay, he was in your care. And you tell me dead?" There was no response from Kay, but his eyes never left Arthur's. "You're sure?" the king demanded. "You saw this?"

"Yes, my lord."

Gawain saw all the king's face tighten. Arthur took a step back. "I must have been mad to trust him to you, Kay. You failed me as you've always failed me." Kay began to reach out a hand, shaking, pleading, but Arthur ignored it. "You're seneschal because I swore an oath to your father," he said. "If I had not sworn that oath, you would be gone from here tonight. As I am bound, stay; but stay out of my sight."

He turned and strode back towards the door to the keep. Kay cried out, but if Arthur heard it he gave no sign. Gawain started forward, but by the time he reached his friend, Kay had collapsed into an unconscious huddle on the stones.

Gawain knelt beside him and raised his head so that it rested in his lap. Kay was limp and motionless; he might have been dead, except that Gawain could detect shallow breathing and, when he sought for it, the uneven fibrillation of his heart.

Kay's cloak was torn and filthy. Under it he wore only shirt and hose, and his sword belt without either sword or dagger. His hair was tangled, straggling round an ash-pale face. Dark blood oozed sluggishly from a wound in his throat.

Alarmed, Gawain was beginning to check for other injuries, when he realised that someone stooped over him. He looked up to see one of the grooms.

"Can I do anything, sir?"

Gawain nodded. "Thank you. Help me to carry him."

They took Kay back to Gawain's own apartments. His servant waited with hot water for Gawain to bathe before supper; he was scandalised when Gawain and the groom laid Kay down on the sheepskins in front of the fire.

"Shall I call the healers, sir?" the groom asked.

"Yes. But tell them I don't want him in the infirmary. I'll look after him here."

Even now, when Gawain had to act quickly to take care of Kay's physical hurts, he could look ahead and imagine that the pain in the seneschal's mind would be harder to heal. At the very least, he would not have Kay wake and find himself among strangers.

As soon as the groom had gone, Gawain took a knife and cut away the remains of Kay's clothes and his scarred riding boots. As he did so, he began to see how badly Kay was injured. His shirt stuck to wounds on his chest, and Gawain had to soak away the last scraps of linen. He uncovered a five-fold gash that ran from Kay's throat almost to his waist, weals dark with dried blood, the flesh around them puffed up and streaked with red.

Gawain could not imagine what could have caused it, except for a bear or some other great animal, and he was sure there were no bears roaming the country around Carlisle.

Helped by his servant, who had been shocked out of his disapproval, Gawain went on bathing Kay's inert body. The sight of his other injuries almost turned Gawain sick. The lacerations around Kay's wrists and ankles showed that he had been bound, and struggled against his bonds. All over his body were shallow wounds that looked as if they had been made with a sharp knife. They fell into some kind of horrible twisted pattern, so that Gawain could imagine the torturer bending over Kay, with the same attentiveness that a woodcarver might give to his design. He wanted to weep.

By the time the healer arrived, Gawain had finished soaking away the filth and dried blood, and was towelling Kay dry. The healer took one look at what had been done to him, gasped, and crossed himself, but after that first entirely unprofessional reaction, set to work rapidly with salves and bandages.

He was a grizzled little man with deft hands; Gawain had worked with him after the siege was raised. He punctuated what he was doing with a commentary spat out between his teeth, disgust in every syllable.

"He hasn't eaten for days . . . cold . . . is there a fire in the bedroom? Dear God, what did that . . . wildcat? Could be poisoned . . . I'll leave you salves, sir. You'll know what to do to change the dressings."

To Gawain's relief, the gashes on Kay's chest, and the small wound in the throat, were the only injuries that looked at all serious. When they were bandaged, he wrapped Kay in a woollen bedgown, and he and the healer carried him through into the next room and settled him in bed.

When the healer had gone, Gawain gave his servant instructions about what he would need for Kay, and while he waited he stripped off his own clothes, which were damp and stained from bathing Kay's wounds, and put on a bedgown. After a little while, his servant reappeared with everything he had asked for, along with some supper for Gawain himself.

"Where are you going to sleep, sir?" the man asked.

Gawain had not thought about that. He did not expect to sleep much for the next night or two, until he was sure that Kay would recover. But his servant, patient and deferential, was waiting for an answer.

"Oh—on the settle in the other room. Or perhaps—yes, we'll bring it in here. I can't leave him alone."

"You should have someone to watch with you, sir."

Gawain knew he was right. If Gareth had been in the court, he could have shared the task with him. But Gareth was far away, on an errand that now was useless, and there was no one else Gawain wanted to ask for help, especially if Kay was out of favour with the king.

When they had moved the bench and his servant had brought extra furs, Gawain dismissed him for the night and settled to his solitary vigil. He mixed milk with honey and spices, and set it to warm in a pot on the fire. He inspected his own supper, and made himself eat some soup and bread, but he felt too disturbed to sit over it for long. He moved restlessly around the room, making up the fire, positioning the lamp so it would not shine in Kay's eyes when he woke, rearranging the bed-furs around him and leaning over to make sure that the faint, wavering breath had not quite died away.

He came to rest at last, sitting on the side of the bed and holding one of Kay's hands between both his own. The hand was scratched, the fingernails broken. Kay still wore Arthur's ring, the carnelian set in gold. Gawain could not remember a time when the seneschal had not worn it, or remember seeing him wear any other ring but this. He thought of the encounter in the courtyard, and prayed that there might be some comfort he could give.

He lost count of time, though the fire burned down and he had to set more logs on it. Returning to the bed, he bent over Kay, studying the pale, still face, and stroked back the thick tangle of dark curls. Kay lay motionless, half buried in the furs. He was a small man, slender and fine-boned, but Gawain had never thought of him as fragile. He had too much vitality, too much nervous energy fuelling him. But now Gawain was afraid that his fighting spirit had died; he thought he had seen it die, out there in the courtyard. He could imagine that Kay would let himself slip out of life, like an exhausted swimmer slipping under the surface of the sea, without the strength or the will to go on struggling.

Unexpectedly, as Gawain leant over him, Kay's lashes fluttered. His eyes opened, closed, and opened again to regard Gawain with a dark, abstracted gaze.

"Gawain," he breathed out. "You're safe?"

"Yes." Gawain clasped his hand, not knowing whether he wanted to smile or weep.

"Gareth?"

"Yes."

Kay let out a long sigh. A slight frown had settled between his brows, a troubled look, as though he fought bewilderment. Gawain thought he understood. Kay knew that he did not need to ask about the king, but as yet he did not remember why.

Afraid of what his face might reveal, Gawain turned away to the fire and poured some of the spiced milk into a cup. When he went back to the bed, Kay was watching him again with that same thoughtful look.

"This is Carlisle," he said.

"Yes, Kay. You're safe here. It's all over. . . ."

Gawain suddenly felt that his words of reassurance were a lie. If Kay was not at peace with the king, it was not all over. Saying no more, he slid an arm round Kay's shoulders to raise him, and held the cup to his lips. Kay drank thirstily.

"That's good," Gawain said. "You can have some more later. Now you're going to sleep again, and get well."

Kay made an effort to focus his eyes on him. "I thought . . . I would die."

"No!" The one word came out too forcefully; Gawain had briefly given way to his own misgivings. Making himself speak quietly, he said, "You're not going to die. Not now that you're here."

Kay still gazed at Gawain as if he only partly comprehended what he was saying. "You won't leave me?" he murmured.

"No. Kay, you know I won't."

Gawain thought that his pity was going to master him, and he did not want Kay distressed by seeing him weep. He knew how hard it was for Kay to accept friendship, to admit he needed anyone or anything. Wanting to offer comfort in more than words, he drew Kay into an embrace; when he released him, the heavy eyes were already closing, and as Gawain settled him back on the pillows he sank into sleep.

Gawain drew the furs closely round him again. Beyond this room there was the death of Loholt, still unexplained, and Arthur's grief and anger. Mercifully, Kay had forgotten, but he would remember soon, and before long he would have to face it. All Gawain could do was shield him now, surround him with such security and love that in the end he would be able to take up his life again. Gawain dared not look beyond that.

He kept watch for the rest of the night. Kay roused twice more, for a few moments, but to Gawain's relief he seemed not to want to talk. He drank more of the milk, and slept quietly between whiles, so that by morning Gawain's immediate anxiety had faded. His other anxieties remained.

Gawain opened the shutter a crack and let the morning light flow into the room. Knowing that Kay was warmly wrapped, he sat for a few minutes in the window alcove, drinking in the cold air and looking out over the towers of Carlisle to the line of hills just visible in the distance. It was too early to hope that Gareth would have given up his search, but Gawain found himself wanting his younger brother very much. He wanted Gareth's cheerful, uncomplicated support, and most of all he wanted someone to talk to who would understand.

He was drowsing in the window seat when he heard movement in the outer room. A moment later his servant came in with a basket of logs, followed by the healer. The old man went over to the bed, examined Kay without disturbing him, and snorted.

"He'll do." Rounding on Gawain, he said, "And you'd better get some sleep now, or I'll have both of you on my hands."

Slightly startled at the irascible tones—almost worthy of Kay himself—Gawain thought he had better obey. He felt bone weary; he needed rest so that he would be ready when Kay needed him. When he had made sure that his servant would call him if he was wanted, he retreated to the settle, pulled the furs around himself, and let sleep take him.

He was woken much later by sounds coming from the bed. At first, still confused by sleep, Gawain was not sure what was happening. Then, as he remembered, the confusion was stripped away. He scrambled out of his coverings, and flung himself across the room.

Kay was still asleep, fast in the grip of nightmare. His arms and legs were splayed out, as if he thought that cords pinioned him to the bed's corners. His head thrashed from side to side. He was muttering something that Gawain could not catch, and then he said clearly, "Loholt."

Gawain bent over him and shook him by the shoulders. "Kay! Kay, wake up!"

"No—no!" Kay's voice was sharpened by terror. "Don't—please, lord. Don't!"

Gawain began to grow frightened as all his efforts to rouse him failed. Kay was still locked into the evil dream, his voice rising now to a gasping scream.

"The Lady—no . . . no!"

Desperate, Gawain struck him across the face. The scream broke into breathy sobs. Kay's limbs convulsed. Gawain tried to catch hold of him, but Kay fought against him, as if terror had driven him out of his mind.

"Don't!" Gawain begged. "Kay, stop it. It's me—Gawain. You were dreaming. Kay—please—listen to me . . ."

As he spoke, Kay's struggles gradually died away, though whether from understanding or simply failing strength Gawain could not be sure. At last Kay leant against his shoulder, panting rapidly, shivering as if he had just been dragged out of icy water. He lifted a hand and stared stupefied at the bandage on his wrist, and then at Gawain's face.

At last he whispered, "Gawain . . . it is you?"

"Yes, Kay."

"I don't know what's real any more," Kay said. "It's really you? I'm not dreaming now?"

"You're not dreaming. You're here with me." Still keeping his arms around Kay, he pulled the furs around him, trying to still the dreadful shivering.

After a moment, Kay said, "I'm sorry." Gawain held him, quietly, heard a long sigh, and then, "You're very good to me."

Wondering if it would help him to talk about it, Gawain asked, "Someone tortured you, didn't they? Was it Briant?"

At the question, he felt a great wave of tension flood through Kay, and another brief spasm of struggling, almost as if his friend were trying to escape from him.

"Don't," Gawain said. "Quiet. . . . Don't tell me if you don't want to."

At first he could not see Kay's face, which was hidden against his shoulder; when Kay raised his head, there was a wild look about him. "Not . . . Briant." The words seemed torn out of him.

"One of his men, then?"

Kay gasped out an assent. "Yes—Briant's man."

"Did he question you?"

Kay was silent for a moment, his eyes fixed on Gawain. Though he said nothing, Gawain thought that he was suddenly more rational than he had been until now.

At last, his voice unsteady, but coherent, Kay said, "He was waiting for Briant. Then they would have questioned me. But he did not ask . . . and I told him nothing. I'm not a traitor!"

The last few words were a desperate plea for understanding. Kay pressed his face into Gawain's shoulder and gave way to a fit of dry sobbing.

"No, of course you're not," Gawain said, and then added, "Dear God, do you mean that someone did this to you for fun?"

Kay made no answer, but none was needed. He rested against Gawain, his chest heaving with his own deep, shaken breathing.

When he was calm again, Gawain dared to ask, "Is that how Loholt died?"

Kay stiffened in his arms, looked up at him—a brilliant, mad stare—and tried to draw away.

Gawain resisted him. "Do you want to tell me?"

"No. . . . Yes!"

But at first Kay said nothing. Gawain held him, patiently waiting, until he began again, slowly, painfully, groping for every word.

"They would have used Loholt. . . ."

"Then why kill him?" Gawain said, genuinely puzzled, forgetting for a minute the delicate control he needed to tease a rational story out of Kay.

Kay's response terrified him. He started to speak, stopped, and then broke down into deep, wrenching sobs. Gawain bent over him, hugging him close.

"Don't, Kay, don't. Don't talk about it now. I'm sorry, I shouldn't have asked you. It doesn't matter."

As he soothed Kay into exhausted quiet at last, Gawain cursed himself for having tried to go too quickly. He wanted the truth about Loholt's death, he wanted a story that he could take to Arthur and use to make the king understand that Kay could not be held responsible. But the pain was still too recent; he, and Arthur, would have to wait.

As he made Kay comfortable again—Kay, who clung to him as long as strength and consciousness would last—Gawain tried to piece together what he knew. Kay's sufferings were all too obvious, but Gawain could not make sense of what had happened to Loholt. It seemed that Briant's men had known who he was, so why kill him when he was so much more valuable alive? Unless Briant's torturer had amused himself once too often. Gawain could see there were large gaps in the story that only Kay could fill, when he was well enough. Gawain remembered one of them now. In his anxiety about Loholt, he had not thought to ask Kay who the Lady was.

When Kay slept again, Gawain washed and dressed and called to his servant, who was hovering in the outer room. "Will you go to the king," he said, "and ask him if he will see me?"

His servant shook his head. "The king's seeing no one, sir."

"I think he might see me."

Dubiously, the man went. He came back within half an hour with an unadorned refusal. Gawain thought briefly. Arthur must know where he was and what he was doing. Probably some of the king's anger with Kay was directed towards him as well.

"Stay here," he told his servant, "and if Sir Kay wakes, tell him I'll be back soon."

In the anteroom to Arthur's private apartments he found Lancelot, with one or two others. Gawain went across to him and drew him aside to speak privately.

"Kay is with you?" Lancelot asked, low-voiced. "How is he?"

"Very ill." Crisply, without fuss, he told Lancelot what had been done to Kay.

Lancelot winced. "Hideous," he murmured. "But it won't change anything. Arthur will still blame him for letting Loholt die."

"And what else was he supposed to do?"

Lancelot shrugged. "However sorry we might feel, we can't deny that Arthur trusted Kay with Loholt's life. It was the wrong choice, but Kay accepted it. If you or I had been in that position, we might never have been taken prisoner at all."

"You and I should thank God that we never have to find out." Gawain was beginning to grow angry, so he consciously calmed himself. "What's happening now?" he said. "I need to speak to Arthur."

"Arthur won't see anyone," Lancelot said. "He grieves for his son."

Gawain thought that over. There were guards outside the inner door that led to Arthur's private room. When he approached, they swung their spears across, barring his way.

"I'm sorry, sir," one of them said. "The king's orders, sir. No one is to see him."

"Please tell him I'm here," Gawain said.

The guard, with a barely concealed shrug, obeyed. Gawain waited. In spite of Arthur's first refusal, he could not help feeling that the king would want to know if Kay had said anything to him, for how else was he to find out how Loholt had died?

His patience was rewarded a few minutes later when the guard came out again and grudgingly held the door open for him.

Inside, Arthur stood with his back to him, gazing down into the fire. At the sound of the closing door he glanced round. "Well?" he snapped. Gawain considered him. All the light had gone out of him; his face looked harder. He was a king still, but Gawain was afraid that the spark that kindled men's hearts might well be quenched.

"Well?" he repeated. "Come to plead for Kay?"

That was so close to the truth that Gawain was almost encouraged; at least Arthur's shrewdness had not been submerged in grief.

"He is ill, my lord," he said. "And deeply distressed over what has happened."

"As well he might be!" Arthur turned from the fire and began to pace jerkily around the room. Gawain watched him, giving him time. At length the king spoke, as if the words were wrung out of him, "My son, Gawain—my son!"

Gawain could not help wondering whether the bright spirit Arthur grieved for was truly Loholt. By losing him now, Arthur might have been spared disillusion later. Gawain felt his own grief for a life cut short so early, but he knew that not every eager boy grows up into a king.

Arthur cut short his pacing at the window and stared out, blindly, into the cold sky. "What excuse has Kay to offer?" he asked abruptly.

"Nothing," Gawain said. "He is too ill to speak of it properly. He feels great pain."

Arthur swung round on him. "And what of my pain? What of Loholt's?"

There was no answer to the challenge; besides, that was not what Gawain had come to say. "My lord, Kay has great need of you," he began carefully. "Your anger will crush him. Just now he is too weak to bear it. Will you not come and speak to him?"

"No."

The one word, snapped out. No hesitation, no compromise. Gawain tried again.

"If you can make peace with Briant des Isles, who is your enemy, surely you can make peace with Kay?"

"Peace with Briant?" Arthur snarled at him. "There'll be no peace with Briant. I'll never make peace with the man who killed my son."

Chapter Twelve

Kay slept for the rest of that day and the following night. Sometimes he would cry out, or mutter a few broken words, but the nightmare did not return, and Gawain was able to quieten him without disturbing his rest. Once, in the evening, he roused and stayed fully awake for about half an hour, long enough for Gawain to give him some soup he was keeping warm, and then slept again.

By the next morning Kay had recovered enough to get up so that Gawain could help him to the privy, and then to wash and sit in a chair by the fire until Gawain had changed the dressings on his wounds. All of them, even the five-fold gash, were beginning to heal. Gawain would have liked to ask Kay what had made a wound like that, but he had imposed a rule on himself: no more questions until Kay himself showed that he wanted to talk.

While Kay was out of bed, Gawain's servant stripped off the stained linen and replaced it with fresh. By the time he had finished, Kay was ready to lie down again, his strength ebbing, head drooping as Gawain supported him across the room. Gawain put another pillow behind him, propping him up a little so that he was not quite so helpless.

"Do you want something to eat?" Gawain asked.

Kay shook his head. "Some water? Thank you," he said as Gawain handed him the cup. "You're very patient with me."

"It isn't patience." Gawain wanted to say more, but he contented himself with resting a hand on Kay's shoulder. "Go to sleep."

He retreated to the chair by the fire. The room was silent for a long time; he thought Kay was asleep, until he heard his voice, very quiet.

"Gawain?"

At once he went back to Kay's side. The seneschal was looking up at him, his dark eyes wide and filled with pain.

"Gawain—I must ask you. Tell me the truth. I am . . . in disgrace, with the king?"

He had remembered, then. Gawain felt pain like a stone in his heart. He bowed his head. "He grieves for Loholt."

Kay drew a long breath. His mouth trembled; so did his voice, though he did his best to steady it.

"I know that—that no one will wish to speak with me while

the king is angry. That is only right. But could you—will you tell Sir Gareth—"

"Kay!" Gawain interrupted him, shocked beyond bearing. He sat beside Kay on the bed and took him by the shoulders. "Do you think Gareth hasn't been to see you because you're in disgrace?" Kay did not reply; he had averted his face, but Gawain caught the glitter of tears. "Kay, he isn't here. He went looking for you, days ago."

Kay stared at him. He had been close to breaking down, but now anxiety drove out his shame. "Then he's in danger! Briant's men—"

"Briant's men are cowering in Roche Dure. We've seen nothing of them since we raised the siege."

"But—"

Gawain shook Kay's shoulders gently. "Will you stop trying to mother Gareth? He can look after himself." Better than you can, he added silently. "Stop fretting and get some rest."

Kay turned his head aside. He had a hand at his throat, as if he found it hard to breathe.

"Forgive me," he said in a whisper. "I meant—I meant no insult to Sir Gareth."

"Of course not." For some reason, the touch of formality, the distance as Kay acknowledged Gareth's title, wrenched at Gawain's heart. "Kay, you know very well that if Gareth were here now he would tell you to stop being such a fool."

Something shook Kay that was either a laugh or a sob. Gradually he began to relax. His hand followed the embroidery on the sleeve of his bedgown; it belonged to Gawain, and was a far finer garment than Kay would ever allow himself to wear.

After a minute, still not looking at his friend, Kay broke the silence. "This is your room."

"Yes. There was no time to get yours ready, and besides—"

"I can't stay here."

He was still not meeting Gawain's eyes. Gawain asked gently, "Why not?"

"Because my shame will taint you, too! Because—"

"Rubbish."

Kay looked at him then, startled by the mixture of affection and exasperation in Gawain's tone. "It's true," Kay said. "Arthur will be angry with you when he finds out—all the others will despise you. . . ."

"Arthur knows," Gawain told him. "And perhaps it displeases him." He shrugged, smiling. "I'll survive it."

"You have spoken to him, then?"

"Yes. I'm sorry, Kay, he won't see you yet. Try not to worry. It can't last for ever."

Kay shook his head slightly. "He doesn't want me." Desolation vibrated in his voice. "He has never really wanted me." He gave Gawain a sideways glance, hesitant, as if he would have liked to say more.

Gawain took his hand. "Tell me if you want to."

Kay swallowed nervously, uncertain still, finding it difficult as he always did to reveal himself freely.

"I was forced on him by accident," he said. "Everyone knows that story! The lord Merlin chose my parents to bring up Arthur—because they were unknown, and unimportant, and a very, very long way away." There was a trace of self-mockery in his tone. "When Arthur pulled the sword from the stone, and we knew him for the king, my father asked him to make me seneschal. Arthur swore that no one else should have that office while he and I lived.

"Even then, I was uncertain. He should have given it to one of the lesser kings, or a king's son. He needed friends, in those days. And I would have followed him without it." His mouth twisted. "Not that you will find many people to believe that."

"I believe it," Gawain said.

Kay smiled faintly and returned the clasp of his hand. "I promised myself that I would be worthy of it," he went on. "I meant to be the best of all his knights. I meant to do such deeds, and win honour in Arthur's name, and lay it all at his feet! And at first I thought perhaps—" He gave a betraying glance at the carnelian ring. "No—everything went wrong. I should have known myself better."

His voice shook, and for a moment Gawain thought he would not be able to go on, but he steadied himself.

"Arthur tolerates me, because of the oath he swore, and—and perhaps a little out of kindness, because we were boys together. But I think he does not hold me in his heart."

"I think he does," Gawain said, afraid that he would break down himself if this went on much longer. "More than you know. Perhaps more than he knows himself. Kay, this will pass."

Kay shifted restlessly against the pillows. Gawain could almost see his pain, like chains binding him. A life wrenched out of true, damaged so that Arthur could be king. It was no one's fault; Kay himself recognised that, only that the imperative demands of Britain's safety could not give way to the claims of a child growing to manhood on the edge of great events.

Kay had shared with Arthur his place in his parents' hearts; he had loved him as a brother; he had been, finally, the architect of a kingdom and a way of life where he felt he could never truly belong.

"I would give him my life," Kay said. "But that has never been asked of me. As it is, I have never given him anything that he has really wanted."

"You can't say that!" Gawain leant forward, willing Kay to look at him, to listen, to understand. "One of your . . . lesser kings would have taken the honour and the power of the seneschal's office, and done nothing to deserve it. But you built Arthur's kingdom for him. You gave him Camelot."

Kay shook his head, blinking tears away. "Even if that's true, it's little enough. There's no honour in it." His voice suddenly choked. "I will release Arthur from his oath and go home to my father's house. My father grows old; there will be work for me to do. I will give up striving for honour, and trouble Arthur no further."

He tried to pull his hand away from Gawain's clasp, but Gawain held it captured.

"You can't release Arthur from his oath," he explained patiently, "because it was not sworn to you." He stifled unsteady laughter. "And if you went home, your father would flay you and pin you out on his barn door. Dear Kay, is it so hard, to stay with us?"

Kay looked up at him, shaken, open to him as he had hardly ever been before. "If I lost you, Gawain," he said unevenly, "I should not wish to live."

"You won't lose me. Don't be absurd."

Kay's eyes were haunted. "But if I had done something—if I were a traitor, or . . . You would turn from me then. You would be right to do it."

"Kay," Gawain said, "are you trying to tell me something?"

He could scarcely bear to see the desperate fear that flashed into Kay's eyes. His friend drew back.

"Tell you—no. . . . I've nothing to tell you. I'm sorry, I'm so tired that I don't know what I'm saying. Leave me to sleep."

Gawain could not go on pressing him. He rearranged Kay's pillows and coverings to make him comfortable, hoping that the simple actions and the touch would be a reassurance when words were no good. But he knew very well that Kay had hesitated on the brink of confiding in him. Gawain had the sensation of looking at something dark and shadowy, something that would have to be revealed before Kay could win free of his fears and his bitter unhappiness.

"Kay," he said quietly, "do you want a priest?"

The seneschal looked startled. "A priest? Gawain, I . . ." His voice died away. He was caught up in some silent struggle. "Not yet," he said at last. I will, but—give me a little while."

Gawain smiled and agreed. Confession might ease Kay's heart, at least. But whether he would ever trust Arthur, or Gawain himself, or anyone else, enough to reveal the story to them, Gawain could not tell.

✥ ✥ ✥

For the next two days, Gawain felt that time had come to a stop. Kay gradually began to recover his strength, but he tired very easily. He slept for long hours; there were no more nightmares. When he was awake, he was listless, and he made no attempt to take Gawain into his confidence again.

In the afternoon of the second day, Gawain was on his way to the infirmary to fetch fresh salves when he heard rapid footsteps approaching. At the turn of the stair he came face to face with Gareth. Gawain cried out his name, and moved to embrace him, but Gareth fended him off with one hand.

"I've been six days in the saddle," he said, "and I stink of horse. And all for nothing. We haven't found either of them, Kay or Loholt." He went on pouring out his story, overriding Gawain's attempt to interrupt. "We went back to the place where they left us, and we found their trail. They took a road leading into a forest, and it looks as if someone ambushed them there." His mouth took on a hard line. "We found the three men who rode with them—all of them dead. And I found Kay's sword. But there was no sign of Kay or Loholt. Briant must have them."

"No, he hasn't." Gawain managed to get a word in at last. "We have. At least—"

Gareth interrupted him, his face a sudden blaze of delight. "Kay is here? Where?"

"In my rooms. But—"

With a brilliant smile, Gareth clapped his brother on the shoulder and went on up the stairs, taking them two at a time.

Gawain called out, "Gareth, wait—"

Gareth pivoted, looking down impatiently. "What is it?"

"Loholt is dead," Gawain said.

"Dead?" Taken aback, Gareth was at least listening now. "How did he die?"

"We don't know. Kay was tortured. He can't talk about it yet."

"Tortured—oh, dear God." Completely sobered now, Gareth stared down at his brother, his face white.

"Go and speak to Kay," Gawain said. "He has wanted you, I know. But don't question him. And Gareth—go gently with him."

Gareth nodded, looked as if he was going to ask something else, then turned and went on more slowly up the stairs. Gawain watched him out of sight before going on his way to the infirmary.

That same night Bedivere returned, after taking Arthur's peace terms to Briant des Isles at Roche Dure. The first Gawain knew of it was the following morning, when he was called into council with Bedivere, Lancelot, and the king.

Arthur had summoned them to his private room. He was more controlled than when Gawain had last seen him, but the hardness was still there. He greeted Gawain formally, and asked nothing about Kay. Gawain withdrew to the window seat. The room was warm, and he was surrounded by familiar faces, yet he felt uneasy, and he knew why. He had hardly ever attended an inner council of this kind that did not include Kay.

Arthur had been pacing restlessly, and came to a stop beside the fire.

"Very well," he said to Bedivere. "Tell Gawain and Lancelot about your meeting with Briant."

Bedivere shrugged. He was a taciturn man, preferring to keep his speeches brief.

"Arthur sent him letters," he explained, "offering him a peaceful withdrawal from Roche Dure. Briant saw that as outright surrender. Didn't like it. Wrote a letter of his own."

He gestured towards the table, where a letter was lying open, as if someone had cast it aside impatiently. Arthur moved slowly across the room and picked it up.

"He offers to come and do me homage, in return for the lordship of Roche Dure and the lands around it. He will hold the lands in my name, and cease to call himself the Pendragon or assert his right to rule in Britain."

He glanced round, inviting comments. Bedivere, staring at his feet, had nothing to say. Gawain, who knew how the king's mind worked, thought there was no point in offering his advice. It was Lancelot who spoke.

"Roche Dure has never been more than a garrison castle. The people who live under its protection have never had a lord to take an interest in their affairs. You could do worse, my lord, than put a loyal man in charge there."

The king smiled thinly, fingering the brooch that held his tunic at the throat. "I notice you say 'a loyal man,' Lancelot. You are talking about Briant des Isles?"

"It would be a risk to trust him," Lancelot agreed.

"And you, Gawain?" Arthur challenged him. "You're very quiet over there. What do you think?"

There was no avoiding it now. Gawain met his eyes. "I should rejoice to see peace and prosperity around Roche Dure, my lord. But I do not think Briant is the man to bring it there."

"Because he killed Loholt?"

"And tortured Kay, my lord."

Arthur's brows went up. He ignored Gawain's reminder about Kay, merely commenting, "Gawain advising war? I never thought to hear that."

"Not war, my lord," Gawain said. A chill ran through him. "But you can insist on your first offer, and allow him to withdraw peacefully from Roche Dure."

Arthur glanced down again at the paper he held.

"He intends to come to the All Hallows' Court, where he will kneel at my feet and do me homage. A most generous offer!" Slowly he closed his hand over the letter and crumpled it into a ball. "Briant has refused my terms," he said. "There will be no peaceful withdrawal from Roche Dure. There will be war, until he is dead and every last man of his who dared set foot in Britain, until my land is clean of them and I have revenge for the death of my son."

He flung the letter into the fire; Gawain watched as it flared up and crumbled to ashes.

Chapter Thirteen

When Gawain returned from the council, he arrived at the door of his rooms at the same moment as the Carlisle steward, an elderly man with a nervous manner.

"Sir Gawain," he said, "I must speak at once with my lord Kay."

Gawain frowned slightly as he showed the man into the outer room. "Sir Kay has been very ill—"

"I pray daily for his recovery, my lord. But I must speak with him. With the All Hallows' Court in three days, and the king here, and everything at sixes and sevens after the siege . . ."

His voice trailed off helplessly. His agitation showed in his face, and his hands, which he unconsciously kneaded together.

Gawain smiled. "Wait here," he said. "I'll see."

He went into the bedroom, and found Kay and Gareth there. Kay sat in the chair beside the fire. There was a bowl of water and a mess of shaving tackle on a table close by; now Gareth trimmed Kay's hair. Amused, Gawain watched them for a moment before either of them realised he was there.

"Has Kay given you your old job back?" he asked his brother.

Kay looked embarrassed and pleased at the same time. "Gareth never stops nagging," he said.

"Now that you're well enough to get up, I want you looking respectable," Gareth said tranquilly.

"Perhaps it's just as well," Gawain agreed. "Kay, the steward is outside, asking to speak with you. Jittering about the All Hallows' Court. Do you want to see him, or shall I send him away?"

"I'll see him," Kay said.

He brushed at hair clippings that clung to his bedgown while Gareth ran a comb through the crisp curls, now restored to their usual neatness. In fact, Gawain thought, Kay looked very much as usual this morning: pale, thinner than before, perhaps, but in command of himself again.

He got up and came to Gawain, reaching out to clasp his hands in a spontaneous gesture that startled his friend. Kay had never found gratitude easy; it encroached too far on his stubborn independence, but this time his defences were down.

"I'll send for some clothes, and have my own rooms made ready," Kay said.

"If you're sure you're strong enough."

"Yes. Thanks to you, Gawain." He gave a little impatient shake of the head. "Thanking you is absurd. I owe you more than I can ever repay."

Embarrassment overcame him again, and he hurried out. Gawain looked after him, anxious when he thought of the amount of work that preparing for the All Hallows' Court would entail.

"I can't imagine what the steward was thinking. He should realise that Kay—" He broke off as he saw that Gareth was grinning widely. "What do you know about this?"

"I sent him."

"You did what?"

Gareth, absorbed in tidying up, was unrepentant. "I went to the steward and told him to come here and panic. I knew Kay wouldn't be able to resist taking over."

"Well, he panicked beautifully," Gawain murmured. "But are you sure Kay is fit to do it?"

"Yes, of course. And I'll run errands for him, just as I used to!" More serious, Gareth stopped what he was doing and came over to his brother. "Kay needs something to take his mind off what happened. You know he's happier when he has a job to do. And besides—" his irrepressible grin surfaced again "—in all the preparation and all the ceremony of the Court, don't you think that sooner or later the king will have to speak to his seneschal?"

Although Kay immersed himself at once in organising the All Hallows' Court, Gawain thought that his brother's optimism had been misplaced. There was no sign in the next few days that the work had brought Kay any closer to Arthur, or even that Arthur was aware of it. Gawain suspected that Kay was being very careful not to force himself on the king.

His suspicions hardened to a certainty at the evening feast on All Hallows itself. It was Kay's duty, as high seneschal, to fill Arthur's ceremonial cup and hand it to him at the start of the meal. On this occasion, Gawain saw that Kay had delegated the task to the Carlisle steward.

On any normal occasion, that might have been no more than a graceful way for Kay to honour his subordinate; this time Gawain was sure that Kay had done it so that he could avoid the king. He sighed faintly. Kay's stubborn pride would not let him do anything that would make Arthur think he was trying to crawl back into favour.

Gareth, sitting at table beside his brother, caught the sigh.

"Kay won't even come and eat with us," he said, nodding at the empty place opposite him. "He's in the kitchen, supervising the serving. I offered to do it, but he threw me out. He won't come." He echoed Gawain's sigh. "I had hoped . . ."

"It's too early," Gawain murmured. The little ceremony was over now, and the cup was being passed among the knights at the high table. "Kay has his pride. He won't put Arthur in the position of having to notice him. Or risk being rejected by the king in front of everyone."

"I don't blame him for that," Gareth said.

"Nor do I." The cup had reached Gawain; he sipped from it and passed it to his brother. "And now I suppose we have to wait to start the meal until the king has heard of some marvel. Unless, under the circumstances, he'll waive that custom for once."

The king had no intention of waiving the custom. At the far end of the hall, just outside the main doors, Gawain could see the servers waiting with their covered dishes, but none of them entered. Gawain caught a glimpse of Kay, who said something rapidly to one of them and then disappeared again. He wore a plain, dark tunic, as he always did; he had not even robed for the feast.

The waiting stretched out. Impatient murmuring rose here and there in the hall. Gawain glanced along the table at Arthur; the king's face was still, unrevealing. His expression did not change even when there was a stir of movement from the entrance.

Knowing about Briant's peace offer, Gawain had expected some word from him, or even for Briant to appear himself, but the newcomer was a woman. She wore the grey habit of a holy order; beneath the white wimple her face was young and clear-eyed. On her upturned palms she bore a wooden casket. Holding it before her she paced down the length of the hall until she stood before the king.

"My lord king," she said. "Hear what I have come to tell you."

Her voice was distinct, though not loud, and it carried to every part of the hall. The low-voiced conversations broke off. At a gesture from the king the musicians ceased their playing.

"Holy sister," the king said, "you are welcome to Carlisle, and to my court. Say what you have come to say, and if I can serve you, I will."

The woman stood before the high table and held out the casket to the king. "It is I who have come to serve you, my lord," she said, "for I have come to tell you of a great wrong which as yet goes unpunished. In this casket is the head of a man, and none may open it except the knight who slew him. I beg you, my lord, will you not try to open it yourself, and then put your knights to the test, so that the truth of this deed can be made plain to everyone?"

Gawain exchanged a glance with Gareth. If the woman sought justice, if she had come to ask revenge for the death of her father or her brother, he would have preferred a straight-forward accusation to this test with the casket. For a holy votaress, as she appeared to be, she was meddling rather too closely with enchantment.

Arthur, however, had no such misgivings, or if he did, he concealed them well. He granted what the woman asked, and called a servant to take the casket and place it on a side table.

"Will you not eat with us, Sister?" he invited. "And when the meal is over we will all abide your test."

The woman sank to the floor in a deep reverence, and then took her seat at the table, Lancelot giving up his place to her so that she could sit beside the king. Lancelot himself came to take the empty place opposite Gareth, that would have been Kay's.

"Well, Lancelot," Gareth said lightly, "have you anyone's death on your conscience?"

Lancelot chose to take the question seriously, and answer it in the same way.

"Not on my conscience. For to kill in battle is no murder. It is some other kind of death that the holy sister speaks of."

"And will you try to open the casket?" Gareth asked.

"I will do as the king commands. But this is one test I will be glad to fail."

There was a buzz of conversation throughout the hall, with perhaps the same questions being asked and answered, but Gareth and Lancelot fell silent as the servants brought the first course to the table. And after that Gawain turned the talk in another direction.

He did not like the thought of this casket. Like Lancelot, he would obey the king and try to open it when the time came, but he had to repress a shiver when he thought of lifting the lid to reveal what was inside. He could not see the casket, where it had been placed at the other side of the hall, but he was aware of it. There was a sinister feeling about it. He wondered if the lady—young, beautiful, pious—was being used by something evil, and the casket was a trap that one of them was about to spring.

Glancing along the table, Gawain could see the lady in her place beside Arthur. She sat with eyes cast down, drinking only water, and crumbling a piece of bread upon her plate. When Arthur spoke to her, she replied briefly, her grave demeanour and austere dress incongruous in the midst of the light and glitter and music of the hall.

The noise was rising now, talk and laughter and the occasional burst of song. Gawain thought there was a hectic quality about the sound. It was not the uncomplicated relaxation that he had expected, on an evening which might have been a celebration of the danger that was past. More people besides himself, he realised, might be apprehensive because of the casket.

At last the meal dragged itself to its close. Arthur rose from his seat, and when there was silence he dismissed, with a gracious good night, the ladies and guests, the musicians, and the servants who were still in attendance, so that only his knights remained, with the doors closed on them. Arthur himself brought the casket and set it in front of him on the high table. Then he bowed to the lady and asked her to repeat her request.

She rose to her feet and looked around the assembled knights with that direct, clear gaze. Gawain had the fleeting impression that she was looking for someone in particular, but he dismissed it as fanciful.

"My lords," she said, "the head in this casket belongs to someone killed by one of Arthur's knights. Only the man who killed him will be able to open the casket, and when he does, Arthur himself has promised me that justice shall be done. Only, my lord—" she turned to the king and laid a hand gently on his arm "—I wish for no more bloodshed. Promise me now, before we proceed further, that you will pass a sentence of exile, not of death."

"If that is your will, Sister," the king responded.

At the words "exile" and "death" the murmurs of interest and speculation sank into a very deep silence. Some of the men present might not have appreciated that this test was serious, but now they began to understand how it could end, for one of their number.

In the silence, King Arthur bent over the casket and took hold of the lid. He tried to raise it, but it held, and he stepped back; Gawain wondered if he imagined that the king looked very faintly relieved.

Arthur glanced around. "Which of you will be next?" he asked.

Lancelot was the first to respond. He approached with a gravity that matched the lady's own, inclined his head to her respectfully, and set his hands to the lid. It resisted him, and he stepped back, bowed, and returned to his place.

Gawain himself followed, eager now to have it over with. As he bent over the casket, he tried to see if there was any lock or mechanism, or if it was truly enchantment that kept it closed. It was small—his two hands could span its width—and quite plain except for beading round the lid. A faint fragrance rose to meet him, like cedar or sandalwood. He fitted his fingers under the rim, and tried to raise the lid. It remained fast. Gawain also retreated to his seat, and hoped no one else could see that his hands shook.

Bedivere came next, brusque and matter-of-fact. Gareth, his natural cheerfulness quenched into wariness. Gaheris, as open and self-possessed as he always was. Agravaine, his face blotched through too much drinking, advancing jerkily and stumbling as he retreated. Ector, looking uneasy, and Bors, unreadable as ever. One by one the knights of the Round Table tried to open the casket. One by one, they all failed.

When the last of them had returned to his place at the table, the lady once more looked around the company.

"Are these all your knights, my lord?"

"Not all, Sister," the king said, "for some of them are away in their own lands, and some are in my service elsewhere. But—"

"But are there no others here?"

Gawain could sense that Gareth was going to speak, and reached out to grip his wrist. There was dismay in Gareth's eyes; Gawain knew it mirrored his own. Into the silence that followed the lady's question came a sharp sound, the opening of the great doors at the bottom of the hall. They swung open part way; in the entrance Kay stood.

The only sound was the regular beat of his footsteps as he walked down the hall and came to a stop before the king. His head was up, with that arrogant tilt that Gawain knew well. "You sent for me, my lord?"

Arthur's voice was mild. "No, Kay, I didn't."

"And why not, my lord, on a matter that concerns all your knights?"

Kay clearly knew what was going on. Of course, Gawain thought, the servants would have heard it all and relayed the gossip back to the kitchens. Gawain's fingers tightened round Gareth's wrist, and he flashed his brother a look with an unmistakable meaning. It would do Kay no good for Gareth to interfere now.

Kay stood locking glances with the king, his challenge laid down, waiting for Arthur to take it up. In his black tunic, the white shirt under it, his face scarcely less pale than the shirt, he made an odd contrast with the other knights, dressed for the feast in their embroidered silks and velvets.

Arthur made no reply to his question, simply gazed at him calmly, a leisurely scrutiny that beat down Kay's arrogance. His control snapped.

"Do you dishonour me, my lord," Kay began, stumbling a little over the words, "by shutting me out of this company when I have a right to be here? Or do you think I lack the courage to kill my enemy? Many of them have been your enemies too, my lord."

Arthur listened, still weighing him up calmly. Gawain thought that such superhuman self-control must have inflamed Kay more than any display of anger.

When the seneschal had finished speaking, the king said, "Kay, there's no need for any of this. If you wish to abide the test with the rest of us, do so. The casket is ready."

He motioned Kay towards the casket, which still stood on the table. Kay took a step towards it. He was silent now, and Gawain realised for the first time that he was deathly afraid. Releasing Gareth, Gawain slid from his own seat and drew near to the casket again, standing just behind Kay's shoulder.

Kay took another step forward, which brought the casket within his reach. As yet he had scarcely looked at it; his eyes had been fixed on the king. Now he glanced down at it, and quickly back at Arthur, as if he expected some kind of instruction from him, but Arthur said nothing. The king must have been able to see, as Gawain could see, that Kay's hands trembled.

With a swift movement, Kay took hold of the casket at each side and pressed upwards on the lid. It rose; he flung it back, and jerked away from it as if the touch were poison. From the casket rose a warm, spicy perfume; Gawain was aware of it before his mind told him what his eyes saw.

In the casket was Loholt's head.

Chapter Fourteen

There was no sign of death upon the head in the casket. The cheeks were faintly flushed; the eyes were open and glistened with the light of intelligence. The mouth was curved in a recollection of Loholt's familiar smile. The golden hair was brushed and shining, the stump of the neck concealed in a fold of silk. Gawain thought it was more horrible than the bloody, decaying relic he had expected.

"This is sorcery," he breathed out.

He did not think anyone heard him. The votaress stood beside the king, her eyes cast down, her hands folded in prayer on her breast. Arthur had stared at the head in one instant of shocked recognition, and then faced Kay, across the casket. For a brief moment they might have been alone in the hall.

Their silence was broken by some of the other knights, who crowded round the casket, exclaiming loudly as they saw Loholt's head. Arthur came to himself. With a gesture he motioned the knights back, and the sudden tumult died into a low murmuring.

Arthur said, "Kay, what have you to tell me?"

Kay's head went up. Now that the casket was opened, the head revealed, his fear was gone, leaving behind it a desperate defensiveness.

"Nothing, my lord."

"Nothing? When you returned to Carlisle, you told me that Loholt was dead. Dishonour enough, when he was in your care. But you did not tell me that you killed him. Is this story true?"

A cry came from among the knights: "No!" It was Gareth's voice, young and desperate; Arthur ignored it totally.

"Kay? Is it true?"

Until now, Kay's eyes had been locked with his king's, but now he bowed his head. Almost inaudibly, he said, "Yes. It is true."

"Kay—why?"

At the confession, Arthur's self-control almost gave way. He leant forward across the table, across the casket and the head, as if he were trying to compel Kay to speak the words he wanted to hear.

"Did he quarrel with you? He drew sword on you once, I know. He was young—thoughtless at times. Did you kill him to defend yourself?"

As the king spoke, Kay raised his eyes to him again. He must have known that Arthur was trying to save him, to create a story for Kay to tell that would not bring on his destruction. Gawain found himself praying fervently that it was so. It must have been so: Loholt's thoughtlessness, Kay's quick temper, and a sudden stroke that had consequences Kay never intended, but left him crushed under a weight of guilt.

Quietly, Kay said, "No. He wore no weapon, my lord, or none that I could see."

"Then why?" Arthur's face hardened, and he stepped back. "Did you decide to start playing politics? I know you never liked Loholt. You thought him unworthy to be my heir. Did you kill him so that Gawain should not be displaced?"

The accusation, revealing what Arthur's plans had been, brought another outburst from the knights who stood around. Kay's denial was swamped in it; even Arthur's command could not restore silence. When he could make himself heard, he turned to the lady, who still stood quietly at his side.

"Since Kay will not speak, Sister, what more can you tell us?"

The lady raised her eyes, and her level gaze reduced the knights to silence more effectively than the king's orders.

"My lord," she said, "when Kay and Loholt were escaping from Briant des Isles, Kay thought that Loholt would hold him back. He would have left him, but he was afraid that the boy's outcry would bring out the guards. And so he stabbed him, with this."

From the folds of her habit she brought out a dagger, and held it out to the king on her open palm. Gawain was close enough to see it clearly, and he recognised it: a broad-bladed anlace, the hilt bound with silver wire. He could not have said how often he had seen Kay use it.

Arthur took the dagger and faced Kay once again. His look was bleak now, remote and unforgiving.

"A coward's murder, Kay," the king said. "A traitor's murder. Are you going to deny it?"

Kay had achieved something of the same icy distance. Gawain wondered how many of the men in the hall knew what it must be costing him. He wondered if Arthur knew.

"No, my lord. I have nothing more to say."

"Then all I can do is pass sentence on you."

"Wait!"

Gawain could not go on watching any longer. He stepped forward to Kay's side and put a hand on his shoulder. He could feel Kay rigid, unresponsive to his touch.

"My lord," Gawain said, "this is no trial. There must be more than this."

The look Arthur turned on him was quite impersonal, more daunting than fury. "More, Gawain? What more do you want?"

"Why not ask this holy sister how she learnt the story she tells? Was she there to see? And how did she come by the head, and this miraculous casket?"

Gawain felt his voice begin to shake, in anger or compassion for Kay's pain, but he managed to finish what he wanted to say. Behind him he heard Gareth urgently seconding his questions. He was suddenly terrified of how the lady would react to a counter accusation, but she paid him no attention at all. Her look, meekly patient, was for Arthur.

"I sought only to help you, my lord, and to see justice done. I ask nothing for myself."

"This is a holy woman, Gawain," the king said, "a votaress, a renunciate. What profit could she have in lying? Besides—" he held out the dagger once again "—there is this. And Kay does not deny the charges."

Gawain turned Kay to face him, grasping his shoulders. "Kay! There must be some treachery here, or some mistake. Why won't you defend yourself?"

Kay's eyes were dark and despairing. His voice was dry. "I cannot."

Gawain let his hands fall from Kay's shoulders. He shared Kay's despair. Arthur trusted this woman, even though she had made no attempt to answer his questions. Kay would not even try to help himself. Gawain could not think of any more that he could do. Standing beside Kay, he braced himself to hear what Arthur's sentence would be.

But when the king spoke, it was to say, "The night grows late. And this affair is too weighty to decide in a few moments. We will all—" his glance took in the assembled knights "—meet here again in the morning, after chapel." He turned to Gawain and Kay, and his formal tones became more personal, more urgent. "Gawain, if you can persuade Kay to say anything that will change what we have heard tonight, I will gladly listen to him. Kay, think well. You have until the morning."

Arthur motioned to the lady to precede him out of the hall through the door at the back of the dais. Before he followed her, he turned slowly back to the casket, and Gawain saw his face convulse with pain. He lowered the lid, and bore the casket out with him.

As the door closed behind Arthur, the other knights surged around Kay and Gawain, loudly questioning. Gareth pushed his way to their side. Together they managed to guide Kay out of the hall, ignoring all the accusations or demands for explanation hurled at Kay.

Once away from the hall, with the clamour dying away behind them, Kay stopped, swaying, a hand to his head. He was shaking convulsively. Gawain remembered that the seneschal

Exiled From Camelot

was still not fully recovered from his hurts, and the work of preparing for the Court must have exhausted him. Gareth put an arm around him, and for once Kay leant on him, accepting his strength, too dazed even to protest.

To come to the hall, to abide the test of the casket, and then to endure the agony of facing Arthur's cold revulsion, had taken all the strength Kay had. Gawain almost asked him why he had not stayed in the kitchens, for he was certain that Kay had known very well what he was going to find in the casket. But before he formed the question, he knew the answer. Kay would not hide away and wait for them to come looking for him, or live in the expectancy of another trap if this first one had failed.

In Kay's apartments, Gawain dismissed his servant; there would be enough gossip the next day without deliberately adding to it. He put logs on the dying fire, while Gareth settled Kay in the chair beside it and brought the furred bedcover from the next room to wrap around him.

Kay tried to thrust him away. "Don't, Gareth," he begged. "You will break me, utterly. I must be ready for the morning."

Gareth sat on a stool at Kay's feet, and gathered the thin hands into his own. Gawain drew up another chair, and set it where he could talk to Kay.

"Now you can tell us what really happened," he said.

Kay did not look at him. "You know what happened," he said. "I killed Loholt."

Gawain did not want to believe it, but he found belief being forced on him. Something had weighed on Kay's mind when he returned to Carlisle, something that had invaded his sleep, something that he had wanted to tell and could not. But if Gawain had to accept that Kay's hand had thrust the dagger home, everything that was in him refused to accept the reason the lady had given. It was not in Kay to murder a boy who needed his help, to silence him so that he could save himself. Gawain rejected that without a second thought.

"Kay, I must know one thing," he said. "Was it for me? Was it so that Loholt could not inherit?"

Kay gave a start of genuine astonishment; anguish flared in his eyes. "Do you truly believe that of me?"

Gawain shook his head. "No. But—that would be more noble, at its root, than this other thing they accuse you of."

Kay murmured agreement. Disengaging his hands from Gareth, he shrank back in the chair, pulling the furs around himself. He reminded Gawain, incongruously, of a snail retreating into its shell.

"Kay!" Gareth said. "You must tell us the truth. It can't be as they said, it can't!"

His young face was filled with distress, tears in his eyes. Kay looked down at him. Gawain thought that something, briefly, warmed the frozen countenance.

"Gareth, I killed Loholt. Arthur's son. Do you think that anything I say now is going to save me?"

Eagerly, Gareth seized on his words. "Then there is something? Something you're not telling us?"

Kay remained unresponsive, not admitting it or denying it.

"You must tell us what it is," Gareth persisted.

"I . . . cannot." The words were forced out painfully.

Gawain laid a hand on his arm. "Kay, tomorrow Arthur will send you into exile."

Kay tried to speak, failed, and tried again. "I know."

"Then tell us!" Gareth begged.

Kay reached out and gently, almost timidly, touched Gareth's hair, for a second only, before he drew back. Gawain's heart went cold; it was a gesture of renunciation.

"I cannot," Kay repeated.

For all their efforts, he refused to say any more. He would not go to bed, but remained in the chair, huddled in his furs. He was trying to stay awake, but exhaustion was dragging him down into unconsciousness. For a while he would drowse uneasily, only to start up with a shaken cry.

Kay's friends watched out the night with him, Gareth curled up on the stool at his feet, Gawain in the chair beside him. Neither of them slept, or talked. To Gawain, dawn seemed late in coming; he was afraid that for Kay there would be no true morning, only the long darkness of his estrangement from the king.

By Arthur's orders, the knights were armed when they assembled that morning. The hall was filled with the shifting sheen of steel mail and the bright flutter of surcoats. The clamour, the questioning of the night before, had sunk to a subdued murmur of conversation as the knights waited for the king. As Gawain took his place, he saw nothing but sombre or apprehensive faces. Kay was not popular, but he had belonged with them; no one was looking forward to his humiliation.

Gareth slid into the place beside Gawain, and clutched at his arm urgently.

"Gawain, I still have Kay's sword! I forgot about it until now, and he'll need it. Have I time to—"

Gawain shook his head. The king's private door was already opening, and the king paced forward to the front of the dais. He was alone; the lady was not with him, and he had not brought the casket.

"Too late," Gawain said in an undertone. "Besides, it's better not." When Gareth clearly did not understand, he added, "The king will break it."

Exiled From Camelot

Gawain could hardly bear to see Gareth's look of horrified comprehension. There was no time to say any more. Already a stir at the far end of the hall announced the arrival of Kay.

He was armed, clothed in black and silver, and he wore a sword belt, but the sheath was empty. He walked quietly down the length of the hall, between the watching ranks of knights, until he stood before the dais. Arthur beckoned him to come up the two shallow steps to his side. Kay knelt in front of him.

"Kay," the king said, "you stand accused of the murder of my son, Loholt. Have you anything to say?"

For a few seconds, Gawain thought that Kay was not going to answer. He was close enough to the dais to see his friend's face. His eyes were unfocused; Gawain thought he might be going to faint. Then he saw Kay's hands clench, and his head went up in that old arrogant gesture.

"I killed him, my lord."

This time there was no response from the knights, nothing to break the hush that had fallen over the hall.

"It is said you stabbed him," Arthur went on, "so that you could escape from Briant's guards. Is this true?"

This time Kay remained deliberately silent. Beside him, Gawain heard Gareth's agonised drawing in of breath.

"Kay," Arthur said, and now his formal tones were touched with a passion he could not conceal, "are you content to be branded a coward and a traitor? Have you nothing to say for yourself?"

Kay was still mute, only his eyes speaking of love, and pain, and despair.

Arthur cried out, "Kay, you know what I must do!"

Hearing him, Gawain's heart was torn for Arthur, who did not want to hurt his oldest friend. The cry almost broke Kay, too; his hand went to his throat, but he remained obstinately silent.

Arthur stood over him for a moment longer, gazing down at the white, set face, and then took a pace back.

To the knights, he said, "I call you all to witness that Sir Kay admits this crime, and offers no defence." And to Kay, his voice hard now, "Get up."

Kay rose to his feet.

"By my promise to the holy sister who brought me word of your guilt," Arthur said, "I may not pass sentence of death upon you, but even if my word did not bind me, I would be merciful, for in the past you have served me well. But I cannot forgive such a foul crime against my son, who would have been my heir and Britain's next king. Punishment there must be."

He raised his voice a little to be quite certain that every knight in the hall could hear him.

"First, I take from you your office of high seneschal, for you have shown yourself utterly unfit to bear it." At the last words, Gawain saw Kay flinch slightly, and then hold himself steady again. "Next, give me your sword."

Kay's hand went to the empty scabbard. Momentarily he seemed confused. "I—I have none, my lord. I lost it in the hills."

"That is well," Arthur said evenly, "for the sword is a knight's weapon, and here I declare that you are no longer knight. Nor have you the right any longer to bear arms."

He unfastened Kay's sword belt and cast it aside. Setting both hands at the neck of Kay's surcoat, with a single movement he ripped it to the hem. Kay never moved, letting the ruined folds slip to the floor around his feet.

"You will go from my court within the hour," Arthur said. "And from my lands within the next three days. I will not raise hand against you myself, but if anyone finds you in my kingdom after the three days are over, he may kill you and have no blame from me. Now go!"

For a moment Kay still stood before him, his eyes devouring the face that was now flint hard against him. Gawain heard someone close to him mutter, "Death would have been more merciful." Then, before Arthur needed to repeat his command, Kay bowed his head, very carefully descended the steps of the dais, and paced slowly down the length of the hall towards the doors, between the ranks of eyes.

Gawain slipped rapidly from his place and walked beside him; a second later Gareth joined them on the other side. Kay never looked at either of them, but he breathed out an agonised, "No!"

Kay remained rigidly self-controlled until they were out of the hall and the doors closed behind them. Then he staggered, and Gareth locked an arm around him, and guided him to a stone seat in a window alcove.

"I'll go with you," Gareth said.

Kay looked up at him, bewildered. "What? No—Gareth, you can't. Think of Lionors, and the child."

Gareth's face twisted in anguish.

Quietly, Gawain said, "Then I'll go. There's nothing tying me to Camelot."

"No!" Kay's voice was shaking. "You're his heir now. He needs you. I can't take that from him, too."

Gawain understood. "Very well," he said. "I'll stay, providing you promise me one thing—no, two things."

"What are they?"

"The first is, that you won't try to harm yourself." From the flicker in Kay's eyes he realised that he had been right to ask that. "The second is that you'll write and let us know where you are." He bent and grasped Kay's shoulders. "Kay, this isn't the end. I know there's something you aren't telling us. Sooner or later we'll find out what it is, and then the king will recall you."

Kay almost smiled as Gawain said the last words, and shook his head regretfully. The words dragged out of a great depth of weariness as he said, "Very well. I promise."

The doors of the hall opened again, and the knights began to disperse. Kay stiffened, and shrank back in the alcove, but none of them looked at him or came towards him, except for Lancelot. He stood in front of Kay and bowed his head.

"I am very sorry," he said. Kay swallowed and tried to respond, but before he could speak, Lancelot went on, "If you wish, you could go to my father's lands in Benwick. I will write a letter for you to take to him."

Gawain thought that Kay would break down then, but he clung to self-control.

"Your father is Arthur's friend," he said. "I would not be the cause of breaking that friendship. But I thank you, Sir Lancelot, for your courtesy."

It was a dismissal; Lancelot nodded and moved on.

"Where will you go?" Gareth asked.

Kay rubbed a hand across his eyes. "I don't know."

"France, perhaps," Gawain suggested. "Or to King Claudas, in Brittany."

"Claudas is Arthur's enemy!" Gareth protested.

"No friend, certainly," Gawain said. "But at present there is no war declared between them. You could—"

He broke off as Kay's servant came up almost at a run. He had brought with him a plain white surcoat, a belt, a cloak, and a pair of saddlebags.

"I've packed spare clothes, and food, my lord," he said. "Enough for—"

"I have no horse," Kay said. "Morial was lost."

"Go to the stables," Gawain instructed the servant. "Tell them to saddle a good horse, and have it ready in the courtyard. On my authority."

The man nodded and hurried off. Gareth slipped the folds of the surcoat over Kay's head and fastened the belt for him.

"You need a sword," he said. "I still have yours. I'll go and fetch it. Gawain, don't let him go until I come back."

"No." The tired, shaken voice stopped him. "Gareth, I've no right to bear it."

"You can't go without a weapon." Gareth would have gone, but Kay reached out and caught him by the wrist.

"That sword was given to me by my father, the day I was made knight. I would dishonour it to bear it now. Will you—will you keep it, and use it, if you feel it is not tainted?"

Gareth looked down at him, tears spilling from his eyes.

"Yes," he managed to say. "I'll keep it for you, until you come again. Provided that you will take mine now."

He drew his sword and knelt, offering the hilt to Kay.

"Oh, don't!" Kay whispered. "Gawain, make him stop."

"Get up, you young idiot," Gawain said. He felt close to tears himself. "But he's right, Kay, you need a sword. Take it, and think of Gareth when you use it."

Kay looked from one to the other; he could see they would not let him refuse. Rising, he took the sword from Gareth and fitted it into the sheath.

Gawain flung the cloak over his shoulders. "You must go," he said.

Kay nodded. Gawain led the way along the passage and through the porch into the main courtyard. A groom was leading a horse round from the stables: a solid bay, not the kind of fiery thoroughbred Kay chose for himself, but a reliable animal. Gawain thanked the groom and asked him to wait.

"Remember, Kay, you're pledged to send us word."

Kay came close to him, and laid his hands on Gawain's shoulders. "My lord Gawain, if I dared ask, of your courtesy . . ." The words were blurred, stumbling.

"Yes?" Gawain said. "I'll do anything I can, Kay, you know that."

"Will you write to my father? I would not have him hear—" His voice broke. "Oh, God, this will kill my father!"

Gawain reached up to embrace him, and Kay tried to thrust him away. As he did so, he saw the carnelian ring that he still wore on his right hand.

"Arthur's ring!" Kay said. Anguish was tearing away his stunned calm. "I can't wear it now, I can't! Gawain, will you take it? It would dishonour you to wear it, but perhaps you would keep it, and remember . . ." He could not go on.

Gawain drew him close. "I'll wear it. But I won't need it, or anything else, to remember."

He released Kay, who pressed his hand, with the ring, to his cheek; when he took it away the imprint of the stone remained on his face. He took the ring off, then, and gave it to Gawain.

"I'll do the same as Gareth," Gawain promised, slipping the ring on, "and keep it until you come back."

He embraced Kay again, and then Gareth came, openly weeping, and held Kay until he wrenched himself away. The gates were already open. Gawain brought up the horse; Kay mounted and urged it forward, and it trotted briskly beneath the archway. Kay did not look back as the gates closed behind him.

CHAPTER FIFTEEN

If Kay had been mounted on Morial, he might have fled from Carlisle at a wild gallop. But he found it took an effort to urge this stolid animal even to a canter, and he did not have the energy to go on making the effort. The horse slowed to a trot, and then to a walk.

The walls of Carlisle were left behind him. Kay rode through a land of green-grey hills, their summits huge and indistinct in a cloak of cloud. Their slopes were clothed in forest and alive with the sound of hidden streams.

For many hours Kay rode without thinking of where he was going. His hands were slack on the reins, and his horse, undirected, followed the road south. Kay's mind held the dull realisation that he must be out of Arthur's kingdom within three days, but he did not know where to go or how to get there. He had stopped making plans.

At last the daylight began to die. Kay did not think about making camp for the night, but he dismounted and led his horse to the side of the road, where he unsaddled it and turned it off to graze. He had not eaten all day, and he felt cold and sick.

There was food in his pack, and a skin of wine. Kay forced himself to swallow a few mouthfuls, but the bread stuck like a hard lump in his chest and threatened to choke him. He drank a little; as he was fastening the stopper of the flask he could make out, on his right hand, the pale band of skin around the finger where he had always worn the ring. He let the flask fall, covered his face, and wept. Darkness gathered around him, thick, unrelieved by moonlight. At last, sleep released him.

He woke the next morning to find himself huddled by the side of the road, his clothes soaked with dew, the possessions from his pack scattered around him. A few yards away his horse placidly cropped grass. Painfully Kay got up and collected his belongings. When he came to saddle the horse his hands were stiff and clumsy.

By the time he was in the saddle and on his way again, Kay had recovered enough to think about what he must do next. He needed to find a harbour and take the first ship out, no matter where it was going. Any more decisions could be deferred until then. The nearest harbour now would be the one guarded by Roche Dure, and Kay did not dare go so close to Briant's stronghold. Farther south, then. It would take more than the two days that were left to him, but Kay doubted that anyone from Arthur's court would take the opportunity to hunt him down and kill him. If they did, he did not greatly care. Still, he urged his horse on at a more determined pace.

That evening, he chose a sheltered spot for his camp, at the foot of a bank where bushes clung to the crumbling soil. Beside it a stream spurted out into a tiny waterfall. Kay would have preferred just to curl up there and hope that sleep would take him, but before the light faded he made himself collect dry wood for a fire, and eat the first real meal of his exile. He finished the wine and refilled the flask at the waterfall before he settled down for the night.

He woke in the dawn light with the sound of the fall in his ears. He focussed his eyes on the tuft of grass beside his face and saw the edges grey with frost. Beyond it were the dead ashes of his fire, and beyond that again, a pair of booted feet and the hem of a cloak. Something caught the light and dazzled Kay's eyes.

Kay blinked, and forced himself up onto one elbow. Looking down at him was a young man, with silver-gold hair and a wild face Kay thought he should remember. His sword was drawn, light glancing off the blade. Kay grabbed for his own weapon.

"I shouldn't," the young man said.

The stranger stepped forward and brought his foot down on Kay's wrist. There was a stir of movement and other armed men appeared from the trees.

"Now," the man said, "you're going to get up, and saddle your horse, and then come with us. My lord Briant has a great desire for your company."

When the horse was ready they bound Kay's hands behind his back and thrust him up into the saddle. The young leader took the reins and led Kay's horse beside his own.

"This won't do Briant any good," Kay said. "I'm not going to tell him anything."

His adversary grinned; Kay realised that even in saying so little, he had made an admission he should not have made. He decided on silence.

The young man led his party at a swift trot. Kay suspected that he hoped his prisoner would fall, but even with his hands bound, Kay had the skill to stay mounted. By midday they came to a river—the same river where Arthur and his men had been attacked, but several miles downstream—and a bridge. Across the bridge the road forked; one branch continued to the south; the other turned and ran beside the river, going westward. An hour later, it left the waterside and began to wind upwards. Kay could see on the hill ahead the dark bulk of Roche Dure.

As his party approached the entrance, the young man called out and the gates were pulled open. Their horses trotted under the archway and came to a stop in the main courtyard. Here the leader dismounted and dragged Kay from his horse. Tossing an order over his shoulder to his men, he thrust Kay in front of him through a side door and to the head of a spiral stairway that led down into darkness.

Kay stumbled against walls of uneven stone, fighting for balance. His feet slipped on the worn stairs. With his hands tied he could not steady himself, and his captor urged him on too quickly. At last he missed a step and fell sprawling on to damp flagstones at the foot of the stairs, the breath driven out of him. Half stunned, he was struggling to his knees when he felt a knife slash away the cords that bound his wrists. Someone hauled him to his feet—someone who was not his captor, for the young man stood in front of him and held a dagger, its point glittering red in torchlight, close to Kay's eyes.

"You can wait here for a while," he said, "until it pleases my lord Briant to see you."

The unseen man who held Kay thrust him forward through another door. Kay caught a glimpse of a cell, bare stone with a stone seat across the far wall, before the door slammed shut, cutting off the light. A bar thudded into metal hasps. Across the echoes of the door's closing, Kay heard the sound of laughter.

He groped his way forward and sat on the seat. Gradually he realised that the darkness was not unbroken. As his eyes became accustomed to it, he could make out the walls of the cell again. They were rough-hewn blocks of stone, damp and glistening faintly red in the torchlight that crept through a narrow slit above the lintel. The door itself was thick oak, bound in iron. There was no window.

Kay knew there would be no escape from here; he wondered how long Briant would keep him prisoner before he brought him out for questioning. He sat rubbing his wrists; the tight cords had opened up the wounds again and they bled sluggishly. He thought of what Briant would do to him, and how much he would have to tell to make him stop. It might be better to die first. Gawain would understand if he broke his word now. But they had taken his sword—Gareth's sword—and Kay had no other means to end his own life.

As Kay sat staring at the floor beneath his feet he felt weariness creeping over him. He was tempted to lie on the seat and sleep. But he did not want Briant to come and find him sleeping. Whatever he had to face, he did not want it to slink up on him in the dark.

But he was very tired. His head nodded, and he jerked awake again, startled, as if he had heard a noise from outside the cell. But there was nothing. Only the unchanging red light, and the damp cold that stiffened and cramped his limbs.

He wondered how long Briant would wait before he sent for him, and with that thought came another. Perhaps Briant would not send for him, perhaps it was enough for him to have Kay in his prison. Kay had to choke back a whimper of fear, and grip the edge of the seat to stop himself from beating against the door and begging to be let out. More than anything Briant could do to him, Kay feared the thought that he would do nothing, just leave him here until life or sanity left him.

The wave of fear ebbed. Kay slumped back against the wall. Sleep dragged at him again and he knew that in the end he would have to give in to it. Already he had lost track of how long he had been in the cell.

His head drooped forward again, his eyes closing. Somehow he felt himself falling, and flung out his hands to save himself, only to cry out in alarm as the flagstones under him dissolved away and he found himself struggling in icy black water. Shocked fully awake, he gazed around and saw nothing but the glittering edge of a wave.

He knew this was impossible. Unknowing, he had fallen asleep and this was no more than a dream. If that was all, there was nothing to be afraid of.

But the leaden exhaustion weighing down his limbs was only too real. Kay seemed to remember swimming for hours in this dark ocean, with no sign of shore. Waves were slapping him in the face, washing over his head and threatening to swamp him. One arm became enmeshed in the clinging folds of his cloak. He gulped in water, and sank.

Below the surface, he tried to let himself drift. Surely if he drowned, the dream would have to break. But fear, and the instinct to survive, and the overmastering need to breathe, were too strong for him. Kay fought his way upwards. His head broke surface; he coughed water, thrashed desperately to stay afloat and find something he could hold on to for help.

Arthur came then, walking over the water, enveloped in a warm, golden light. Kay gathered his remaining scraps of strength and struck out feebly towards him. He wanted to cry out, but the sea choked him. He reached out and tried to catch hold of Arthur's mantle, but the golden light seared his hand. He could not touch the robe. He gazed up into Arthur's face; it was hard and unforgiving. No hand stretched out to save him as the black waves closed over his head.

Once again, Kay found himself in the cell, lying face down on the floor. His breath came in deep, sobbing gasps. He was exhausted, every muscle aching as if he had really been fighting for his life in dark water.

As his vision cleared, he realised he was not alone any more. He saw before him feet, in leather ankle boots, and the furred hem of a velvet robe. "Briant?" Kay wondered vaguely. He raised himself on one elbow and looked up, past a jewelled belt, to hands folded on the breast. Long, clawed hands.

Kay's eyes flew upwards. The lips were parted, and from them came that laughter like the melody of a bone flute. The eyes gleamed with the cold, exultant evil of the Lady. The face was Arthur's. Kay screamed, and fell back into night.

Warmth, and the faint scent of sweet herbs. Kay stirred; one groping hand encountered linen, soft fur. He opened his eyes.

He thought at first that he looked down a long forest ride. Trees arched over it, bearing golden fruit. Beneath them, on its knees, was a white stag with an arrow in its breast. Hounds were pulling it down.

Kay reached out a hand in protest, and his fingers met ridged wool. He recognised that he was looking at a tapestry, a hanging on the wall of the room where he lay in bed. He turned his head and pain shot through it, blurring his vision. The lamp by the bed seemed to fill the room with a golden haze. Kay gave up trying to penetrate it, and slept again.

When he woke for the second time his head had cleared. He could see that the room where he lay was small but comfortable, the kind of room where they would lodge guests at Carlisle or Camelot. The lamp was quenched now, but a fire leapt in the hearth. The scene on the tapestry looked flat and lifeless; Kay could barely remember being deceived by it when he woke in the night.

Across the room a servant opened the shutters, letting in a cold, pale light. As he turned, he was outlined against it; Kay could not see his face, but his manner was deferential.

"There's hot water, sir, and fresh clothes for you. You're to get dressed, if you please, and then come and speak to my lord." He turned to go.

"Wait!" Kay said. "Who—"

It was no use. The man had gone, closing the door softly behind him. At first, Kay did not move. As his mind shook off the last clinging shreds of sleep, he began to remember. The cell. The dark ocean. And the last, unspeakable vision. Kay felt his heart begin to race, and his gaze flickered from side to side as if he wanted to make sure that the thing was not in the room with him now.

The room. He had no memory of coming here. He found it hard to believe that he was still in Roche Dure, and with that thought came a sudden, breathless hope. Was it conceivable that he had been rescued without knowing it and taken to—no, not to Camelot, that was impossible—to Carlisle? How much time had passed while he lay unconscious?

Kay knew that if he was to gain any answers to his questions he must obey the servant's carefully worded command. He got out of bed; he felt shaky, the floor not quite steady under his feet, as if he had been ill for a long time. He saw that his wrists had been bandaged again. As he washed, shaved, and dressed himself, the questions still beat at his brain. He could not believe that Briant des Isles would treat an enemy like this. But Arthur—perhaps Arthur had not quite cast him off, perhaps he would be a little merciful.

The clothes were of good quality: a fine linen undershirt, a tunic of dark blue wool with a woven pattern on the hem and on the edges of the sleeves, and a silver pin to fasten it. There were soft kidskin slippers and a belt of embossed leather with a silver clasp. Clothes for a guest, not a prisoner.

When he was ready, the servant had still not returned. Kay went to the window and looked out. His room was in a tower. Below him he could see an untidy huddle of rooftops and a section of crenellated battlement. Beyond it was only sky. Kay did not recognise the view. It could have been Carlisle; he was not sure.

Moving softly, as if afraid of being overheard, he made for the door, wondering whether he would find it unlocked. Before he reached it, it opened; the servant stood there. Kay got a good look at his face for the first time. It was flat and inexpressive, under a thatch of brown hair. Kay had never seen him before, but he did not know all the Carlisle servants.

"Well?" he said abruptly. "Where must I go now?"

The servant bowed. "If you will follow me, sir. . . ."

Kay followed him, out into a passage and down a flight of stairs. At their foot, the servant pushed open a door and motioned him inside. Kay went in and heard the door close behind him.

The room was a long hall. Along one side were windows, their shutters folded back to let in a flood of light. On the opposite wall were sconces that still held burnt-out torches from the night before. Banners hung from the ceiling, stirring in the moving air. Kay felt cold. He knew now that he was not in Carlisle.

At the far end of the hall was a hearth where a fire blazed up. Three or four wooden chairs were drawn close to it. Kay could see no one, but he gathered his courage and walked firmly down the length of the hall towards the fire.

As he approached, a man got up from one of the chairs; its high back had concealed him from Kay until he moved. He was a tall man, broad-shouldered, with curling golden hair and beard. He wore a bright emerald robe, splashed with embroidery and trimmed with fur. His hands were hooked in his belt: broad hands, with glistening golden hairs springing out of the backs, and rings pushed on to thick fingers. His eyes watched Kay with a bright interest.

"Welcome to Roche Dure," said Briant des Isles.

Chapter Sixteen

Kay halted. Briant, smiling, held out a hand.
"Come to the fire, Kay. It's a cold morning. Wine?"

Once again Kay advanced, warily. By the time he reached the fire, Briant had a cup of wine ready, and thrust it into his hand.

"Don't look at me like that," Briant said with rough good humour. "I'm not going to bite you. See, my lady bids you welcome, too."

Seated in one of the other chairs, and visible to Kay only now that he moved into the space before the fire, was a woman. She was slender; black hair flowed over her shoulders like dark rain. Though she was more than a girl, Kay would have been hard put to tell her age. Her skin was pale and translucent, her mouth red. She was very beautiful, and yet Kay felt an unexplained prickle of revulsion.

She did not rise from the chair, but she inclined her head. "Greetings, Kay." Her eyes laughed at him. "We have waited for a long time to see you in Roche Dure."

"Then you might have couched your invitation in more courteous terms," Kay said tartly.

This time her laughter was real. "A lesson in courtesy from Kay! We have been remiss indeed. But now you are here, perhaps we can make amends."

"Sit down," Briant said. "Sit down, and we'll talk."

He urged Kay towards a chair, clumsily, so that Kay barely saved his wine from spilling. Briant poured another cup for his lady and one for himself; he did not sit, but paced back and forth in front of the fire, gesturing with the cup as he talked. Kay had the impression of a crude strength, chafing at inaction and ready to break out.

"Arthur defeated us at Carlisle," Briant said. "If I'd been there myself, things might not have gone his way. Who can tell? But the men I sent to deal with Arthur failed me, and I was called away, and in the end you slipped out of my nets. Arthur had more good fortune there than any man has the right to. But now—" he gave a short bark of laughter "—now you won't be quite so eager to leave me, eh?"

He waited for a response, but Kay had nothing to say. Shrugging, Briant went on.

"I made Arthur an honest offer—to be lord of Roche Dure and care for the lands around it. He refused, because he thought I'd murdered that son of his. If he'd only known I cared for Loholt as much as he. I'd have put him on the throne of Britain."

Kay could not repress a small sound of disbelief. Briant regarded him with good-humoured contempt.

"A man of your experience shouldn't value the name of king more than—" he snapped his fingers "—that. But where the power lies—now that's a different matter."

"Oh, now I see," Kay said. "Loholt as a puppet king, with you as seneschal. . . . Yes, my lord Briant, that makes very good sense. A plan worthy of you."

Briefly Briant's eyes narrowed, as if he detected the covert insult, but then he shrugged it off and clapped Kay on the shoulder.

"Good! Now you understand—except that with Loholt dead, the plan comes to nothing. We need another."

He stood looking down at Kay as if he expected him to ask the obvious question, but Kay kept silence, sipping his wine and pretending to a detachment he did not feel. Across the hearth, the lady watched him over the rim of her cup, a sharp amusement in her eyes.

"You make it hard work for me," Briant complained. "Listen. If I made a push, I could dislodge Arthur from his throne. I could make myself king. And now, in this crisis, when everything hangs on the next few days—now, Kay, you come to me."

Evenly, Kay said, "I will tell you nothing that will help you gain one foot of ground from Arthur, or kill a single one of his followers."

He expected that Briant would let show the ugly reverse of his good mood, but Briant made only an irritable gesture, as if he brushed flies away in summer.

"Trivialities, Kay. You're no warrior, so I'll not talk warrior's business with you. I'm not a fool, and I have spies who can tell me all I need to know. That isn't why I want you."

Kay felt a sudden dismay. He had been ready for that threat, ready at least to spend all his strength in trying to counter it, and to have his defiance dismissed as unimportant left him at a loss. He could see that the lady could read his thoughts, and was enjoying his discomfiture.

"Why, then?" he asked.

Briant went to pour more wine for himself, and stood looking down into the cup, twirling the stem thoughtfully.

"I've a man in my service," he said, "who can build me a mangonel so accurate that it will hurl a rock within a handbreadth of any target I name. I know where to strike, but could I put together the beams and crosspieces and the ropes so that all runs smoothly and the rock flies through the air and strikes— there?"

Briant brought down his hand on the table, making the wine jug shake. Kay watched uncomprehendingly.

"I have no expertise in siege engines, my lord," Kay said, "if you are looking to replace this man of yours. Clearly his skill failed him at Carlisle."

As he planted the barb he caught a flicker of the danger under Briant's affability.

"I tell you this, Kay, so you can understand me. As my servant builds his siege engine, so you have built Britain, so that all the parts move together smoothly and the whole land is ready to answer to Arthur's command. That's what I want of you, Kay, when I am king."

Kay stared at him, genuinely taken aback. For the first time he asked himself if Loholt had lied to him, if his threats of torture and questioning from Briant when Kay was his prisoner had been no more than a cruel game.

"I could make you seneschal again," Briant offered.

His lady's face was vivid with expectancy.

"No," Kay said.

Briant came to stand over him. His handsome, florid face was harder now, but he was not hostile, or not only that.

"You're finished with Arthur," he said. "Or Arthur's finished with you. He'll never forgive you for what you did to Loholt. And he'll never forgive himself. He'll never be able to look at you again without remembering that he made a mistake when he set you in command to take care of the boy. He's taken everything from you, but I could give it back. I can make you knight again, here, now, before we leave this hall. You shall be seneschal again when I am king. I will give you back your sword."

Briant made a gesture and Kay turned his head to see his sword belt, with the sword Gareth had given him in Carlisle, lying on a chest against the wall nearby. He had begun to wonder, as Briant spoke, how he knew so accurately that Arthur had stripped him of his honours before he sent him into exile, but the sight of the sword drove all such questions out. Kay wanted it too much. The need rose in his throat and he raised a hand so they should not see his mouth quivering. Inwardly he raged at himself. He would not let Briant and his lady see him weep.

"No," he said.

He felt Briant's hand rest on his shoulder. There was warmth in the gesture, harder to bear than pain.

"It's over," Briant said. "You and Arthur. He won't receive you again, nor will any of his friends. What else is there?"

Kay looked at the sword. It was very familiar to him. Firelight glinted off the big, rough-cut topaz in the pommel. Once, in Gareth's hands, it had saved his life.

"No."

"Kay, if you cross me, I—"

Briant broke off as the doors at the end of the hall were flung open, his threat left hanging in the air. A servant stood there.

"My lord Briant," he said, hurrying forward. "An envoy from King Claudas has arrived and is waiting to see you."

Briant's face clouded. He bit off an exclamation, perhaps a rebuke, and Kay, managing to tear his eyes away from the sword, saw that he had been given a respite. All Briant's thought now was for this envoy; he was not pleased at his coming, or perhaps he was not pleased that Kay had heard the envoy announced.

He frowned, hesitating. "Tell him—"

His lady interrupted by rising from her seat, a fluid movement that set firelight glancing on her silks. She laid a hand on Briant's arm and smiled sweetly at the servant.

"Take him to the council chamber," she ordered, "and say that my lord Briant will come to him at once. My lord," she went on, as the servant retreated, "go and deal with this tedious piece of business, and let me talk awhile with Kay. Perhaps I can make him understand your point of view."

Briant's frown had been smoothed away as soon as she started to speak. He covered her hand with his own, and smiled down at her, a hint of foolishness on the handsome features that had been shrewd enough until now.

"I will, lady," he said, "for if anyone can bind Kay to us, it is you."

He bent over her hand and kissed it, and then left the hall. Kay had already risen tensely to his feet. He was afraid of Briant with the straightforward fear of facing a man who could, if he chose, inflict on him any pain, any humiliation. But he recognised that Briant had—according to his lights—offered him the chance of friendship, that Briant himself could see no good reason for him to refuse. Kay's fear of Briant's lady, threading through his every sinew, was a thousand times harder to conceal.

From her look of cool amusement, Kay realised he had not concealed it very well. She stood in front of him, her hands extended a little way towards him, the palms upwards.

"Shall we have friendship, Kay?"

Nothing would have made Kay touch her. He took a step backwards.

"You fear me?" she said. "You do well. Yet so far you scarcely know me. My lord Briant did not even tell you my name. It is Brisane."

For a moment she waited, as if she expected the name to draw some response from him, but Kay could not recall ever hearing it before. His bewilderment seemed to displease her; the red lips thinned.

"You know what I can do to you if you refuse," she said.

As Kay gazed at her a darkness swept over his eyes. He saw the crest of a heaving wave, and tasted the salt sea in his throat. Briant's lady was laughing softly.

"It was you," Kay said. "In the cell. It was no dream."

She swept him a mocking curtsey. "It was I. And I can conjure it again, or any death you care to name. I can kill you a thousand times."

Kay fought in the grip of an icy terror. "Illusion," he managed to say. "I don't believe you can do anything that would really harm me."

Brisane's eyes grew cold, though her smile remained fixed. "Indeed," she said. "So you dismiss illusion, Kay. Yet illusion can be very powerful, and perhaps death is the least that you have to fear. See."

She gestured towards the bottom of the hall, where Briant had gone out. The door opened again. At first, Kay thought that Briant had returned, for the man who stood there was tall, broad-shouldered, fair, as Briant was. Then, as he moved, Kay knew.

A cry was torn out of him. "Arthur!"

The king strode down the length of the hall and caught Kay by the shoulders.

"Kay!" In Arthur's eyes flared a terrible fear that Kay recognised, wonderingly, as fear for him. "Kay—Brother—I thought I'd never find you. Dear God, I've been half out of my mind. . . ." He enfolded Kay in his embrace.

Kay clung to him, all caution, all calculation, swept away. "My lord, forgive me!" he gasped out.

Arthur's arms were tight around him. Kay leant into his strength. He was acutely conscious of the linen surcoat beneath his clutching fingers, the fine mesh of the mail beneath it, and the clean, sharp scent of Arthur's hair.

"Forgive?" Arthur was saying. "Kay, that's just a word. I need you. I can't do without you. I want you to come home."

As he listened to the words he had longed all his life to hear, the words he had never dared hope for, Kay understood. He tried to draw back, and as he did so Arthur's warm clasp gave way, the body under Kay's hands crumbled into dust, and the whole bright form of the king dissolved into a sparkling mist before Kay's eyes. He caught at the arm of his chair and managed to lower himself into it. Looking up, he met Brisane's cruel smile.

"Well?" she said. "Do you despise illusion now?"

Kay could not answer her. He was frozen in contemplation of what she knew of him, and what she might be able to make him do, for part of him wanted to fling himself at her feet and beg her to bring the illusion back. And that, too, she knew.

"I could give him to you," she said. "Think of it, Kay. You and

Arthur, together at last, for ever. An Arthur who would do whatever you wanted, who would be whatever you wanted him to be."

Kay flung his head up. "Then he would not be Arthur."

He was ready for the lash of her anger, but she merely stood gazing down at him, with the amused, speculative look she had worn at first.

"Are you still defying me? Do you still imagine that you have any choice? Don't you know that if I wish it, I can take your mind and twist it until the last threads of sanity snap? Don't you know that I have defeated better men than you? Do you really not recognise me?"

As she spoke the last few words, her form blurred in front of his eyes and she changed. Before him was standing a dumpy little woman, robed brown as a sparrow, with brown hair braided around her head and eyes cast submissively down. Kay caught at memory, and suddenly recalled where he had seen her before.

"You were . . . with Elaine. You came with her to Camelot. You were her waiting woman. It was you who deceived Lancelot into her bed!"

"Yes!" The sudden angry challenge in her voice, coming from that insignificant creature whose shape she still wore, startled and daunted him. "So long dancing attendance on that whining, whey-faced bitch—and for what? So Lancelot could slip away from me in the end, his guilt still hidden." The dull eyes narrowed. "That was your doing, Kay. I don't forgive, or forget, and I can learn from my mistakes. I made sure your guilt would be brought home to you in front of everyone."

She whirled, and as she turned she changed again, and stood before him the tall young votaress in the grey habit, who had brought the casket to Carlisle. Her fierce spirit looked out at him from a face of purity and innocence.

Kay leant forward, hands gripping the arms of his chair. "Now I understand," he said.

The figure rippled, and was Brisane again. "I think not," she said. "Not yet. Not quite."

"You tried to destroy Lancelot," Kay said, "because you knew that without him Arthur would be weakened and Briant's way would lie open to the crown. But for all your efforts, Lancelot was not destroyed. So you tried your arts on me, and found me an easier victim." A bitter self-loathing crept into his voice. "You must have rejoiced at Loholt's death, lady, when it gave you a weapon to use against me."

Brisane made no response, except for a slight movement, a glittering of her silks. She was watching him intently now, as if she waited for something.

Kay was deathly afraid, but nevertheless he made himself say, "You are not all-powerful. You failed with Lancelot. With me you succeeded, because you divided me from Arthur, but you will get no more of me. I will not betray my lord and serve Briant."

Brisane's brows arched. All her power and beauty was bent on him. "You will not, Kay? You will not? Have I not frightened you enough?"

Her lips drew back in a snarl as the last, fearful change came over her. The skin shrank back on her bones. Her eyes grew cold and exultant. Her hand, extended towards him, unsheathed claws.

Kay flinched away. "The Lady haunts you, too," he said in a whisper.

"The Lady haunts me?" The words were pronounced in that inhuman melody that owed nothing to flesh or breath. "The Lady haunts me? Are you really as stupid as all that? No, the Lady does not haunt me. Kay, I am the Lady."

Kay's eyes darkened. The calcined laughter was all around him. The room sang with power. A voice spoke in his ear—or was it inside his own head?

"I am the dark tide in your blood. I am your thoughts in the silent hours, when sleep eludes you. Know me, Kay. I am yourself."

Kay fought to choke out a denial. He felt as though bone, nerve, and sinew unthreaded, refused to obey the control of his will, so that like Brisane's illusions he would dissolve into the surrounding dark. He tried to cling to the chair but he could feel nothing beneath his hands. A black wind was sweeping him away. His mind was spiralling into nothingness, when across the tumult and the night came a voice, loud, expostulating, and on the edge of being amused.

"By all the blessed saints, lady, what have you done to him?"

It was Briant's voice. The darkness rolled back. A brilliant green-gold dazzle before Kay's eyes became Briant, stooping over him where he crouched in the chair. Beyond him, Brisane was standing, in her own shape again, or at least in the shape she chose to show herself, for Kay was no longer sure which was her true appearance.

"She—changed," he gasped out.

Briant glanced over his shoulder at his lady. He laughed indulgently.

"Women's magic. Useful, but you and I can disregard it. Be easy, Kay. She will not harm you."

Kay felt a cup of wine being put into his hands. He gulped at it. Briant looked down at him, smiling, a little contemptuous, and, as Kay realised, completely unconscious of what he had interrupted.

"Evil." Kay was still incoherent. "My lord, you know not . . ."

He felt Brisane's eyes on him, bright with confidence. And

how will you tell him? she seemed to be asking. And will he believe you?

Kay stammered into silence. Briant patted his shoulder and turned away.

"The envoy is dealt with," he said to Brisane, "and goes back to his master tomorrow. I have sent Meliant to entertain him."

Brisane nodded a gracious approval, and Briant, dismissing the matter, swung back on Kay. "Well? Your answer? Will you serve me?"

Kay looked not at him, but at Brisane. He could not hide the truth from himself. He knew what he could expect from her if he refused, and he knew that he could not face it. In comparison, Briant was a rock of blessed sanity in a tossing sea of madness and evil. But Briant would still do nothing to save Kay if he withstood him now.

Shakily, Kay said, "I will not . . . I cannot . . . raise sword against Arthur."

"I won't ask it of you. Kay, it's not your sword I need. Come, kneel before me. Courage, man—it's the only way now."

Somehow, Kay found himself kneeling on the flagstones at Briant's feet. He did not know what to say or what was being asked of him.

"Give me your hands," Briant said, suddenly, unexpectedly gentle. "Dear God, you're ice cold! Now swear to me—to be my man, to serve me, in everything I ask, save that I will never ask you to fight against Arthur."

Kay gave his oath. The words were like stones, falling into black water. The last of his honour went with them. When he had finished, and Briant had released him, he still knelt. He had no strength to do anything else.

Briant moved away and then came back. He had Gareth's sword in his hands, and was beginning to draw the blade from the scabbard. Kay realised what he meant to do.

"No!" he protested. "My lord Briant, I can never receive knighthood again, except from the hands of the man who took it from me. And that will never be." That "never" stretched out in front of him like a bleak wasteland. "I beg you, excuse me."

Briant grunted. "If that's what you want." He drove the blade back into the scabbard. "The sword's yours, in any case. Here, take it."

He stooped and laid Gareth's sword into Kay's outstretched hands.

Chapter Seventeen

Kay returned to the room where he had spent the night. The servant was there again, doing something with the fire. Kay dismissed him and sat in the window alcove to think.

He was calm. Like a man who has a mortal wound and dares not probe it, his mind shied away from his recent encounter with Briant. Instead, he considered what he had learnt. Brisane was the Lady. A supernatural being, or a mortal woman who had given herself as host to a demon for so long that they had become indistinguishable? Kay could not tell, and did not think it made much difference.

What was clear now was how Briant had known about his exile, and how his men had managed to find him so easily; although Brisane had not been present at his final dismissal or his departure from Carlisle, Kay had no doubt that somehow she had been watching.

He understood too how Briant's men had known where to ambush Arthur at the river crossing, and how they had tracked the company across the fells. The Lady had sent out her spirit into Loholt and seen what he had seen. Kay frowned slightly. That would mean—unless Brisane herself had taken horse and joined Briant's war band—there must be another. At least one other. A man who, possessed by the Lady, had known where to lead Briant's troops.

Kay shivered. Could she enter where she wished, bend anyone's will to hers? Could she possess him? Unconsciously, his hand moved in the sign of the cross. Loholt, he remembered, had consented. Kay would never be sure whether, at the end, the boy had repented and tried to go back, but the consent had come first. The evil could not take him unless he opened the way for it. And he had at least withstood her first assault, or Briant's interruption had saved him.

Sighing, he leant against the stone sill, his head supported on one hand, and breathed in the cold air. Kay knew he was still a prisoner, though the prison was comfortable and the bars were unseen. He would have liked to ride, to gallop across the moorland with a good horse under him, but he knew very well what would happen to him if he tried to pass the gates of Roche Dure.

When he sat down, he had laid Gareth's sword across his knees. Lightly he caressed the hilt. He should not bear it now, he knew. Gareth would not wish it. What little right Kay had to the blade, he had thrown away when he swore fealty to Briant des Isles, along with his honour and his last hope of Arthur's forgiveness. His enemies had been right when they called him coward.

Kay flinched away from that train of thought. A mortal wound; his life-blood pumping away. Instead he made himself reflect on something else he had learnt: An envoy from King Claudas of Brittany had just arrived at Roche Dure. Briant, Kay knew, held lands in Brittany from Claudas. The envoy might be no more than a routine messenger. Or was Claudas backing Briant's attempt to conquer Britain? Certainly Briant did not have the resources to take on Arthur alone; was Claudas sending him men and supplies? Kay had begun to work out ways in which he might send a warning to Arthur before he remembered that Arthur would not welcome any warning that was sent from him.

Meanwhile, Brisane worked a subtler plan. She had tried to weaken Arthur by destroying Lancelot, but the plan had failed. Lancelot's love for the queen had remained private, and Lancelot had been able to return. Her second plan, to destroy Kay himself, had been triumphantly successful. And now? Would she turn to Lancelot again, or would she pit her arts against the third of Arthur's closest councillors, against Gawain himself? A cold hand closed round Kay's heart as he realised his friend's danger.

Engrossed in his own thoughts, he did not hear the tap on his door, or the door itself open a moment later. The first he knew of someone entering his room was when he heard a voice close by.

"Kay, are you dreaming? Or rapt in amazement at the power of Roche Dure?"

Kay started, and looked up into the face of the young man who had taken him prisoner on the road to Carlisle. It was a wild face, almost beautiful, with long, slanting eyes beneath flaring brows and curling, silver-gold hair. Suddenly Kay remembered where he had seen the face before. This was the man who had led the ambush, when Kay and Loholt had left Arthur's troop on the fells above Carlisle.

Both times that Kay had seen him, the young man had shown savage delight in their encounters; now he smiled, though there was still a hint of mockery in his eyes. Kay laid aside the sword and rose slowly to his feet, in no doubt that he still faced an adversary.

"My lord Briant sent me to talk to you, to welcome you to Roche Dure and see that you have all you want. My name is Meliant de Lis."

The name was familiar; Briant had told his lady that he had sent Meliant to entertain the envoy from King Claudas. And now Meliant was here. So where was the envoy? In conference with Briant, or already on his way back to his master?

Warily, Kay said, "I thank you for your courtesy, my lord Meliant."

Meliant laughed, showing white, even teeth. "I think neither of us esteems courtesy, Kay. Let's have honesty instead. We met as enemies, but surely we can be friends. I have a quarrel with Arthur, and you can have no cause to love him now."

Grief rose in Kay's throat, almost preventing a reply. No cause to love Arthur. . . . He needed no cause. The love was there, the rock he built his life on. Not banishment, treachery, separation, nothing was strong enough to eradicate it. But Kay could not have confided that to anyone, could scarcely put words to it in his prayers, much less speak of it to someone like Meliant, or even let him guess.

"Friends?" Kay said coldly. "That is not a word I let fall easily."

He had rather expected Meliant to take offence, but the younger man's laughter returned, and he put an arm round Kay's shoulders. "Shall we say 'allies,' then?"

Kay would as soon have allied himself with a viper, but he did not say so, only detaching himself from the encircling arm. "You wished to speak with me?" he said.

Meliant did not answer for a moment. He took the seat Kay had left vacant and sat with his feet drawn up, hugging his knees. His glance fell on Gareth's sword; Kay thought he was going to touch it and wondered how he would keep his hands away from the man's throat if he did. He made himself stop watching, and paced slowly to the other side of the room.

"My lord Briant," Meliant began, while Kay was still turned away from him, "has dreams of grandeur. He wants to be King of Britain, and not only king, but High King. He aspires to be a second Arthur."

Kay looked back to see the vivid face alive with amusement.

"I help him," Meliant went on, "for reasons of my own. But it isn't my help he wants just now. It's yours."

Kay raised his brows and waited.

"He wants you to take up your duties as seneschal. He wants you to create a court, here at Roche Dure, that will shine as brightly as Camelot. A court to rival Camelot."

"Impossible," Kay said.

Meliant's smile grew gentle. "That will disappoint my lord Briant."

"That I regret," Kay retorted austerely. "The light of Camelot was not kindled overnight. And not by one man alone. Even Arthur only played one part." His voice grew vibrant, as he forgot where he was and spoke from his heart. "Camelot shines so brightly because we built it to hold back the dark. And I think when that light is quenched at last, it will never be lit again in this world."

Exiled From Camelot

Kay was afraid that he had betrayed himself, but Meliant was looking at him with a mischievous expression, as if he had not heard what he said, or hearing had failed utterly to understand it.

"So, no light for Briant. But you and I, Kay—could we not contrive him a little hearth fire?"

Kay shrugged. "What do you want me to do?"

Roche Dure had never been more than a garrison castle, commanding the estuary against raiding parties, the pirates from the North. The troops on their tour of duty had been content to have their quarters plain and simple, and no one had ever tried to change it.

Now Briant had chosen it as the seat of his court. As Meliant escorted Kay around the building, Kay saw that some rooms, like his own, were well-furnished, while others remained bare. Briant had wealth enough to import fine hangings and furniture, and Kay could not help asking himself where both the wealth and the furnishings came from. Claudas in Brittany, perhaps?

Crossing a courtyard, Kay and Meliant paused briefly, and watched workmen taking up the flagstones.

"My lord Briant will make a garden," Meliant said. "He is ever eager to please my lady."

"And a garden will please her?" Kay inquired, and added tartly, "To grow wolfsbane and mandragora, no doubt."

Meliant laughed. "No doubt. Though you would be well not to say so in my lady's hearing."

The earth beneath the flagstones looked hard and infertile. All around, the walls of Roche Dure rose, a sheer, forbidding grey. There would be little sunshine; Kay could not imagine the garden flourishing.

"I wonder that my lord Briant cares for this gloomy place," he said. "Has he not a fair castle of his own, in Brittany? And does he not hold it from King Claudas, and owe him service?"

Meliant gave him a glinting look, penetrating beyond the innocence of Kay's remark. "And what do you know about King Claudas?"

Kay knew many things about Claudas, none of them to the king's credit, none of which he felt like discussing with Meliant. He decided on directness. "I know his envoy is here to speak with Briant."

Meliant's eyes were very bright and fixed on him as he murmured, "Indeed. . . ." Kay had a second or two to wonder whether he had been too direct, before Meliant relaxed and went on blandly, "Indeed, my lord Kay, the envoy is here, but he came to see me. I am Claudas' sister's son, and he brought me letters from my dear uncle."

The light, caressing tone invited Kay to contradict him. Kay declined the bait.

"Forgive me," the seneschal said, "I had no idea of what exalted company I'm keeping. You overwhelm me."

He thought it wiser to say no more, though he believed little of what Meliant told him. The relationship, perhaps—for Meliant had the inbred self-confidence of the high nobility—but not that the envoy had come for such an innocent reason. He was more sure than ever that there was conspiracy between Briant and Claudas.

"I overwhelm you?" Meliant was amused, or pretended to be. "Then perhaps we had better go and inspect the kitchens. You may feel more comfortable there."

By the evening Kay was beginning to feel more comfortable, if only because he had found himself a job to do. He did not know where Briant had come upon his servants, but Kay doubted that any one of them had the slightest idea of how a lord should be served, or how a lord's household should be run. If Briant really had it in mind to rival Arthur, there was a long way to go.

Kay spent the rest of the day supervising the preparations for the evening meal. Briant would dine in state, with the envoy as his guest. Kay became determined that the evening would at least fall short of total disaster, though when he saw what he had to work with—the kitchens filthy, the cooking pots inadequate, a cook who had apparently never heard of seasoning, and sewers who thought that the proper way to serve a lord was to slap the dish down on the table and leave it there—he wondered if a month, rather than half a day, would be long enough. Briant's lavish provision in his own part of the castle did not extend to the kitchens, but Kay suspected that a great lord such as Briant envisaged himself would not even know where his kitchens were, much less visit them.

As the time of the meal approached, Kay inspected the tables that had been set up in the hall. The tableware—silver and some pewter—was barely adequate but now it was at least clean. The linen cloths, with luck, would escape too close inspection in the torchlight. Kay sent one of the kitchen boys scurrying back to the kitchens for more salt, and decided that the rest would have to do.

Meliant, who had lounged in to see what was going on, openly grinned. "You're enjoying yourself," he said. "Admit it."

Kay gave him a look of austere disapproval. He had no intention of admitting anything to Meliant. But to himself he owned that his activity had done one thing—distracted him from what he could not bear to think of.

He was able to turn away from Meliant as Briant himself

came bustling through the door leading to the dais. He wore a loose robe, as if he had interrupted himself in the middle of dressing. He had a gold cup in his hands, the rim and the base set with emeralds.

"My lord," Kay said, "you should not be here. It is not fitting."

Briant ignored the rebuke. "Kay," he said, "is it true that Arthur never sits down to eat until he has heard tell of some marvel?"

Kay, for the first time in days, felt like smiling. "Only at the great courts, my lord."

Briant nodded and looked relieved. Kay could not help wondering whether he was really as stupid as the question suggested, or whether he had some purpose in copying the customs of Arthur's court. A charade to impress the envoy, perhaps, or to convince anyone who was present that Briant could replace Arthur as King of Britain?

Meanwhile Briant gazed round the hall. Kay saw him visibly expanding, his mood growing more genial.

"Wonderful," he said. "That's what I've needed, Kay, a man who knows how these things should be done. Have you found all you wanted?"

Kay forbore enumerating all the things he had failed to find, only remarking, "We have no musicians, my lord, to grace your entry and to entertain your guests."

Briant looked momentarily worried, and then shrugged. "Too late now. But see to it for next time."

Was he supposed to produce musicians with a flick of the fingers? "No doubt, my lord," Kay said, a satirical edge to his voice, "once they learn that Briant des Isles holds court in Roche Dure, they'll be along here in droves."

Impervious to his irony, Briant slapped him on the shoulder. "Wonderful!" He held out the gold cup. "Now, Kay, I want you to take this, and when all the guests are assembled, fill it with wine and bring it to me, as the signal for the feast to begin. And tell the fellows who serve to be ready when I drink."

Kay looked at the cup as if it already had poison in it. This was Arthur's custom, too, or a version of it. In his court, Arthur would drink from the cup and then pass it among his knights as a symbol of their fellowship. That idea was probably too subtle for Briant. But filling the cup and handing it to the king had always been Kay's office. His whole spirit revolted against the thought of doing for Briant what he had once done for Arthur.

He took the cup. Evenly he said, "Very well, my lord. And if you do not want your guests to see you in your bedgown . . ."

Briant took a hasty leave. Kay returned to his own room, meaning to wash and tidy himself before the meal began. In his room he found his servant laying out a robe for him to change into. Kay eyed it with distaste. It was scarlet velvet—a colour he never wore—trimmed with ermine.

"Please take that," he requested, "to the room of my lord Meliant. Give it to him, with my compliments."

The servant went. Kay made his preparations and then went down to the hall in the blue tunic he had put on earlier.

By the time he arrived, Briant's company were already assembling. There were not many of them; not many people at Roche Dure would have the status to sit and eat with their lord. Meliant was already there; he was wearing the scarlet robe, and looked magnificent in it. His eyes danced at Kay as he patted the place by his side.

"What's this, Kay?" he said, with a flourish of his velvet sleeve. "A gesture of humility?"

"It suits you, my lord," Kay replied, "much better than it would suit me."

He ignored the seat Meliant offered him and went down to the doors at the end of the hall to make sure his servingmen were in position. They were; he must have terrified them adequately.

As Kay returned to the hall, the doors to the dais opened to admit Briant, his lady, and a tall, elderly man whom Kay assumed was Claudas' envoy. Although there were no musicians to play a fanfare, the noise of conversation in the hall died away. Briant advanced to the high table, holding his lady by the hand. Brisane was splendid in a robe of golden silk; emeralds flashed in her hair and on her fingers. She smiled graciously at Briant as he settled her in her seat, with the envoy on her other side. Briant spoke a few words of welcome—pompous, Kay thought, but with a warmth that sounded genuine. Briant was enjoying himself.

Meanwhile Kay had made his way rapidly along the edge of the hall to the table at the side of the dais where he had left a jug of wine and the golden cup. There was only one way to do this, with all the formal ceremony he could muster. Then he might be able to forget the last time he had done the same, on the night before Arthur rode from Camelot.

As Kay poured the wine and brought the cup to Briant, there was a stir just outside the main doors of the hall. A herald came forward and announced, "My lord Briant, an embassy from the court of King Arthur at Carlisle!"

Kay froze, standing utterly still except for his shaking hands, which set the surface of the wine shivering in the cup he held. Two men came forward into the hall. Under his breath Kay murmured words he could not repress—a prayer, or a desperate rejection of what he could not deny he saw. The newcomers were Lancelot and Gareth.

Chapter Eighteen

Kay never knew how he got through the meal. He was aware from the first that Gareth's eyes were on him, although after one look he could not face his friend's anguished gaze. Lancelot, his expression shuttered as always, gave nothing away.

Briant's servants found them both places at one end of the high table, well away from Kay himself, and well away too from Claudas' envoy. Kay could guess that Briant would want to hide from Arthur that he was receiving messages from Claudas.

Kay himself took his place between Briant and Meliant, and tried to make a pretence of eating. Every mouthful turned sour, and he thought he was going to be sick. He was thankful that Briant, after a hearty compliment on the serving of the meal, ignored him, being too wrapped up in his lady, until she excused herself and moved down the table to charm her lord's latest guests.

Meliant, too, paid Kay little attention, although Kay had braced himself to endure his jibes about the presence of Arthur's knights. Although he still smiled, still made a pretence of vivacity, there was a glint of steel about Meliant that Kay had not noticed before. More than once Kay caught him with his eyes riveted on Lancelot at the opposite end of the table.

Towards the end of the meal, a servant approached Lancelot and Gareth again, and conducted them away. Lancelot, before he left, bowed over Brisane's hand and kissed it, and she smiled up at him, all gracious warmth. When he had gone, followed by Gareth, who still looked too stunned for courtesy, she came back to her lord. For some reason, she looked well pleased with herself.

Briant's eyes caressed her as she reseated herself. Draining his wine cup, he turned to Kay.

"There are guest rooms at the top of the main stairway," he said. "That's where your friends will be. Go and welcome them from me, and tell them I'll attend them in a little while."

He seemed honestly oblivious of what he was asking. Kay opened his mouth to protest, but Briant had already turned away. Kay caught a glance of sparkling malice from Brisane and let his protest die. Whatever came now, he would have to bear it.

Quickly, wanting it over with, he left the hall and mounted the main stair. Along the passage above, he caught up with a man carrying a tray with wine and little spiced sweetmeats; he took the tray and dismissed the servant. Kay was beginning to realise that provided no one else was in attendance, he would have the chance of speaking to Lancelot and Gareth alone; he would at least be able to warn them about what he knew. Perhaps, for that, his own pain was not too great a price.

Outside the door of the suite of rooms Briant had pointed out to him, Kay paused. He could hear a low-voiced murmur of conversation. Bracing himself, he tapped at the door and went in.

Lancelot had his back to him, the huge, bony hands spread before the fire. Gareth was speaking to him, something urgent in his stance and his voice, though Kay could not catch the words; he broke off as the door swung open. Gareth spun round and stood rigid, facing Kay. A further door, on the other side of the room, stood ajar; Kay could hear sounds of movement inside.

He took his tray across to the table where he set it down and poured two cups of wine. "Welcome to Roche Dure, my lords," he said neutrally.

He took one of the cups and carried it to Lancelot, who accepted it, eyes narrowly on him, but said nothing.

Kay went to hand the other cup to Gareth, but Gareth stepped back, tense as if someone had drawn a weapon on him.

"Kay, don't," he said. "Stop pretending . . . you can't—" Growing incoherent he broke off, and then gathered himself. "I never thought we would find you here."

Kay put the cup down, before he spilt it, and bowed his head a little. "As you see."

It was hard to look at Gareth now, but all too easy for Kay to remember the last time he had seen him, distraught at their parting in the courtyard at Carlisle. Easier still to recall Gareth at Camelot, the light heart, the warm affection that had encompassed even Kay himself. He wanted that now, wanted to see the laughter alive in Gareth's eyes, but he knew he had thrown away all right to it when he swore oath to Briant.

For all his efforts to steady it, Kay's voice was shaking as he said, "Sir Gareth, you will wish me to return your sword."

"What?" Gareth started. "Oh—no. No, it doesn't matter," he finished miserably.

Kay was not sure what he would have done or said if they had been alone, if Lancelot had not been standing there in watchful silence. As it was, he forced himself not to move, not to reach out to Gareth, and he could find no words that he dared speak.

As he still stood there, a servant came from the bedroom carrying a jug of lamp-oil, bowed to his lord's guests, and went out.

Kay struggled to throw off the paralysis of his body and mind. "Listen," he said. "Before Briant comes, I must—"

"Wait." Lancelot interrupted with a calm assumption of authority. "Why should we listen to you? Why should we have anything to do with you, when there's nothing in Arthur's law that would stop us killing you?"

Kay glanced from one to the other. He could not bear to look at Gareth's white, stricken face. It was easier to confront Lancelot.

"I grieved for you in Carlisle," Lancelot continued. His tones were coolly formal. "I thought you were—not wronged, but unfortunate. And now we find you here, in Briant's service. You must have ridden straight to Roche Dure."

"I was made prisoner," Kay said wearily. "Briant's men brought me here. Do you think they would let me leave?"

"But you have sworn service to Briant?" Lancelot persisted.

"Yes."

There was a sudden movement from Sir Gareth, his head averted; Kay felt it like a blow thrusting him away.

"Kay, why?" Gareth said.

"I was afraid."

Lancelot turned from him with a tiny shrug and put down the wine cup, untasted, on the table. Kay did not overlook what the gesture meant, but he could not afford to take notice of it.

"Sir Lancelot," he said, "whatever you think of me, there are things I must tell you. Arthur is in danger. He must not make peace or compromise with Briant des Isles."

Lancelot flicked a glance at him, but made no other response.

Faintly encouraged, Kay went on, "Briant's lady is an enchantress, and she is wholly evil. Her purpose is to destroy Arthur by destroying the men closest to him. Myself; you, Sir Lancelot; and my lord Gawain."

As he spoke Gawain's name, Kay could not help seeing that Gareth had turned towards him again. The younger man's distress had not ebbed away, but a different feeling had invaded it, a sudden alarm, and he was listening closely.

"What proof have you of this story?" Lancelot said. "For Brisane seems to be a lady both noble and beautiful, and such slander of her surely needs proof before any honourable man will believe it."

Inwardly Kay flinched at the contempt that seared through Lancelot's words. Outwardly he remained calm.

"When you were at Corbenic, my lord, and again at Camelot, you were deceived, were you not, into the lady Elaine's bed?"

He could not help starting back a little as Lancelot turned on him a face of fury. He had never been a match for Lancelot, even in a practice bout when he knew Lancelot would hold back so as not to hurt him. Now there was nothing, no shared service, no last shred of respect, to stop Lancelot from tearing him apart.

"You will not speak of that!" Lancelot commanded him. "Though I cannot love her, Elaine of Corbenic is a lady of high esteem. You will not soil her name by speaking it. What passed between us is not for you to know."

"But I do know," Kay retorted, angry with himself for betraying his fear. "I know what happened, and I know why. And if I had not been there, in Camelot, the rest of the court would have known it too."

Lancelot relaxed, a look of shame in his eyes. "True. And for that I am grateful. But why do you speak of it now?"

"Because, my lord, it was the lady Brisane who deceived you."

Lancelot stared at him; a frown gathered on his face. "This is nonsense," he said. "The lady Brisane was not with Elaine. Do you think I would not know her again?"

"You would not, my lord, for she shows you the form she wishes you to see. As she did again, in Carlisle. She was the votaress who brought the casket with Loholt's head. She has destroyed me, and she has tried to destroy you. Do you think she will not try again?"

Lancelot was still staring; his expression, that had been puzzled, considering, settled into one of profound distaste.

"I'd like to think you were mad, or drunk," he said. "That might be some excuse for these foul lies. But I can't believe it. You're fabricating this vile story, the blackening of a noble lady's name, in the hope of excusing yourself, as if somehow you could still crawl back into Arthur's favour. That's a coward's trick, Kay. There's no hope. Since you've betrayed one lord, you might at least try to stay faithful now you have another."

Kay felt himself shrinking, for he could not defend himself. Lancelot was right—even, perhaps, as far as recognising some tenuous dream that Kay had not even admitted to himself, that Arthur might turn back to him. He knew himself, his life and his honour all laid waste, save only for one thing.

"I have told you the truth," he said.

"Truth? Forgive me, Kay, but truth is something we have learnt not to expect from you."

Desperate in the face of his cold disbelief, Kay turned to Gareth, who had withdrawn and was sitting in the window seat, his eyes fixed on his clasped hands.

"Gareth, you'll listen to me! You must—"

He had taken only a step towards him when Lancelot was there, intercepting him, grabbing at his shoulders. Kay gasped out a curse at him and twisted in his grasp, the struggles futile.

"No," Lancelot said. "You'll have no more to do with Sir Gareth. When he first came to Camelot, you put him to work and humiliated him. He forgave you, out of a generous spirit, even offered you friendship, but you showed what you thought of the worth of that. Haven't you hurt him enough with your treachery?"

Kay stopped struggling. Briefly Lancelot's grip was all that kept him on his feet. Everything was swallowed up in a vast wave of pain. As if through a mist, he saw Gareth get up and begin to cross the room towards them, but before he could speak the door opened. Briant stood on the threshold, with Meliant behind him. Kay tore away from Lancelot's hands and flung himself on his knees at Briant's feet.

"My lord, let me go away from here!" he begged. "Send me away, for truly I cannot bear this!"

Briant bent over him, a look of bewilderment on the broad, genial face. "Get up, Kay," he said. "You expected it, surely. You didn't think you could go for the rest of your life without meeting Arthur's men?"

He raised Kay to his feet. At the same time, Meliant thrust past him into the room and planted himself in front of Lancelot. His liveliness, his smiles, were gone. He was cold and fierce.

"Sir Lancelot of the Lake," he said. "I've waited long to meet you."

Briant tried to interrupt, but Meliant ignored him; with a shrug Briant gave up the attempt and stood watching. Momentarily, to his shame, Kay had leant on his arm, but now he straightened up and drew away. He was acutely conscious of Gareth standing a foot or two away from him, though he did not turn his head.

Meanwhile, Lancelot was saying to Meliant, "You have the advantage of me. May I know your name?"

His quiet tones did nothing to abate Meliant's fury.

"It is Sir Meliant de Lis, my lord. That was my father's name, too. You may have heard it, perhaps?"

Lancelot looked confused. He could not be unconscious of Meliant's hostility, but Kay could see that he genuinely could not account for it.

"No," he said. "For all I know, I have never heard it. Or if I have, I don't remember it."

Meliant spat on the ground at his feet. "You have never heard it!" he echoed. "Or you do not remember it! No, my lord Lancelot, how should you, for it would be but one more name in the lists, one more victim to Sir Lancelot's all-conquering sword. You killed my father, Lancelot, and you don't even know that you killed him. You don't even remember his name!"

Lancelot's bony features had grown gaunt, and he spoke with a deeper seriousness. "If that is so, then I am truly sorry for it. Will you tell me how it was?"

"It was, my lord, in a tournament at Lonazep, two years ago. You unhorsed my father, and in his fall he broke his neck. But no doubt, my lord Lancelot, such things happen to you so often that we do you wrong in expecting you to remember."

Lancelot was silent for a moment and then held out his hands to Meliant. "What penance will you have me do?

"No penance," Meliant spat at him. "But I will have revenge."

"Revenge?" Lancelot might never have heard the word before. "Are you challenging me?" he asked slowly.

"Yes!" There was nothing hesitant about Meliant's reply. "I challenge you to combat, Sir Lancelot. To the death."

Lancelot paused in helpless silence. Taking advantage of the pause, Briant stepped forward and caught at Meliant's arm.

Meliant shook him off savagely. "You'll not cross me in this, my lord," he said, and to Lancelot, "Well?"

Coming to himself, Lancelot shook his head. "I don't fight unfledged boys."

"Don't call me 'boy.'" Meliant's fury had a harder edge now. He was managing to hold on to his temper. "I'm knight as you are, and you have no excuse for refusing to fight me. Unless you're too much of a coward."

The last taunt was absurd, but it reached Lancelot. His eyes kindled. "No one calls me 'coward,' boy."

Kay found himself exchanging an anxious glance with Gareth, as they stood on the edge of the encounter, unable to do anything to intervene. It was almost as if the last few days had never been, until Gareth, remembering, flushed and looked away.

Kay made himself concentrate on Meliant; he was feeling more sympathy for him than he would have thought possible earlier in the day. Though Meliant had no true quarrel, for his father must have accepted the risks of the tournament as all knights did, he had good reason for his bitterness, especially when Lancelot had utterly forgotten what he had done.

"Stop it, lad," he found himself saying impulsively. "If you fight with Lancelot, he'll tear you in pieces."

He might not have spoken, for all the notice Meliant took of him. The younger man was all coiled tension, waiting for Lancelot's reply, and Lancelot was on the verge of speaking when Briant pushed himself forward, between the two adversaries.

"I'll not have this," he said. "Meliant, I forbid it."

"You forbid it!" Meliant burst out. "When I asked you for knighthood and gave you my sword and my service, you knew it was so that one day I would come face to face with Lancelot. You knew I wanted revenge. Don't take it from me now. I've deserved better of you than that, my lord."

"You've deserved better than being spitted on Lancelot's sword," Briant said. "Kay's right. He'll make crows' meat of you. Get out of here. Go and cool off somewhere else."

He took Meliant by the shoulder and thrust him towards the door. Meliant turned on him, eyes snapping fury, his hand on the dagger at his belt.

Kay started forward, grasping Meliant by the arm. "Stop it. You young fool, you can't draw weapon on your lord. Do as he says; I'll come with you."

Briant gave him a nod of thanks, not without a faintly surprised look, and stepped back. Beyond him, Lancelot relaxed again, breaking from the stance of the fighting man and moving away towards the fire. Meliant flung a vicious curse at all of them and fled, head down, out of the door.

Kay was left facing Gareth. Shakily, he held out a hand, not as if he expected Gareth to take it, but palm upwards, a plea.

"Sir Gareth," he said; impossible to beg him openly with Briant in the room. "Sir Gareth, will you speak with my lord your brother?"

Gareth hesitated, and shot an anguished glance across the room at Lancelot, but Lancelot had withdrawn into brooding silence. His eyes went back to Kay. "Yes," he said. "Yes, Kay, I will."

He almost reached out to clasp Kay's hand, but remembered himself in time. Kay, struggling with relief almost impossible to bear, could still find space to be thankful Gareth had remembered. He would have nothing to reproach himself with afterwards.

"Kay," Briant said, "get after that young idiot and make sure he doesn't do anything else stupid. You can have what you asked for. Tomorrow. I'll send you both away from here tomorrow."

Chapter Nineteen

Kay passed a sleepless night. Knowing that Lancelot and Gareth were under the same roof, so close to him and yet so distant, would have banished sleep in any case, but Kay could not help worrying about the warnings he had tried to give. He had been interrupted before he had the chance to mention Claudas' envoy, but perhaps that was less important than the truth about the lady Brisane. And there Lancelot had utterly refused to believe him.

Kay was not quite without hope. Perhaps Gareth believed; whether he did or not, he had promised to tell Gawain what Kay had said, and Gareth would keep his word. Of all Arthur's knights, Kay thought that Sir Gawain was the one most likely to listen, and the one with the best chance of convincing Arthur.

Lying still, his bed-furs clutched around him, Kay was shaken with a sudden agony of wanting Gawain. He vaguely remembered—the memories scalding him now—Gawain's gentle care of him when he was ill in Carlisle, half out of his mind with fear and guilt. Clearer, though just as painful, were his memories of Gawain in Camelot, the unconscious grace and generosity, the compassion, the warmth. Kay had never fully understood why Gawain should have cared at all for him, who was so utterly different, but he had given friendship without stinting, and Kay, half afraid but finding him, in the end, impossible to resist, had managed to respond. He had lost all right to that now, and yet Kay knew that if Gawain had been here, he would have listened, and understood, and perhaps found it in his heart to forgive.

Kay did not find relief from his black thoughts until his servant came in the next morning with hot water for him to wash.

"My lord Briant asks you to pack for a journey, sir," the servant reported. "He's sending you home with my lord Meliant."

Home with Meliant? Kay asked himself as he got up and washed. To Brittany? Perhaps that would be best, to be far away from Arthur and from anyone else, or anything, that would remind him.

The clothes he had been wearing when he was brought to Roche Dure had been returned, neatly folded in the clothes chest, along with the few possessions he had brought from Carlisle. Kay dressed, but he left off his mail shirt and surcoat. He was a warrior no longer; he would not dress as a warrior when the only attack he might have to face would come from Arthur's men. He packed the change of clothes Briant had given him, and then, half ashamed of himself, bundled in the mail and surcoat as well.

By the time he was ready, the servant had returned with his breakfast. Kay was sitting in front of it, crumbling a piece of bread, when the door of his room opened to admit Briant des Isles. Kay rose to his feet.

"You're ready?" Briant said. "Good. Come with me. I've a gift for you." He seemed full of energy and good humour.

Kay eyed him warily. "A gift, my lord?"

Briant let out a bark of laughter. "Maybe not a gift, at that. Come on, I'll show you."

Kay caught up his cloak and the bag and, after a brief struggle with himself, the sword belt with Gareth's sword. Buckling on the belt, he let Briant shepherd him out of the room and down the stairs. They went along a passage and out into a courtyard Kay had not visited yet; the sharp tang of the stables reached him from the opposite side. Hunting dogs were milling around the feet of the horses; the courtyard seemed packed with them and with the riders.

Near to the doorway where Kay stood with Briant, Meliant was mounted on a rakish chestnut—a showy animal, Kay thought disparagingly. Beyond him, a groom led another horse up and down, a black that fought against the rein, flinging up its head and trying to veer away, hooves beating impatiently.

Kay stood still. "Morial!"

Briant grinned. He stood with feet apart, thumbs tucked into his belt, radiating self-satisfaction. "My men brought him in. He's a fine horse, Kay, but no one can ride him. He's been taking up space in my stables, stuffing himself with corn, and I haven't got a scrap of good out of him. He threw one of my best horsemen and broke his arm. If you can manage him, take him and welcome."

Kay was already moving forward, skirting Meliant, who kept his horse standing with a tight rein. He wore a savage expression and took no notice of Kay.

As Kay reached out to take Morial's reins from the groom, the man said, "Steady, sir. He's a devil."

"Rubbish," Kay said absently. He was already stroking the silky neck, quieting the horse. "Morial, my beautiful Morial," he murmured.

Tears threatened him, and inwardly he lashed himself. He was not going to make a fool of himself here. Swiftly he swung himself into the saddle and brought the now-docile horse up beside Meliant.

"Thank you, my lord," he said to Briant. "This is a noble gift."

Briant looked surprised, too surprised to pick up the hint of satire that Kay could not keep out of his voice. "Well, if you're pleased, Kay. . . . I'm not sure but what I thought the beast would kill you." He beckoned to Kay to bend down so he could speak without Meliant's overhearing. "Keep an eye on the boy. He's a good lad, and if he wants a chance at Lancelot he may well get it, but not now. I'll not have him breaking up the peace talks with Arthur."

"Forgive me, my lord," Kay could not resist saying. "I didn't think that peace with Arthur was what you had in mind."

Briant laughed. "Maybe. But if I want war, I'll have it in my own time, not in Arthur's—or Meliant's. So keep him out of trouble. I'll send word to you when I'm ready."

He moved off to speak to Meliant, leaving Kay to think over what he had said. He was wasting time, Kay thought, delaying the onset of another battle with Arthur, delaying until . . . what? Until Claudas could send him reinforcements? Kay wished he could have passed on his suspicions to Gareth, but there was no time.

Meliant and Briant were in the middle of a low-voiced quarrel.

"I'll not be packed off like this," Meliant said. "You promised me my revenge on Lancelot. Are you breaking your word now?"

"Don't accuse me of breaking my word." Briant was in better control of himself, and sounded all the more dangerous. "There are more ways of taking revenge than hacking the man to pieces. I'll give you what I promised in my own time."

"I've served you!" Meliant was raising his voice in protest. "I've given you what I could, and done your bidding—"

"Done my bidding! If you'd done my bidding, lad, Arthur would never have reached Carlisle."

At that, Meliant was silent, lapsing into a furious sulk. Briant slapped his horse on the neck and stood back. The small party formed up, the confusion in the courtyard suddenly vanishing as the men-at-arms mounted and whistled up the dogs. There were four men in their escort. Or guard, Kay thought. And were they guarding him, or Meliant?

The group of horsemen moved off, beneath an archway that led to the main courtyard, and out of the gates, which already stood open for them. Meliant led the way down the hill—not towards the harbour, but down to the river, along the road Kay had travelled as a prisoner two days before.

"Where are we going?" the seneschal asked.

At first he thought Meliant was too furious to speak to him, but after a pause he tossed one word over his shoulder. "Home."

"Not Brittany?"

"No."

He would say no more. Kay was glad enough not to talk; he wanted time to think over that last conversation between Meliant and Briant. Briant had almost admitted that he was making plans against Lancelot, which must by their very nature be plans against Arthur. Destroy his best men. . . . Kay was more than ever convinced that he was right, and was shaken once again by fear for Gawain.

The other thing that Briant had let fall was new to Kay. It sounded as if Meliant had been responsible for tracking Arthur across the fells on the way to Carlisle. He had certainly been among the men who had lain in wait for Kay and Loholt. And Briant was blaming him for letting Arthur get through. Kay found his eyes resting on Meliant, who rode just ahead of him, a host of uncomfortable speculations rising in his mind.

When they reached the bridge, Meliant led the way across, following the road to the north.

"Where are you taking me?" Kay asked, with a jolt of fear at the thought of coming any closer to Carlisle.

At the far end of the bridge, Meliant reined in and waited for him to catch up. He was smiling, but there was no friendliness in his face.

"Home," he said. "To my manor. Where you will be royally entertained, Kay, I promise you." His tone contradicted the promise in his words, but he made no attempt to explain.

"You have lands in Britain?" Kay fell into step beside him as Meliant urged his horse forward again.

But Meliant did no more than mutter an assent. His foul mood after the quarrel with Briant had still not dispersed.

He remained uncommunicative, even when they stopped for food at midday. Kay found that he missed Meliant's liveliness, even the derision that had been directed at him. It was at least easier to counter than this brooding silence.

After the halt they went on, through wooded country at first. To Kay's relief, they turned off the main road to Carlisle, and followed a track that led up into the hills. Trees gave way to moorland where sheep were grazing. They crossed a ridge; here Meliant drew rein again and threw out one arm in an expansive gesture. "Welcome to my manor, Kay."

Kay looked at the landscape in front of him. Some way ahead the moorland gave way to cultivated fields. The stubble of the last crop still stood; no one had done the autumn ploughing. Beyond the fields was a belt of woodland and, just on the edge of sight, the glimmer of a lake. There was no sign at all of any human habitation.

"Do you live in the trees?" Kay asked.

Meliant laughed, a more natural sound, as if he was at last emerging from his sulk. "You'll see where I live soon."

He led the way down the track that continued into the valley, through the neglected fields. The sun began to set behind the horsemen, casting their shadows forward. As twilight thickened, they came to a village, which until then had been hidden by a fold in the land and by the forest that stretched its arms around it, almost enclosing the village in a circle of trees.

The houses were humped shapes against the dying light. At first sight Kay thought they had been abandoned, they were in such poor repair. Walls gaped, roofs were uneven, as if the village had been battered by a storm and then left to decay. Then he saw wavering lights in windows here and there, and the smoke from a few hearth fires.

No one appeared to greet the horsemen or even to watch them pass, but Kay could feel watchful eyes on them, and his hair prickled with their hostility. He had to make a conscious effort not to look round.

At his side Meliant rode unconcernedly, as if none of this was unexpected, or bothered him at all.

Kay could not resist asking, "What has happened here? What can your steward be thinking?"

Meliant ignored the question.

They left the village behind as the road led into the forest. Kay had expected to feel relief once the eyes were gone; instead, he grew even more uneasy. The trees had a kind of dreadful familiarity, and as he passed more deeply among them he thought he could hear, beneath the movement of the horses, the lapping of lake water against stone.

Abruptly the trees ended. The riders emerged on the shore of a lake. Kay could see ahead of him the causeway leading to the gate of the manor house where he had been Loholt's prisoner. He jerked Morial to a halt, and the horse, resenting the unusual clumsiness, threw up his head, snorting. Kay was seized by an uncontrollable fit of shivering, and he turned to Meliant.

"No!"

"You recognise it?" Meliant said carelessly. "Of course, you've been my guest once before, I believe."

He gestured for Kay to precede him on to the causeway, but Kay made no move. His hands gripped the reins. He struggled with an irrational fit of terror. The last thing in the world he wanted to do was cross the causeway and enter that building.

Meliant reached across and laid a firm hand on his bridle. "You wouldn't dream of being difficult, would you, Kay?" he said silkily.

"Were you here?" Kay asked. "Do you know what happened?"

"Of course I was here. Of course I know."

His voice had changed. Ice thrust along Kay's veins. The hand that tugged now on his bridle was clawed. As Morial's hooves rang on the stones of the causeway, the eyes of the Lady laughed at Kay from Meliant's face.

Chapter Twenty

Kay stood with Meliant at the entrance to the great hall of the manor. Their escort had taken the horses round to the stable yard. The dying sun slanted through narrow windows in staves of fire, falling on the dark shape of the bier where the dead knight still stared blindly upwards.

Meliant paced forward and stood beside it. "My father, Kay. I have sworn that he shall not be buried until I have taken revenge on Lancelot."

He was Meliant again. After her brief appearance on the causeway, the Lady had withdrawn, her presence no more than a warning, or the flick of a cat's paw, a reminder to the mouse that it has not escaped.

Kay followed Meliant until he also stood beside the bier. When he had first seen it, the skull with its few remaining flaps of skin had been just one more part of the terror of that night. Now it filled him with a profound sadness.

"My lord, that is blasphemy. Let him go to his rest."

Meliant's eyes flashed fury at him. "I have sworn."

Tentatively, Kay reached out and rested a hand on the other man's arm. "Lancelot would make peace if you would let him. He has offered you penance."

Meliant laughed, an angry sound. "Are you pleading for Lancelot? Is he really so dear to you?"

Kay shook his head. Painfully, he said, "Lancelot and I have never been friends. We are . . . too different. But he is a noble man. Your father's death was an accident. If Lancelot made amends—"

"All I want from Lancelot is his body at my feet," Meliant interrupted. "And that I will have. I have sworn it."

"If you fight Lancelot, he will kill you."

Meliant pulled away from Kay's touch on his arm, and stood with his back to him. "I'm not as helpless as you think. But if he does kill me, then I will have died keeping my vow."

Kay stood looking at him in silence for a moment. He could feel the grief radiating from Meliant, and it almost made him forget that Meliant was his enemy. He was not wholly given up to evil. He had loved his father, and now he showed courage in pursuing his revenge, for he must have known that Lancelot was an adversary he could never overcome. Kay felt pity, and an urgent need to salvage something from that wrecked nobility.

Fearful of the reaction his words would provoke, he said, "My lord Meliant—when we were on the causeway . . ."

Meliant turned back to him. His eyes were alive, and he smiled in pure triumph. "You saw her, Kay? You saw the Lady?"

Kay nodded. Dry-voiced, he asked, "You know what she is?"

"She is the power of the lady Brisane. And she will give me my revenge."

"No!"

Kay was beginning to understand. Some of Meliant's courage was drawn from his awareness of the Lady's presence within him. It would not be Meliant alone that Lancelot would have to fight. Kay wondered if even Lancelot could withstand the Lady, especially when he had no concept of his own danger.

"Meliant," he said, "the Lady is darkness—evil. She comes from hell."

Meliant stared at him. Something like fear flared in his eyes.

"Pray for release," Kay said urgently. "It's not too late. It's never too late to go back. God will forgive you."

As he spoke he relived the moment when he had made the same plea to Loholt. Loholt had denied him through the ecstasy of his possession, but there had been a moment, Kay believed, when the boy had thought of going back. Now he thought he saw the same indecision in Meliant. He was staring at his hands, washed in blood from the rays of the dying sun.

"Please, my lord, think of—" Kay broke off as Meliant flung his head up. He knew that he had failed.

"I'll not turn back," Meliant said. "Why should I care what the Lady is, if she gives me my revenge? Afterwards—when I've torn Lancelot's living flesh from his bones—afterwards I can drive her out."

"Afterwards it may be too late," Kay said, but Meliant no longer listened to him.

The young man strode down the length of the hall, towards the hearth at the far end, shouting for his servants. His voice raised echoes, but no one came. Impatiently Meliant stripped off his gloves, and stood slapping them against his palm.

"Has everyone left this God-forsaken pigsty?"

Kay did not attempt to answer. As he moved more slowly down the hall to join Meliant, a door at the far end opened. Through it came a girl; Kay recognised, with a sudden beating of his heart, the lady Alienor.

She paused, gazing at Meliant with a swift, brilliant smile, and Kay understood the fugitive familiarity he had seen in Meliant. Alienor had spoken of a brother, but until now, Kay had forgotten. They were very like.

Alienor sank to the ground in a formal curtsey. She still wore her ruined finery, her pale hair looped up as before in a tangle of withered leaves. Her voice was joyful. "Brother, you're most welcome."

For a moment Meliant did not respond. He stood looking down at his sister with a kind of sick dismay. When he spoke, it was to Kay.

"You see one more reason I have to thank Lancelot. When my father died, grief drove out her wits."

More gently than Kay would have thought possible, he bent over Alienor and raised her to her feet. "Come, Sister. Bid our guest welcome, too."

Alienor turned to Kay and swept him the same deep reverence. "I must welcome all my brother's friends, sir."

Nothing at all in her look, her voice, her behaviour, suggested that she had ever seen Kay before. Kay did not know if she had truly forgotten, or if she dissembled. Bending over her hand, murmuring the customary courtesies, he did nothing to betray her. If Meliant did not know it was his own sister who had released Kay from his imprisonment, Kay would do nothing to tell him.

"Sister," Meliant said, when the greetings were over, "Kay and I have travelled from Roche Dure, and we're tired and hungry. We need food, and fire, and beds for the night."

Alienor gave him a look of bewilderment, as if he had asked for dragons' teeth. They might, Kay reflected, have been just as easy to provide, here. Then she smiled again.

"I'll ask Avice," she said, as if that were the solution to all difficulties.

Alienor clapped her hands. The summons was more effective than her brother's had been. Almost at once, a side door opened and an old woman came in. Kay visualised her as she might have been the moment before, with her ear to the keyhole. She was small and shrunken, with wispy white hair skewered in a bun; her eyes gleamed black and malevolent from a wrinkled face. She bobbed a perfunctory curtsey and said nothing.

"Avice," Meliant said, "why is there no fire, no light here, no attendance for your lord and his guest?"

Avice glared beadily at him. "Because you sent no word," she said, and added, "my lord," as an afterthought.

Kay could see Meliant grow angry at the insolence, but he kept his temper.

"You should be ready to receive your lord at all times," he said.

Now Avice's look was pure contempt. "You might have thought of that when you sent your menservants to the Breton's wars."

Meliant's nostrils flared in anger. His lips thinned; he took a step forward. "Old crone, I could have you whipped."

Alienor gave a tiny gasp of distress, and Kay found himself taking her hand, as if there was any comfort he could give her.

Avice herself was unimpressed by the threat. "Maybe," she said, "but you won't, if you want to eat tonight. There's nobody else to cook for you."

For a moment, Meliant quivered on the edge of fury. Kay almost expected to see him unleash the power of the Lady, but there was no change in him.

At last he snapped out, "Go, then. And make all speed."

Avice turned and shuffled out, elaborately slowly. Over her shoulder, she tossed the words, "There's a fire in my lady's solar. I'll serve you there."

Meliant snarled something at her back and strode out by the other door. Alienor drew Kay after him, her serenity restored again.

"Come, sir. You're welcome to our home." Enigmatic again, with one of the dizzying changes that had bewildered him before, she said, "At least we shall be kinder to you this time."

His breath taken away, Kay did not reply, and by the time she had conducted him up a stairway and into her solar, where Meliant already waited, she had slipped back behind her courtly mask. Kay could not help wondering whether her changes were deliberate, whether she had herself under control and for whatever reason was pretending madness, or whether there was some more complex cause. He wondered, too, where she had learnt her manners; not here, in the depths of the country, even before the manor was laid waste. In Brittany, perhaps, in Claudas' court?

The solar was the nearest Kay had seen here to a normally furnished room. It was bright with lamps. A fire blazed on the hearth. The chairs were cushioned and the walls covered with hangings. The shutters were open; as Kay and Alienor entered, Meliant was closing them, and they fastened and fitted snugly. But as Kay took in his surroundings more carefully, he realised that the lamps burnt smokily, with a reek of oil, and nothing was as clean as it should have been. Like Alienor's dress, the fabric of the cushions and hangings was beginning to rot away, their embroidery unravelling. The room fitted Alienor as a setting fits its jewel.

Alienor took her brother's cloak, and Kay's, and invited them to sit by the fire. Kay sank into a chair feeling that he might never have the strength to get up again. He still fought irrational terror brought on simply by being within these walls again, and by the thought of the Lady lurking within Meliant. The strangeness of his welcome and his surroundings added to his fears; it was almost more than he could bear.

To his relief, Alienor asked Meliant for his news, so that Kay did not have to talk. He was half aware of their conversation, but

Exiled From Camelot

the chance to rest and the warmth of the fire meant that sleep began to creep over him. He was drowsing uneasily when the door opened to admit Avice bearing a tray with an earthenware jug and cups.

"The meal's cooking," she said sourly. "And I'll thank your men to stay out of my kitchen."

"Dear Mistress Avice," Meliant said; he had recovered his usual derisive tones, "I'm sure you could deal with a whole army and not need my help."

Avice grunted and slammed her tray down on the table by the window.

"Wine, gentle Avice?" Meliant asked.

"It is not," she snapped. "You sent the wine to the Breton's cellars. And there's no ale, for there's naught to brew. That's mead, though it's not right for my lady, or there's water."

Meliant looked for a moment as if he was going to lose his temper, but instead he laughed. "Truly, Mistress Avice, this is a worthy homecoming!"

Avice sniffed. "You can serve yourselves," she said. "I've a pot on the fire."

When she had gone, Meliant lounged across the room and investigated the jug before pouring three cups. He handed one to Alienor and one to Kay. Kay sipped cautiously; the mead was surprisingly good. Not a fit drink for Arthur's table, of course, but Kay could imagine offering it to his men without feeling ashamed. Then, with a sudden pang, he remembered that he would never have to choose wines for Arthur again.

After a while Avice returned with bowls and plates that she distributed around the table. Meliant drew up chairs and conducted Alienor to her place. Alienor's eyes sparkled; in her own mind she was a great lady entertaining noble guests at her feast. Kay, rising from his fireside seat, tried to share the illusion with her, for her comfort and his own, but it was difficult in this decaying room.

The plates were made of wood; good craftsmanship, but not suitable for a lord's table. Kay wondered what had happened to the silver, or at least pewter, he would have expected to see, and answered himself in Avice's phrase: "sent to the Breton." "The Breton" must be Briant des Isles, and Meliant was impoverishing his own estates to help Briant in his war against Arthur. Kay did not have to look far to find the reason: Meliant's terrible obsession with revenge. Would it drive him on, Kay asked himself, until he had lost everything, even his immortal soul?

An earthenware pot contained a stew of pork and beans; again, it was good of its kind, but not fit for a lord's table. Meliant served it with a mutter of contempt. The bread was coarse; Kay guessed the flour had been mixed with something else. But he was grateful for the hot food, and found to his surprise that he was hungry.

Soon Alienor left the table and went back to the fire, where she took up a little lap harp, and played, and sang courtly songs of love betrayed. But some of the strings were missing from the harp, and the rest out of tune, and so the music was a jangling discord, a counterpoint to the sweet, true voice.

Meliant pushed away his plate and sat with his elbows on the table, his head resting on his hands, fingers digging into his hair.

"I remember how she was." His voice was scarcely above a whisper. "Gentle, beautiful, happy. . . . All the men at Claudas' court were wild to wed her. And look at her now! What man will ever want her again?" He groaned. "Dear God, Kay, do you wonder that I want revenge?"

Kay leant closer to him. "Take her to Arthur. Tell him what happened. He will make a settlement for you with Lancelot. He will find healers for your sister."

Meliant looked at him, his face twisted, eyes bright with tears. For a few seconds Kay thought he was taking the advice seriously. But all he said was, "I will tear out his living heart!"

He rose, tipping over his chair, and slammed out of the room. Alienor broke off her song and gazed after him wonderingly, but then she dismissed his unaccountable behaviour with a tiny shrug and a sweet smile for Kay.

"You must forgive my brother, sir," she said. "He has much to trouble him."

Meliant returned an hour later—an hour in which Alienor entertained Kay as if she were a great lady welcoming an equally noble guest. Kay had never been good at courtly trivialities—in Camelot he had usually managed to find a good reason to be somewhere else—and now pity made him even less articulate. Meliant's return was a relief.

He carried a lamp and jerked his head peremptorily at Kay. "I'll show you where you can sleep."

Even as Kay wished Alienor good night, his fears rose again. All evening he had wondered, at the back of his mind, what he would do if they expected him to spend the night in the room where he had been imprisoned. He knew that he could not bear it.

To his relief, the room where Meliant led him was not the same. It was larger and less neglected, though still bare and cheerless. When Meliant and Kay went in, there was dust in the air, as if the floor had been newly swept. One of Briant's men, who had ridden with them that day, knelt on the hearth piling logs on a fire that gave out smoke but little heat. There was a bed, a chair, and a clothes chest; no other furnishings or hangings. Kay's saddlebag with his few possessions had been brought up and placed on the clothes chest.

"Do I have to leave a guard on your door?" Meliant said. "Or are you going to be sensible?"

Kay sighed and shook his head. He felt too exhausted even to argue, much less try to escape. "Where would I go?" he said.

Meliant laughed. "Where indeed? Very well, I trust your word."

There was an edge of derision in his tone, more like the Meliant Kay had known until they arrived here. He was recovering from his grief over his sister. He dismissed the man-at-arms, set the lamp down on the window ledge, and left Kay alone with an ironic wish that he might sleep well. He did not even lock the door; Kay did not know whether that meant trust or contempt.

The following morning, Kay was woken by the cold. The fire had burnt out; no one had come to reset it, or to bring hot water for him. He had not expected that they would.

He pulled on his clothes rapidly and found his way down to the hall. A table and benches had been set up on the dais, where Meliant sat eating. He beckoned to Kay as he came in. "Come, share in this feast."

Kay approached and inspected the food. There was a loaf of bread and a wedge of dry-looking cheese on a wooden trencher, and a jug of water. Kay took a portion for himself and sat on the bench opposite Meliant. "Good morning, my lord," he said.

The younger man looked sour. He did not reply to Kay, and ate in silence for a while. Kay took the opportunity to look around him. In daylight, the derelict state of the hall was even clearer. Dust hung in the air. The hangings sagged on their fastenings. The sconces held burnt-out torches that Kay guessed had been there for weeks if not months. The table where he sat to eat had food scraps lodged in the grain and sticky rings from mugs and cups. Kay dared not think how long it might have been since someone had scrubbed it. A faint impatience stirred within him; had Meliant no more care for his estate than this, or had he no steward to do the caring for him?

He almost asked Meliant what he thought he was doing, but he knew the answer already. That hopeless, sterile impulse for revenge. Kay had already realised that nothing would turn Meliant aside. He did not try to talk; Meliant showed he was in no mood for conversation, until he said, "I'm going hunting. Do you want to ride with me?"

"With your leave, no, my lord."

Meliant gave him a narrow look, hostile and suspicious. "You'll remember you've given me your word not to escape."

Kay nodded. He had no other reason for refusing to join the hunt but that he was bone weary, his mind a tangle of confused impressions and ideas. He wanted to rest, to be alone. He wanted to explore his own mind, and try to discover whether there was anything left, any point to the continued existence of the man who had been Arthur's brother, Knight of the Round Table, and High Seneschal of Britain, and now was only Kay. Nothing would have made him admit that to Meliant.

"Stay, then," Meliant said carelessly. "And if I have good fortune, we'll eat better tonight. If I can persuade that old witch to cook my kill."

As if she had been listening outside—and perhaps she had—the old witch, Avice, appeared in the doorway. She gave the two men a disgusted look. "I thought you'd be finished. I'm not running around after you all day."

Meliant gulped down the last of his bread and cheese, and got to his feet. "I go hunting, Mistress Avice. And no doubt you'll be glad to see the back of me. But Kay stays here to get under your feet."

He gave a short, unpleasant laugh, and disappeared by the door to the stairs. Avice came up to the table to take the cup and plate he had used.

"Mistress Avice," Kay said, "may I have some hot water to wash?"

Avice sniffed. "You can if you fetch it."

She turned to go, but Kay called her back. His impatience with the grime and neglect and poor service, and with Meliant's carelessness, welled up again.

"Mistress Avice, sit down," he said. "I want to talk to you."

Avice eyed him, her look unfriendly. "I've work to do, sir."

Kay was undaunted. He might not have a silver tongue to entertain court ladies, but he knew how to talk to women like Avice, and he had not missed the title of respect she had given him for the first time.

"Sit," he said. "If you please. Have you eaten this morning?"

Still reluctant, wary of him, Avice sat on the very end of the opposite bench. "I have, sir. More than two hours ago. What is it you want?"

Kay leant forward, elbows on the table, chin resting on clasped hands.

"Tell me, Avice," he said, "what has gone wrong here? Why is everything so . . . filthy?"

Avice was giving him a look as if she thought he was wandering in his wits. "Because there's nobody to clean it."

"Why? Tell me, Avice."

The black eyes kindled; Kay almost flinched at the force of her anger, though he recognised it was not directed at him.

"What good will it do to tell you? The young lord's men, they say you're his prisoner—and other things I wouldn't soil my tongue with. Why should you care what happens here? And what can you do?"

"I don't know, Avice," Kay said honestly. "Tell me, and let's see."

He was beginning to feel an enormous respect for her. He recognised her vitality, still strong in spite of her age and the poverty around her. She had not given in. Now she began to speak, in a grumbling tone that became more fluent as she went on.

"When the old lord was killed—" she flicked a glance down the hall towards the bier "—the young lord brought him here, along with my lady his sister. He was always a wild lad, the young lord, and he was set on revenge. Then the Breton came—sent for, I reckon—"

"Briant des Isles?"

"Aye. They planned war against Arthur. Young Meliant gave him money at first, and then last summer he sent our men away, to fight for the Breton. Some we heard had died, sir, and some we never heard nothing of. And then a few came back, but they're not as they were." She stopped, mouth clamped shut, as if she might have shown weakness if she had tried to continue.

"And then?" Kay prompted after a minute.

"The young lord, he'd gone to join the Breton, too. But he sent men that took the stored food, sir, and the grain, and they took the wool clip to sell."

"And no one tried to stop them?"

Avice shrugged. "It were our lord's orders, sir. Our steward, he stood up and protested, and they whipped him. He was an old man, sir, and he took sick after and died. And Margery—my daughter's girl—she spoke up, and they—sir, they did to her what soldiers do to women, and when they'd gone, we found her in the lake."

Kay felt sick. Almost unconsciously, he reached out and laid his hand on Avice's. For a few seconds she let it rest there before she shook him off and stood up.

"It's no good, sir," she said. "We've tried, but we're mostly women now. We can't do all the men's work as well as our own. And where's the point of it? Why plough, when the seed corn's gone? We've kept going, but we can't do it much longer."

Kay looked up at her, recognising the indomitable courage, and the anger that fuelled it.

"There must be a way," he said. "We must look at what we have and how best to use it."

The "we" had been quite unconscious. Kay hardly realised what he had said, until he heard laughter behind him. He turned to see Meliant lounging against the doorpost, a cloak over his arm. "Taking over, Kay?" he asked.

"No man should let his lands go to ruin like this," Kay said. "He should know that he has duties as well as rights."

Meliant laughed again. "And you're going to teach me? Very well, if that's what you want. I appoint you my steward, Kay, and may God give you joy of the task!"

Kay thought he was half joking; certainly Meliant expected that he would back out of the job. Instead Kay rose and bowed. "I accept, my lord. If it please you to hunt, I will arrange a feast for you tonight."

"Now that, Kay, I can't wait to see!"

The voice was taunting. Kay said no more, but stood in a respectful posture as if awaiting further orders. Meliant seemed about to speak again, but instead he spun round and made off, almost running, down the length of the hall to the main doors.

Avice was staring. Kay smiled at her.

"Mistress Avice, put your cloak on, if you please, and take me down to the village. I wish to meet my people. Tonight we will all feast with our lord. And tomorrow," he promised, "we will hold a Manor Court."

Chapter Twenty-one

The next morning, as Kay made his preparations for the Manor Court, he began to wonder what he had undertaken. In his visit to the village with Avice the day before, he had seen the results of what Meliant had done, draining the wealth of his manor to aid Briant in his wars. There was poverty and hardship that were bound to get worse as winter drew on. More difficult still to cope with was the hostility of the villagers; they would not easily trust anyone that they thought was Meliant's friend.

At first he had been afraid that they would not come to the evening meal in the hall. But they had come, some of them at least. There had been a fire, and torches along the pillars of the hall. Kay himself had rehung the tapestries, on a ladder that he had to mend before he dared set foot on it. Avice had swept the floor and laid fresh rushes.

Meliant had done his part, too, returning from his hunting with two plump hinds that formed the main course of the meal. For dessert there were apples, and Kay had persuaded Avice to bake honey cakes. Soon, he knew, he would have to take an inventory of the remaining food stores, but for one night they would feast.

Kay had made sure that the jugs of mead on the tables were kept filled. At least there seemed to be plenty of that, if nothing else. And gradually the people's wariness had relaxed; the sound of talk rose, and laughter rang that not even the presence of the old lord, silent on his bier, could stifle. Kay would have given his right arm for a good musician.

Meliant had sat at the high table with a sardonic look and said little. Alienor had been charmed. For her it was as if she had been taken back to the happier days at Claudas' court. Towards the end of the meal she passed along the tables, speaking to her people. At first Kay had been afraid for her, wondering if they would answer her kindly, but then he realised that it was the best thing she could have done. The villagers might blame Meliant, and hate him for what he had done, but they had nothing but pity for his sister.

Now Kay asked himself whether the warmth of the feast would survive into the bleak light of another day. He set up a table on the dais, with a chair for himself, and pen, ink, and paper brought from the steward's room. He did not know what he would need to write, but he felt more comfortable with a pen in his hand.

To his relief, Meliant had taken himself off to the hunt again. Kay was pleased with the promise of the game Meliant might bring, and even more pleased at the thought of his absence. He did not want Meliant interfering in what he meant to do.

The main doors of the hall stood open, and soon the villagers began to arrive, warily, in twos and threes and little knots of them together, taking their places on the benches in the hall and eyeing Kay with a mixture of suspicion and curiosity.

They were mostly women, Kay saw, with a few older men. Some of them brought children. There were no men of fighting age, which meant that there were no men with the strength to do the heavier work. Kay could guess, too, that most of the skilled craftsmen had been forced to go and fight.

When the last of the villagers had straggled in, Kay prepared to speak. The first few minutes might decide, he thought, whether he could persuade them to co-operate with him. It would have to be co-operation; he had no other way of enforcing any orders he might give.

He seated himself at the table, took up his pen, and let his gaze travel across the hall. The murmuring voices sank to silence.

"As most of you know," Kay began, groping for the right words, "my lord Meliant has appointed me his steward, and I have seen how much needs to be done here. I know that—"

He broke off as a woman near the front of the hall rose to her feet. She was tall, strong featured, in early middle age. The woman beside her grasped her arm and tried to persuade her to sit down again, but she shook her off.

"Is it true what they say," she said, "that you're Sir Kay who was Arthur's seneschal, and you betrayed Arthur to serve the Breton?"

For a moment Kay was taken aback by the direct accusation. While he hesitated, the woman's neighbour made a fearful protest, but again the speaker refused to be silenced.

"I'll know what manner of man we have set over us," she said.

Kay came to his feet. He should have expected this, he supposed, should have known that Briant's men would have passed on what they knew. He felt a brief stab of fear; if the villagers wanted to, they could tear him to pieces.

He took a breath and faced the woman who had spoken. "May I know your name, mistress?"

She looked startled, as if she had not expected him to ask that. "They call me Estrildis," she admitted grudgingly.

"Then, Mistress Estrildis, I will answer your question. I am the man you speak of, but I am not Sir Kay, for I am no longer knight. Arthur took that from me, along with the seneschal's office, when he sent me into exile. True, I serve Briant des Isles, but I am his prisoner, too." Suddenly he found that he could cast off restraint and speak from his heart, as if he were alone with his accuser. "I have lost everything that made me value my life. I would die tomorrow if I could die in the service of my king. But if I must live I will do it with dignity, like a man, not a beast." His eyes had been locked with Estrildis'; now he looked around the hall, aware of the stunned faces staring at him. "You have suffered loss, too," he said. "And I see you have not given in. Can we not work together?"

There was no direct reply. The murmuring talk broke out again. Estrildis still eyed him with a look of suspicion, but she gave him a little nod, almost a sign of respect, and sat down.

Kay took his own seat again. "What do you want of me?" he said.

From the back of the hall someone unseen spoke up. "We want our men back."

Another unidentified voice broke in with a ribald response, and there was a gust of laughter. Kay caught a hysterical note in it.

He rapped the table. "That is beyond my power."

Renewed laughter told him that someone had picked up a double meaning; well enough, he thought, if they would relax towards him.

When there was quiet again, he said, "Tell me about the food stores."

More talk, more purposeful now, and then Avice stood up from her seat at the side of the hall.

"The young lord took most of it for the Breton. All the grain, the stored vegetables, most of the apple crop—"

Kay raised a hand. "You baked honey cakes last night, mistress. The flour?"

Avice glanced at someone behind her, and then faced him again. "When the Breton's men came and started to load supplies, there was flour stored at the mill. We . . ." She hesitated.

"Removed it to a safer place?" Kay suggested.

Avice nodded. Kay noticed that she did not tell him where.

"It's not enough," she said. "Not to last the winter. We've mixed chaff with it to make it go further, but it's still not enough."

"And there was no autumn ploughing," Kay said.

"There was no seed corn," Avice snapped. She sat down again.

"It's too late now to plough and plant wheat," Kay said, "even if we had the seed. In the spring we can plant oats and barley. He hesitated, and then went on, "I promise you, by the time of the spring ploughing, we will have seed."

"How will you do that?" someone asked.

"I don't know." Kay knew he had to be honest. "But I will do it." He paused again, but no one else questioned him. "What other food have we?" he said. "Livestock?"

A fat, untidy-looking woman hauled herself to her feet at the back of the hall. "We've pigs, sir," she said. "A herd of pigs. We pasture them in the forest." She grinned at him. "Funny thing, sir, when the Breton's men came, all the pigs ran off. It took us days to round them up, after they'd gone." She sat down again to a murmur of appreciation.

The next speaker was a man, old and shrunken, thrust to his feet by the younger woman at his side.

"Wildfowl on the lake, sir," he said. "I were a fowler once. I know all about nets and springes. But my joints pain me; I'm no good for work no more." He gave Kay a crafty look from small, twinkling eyes.

"You have my sympathy," Kay said silkily. "But in our present need, perhaps I could ask your . . . daughter?" The younger woman nodded at him. "Ask your daughter if she will make you a salve for your aching joints. Or I have a very good recipe myself."

He met the man's eyes, which slid aside as he resumed his seat, muttering. His daughter had a broad smile on her face. Kay glanced round as another woman got to her feet, on the opposite side of the hall—a pretty woman, neater and cleaner than most of the others, with flame-red hair braided round her head.

"I keep the bees, sir," she said. "There's honey, and—"

"And you brewed that excellent mead?"

The woman flushed with pride and dropped him a curtsey. "Yes, sir." She gave a little gurgle of laughter. "The Breton's men, they left the beehives alone."

Others volunteered suggestions now—nuts in the forest, the last of the apple crop still on the trees, fish in the lake, a few hens that had escaped the Breton.

At last Kay rapped the table again. "Last night," he said, "we all ate together at my lord Meliant's table. We will do the same every day. All the cooking will be done in the manor kitchens, and Mistress Avice will choose some women to help her and supervise them."

He had wondered if he would get agreement to this, and he could see that some of his listeners were doubtful, although they made no protest aloud.

"That will mean less waste, and free the time of most of you for other work than cooking for yourselves and your families. Mistress Avice, you are in charge of provisions, and you may store the food where it pleases you."

It struck him that he should have consulted Avice first; he glanced at her, and was profoundly relieved to receive a curt nod from her.

"Next," Kay said, "my lady Alienor must have a waiting woman to take care of her."

"What did she ever do for us?" an unidentified voice asked.

Kay did not have to reply; there were enough of the villagers hushing the speaker.

When the voices died, he said levelly, "Because my lord Meliant has failed in his duty to you, it does not mean that you must fail in your duty. You will show him how civilised people must live."

They were thinking about that; meanwhile, a woman near the front raised her hand uncertainly. Kay thought that she looked tired, even ill.

"I was a weaver, sir," she said, "but there's naught to weave, since the Breton took the wool clip. I'd be willing to care for my lady. She never did us harm, that I know of."

Kay thanked her. He sat leaning on the table, chin in his hands, and looked around. They were coming together; he could feel it. His people; his responsibility. His resolve hardened. He would make good his word, about the seed for the spring planting, if he had to go down on his knees to Briant for it.

"Now that we can feed ourselves," he said, determined on optimism even though he knew that the problems were not solved by a long way, "we can start to think about the houses and the barns. They need repair. What can you tell me about the smith and the carpenter?"

"The smith's dead," someone called. "Killed when the Breton took Roche Dure."

"I am sorry," Kay said. "And the carpenter?"

A thin, grey-haired woman stood up. She twisted her hands together nervously.

"The carpenter's my man, sir," she said. "He should be here, but he—he said he'd not bow to any servant of the Breton's. I think you'd not hold it against him, sir. . . ."

Kay shook his head impatiently. "I'll come to speak with him. Whatever he thinks of Briant des Isles, he must do his work, if only for—"

"No, sir," the carpenter's wife interrupted. "You don't understand. He was at Roche Dure, too, sir. He came home after, because he was no use to the Breton any more. He's lost an arm, sir. How can he do carpenter's work with only one arm?"

Her pain, the pain of her absent husband, struck Kay like a wave.

"I am sorry," he repeated. "I will think of this. And I will come and speak with him."

He felt discouraged. The carpenter and the smith were the essential craftsmen of the village, and without them, there was little hope of making the repairs that were so urgently needed.

"We're not helpless, sir," one of the women said. "We can nail a board over a hole to keep the wind out—if we had the nails. We haven't, and that's smith's work."

Kay nodded slowly. "Before you leave," he said, "you will come to me, each one of you, and tell me what skills you have, and I will write them down. And then I will see what can be done. But now, go to your homes and think of what we have said today. If you—"

He broke off as Estrildis, his first adversary, got to her feet again. She was not looking hostile now, but her voice was abrupt as she said, "Sir, we must hear Mass."

Kay was startled, and before he could reply, she went on, "We've no church, sir. We used to hear Mass in the chapel here, but there's been none since the Breton came. That's not right, sir."

"But if we have no priest—"

"We have a priest, sir," Estrildis interrupted him.

A confused murmuring sounded again; Kay could hear protest in it, and distress. Estrildis ignored it. She turned and scanned the hall, and then made her way purposefully towards the back. She said something Kay did not catch, and then returned, a man with her, plucked out of the group nearest the doors. Though she was not touching him, she had the look of a jailer with her prisoner.

The man was small, and Kay thought he had once been plump, though his face now was grey and crumpled, and his cassock hung in baggy folds. He had wispy fair hair in a tonsure, and blue, bewildered eyes. He was trembling as he approached the table; without being asked, someone set a stool for him so that he could sit opposite Kay. He gripped the table with both hands as if it kept him afloat in a torrent.

"You are priest here?" Kay asked him.

Nothing but an unformed, whimpering sound came from the man, and it was Estrildis who replied.

"He was Lord Meliant's chaplain." Kay understood she spoke of the father, not the son. "When the Breton came here, he brought his lady, and she and young Meliant did vile things in the chapel. Father here tried to stop them, and they cut out his tongue."

Kay caught his breath in a gasp of pure pity. The hall was silent. He looked at the man opposite him. The hands that clung to the edge of the table were soft little paws, scratched now and engrained with dirt. A pliant man, Kay thought, a man who loved good living and took the easy road, until he had at last discovered there was something he could not bear. And the discovery had almost destroyed him. Kay thought he had never seen a man so close to disintegration.

Exiled From Camelot

He wished that he were Gawain, the gentle healer, but he was only Kay, and Kay's skills were all he had to use.

He nodded to Estrildis. "Thank you, mistress," he said crisply. "You may leave us."

Estrildis looked taken aback; she retreated reluctantly to her seat again and left Kay with the priest.

"This story is true?" Kay asked.

The priest nodded. Kay regarded him levelly. "Tell me your name."

The priest's eyes grew wild, and his mouth started to tremble. Kay held out the pen to him, and slid a sheet of paper across the table. "Write."

A spark lit in the blue eyes. One hand released the edge of the table and reached for the pen. A second later the other, to steady the paper. He was shaking, but he managed to scrawl, in huge, uneven letters: *Father Paulinus.*

Kay smiled. "Thank you."

He was aware of a gentle exhalation, a release of shared tension, from the hall, but he looked at nothing but the priest's face. "Father Paulinus," he said, "you must return to your duties as chaplain."

The priest wrote more quickly now, the writing becoming more controlled. *I cannot say the words.*

Kay leant forward again. "If I pray with my lips, but have no care for God in my heart, will he hear me?"

No need to write a reply to that; an emphatic shake of the head was enough.

"But if I pray in silence, in my heart, God will hear me then?"

Father Paulinus nodded; tears were gathering in his eyes as he began to understand where Kay was leading him.

"Then if you pray in your heart, Father, the bread and the wine will become the body and blood of our Lord Christ, for God will hear you."

Father Paulinus thought for a moment, scrubbed at his eyes with a filthy sleeve, and then wrote, *The people should hear the words.*

"They will hear them in their hearts," Kay said. He rose. "Mistress Estrildis, you are right. We must hear Mass, and we will. Tomorrow, at noon, in the chapel. A Silent Mass, for none of us have voices to be heard, and yet God will hear us."

He did not wait for any comments, but dismissed them, reminding them to come and offer their skills before they left.

"Father Paulinus," he said, sliding another sheet of paper across the table, "of your courtesy, be secretary for me, and write what these people tell me." He did not want to look at the man's exalted face, or give him a chance to go to pieces after all, in the stress of recovering his life and his vocation. Kay wanted him busy, busy and self-controlled. "And later—" he lowered his voice so as not to be heard by the villagers who were already gathering around the table "—later, I would have you hear my confession."

Chapter Twenty-two

When the last of the villagers had gone, Kay cleared away his writing materials, and then let Father Paulinus take him to the chapel. In the steward's room he found a pair of wax tablets and a stylus, and gave them to the priest, as being easier to carry around than pen, ink, and paper.

The crumpled lines of Father Paulinus' face were miraculously smoothing out, and he was smiling. He received the wax tablets with delight, a precious gift. Diligently he scratched away with the stylus, and held out the result for Kay to read. *The chapel may be defiled.*

"This we will see," Kay said.

Father Paulinus directed him up the stairs and along the passage that led past Lady Alienor's solar. The door to the chapel was at the end. Father Paulinus hauled a massive key out of the folds of his cassock and unlocked it. The door swung open, and Kay let the little priest go before him into the chapel.

It was cool, and quiet. Dust motes danced in shafts of pale sunlight from windows beneath the roof. The altar was bare of hangings, but there was no sign that anything had been damaged. Kay felt no sense of an evil presence there, nothing but a waiting stillness.

Father Paulinus scurried across the flagstones until he came to the altar steps, where he stopped and beckoned to Kay. Kay joined him. On the steps, as if it had flowed down from the sanctuary and congealed as it flowed, was a dark, sticky mess. Kay suspected it was blood, but he did not want to investigate it more closely or ask where the blood had come from.

"We will have it cleaned," he said evenly.

Father Paulinus tapped himself on the chest, the ghost of an old self-importance waking in him.

Kay smiled and nodded. "Then we will say such prayers that will drive out all memory of evil."

For the first time, Father Paulinus looked uncertain. He wrote again with the stylus. *It should be done by a bishop.*

"Unfortunately," Kay said, "the nearest bishop is in Carlisle, and he is unlikely to come if I send for him. We must hope, Father, that you and I and the rest of the good folk of this manor are at least equal in the sight of God to one bishop."

Father Paulinus looked scandalised, though Kay thought he was more inclined to laugh. But when he next took up the stylus and wrote, it was about something different. *Kneel, my son. I will hear your confession.*

Kay was momentarily startled; a show of authority was the last thing he had expected from Father Paulinus. But he obeyed, and knelt on the altar steps, avoiding the dark stickiness. With Father Paulinus standing before him, he made his confession.

It took a long time. Kay had not realised how much guilt and fear and pain were coiled up inside him, or how deeply he had needed to let it all go. When he had finished, and saw Father Paulinus tracing the sign of absolution in the air over his head, he was weeping.

"What penance must I do, Father?" he asked.

Father Paulinus took his tablets again, and wrote swiftly, one sentence only: *Are you not doing it already?* He let his hand rest on Kay's head, and the touch was a blessing.

When Kay left the chapel, Avice already had the midday meal ready for him: bread and cheese and small, wrinkled apples. Afterwards Kay walked across the causeway and through the wood into the village.

He felt as if his mind had been scoured clean, and he himself exposed as if his body had been naked. He was surprised that no one else could see any difference in him.

One or two of the villagers nodded to him, not entirely friendly, but their suspicions tempered since the day before. The pretty bee-keeper, whom he met towards the centre of the village, smiled frankly at him and dropped a curtsey. "Can I help you, sir?" she asked.

"I was looking for the carpenter," Kay said. "Can you tell me where he lives, mistress?"

She pointed. "The third house, down there, sir." Her smile faded. "He's a hard man. Always was. And terribly bitter against the Breton." She laid a hand on his arm—a shapely hand, though roughened by work. "Take care, sir."

Kay thanked her and went on, aware that she watched him go. The carpenter's house looked empty, the door closed, the windows shuttered. Kay knew that the carpenter's wife was helping Avice in the manor kitchens, but somewhere in that dark house the carpenter must be sitting. Kay approached cautiously, skirting round a couple of urchins who were happily wrestling in the dust of the path, and knocked at the door.

There was no reply. Reluctant to try the door, Kay paced to the corner of the house and saw that built onto the back of it was a lean-to, partly open and sheltered by an overhanging roof. As Kay drew closer he saw a rack of tools hanging on the far wall, and realised that this must be the carpenter's workshop.

The carpenter sat on a stool beside his workbench. One

sleeve of his jerkin was tucked into his belt; with the other hand he beat out an insistent, repetitive rhythm on his knee. Kay could not see his face, for his head was bent. The hair was grey, thinning. On the floor at his feet were sawdust and curled wood shavings. A layer of dust lay over everything. As Kay drew closer he could see that the tools on the wall were blotched with rust.

"Good day," Kay said.

The carpenter's head jerked up. He looked at Kay for a few seconds out of ice-grey eyes, and then dropped his head again.

"They tell me you're the carpenter," Kay said. "What is your name?"

"Then they tell you wrong," the man snapped back, not answering the question. "What sort of carpenter has only one arm?"

"Your wife told me you were hurt at Roche Dure," Kay said, avoiding the question in his turn, for he had no answer to it.

"Aye. And I should have died at Roche Dure. There were plenty who did."

"Too many," Kay agreed.

That got him another flickering look, as if the carpenter had not expected him to say it. Encouraged, he repeated, "What is your name?"

The man jerked his head as if shaking a fly off it. "They call me Thomas."

"And I am Kay. I am Lord Meliant's steward."

This time the carpenter gave him a straight look, with nothing to temper the hostility in his eyes. "Aye. My wife told me so. Steward or no steward, you can take yourself off. I'll not serve the Breton's man."

Kay paused, thinking. After a moment the carpenter's gaze dropped, and he went back to the obsessive drumming on his knee.

"Thomas . . ." Kay said.

"I told you, I'll not serve the Breton, or any of his. I'll not take your orders." He stood up, and spat on the ground at Kay's feet. "Take yourself off."

Kay looked up at him. For the first time, he felt a hint of fear. The carpenter was a tall man, broad-shouldered, and even though he had only one arm, Kay was not sure he could save himself if it came to a fight. He was unarmed, and in any case he would not have drawn a weapon on any of the villagers. He realised that the fragile authority he was building could be utterly shattered if he took a public beating from the carpenter. He stood his ground.

"I have given you no orders," Kay said. "I came to ask you to serve—not me, or the Breton, but your own people."

There was a subtle change in the carpenter's stance. Kay breathed more easily.

"Do you think I don't want to?" Thomas said. "I know what's happening, better than you. Do you think you'd need to come here if I was a whole man? But my skill was in my hands, and now I've lost an arm, what can I do? Tell me that, steward. What can a one-armed carpenter do?"

The answer slid into Kay's mind as if all he had waited for was the right form of words. "He can teach."

For a few seconds the man stood immobile. Then he sank down onto the stool again. A formless sound of contempt came from him. But there had been that brief hesitation.

"Listen," Kay said. "Your skill was in your hands, true. But it's in your head as well. And there's nothing wrong with that. Or did Thomas the carpenter lose his wits when he lost his arm?"

The words were near enough an insult for Kay to feel misgivings about his own safety again, but the carpenter only made the same dismissive movement of his head.

"Teach?" he said. "Teach who? The men are all gone to the Breton's wars."

"Then you must teach those who are not men," Kay said. "But not yet. You need an apprentice."

He turned his head. Behind him on the path, the two boys were still locked into joyful combat. Kay felt himself beginning to smile. He walked over to them and inserted the toe of a booted foot into the place between the two intertwined bodies where he thought it would do most good. The boys broke apart and sat up, staring at him with identical gap-toothed grins from identical filthy faces.

"Get up," Kay said. "And get in there. Do as Master Thomas tells you. You're apprentices."

He was amazed that they obeyed, trotting unquestioningly into the workshop and standing one on each side of Thomas.

"Get them to start by cleaning your tools," Kay suggested.

"They can start by cleaning themselves."

The carpenter's voice was a growl, but there was a new energy in it. Kay did not wait to see the result of his experiment, but quietly left.

Kay spent another hour in the village, exchanging a few words with the villagers he met, all the while adding to the picture of the manor that was forming in his mind. He walked upstream as far as the mill, desolate now as the miller, like all the others, had been forced into the Breton's wars. Kay inspected the machinery. It was in good order; there would be no difficulty in getting it working again, but there was no corn for it to grind.

More depressing still was the other derelict house he found, that had once been the smithy. The forge was still intact, the tools were there, but there was no one to do the work. Kay felt that he was facing a blank wall. There were some problems that could not be solved, and this looked to be one of them. He needed a strong man with smith's skills, and there was none in the village.

The smithy was the last house on the far side of the village, near the edge of the forest. As Kay turned away, he heard someone calling his name, and saw Meliant emerging from the trees, followed by his men-at-arms and the hunting dogs. They had killed again; the deer was already flayed and slung on a pole between two of the men.

Kay waited for the huntsmen to come up with him, and fell in beside Meliant. "You had good sport, my lord?"

Meliant gave him a brilliant smile; he seemed in a better humour than Kay had seen lately.

"Very deferential, Kay! You play your new part well." He laughed. "I suppose we're to have company again at supper tonight."

"Indeed, my lord. Especially as you have furnished the feast."

They were drawing slowly closer to the centre of the village. Meliant reined in and looked around. Though the tumbledown houses were no different from how they had looked two days before, when Kay and Meliant had first arrived, there was a difference, in spirit if nothing else. The sense of watchful hostility was gone. Kay wondered if Meliant could sense it as he could himself.

"And how was your sport, Kay?" Meliant said. "Did you have good hunting at your Manor Court?"

"Excellent, my lord," Kay replied in the same vein. "I started a priest and a carpenter from their coverts. The only beast that eludes me now is a smith. The village has none."

Meliant shrugged, carelessly. "Then you must make do without."

Kay thought, but did not speak his thought, that it was easy enough to say, but harder to do. Meliant was not inconvenienced by houses falling down for lack of nails, or by all the equipment that must be awaiting repair. He did not think there was any point in protesting, and was ready to continue back to the manor house, when one of Meliant's men-at-arms said, "I can do smith's work, sir. It's my father's trade."

Meliant shot him a glance, good humour battling with exasperation. "Your job is to wield a sword, not to forge one," he said.

"But while we're waiting here, my lord . . . It couldn't do any harm." The man's fingers twitched on the reins.

Kay stepped up to his horse; he was a young man, muscular, with a fresh and eager face. Kay could see him as a smith much more easily than a warrior. "You would have my thanks," he said. "And the thanks of all the village. There's much to be done."

The man was looking at Meliant for permission. Meliant waved his hand. "Oh, go if you must. Go and play with the forge. But be ready to ride at an hour's notice when my lord Briant comes."

Already the man was dismounting, tossing his reins to one of the others. Kay walked back with him a little way to point out the smithy. The avid look the other gave the disused forge was almost laughable, if the need had not been so great.

"I'll get started right away, sir," he said, stripping off his gloves. "There's still an hour or two of daylight. I can get ready for tomorrow, at least."

Kay nodded, and clapped him on the shoulder. "I'll find you someone to work the bellows," he promised.

Kay was turning away when the man asked, "And what shall I make, sir?"

"Nails," Kay said. "Nails for repairs. Start with that."

On the following day, the people of the manor assembled in the chapel for the Silent Mass. Kay stood to greet them as they arrived. Avice, first of all. Estrildis, with two grown daughters, neat and modest looking. The bee-keeper, with a tiny girl, her hair flame red as her mother's. The fowler and his daughter. Thomas the carpenter—rather to Kay's surprise—and his wife. The pig woman with a whole brood of children, including the carpenter's two newly enrolled apprentices.

Kay had wondered whether Meliant would come to Mass, and what that would do to the presence of the Lady within him, but the young lord had ridden to the hunt as usual that morning. He had taken his men-at-arms with him, all but the smith, who arrived in chapel in a hurry, content and still flushed from the heat of the forge.

Last of all came Lady Alienor with her waiting woman. Kay could not help staring at the transformation. Instead of her rotting silks, she wore a gown of fine linen with embroidered flowers at wrists and throat. Her hair was brushed and shining.

There was warm laughter in her eyes as she gave Kay her hand and sank in a curtsey. "Do I please you now, my lord?" she said.

Kay found himself bending over her hand and touching it with his lips. "More than I have words for, lady."

He was thankful that at that moment Father Paulinus appeared to begin the service. The altar silver had been sent to Briant, but the candles burnt with a pure flame in their wooden holders. The chalice and paten were earthenware, a cup and plate from the manor kitchens. Avice had baked the bread that morning; the chalice was filled with mead.

Before Father Paulinus began the mass, he lit candles, and

sprinkled the chapel and the congregation with holy water from a rosemary sprig. Kay spoke a prayer for the driving back of evil. Then he served at the altar and led the responses.

Father Paulinus became more than himself, both remote and immediate, a figure clothed in dignity and light. The great symbols were present and real; many of the congregation were weeping. Refracted through tears, the earthenware cup could have been the Grail itself. The prayers of the Silent Mass rose up like the smoke of incense, and no one could doubt that God would stoop to hear.

Chapter Twenty-three

The manor house was built on the shore of an island, separated from the mainland by a short causeway. Behind the house were neglected gardens and an orchard, and beyond that, lightly wooded ground stretching down to the lake.

Kay was walking there among the trees, about a week after his arrival. He had begun in the orchard, assessing the state of the late apple crop; exchanged greetings with Clemence the beekeeper, who was doing something with the wintering colonies in the hives; had gone on to the lake with some idea of looking for a good place to site a fishing net; and now he was merely idle.

The sun had gone down; the surface of the lake was ridged steel. A faint breeze blew off the water. Kay halted, leant against a tree, and rested his forehead on his arm. If he kept busy, he could get through the days. It was in these quiet moments that the darkness would be on him with a bound, and he found himself looking down its throat.

He took a deep breath; another, and he could straighten up again. He must go back to the kitchens and see if Avice needed any help with the evening meal. He was turning towards the house when he heard a woman scream.

Kay raced through the trees and across the grass. Beside the beehives Clemence struggled with one of Meliant's men-at-arms. She screamed again, and her hands went for his eyes. Kay saw the man crash one hand across her face. Her little daughter sat in the grass, howling.

Kay shouted, but the man ignored him. He drew his belt knife, his only weapon, and flung himself forward, tearing at Clemence's attacker. The man pivoted, and fell on top of him, bearing him to the ground.

"Run!" Kay gasped, hoping Clemence could hear him. "The house—take the child. . . ."

He was pinned down, without space to wield the knife. He felt it snag on the man's leather jerkin, and slip sideways. Then the man was on him, a knee on his chest, one hand at his throat and the other gripping his wrist, pounding it against a stone so that he would let go the knife.

Kay writhed vainly. His adversary was more than a match for him in weight and reach. Kay could see his face, pouched and reddened with drinking, and hear the steady stream of obscenities that poured out of his mouth. A question flickered into Kay's mind, but as his air was cut off and his senses swam away he could not pursue it; all that was left to him of rational thought told him he was going to die.

He thought he could hear shouting and the thud of footsteps, but they were very far away. Then the weight on his chest, the constriction on his throat, eased so that he could breathe again. His vision cleared in time for him to see his adversary shambling away towards the house. Looking down at him were Clemence and Briant des Isles.

Briant had a broad grin on his face as he held out a hand to help Kay to his feet.

"Good evening, Kay," he said. "Why do I keep finding you in these . . . little difficulties?"

Kay ignored the question and the hand. He thrust himself to his knees, and then managed to gain his feet. He realised what had disturbed him about the man; he was not one of Meliant's, but a stranger. He must have come with Briant.

Coughing, Kay fought to speak. His voice rasped; his throat was painful. He forced disdain into his tone. "Have you no better control over your men, my lord Briant?"

Briant shrugged indulgently. "Men will be men, Kay, you know that."

"Not on any manor where I am steward."

Briant's eyes widened, and he laughed. "Where you are . . . is that Meliant's latest idea! Good God, the boy doesn't lack impudence. The High Seneschal of Britain, steward of his manor. . . ." He took no notice as Kay winced at the use of his old title, or perhaps he did not see it, and Kay hid his face by stooping to pick up the belt knife. "Then, Master Steward," Briant went on genially, "come up to the house and prepare some entertainment for your lord's guests."

All this while Clemence had stood silently by. She had pulled her torn gown around herself, and was soothing her daughter, whose wails had sunk to snuffling against her mother's shoulder. Now she stepped forward, looking up at Kay, and dropped him a curtsey. "Thank you, lord," she said softly.

She was gone, hurrying up the path between the trees before Kay could think of how to respond.

Briant guffawed and clapped Kay on the shoulder. "She'd give you, what she wouldn't give to my man."

Kay was astonished. "She's a decent woman," he said.

For some reason Briant seemed to find that even more amusing. He was laughing quietly to himself as he preceded Kay up the path. Kay had begun to follow before he found himself, against all expectation, shaken with desire for what Briant had just suggested. There would be warmth, and comfort. He would not be alone. Emphatically he shook his head. He had no right to make demands on a woman whom he had, perhaps, put under an obligation and who was under his authority, a woman he could never wed. But then, he reminded himself, disgraced as he was, no lady of stature would wed him. With someone like Clemence, though, there could be a little house, firelight on her hair. The child was surely young enough to turn to him. . . .

As he approached the postern gate in the manor's wall, Kay choked down all such foolish imaginings, and by the time he stepped through into the lighted courtyard, following Briant, he was the crisply efficient steward again.

"How many of your men must we feed and lodge, my lord?" he asked. "Our resources are few. We cannot support an army."

Briant was still chuckling. "No army. Just myself and half a dozen men. I've come to fetch Meliant. Maybe I'll be able to keep my word to him at last."

He strode off across the courtyard to the house door. Kay followed and caught him up on the threshold.

"What do you mean?" he said, grasping his arm. "Has Claudas sent you troops? Are you moving against Arthur?"

Briant shook off his hand. Briefly Kay glimpsed the cold undercurrents beneath the surface geniality.

"Don't speak of that," he said. "It doesn't concern you. I'll keep my word to you, too, Kay, and not ask you to ride with us. But yes—" He glanced along the passage; no one was in sight. "For your ears only: you may soon find Meliant's manor too small to hold you. Within a few days, you could be High Seneschal of Britain again."

Kay wanted to question Briant further, but at the supper table the Breton lord sat between Meliant and the lady Alienor, and Kay had to content himself with the company of Father Paulinus. At first the little priest had been pitifully frightened at Briant's return, though he grew calmer when he realised that their visitors were fighting men; the lady Brisane was not with them.

An extra table had been set up in the hall for Briant's men-at-arms. The men who had come with Meliant had joined them, all except for Yann, the young smith, who still sat among the villagers, with Estrildis and her two daughters—or to be more accurate, Kay thought, half smiling, with one of Estrildis' daughters. An excellent young man, Yann, and he wasted no time.

There was a more hostile atmosphere in the hall than Kay could remember, even on the first night. None of the villagers wanted Briant there, and no one, even Kay himself, was sure what he would do. They had begun to build; would Briant destroy it all again?

At the end of the meal, when the villagers were beginning to withdraw in sullen silence, Kay managed to speak to Briant. "Will you be staying long, my lord?"

The question meant: How long do we have to feed you? Kay doubted that Briant understood that, or that he would have cared if he had.

"I told you, Kay," he said, "I'm only here to fetch Meliant. We'll ride in the morning."

He turned away; Meliant and Alienor were waiting to conduct him to the solar. Kay caught him by the arm.

"My lord, you see how it is here. The food supplies are low, and there aren't enough men to do the heavy work. We need seed for the spring planting—"

"These are your affairs, Master Steward," Briant said, pulling his arm away. "Don't bother me with them. Besides, you've just set a decent meal on the table before your lord; you're managing very well."

"But don't you see—"

"You worry too much," Briant said indulgently. "In a few days the whole of Britain will be your storehouse. Ask me then, and you can have everything you want."

He went with Meliant then, leaving Kay standing by the door, looking after him in frustration. After a moment, he realised that Avice had joined him.

"Don't worry, sir," she said. "We'll see the back of them, that's the main thing. We'll come through, if they leave us alone."

She went back to her task of clearing the tables. Kay was mildly surprised. He had changed sides, he could see, in the way the villagers thought of him. He was not "the Breton's man" any longer. He was one of them, to stand or fall with them. Encouraged, he went to see what was happening in the kitchens.

Very early the next morning, Briant left with Meliant and the fighting men. No one bothered to inform Kay, but he was roused from sleep by the noise of their preparation. He pulled on his clothes and went down into the courtyard.

The men were already mounted. Meliant's horse fidgeted as the men formed up into a column; Meliant himself looked exultant, as if he could already feel his sword biting into Lancelot's flesh. Lady Alienor had come to bid him farewell, and stood close to his horse's head without even a cloak against the icy wind. Meliant paid no attention to her.

Kay's heart jolted as he saw that among the mounted men was Yann the smith. He supposed he should have expected it, but it was hard to accept. Yann had given them his work for so short a time; he had seemed to be fitting in, to be happy, and now he was riding away.

Kay walked over and stood beside his horse. "Yann, I'm sorry to see you go," he said.

The fresh face looking down at him was distressed. "It's not my choice, sir," he said. "I'd stay if I could. I asked my lord Briant, and he called me coward." He reddened. "You know it's not that, sir."

Kay murmured agreement. He turned to Briant, to see if his pleas would do any good; the Breton lord was already listening.

He shook his head. "Don't ask, Kay. The answer is no. I need every man I can get."

"And we need his skills—" Kay began, but his voice was drowned as Briant, wheeling his horse, yelled an order for the gates to be opened.

"I'll come back, sir," Yann said, leaning over urgently towards Kay. "If I live, I'll come back."

Kay clasped his hand and stood back. The two men who had pulled open the gates remounted; the column formed up and began to trot across the causeway. At the last second, Meliant stooped and said a word to Alienor before he set his mount in motion. Kay crossed the courtyard and stood at Alienor's side to watch them go.

As they crossed the causeway and entered the strip of forest between the manor and the village, they met some of the villagers on their way to Mass. Kay saw Estrildis and her daughters; one of the girls caught at Yann's bridle and ran beside his horse for a few paces. He leaned over to talk to her. She had to turn back, and as she approached the house Kay could see that she wept. Kay took Alienor's hand and escorted her into the house.

After the first day, Mass had been celebrated in the early morning, before the villagers went to work. As they gathered now, Kay could sense their disturbance. He felt disturbed himself, and wondered if they could see the future as he saw it.

When Mass was over, he stood on the sanctuary steps and spoke to them before they left the chapel.

"My lord Briant rides to battle against Arthur, and no one can tell what the result of that battle will be. If Briant wins—" he lifted his shoulders in a shrug more eloquent than his words "—if Briant wins, then there will be no law left in Britain. If Arthur wins, as I pray to God he will, then Briant's men will be hunted across country, with nowhere to flee to, except perhaps Roche Dure. And we lie on the route from Carlisle to Roche Dure." He held out his hands. "We are not safe any longer."

They were silent for a moment, exchanging glances. To his relief, no one looked ready to panic.

"What shall we do, sir?" Clemence asked.

"We cannot fight," Kay said. "I am the only one here who is trained, and truly my reputation was never great. It would be better for you if you had Sir Lancelot here with you now."

There was a ripple of warm laughter; Kay was startled, for he had not thought he had said anything amusing.

Out of the murmur came Estrildis' voice. "I'll fight. I'd slit the Breton's throat without thinking twice."

Kay smiled. "Indeed, mistress, I believe you would. And in the end it may come to that. But we may try better ways of defending ourselves."

"What ways?" Avice asked.

"Abandon the village."

Kay raised a hand to still the instinctive protest that broke out; to his astonishment, the villagers grew quiet at once.

"We can't defend the village," he explained, "but we can defend this manor house. If we bar the gate to the causeway, then we should be safe. We're not expecting an army. If they come, they'll be in ones and twos, small groups at most. If they're fleeing, they won't have time to break in, and I doubt they'll be eager to swim the lake."

He came down from the steps and moved among his people in the body of the chapel.

"We have twenty-four hours, maybe more," he said. "Avice, have all the food moved into the storerooms here. Clemence, whatever you need for your bees. And livestock—Ursula, you can pasture your pigs in the orchard. All of you, bring clothes and blankets and anything else you need. Tools—there may be work we can do. And anything we can use for weapons."

"If they do break in, they'll wish they hadn't." That was Estrildis' daughter, the one who had wept to part from Yann.

Kay reached out to her and took her hand. "Truly, mistress, they will."

They were all round him then, warm, supporting, one with him. Kay felt his throat tighten, and struggled not to show weakness now.

"Go, then," he said. "By nightfall I want us all back here, safe under one roof."

All that day, a line of bowed figures, bundles on their shoulders, trudged through the trees from the village and across the causeway to the manor house. Lady Alienor welcomed each of them as if they were noble guests, while Kay showed them where they could sleep; there was enough space for each family to have a room of their own. They settled in cheerfully enough. Though the house was bare and comfortless, the stone walls kept out the weather better than the mud and wattle and wood of the village houses. As if to remind everyone of that, it grew colder, and a thin sleet whipped down.

The food stores were moved, and the livestock. Ursula and her brood drove the pigs across the causeway, and for a while the courtyard became a sea of long, squealing bodies, until she managed to coax them round the house and out through the postern. A couple of goats and a wire coop of chickens followed more sedately. Kay had put extra bedding down in the stable, empty now except for Morial. He stood for a moment stroking Morial's nose, and feeding him with a windfall apple, imagining that he could see a thoroughbred disdain in his mount's face.

"Never mind, Morial," he murmured. "It won't be for long." He added silently, "It had better not."

Thomas the carpenter put himself in charge of gathering weapons, and later in the day exhibited his armoury for Kay's approval. A business-like collection of staves, long knives, daggers. Best of all, three bows, with their quivers of arrows.

"For hunting, like," Thomas said.

He did not explain what the villagers had been hunting, or whether they had their lord's leave, and Kay did not ask. He took the bows to the room above the main gates, where, he decided, there must always be someone on watch who knew how to use them. The forest end of the causeway was well within bowshot; a well-placed arrow would discourage most unwanted visitors.

Kay armed himself once more with Gareth's sword; he thought his former friend would not mind its being used in this urgent need. He went round distributing weapons so that each family was armed, and made sure there was at least one person in each who knew what to do and was prepared to do it.

He permitted himself a grim smile as he wondered what Sir Lancelot would think of Kay giving weapons instruction.

By that night, as he had hoped, everyone was settled in the manor house. Kay went to bed with his mind whirling over everything still to do. From the next morning he must set a watch; he must draw up a list of duties so that everyone had something to do and no one had time to worry. He must speak to Avice about rations of food and fuel. Towards morning he managed to snatch a little sleep, only to dream of trampling feet and the clash of swords.

He rose in time for Mass. Feeling tired himself, he was surprised to see how bright-eyed and optimistic his people were. They crowded into the chapel, even those who had not attended before. Father Paulinus began the service.

Kay, who had given up the altar serving to one of the younger women, tried to keep his mind on the ceremony. It was quite possible that even now Arthur and Briant were joined in battle, and the future of Britain was being decided. Kay prayed earnestly for Arthur's victory. His mind was so turned inwards imagining that battle that at first he did not think it strange when the silence of the chapel was cut by a scream.

Lady Alienor, kneeling at the sanctuary steps to receive the sacrament, had flung herself backwards. She writhed on the flagstones, her head whipping from side to side, her lips snarling. In consternation her waiting woman bent over her, trying to catch at her hands, but Alienor threw her off. She kept on screaming; her lips were flecked with blood and foam.

Pulling himself back to reality, Kay knelt beside her, and tried to raise her head. He could not account for this. This mad fit was not Alienor; her strangeness was gentle and kind. Yet now her arms were flailing and, as he bent over her, the nails of one hand scored across his face. He jerked back, barely saving his eyes, and saw the fingers crooked into talons. Claws flexed like a cat's.

Ice formed round Kay's heart. Bending over, he saw the Lady's cold eyes like a shifting veil over Alienor's own clear gaze. She had stopped screaming now; harsh splinters of sound were coming from her, interspersed with a pure, melodic bubbling.

"No," Kay whispered. "Dear God, no."

Alienor's woman was still vainly trying to catch hold of her. Around her the villagers clustered, their faces white and frightened. The two who stood closest gave backwards as Father Paulinus pushed between them. He had the earthenware chalice in his hand; stooping, he spilt some of the consecrated mead into Alienor's gaping mouth.

The presence within her howled. The lips spat. Her body arched in a spasm of agony. Her hand lashed out and caught the pectoral cross that hung from Father Paulinus' neck as he bent over her.

Kay half expected the grasp to splinter the wood or blacken it. But the fingers closed gently, Alienor's hand again. Her body went limp. She let out a great sigh, and let her head fall back on to Kay's knees. Her eyes closed. There was silence.

Father Paulinus slipped the cross from his neck so that Alienor could go on holding it. His lips moved in a rapid prayer as he traced the sign of the cross over her. Her eyes opened again—clear, blue, untroubled, and then, as she focused on the frightened faces around her, flooded suddenly with intelligence. Kay drew a painful breath.

"Lady?" her waiting woman said uncertainly.

Alienor sat up, and pushed back her dishevelled hair. "My brother is dead," she said, "and thinks no more of vengeance. Father Paulinus, Kay, will you help me to bury my father?"

Chapter Twenty-four

When dawn came it was dull, with cloud low on the hills. Freezing wisps of it fingered their way through the edge of the trees where Sir Gawain stood waiting, a hand on the bridle of his horse. The men under his command were bunched beside and behind him. In the valley bottom a stream tracked through sedge, and the road wound alongside it. There was no sign yet of the approach of Briant des Isles and his men.

The peace embassy had been a failure in the end. There had been nothing but letters sent back and forth, offers and suggestions from Briant that had ended in defiance after all. Arthur's scouts had reported fresh troops arriving at Roche Dure by sea, and now everyone could understand that Briant had never truly wanted peace; he had just been wasting time until his reinforcements could arrive. Now he was marching on Carlisle.

From his vantage point on the hillside, Gawain could see Arthur and the main body of his troops, drawn up across the end of the valley. As he watched there was a stir of movement, as the knights mounted. Gawain felt his breath come faster. Perhaps a scout had brought word that Briant was close by, but as yet he had not come into sight.

Gawain could make out Arthur in the centre of the line, and beside him Lancelot, bearing the great Pendragon banner, scarlet and gold. Gawain suppressed a pang of regret as he remembered that the king's standard bearer had once been Kay.

Farther down the valley, visible to Gawain but hidden from the road by rocks and thickets of gorse, were Gaheris and his archers. They crouched motionless, all their attention on the road where Briant would appear.

On the opposite slope, concealed like Gawain and his men by the edge of the trees, was another band of horsemen led by Bedivere, who stood watching the road below. As Briant marched north, he would see his way blocked by Arthur and his men. But before he could reach them he would be exposed to Gaheris' arrow storm. Gawain's orders, with Bedivere, were to hold back until battle in the valley was fairly joined, and then attack Briant's troops from the rear.

The rattle of a bridle just beside him startled him; he turned to see Gareth leading up his horse.

"Any sign?" Gareth did not wait for an answer. "Do you think he's with them?"

"Kay?" There was no real need for Gawain to ask that. He shook his head uneasily. "If he's sworn to Briant . . ."

Gareth made an impatient sound. His voice muffled, he said, "He could never swear oath to Briant, not in his heart."

Gawain sighed. The raw cold of the morning mist was eating into him. There was nothing he could say. Instead he reached out and touched Gareth on the arm, but it was an empty comfort he had to offer.

"I wish I could have spoken to Kay again," Gareth said, his face averted. "I should have liked to tell him . . ." His voice trailed off.

Gently, Gawain said, "Kay already knows anything you could possibly want to tell him."

"After the way I treated him at Roche Dure!"

"Even so."

Gareth had come back from Roche Dure in an agony of guilt, and he had not managed to throw it off. Gawain wished he had been chosen to go instead. Gareth, as it turned out, had been the wrong person: too inexperienced, too emotional, and respecting Lancelot enough to follow his lead, even if his heart told him something else. And yet, Gawain thought, was he being arrogant to think that he would have handled the meeting any better?

"I scarcely spoke to him," Gareth said, voicing his regrets as he had done so often since his return. "I wouldn't take his hand."

"Kay would know why."

"I know why!" Gareth snapped back at him. He flung his head up, flame in his eyes. "Because I put honour before friendship, because I was thinking about my own loyalties. I could see what he was feeling—and I still failed him."

"Kay would understand," Gawain repeated.

Gareth shook his head, the fire going out of him. "I don't want it to end like this." He put a hand on the hilt of his sword. "This is Kay's."

"He bears yours," Gawain reminded him. "It isn't ending."

"And if I have to use it to kill him?" Gareth asked bitterly.

Gawain found no reply to that.

All the while they had been talking, Gawain had kept watch on the road. Watching—waiting. . . . He swallowed a tightness in his throat and prayed for something to happen.

Then he was aware of a ripple of tension passing across the men in the valley, an added alertness, and saw round the curve of the road the first of Briant's troops. Even at that distance, he could make out Briant, openly wearing the dragon surcoat he had usurped from Arthur, but none of the other leading horsemen was familiar to him. He did not see Kay's black and silver, or anyone wearing a plain white surcoat.

He heard Gareth mutter, "Where is Kay?"

A sick feeling began to gather in Gawain's stomach, more than his usual tension at the start of a battle. They had set their trap and Briant seemed to be riding into it, but perhaps this was a feint; perhaps there were other troops working round to come upon them from behind, or some further treachery they had not seen, but surely Kay could not be behind it? Gawain could not believe it, but he was desperate to be on the move, because then he would not have to go on thinking.

Briant's column drew closer. They had seen Arthur now; Gawain saw Briant gesture, and the column deployed into a line. The pace quickened. Faintly now he could hear the thunder of the horses' hooves and the cries of their riders.

Gawain gave the order to mount and manoeuvred himself next to Gareth. He remembered Kay, in his bitterness, saying that if he had to be slaughtered, he would prefer to choose his company. Gawain knew what he meant.

Arthur's line, horsemen and foot soldiers, still stood firm. For a few seconds it looked as if Briant's troops would trample them down. Then the archers let fly their arrows. Gawain was too far off to hear the twang of bows or see the arrows in flight, but he imagined both as he saw Briant's well-disciplined charge begin to break up. Men were falling, and horses, getting in the way of others. Riders on the flanks tried to bunch into the centre of the valley. The line became ragged, its impetus gone.

Briant's foot soldiers, left behind as the horsemen charged, were battered by the arrow storm. Some dived for cover; others tried to flee back the way they had come. Few of them tried to retaliate, and even those with bows or throwing spears could not hit targets farther up the slope and protected by the rocks and gorse. Gawain could hear their screaming.

When Briant's line hit Arthur's it was like a wave smashing into a rock: all scattered fury, but the rock stands firm. Almost at once, Arthur's line began to curve, to encircle Briant and his men. For a few seconds, Gawain saw the battle almost as he believed the king and Lancelot saw it, as a great pattern, almost a dance.

Across the valley he could see Bedivere, mounted and ready, and felt his impatience like a rope tugging at him. But it was for Gawain to give the order. He knew he had to hold back until the arrow storm had done its work, because once the attack began from the rear the archers would risk hitting their own men.

He held back. Strategy—prudence—cowardice? Gawain's mind reeled. Below, the foot soldiers had scattered, some into cover, some managing to come up with the main conflict that now swayed back and forth along the valley bottom, some frankly fleeing. The road and the turf beside it were littered with bodies. Gawain took a breath. He drew his sword, raised it, and brought

Exiled From Camelot

it flashing down. Across the valley, Bedivere and his men poured down the slope. Gawain set spurs to his horse and led out his own men.

The valley rushed up to meet him. He caught glimpses of one or two faces, stupid with terror, as he rode over foot soldiers on the edge of the conflict. An arm, swinging a spear; he slashed at it and never saw what happened in the downward rush.

As they reached the stream, his men drove like a wedge into the rear of Briant's troops. Gawain galloped through the water, his horse's hooves throwing up spray, as the line of his adversaries broke in front of him. He found himself beginning to climb the further slope. Within seconds the press of men halted him; a quick glance behind showed him that he was hemmed in. His sword jarred against the sword of an enemy knight as he flung it up to defend himself.

The pattern was shattered now. Behind Gawain was a heaving mass of men, churning the stream and its banks to a morass as they fought and died. Their screams and the clash of weapons pressed up against him like a smothering blanket; his stomach heaved at the stench of blood. His own fear darkened his eyes, and what he did was automatic, as if something else had taken over his body and animated it. He lost all sense of time passing; this could be an eternity, hell itself, and there would be no escape from it.

Gawain could see no one he knew. He thought he had overreached himself, cut himself off from his own side so that his enemies could surround him and pull him down. But soon he became aware of Gareth, thrusting forward at his shoulder, yelling something that Gawain could not catch; then he saw ahead of him a mounted knight, his sword already shearing the air towards him.

The shining blade seemed slow, like movement in water, and Gawain felt that he had all eternity to raise his own sword and parry it. The sound of the battle pulsed faint and distant. In the last second he snapped back to awareness, twisted sideways out of the line of the blow, and drove his own sword forward beneath his enemy's shield. The knight doubled over, slid from his horse, and crashed to the ground among the flailing hooves.

Gareth pushed up his own horse next to Gawain's, urging him to the edge of the skirmish. "Never do that to me again."

Gawain caught his breath. The press of the fight was thinning out. He looked around him and realised that the battle was as good as over. Now Briant's men were scattering along the banks of the stream in both directions. Here and there little knots of them were locked into separate skirmishes, but all the while giving backwards; it was flight they had in mind. Arthur's men let them go.

Only the fighting at what had been the centre of the lines continued. Arthur and Briant clashed together in the middle of the stream; on the far bank, Lancelot fought with another mounted knight.

Gawain picked his way down the hillside towards them, but as he drew closer, along with Gareth and some of the others, he heard Arthur shout, "Keep back! Briant is mine!"

Gawain drew rein. He was still alert, his sword still in his hand, but all their adversaries had melted away.

Gaheris, who must have mounted and joined the battle once his archers had done their part, brought his horse to a standstill beside him and said, "It's all over. What does Briant think he's doing?"

Gawain could not answer the question. With Gaheris and Gareth, he watched the fight. Arthur had the end of Briant's shattered spear dangling from his shield; now they fought with swords, manoeuvring their horses in a tight circle to stay within reach of each other. Gawain felt as if he watched a display of skill instead of a mortal combat.

He was not in any real doubt about the outcome. Briant would have to be a finer warrior than he was to be a match for Arthur. Gawain could not see why Briant did not yield, for even if he killed Arthur now he must know that he would never leave the battlefield alive.

When the end came, it was quick. Arthur pressed Briant back, along the bed of the stream. Briant's horse slipped on a loose stone and went down, rolling over Briant, who could not scramble clear in time. He lay in the stream, struggling to rise, while the horse pulled itself up the far bank. When Arthur leapt down beside Briant, his sword raised, Briant reached out a hand, at last, in a gesture of surrender.

Gawain sheathed his sword, breathing a prayer of thankfulness. It was over, except for where Lancelot still fought his unknown adversary.

Their fight had taken them farther upstream. Leaving the others to deal with Briant, Gawain set out towards them, following the stream up the valley where Arthur's men were already beginning to regroup. He would take word of the surrender; he might be able to save the life of Lancelot's opponent. He had time to be surprised that the pair still fought. The unknown must be a fine knight to hold Lancelot for so long.

When Gawain approached, the sight turned him sick. Lancelot's opponent had a spear through his body, a body mantled in its own blood. The wounded man reeled in the saddle, but he still fought on. His strokes were weak and wild, and Lancelot parried them easily, forcing him steadily backwards.

Gawain heard Lancelot shout, "Yield to me!"

Exiled From Camelot

If there was a reply, Gawain did not hear it, but there was no sign that the warrior meant to give up the struggle, hopeless as it was.

"Lancelot!" Gawain cried out. "Briant has surrendered!"

Even as he called, Lancelot raised his sword to strike. Gawain was not sure if he had heard, or was aware of anything except the rhythm of the fight and his adversary's broken body. Or perhaps it was too late for him to hold back the stroke. His sword scythed down through the knight's shoulder to the ribs, a cut so deep that the shards of the broken spear fell away. The knight swayed and collapsed out of the saddle. Gawain was beside him as he hit the ground.

Lancelot had trotted his horse round in a wide circle and came up again as Gawain eased the helmet from his opponent's head. He was a young man, with silver-gold hair and a wild, beautiful face. Incredibly he lived; the sea-green eyes were open and he tried to get up.

Gawain found his hand and held it. "Lie still," he said. "You fought well. It's over."

"No!" the young man spat out. "Never over. Not until Lancelot lies dead."

Gawain glanced up at Lancelot, who had dismounted now and stood beside him. He was remembering what Gareth had told him about their visit to Roche Dure, and a young man who had challenged Lancelot.

Now Lancelot had his familiar closed-in look, revealing nothing. "Meliant, I didn't want this," he said. "I would have had peace with you."

"Peace!" It was as if his hatred was all that gave Meliant strength. "Did you speak of peace to my dead father?"

"I am sorry," Lancelot said. "I would have done penance. I can do no more."

Others gathered now. The only one Gawain really noticed was one of Arthur's men-at-arms, who knelt at Meliant's other side and held out a water skin. Gawain took it and raised Meliant's head; blood surged from his ruined side. The dying man drank, coughing weakly.

"Meliant, give up this hatred," Gawain said. "Make your peace with God."

The glazing eyes focused on him and for an instant Gawain thought he saw something else in their depths, a flicker of something cold, alert, and self-possessed.

"God?" Meliant said. "I renounced God."

Gawain drew a breath of horror and pity. "What do you mean?"

Instead of answering, Meliant raised a hand to Gawain's shoulder, the fingers crooked like claws. He drew his nails down

Gawain's surcoat, the lightest of touches, but the fabric slit as they passed. A five-fold gash. Gawain shuddered.

"The Lady promised me vengeance," Meliant said piteously. "She cheated me. Lancelot lives." A sob escaped him. "No way back. . . ."

Gawain crouched over him. He knew that there was nothing a healer could do here; what Meliant needed was a priest.

"God has not renounced you," he said urgently. "It's not too late. Make your peace—but quickly."

The young man's eyes focused on him again, clouding now with the approach of death, but free, Gawain thought, of that other watchful presence. Meliant said, the words breathed out on an exhausted sigh, "I will. . . ."

His body arched. He clutched at Gawain, who held him in a hard embrace. A cry was torn out of him, and then he relaxed. He said, very clearly, "Alienor."

Then blood gushed from his mouth and he died.

Gawain looked up and saw a circle of men surrounding him: Arthur, Gareth supporting Briant, Gaheris, Bedivere. . . . Their faces blurred. He got to his feet and swayed as the hillside lurched round him. He felt a hand under his elbow, steadying him: Lancelot's. For a minute Gawain leant against him, grateful for the support.

"He fought well," Lancelot said. Gawain knew it was the best epitaph he could give. "For a while there," Lancelot went on meditatively, "it was as if I fought some—some clawed thing, not a man at all. I could see its eyes. I never want to see the like again."

He fingered the shredded fabric of Gawain's surcoat, and shook his head, confused at first, and then dismissively. "Are you all right?" Lancelot asked. "I must attend the king."

Gawain nodded. When Lancelot had gone, he stumbled down to the stream and dropped to his knees in the midst of it. He pulled off his helmet and poured water over himself, trying to wash away the gouts of Meliant's blood. It was no colder than the sweat that broke out all over his body. As he fought back a spinning darkness, willing himself not to faint, he remembered that Kay in his nightmare had screamed out something about the Lady.

Chapter Twenty-Five

"He'll do, sir. Let him sleep now." The healer drew Sir Gawain out into the passage; Gawain caught a final glimpse of Briant des Isles, shifting restlessly among the bed-furs, before the door closed.

"Just as well," the healer said, "that Arthur doesn't fling his enemies into the dungeons."

He was the same grizzled, elderly man who had helped Gawain to care for Kay. Now he had set the broken bone in Briant's leg with the same efficiency, though disapproval came off him in waves, as it had since Arthur returned from battle earlier that day with Briant as his prisoner. "I'd appreciate it, sir, if you could look in on him later tonight," the healer said. "I've got the rest of the wounded to see to in the infirmary."

He set off down the passage. Gawain walked beside him, murmuring agreement.

"I'll find a servant to sit with him. Or a guard. Someone who'll make sure he stays where we've put him."

The healer gave him a sharp smile. "You don't trust Lord Briant, sir? No more do I—but he won't be going anywhere for a while yet."

Gawain sighed. "That's what I don't like. If he were whole, we could put him on the next ship for Brittany and be rid of him. As it is—Arthur won't turn out a wounded man, even his enemy. Briant has a claim on our hospitality for as long as he needs it."

The healer sniffed. "And no longer than needed," he said as they paused at the foot of the stairs that would take him to the infirmary. "But he'll not walk on that leg inside a week, nor a fortnight neither. His horse rolled on him. He's lucky to be alive."

He gave another sniff and disappeared up the stairs. Gawain strolled on down the passage. It was late now, on the day of the battle; Arthur and his men were already settled again at Carlisle. Gawain had missed the evening meal because he had thought he should go and make sure that Briant was being cared for. He was tired; he would beg some supper from the kitchens, and then go to bed.

As Gawain continued down the deserted passages, the healer's last words repeated themselves in his mind. It went hard with him to wish any man dead, but if anyone had courted death in battle it was Briant des Isles. Alive, even though he was injured and a prisoner, Gawain found it hard to trust him.

He called in at the guard room and arranged for a man to watch Briant, and then went to the kitchens, where a maidservant found him bread and cold meat and apples, and had to be dissuaded from carrying the tray to his rooms. While he was eating at his own fireside he still went on turning over in his mind a whole series of vague anxieties, none of them definite enough to put into words. At last he had to admit to himself that he was using Briant to stop himself thinking about something else.

Meliant. The young man Lancelot had killed. An uncanny death. Gawain shivered as he remembered the cold presence in his eyes. Had he turned to God at the last? Gawain caught his mind veering away again, and focused it on what he knew he had to consider.

The Lady. Meliant had said that the Lady had promised him vengeance. Was that his name for the evil within him? Kay had named her, too. Gawain shivered. It could not be—he would not believe it—that Kay had allowed the evil to enter him.

Gawain remembered the five-fold gash from Kay's throat and across his chest, the wound that had been so hard to heal. Meliant had shredded Gawain's surcoat; perhaps if he had not been so enfeebled, at the point of death, or if Gawain had not been wearing mail, he would by now be bearing a wound like Kay's. Perhaps Meliant had been Kay's torturer. Gawain found he would rather think of Kay as the victim of evil than a partner in it. He murmured a short prayer.

Although he sat alone until the fire burned down and the lamp guttered, he found no answer to any of his questions. The rest of the court, he knew, was celebrating victory. Gawain wished he could join them, but he knew in his heart that victory was still a long way off.

Several days later, while the court assembled for the evening meal, there was a stir of movement at the main doors of the hall that heralded the arrival of a guest. Gawain, already seated at the high table, felt a jolt of apprehension. This was a favourite time for visitors and petitioners, who could be sure of gaining the ear of the king, but with the country at war there had been no one since the All Hallows' Court, when the young votaress had appeared bearing the casket that held Loholt's head.

Unwillingly alert, Gawain watched as the steward halted the sewers with their dishes and came forward himself into the space between the tables.

"My lord," he said to the king, "the lady Brisane of Roche Dure begs to enter your presence."

He looked sour as he said it; Gawain could understand why. It sounded as if the lady claimed a title she had no right to. Her humble approach would have been more convincing without it.

"Let her come in," Arthur said. "You know that no one is barred from my presence at this time."

His voice was flat and expressionless, as if he repeated a formula he did not believe. Gawain's heart tore for him. Ever since All Hallows, Arthur had been tired and remote. Even victory over Briant had done nothing to change him. Everyone said he grieved for Loholt; Gawain wondered if he also grieved for Kay.

The steward left the hall again; Gawain watched curiously as the lady Brisane made her entrance. She was a tall and slender woman, with a lustrous fall of black hair. Supremely beautiful, and yet she used no arts for beauty. She wore nothing but a garment of coarse wool, dead black, tied with a rope girdle. Her head and her feet were bare, and the wide sleeves fell back from bare, white arms. She had no jewels. Unworthily, perhaps, Gawain wondered if she knew how well this penitential austerity set off her flawless loveliness.

She paced down the length of the hall until she stood before the high table, and then prostrated herself in front of Arthur, face down on the flagstones, with her arms spread wide.

"My lord, I beg your pity," she said.

Arthur was jerked out of his apathy; there was pity and wonder in his voice as he said, "Rise, lady. I will have no one so noble abase herself before me."

The lady rose, but only as far as her knees, and held out her hands beseechingly. "My king, I will not rise from here until you grant forgiveness to my lord Briant des Isles."

Gawain was distracted from the king's reply by the arrival of Gareth, who had come rather late to the meal and now skirted the tables beside the wall and slid breathlessly into his place. He reached out and gripped Gawain's wrist. "Gawain—Briant's lady," he said.

Gawain nodded, still looking at the lady and not at his brother. "You saw her at Roche Dure?"

"Yes—I told you. Gawain, Kay said she is evil."

He made the accusation in a low voice; Gawain did not think that anyone else would have heard it, but he put a hand over Gareth's for a moment, a gesture for silence.

"They tell me," the lady was continuing, "that my lord Briant is your prisoner, and wounded. My lord, I beg you not to take revenge on an injured man, who can do you no more harm. Forgive him so far as to let me stay here and care for him, even if I must share his imprisonment."

Her distress and her beauty was having their effects; Gawain could hear a low murmur of pity arising in the hall, almost as if the knights gathered there might really believe Arthur was the tyrant she painted him. Arthur's own face showed nothing but sympathy.

"Lady, there is no need for this," he said. "Get up, I beg you. Your lord Briant is lodged here as well as I, and cared for by my own healers. Sir Gawain himself has made sure of his comfort."

Still on her knees, the lady Brisane turned her gaze on Gawain, all tremulous hope now. Gawain wanted to pity her and reassure her, but he could not stifle the suspicions roused by Gareth, and through Gareth, Kay.

He rose in his place and bowed to her. "True, lady. Your lord is well cared for. He was not wounded in the battle, but he broke his leg when he fell from his horse. The bone has been set, and mends well, the healers tell me."

Brisane let out a long sigh of relief. "And I may see him?"

"Of course." It was Arthur who replied, and Gawain was glad to reseat himself. "You may stay here as our guest for as long as you choose, until your lord is well again. Do you wish to go to him now, or will you sit here and take supper with us?"

Rather surprisingly, in Gawain's view, the lady elected to stay for the meal. Lancelot himself came to raise her to her feet and escorted her to a seat between himself and the king. Conversation started up again as the steward sent the servingmen into the hall and the meal began.

Gareth still frowned, a strained look on his usually cheerful face. "Kay thinks she is evil," he repeated, still with the good sense to keep his voice a murmur for Gawain's ears alone. "I told you what he said. She means to destroy Arthur by destroying his chief men: Lancelot, and Kay, and you."

Gawain nodded, remembering Gareth's outpouring when he returned from Roche Dure. "She has done nothing to harm me," he said.

"Yet."

Gareth took the cup a page offered him and gulped the wine.

"Kay said she was with Lady Elaine when she visited Camelot. He said she was the votaress who brought the casket. He begged me to warn you—"

His voice was rising. Gawain signed him to silence again.

"And you have. But you saw this lady at Roche Dure. Do you believe what Kay said about her?"

Gareth's shoulders slumped. "I don't know. I don't think Kay was lying. But I don't know if he was right."

Gawain rested a hand briefly on his arm. Glancing along the table, he could see the lady Brisane as she talked with Lancelot and the king. Lancelot's austere face was alight, so that Gawain reflected it was as well Guenevere could not see him. Even Arthur was more animated than Gawain had seen him since word had come of Loholt's death.

The lady Brisane. Gawain startled himself with the form of words. The lady Brisane . . . the Lady. Could it be? Could she have terrified Kay, and sent that cold intrusion into Meliant's eyes? There was no sign of it now, no sign of anything but graciousness and courtesy. Yet Kay had said she could change form.

Gawain felt cold fear fastening round his heart. Yet he knew that whatever he himself might suspect about the lady Brisane, there was no point in voicing his suspicions. No one else in the court, except for Gareth, was likely to believe him.

After Brisane's coming, time seemed to drag at Carlisle. The year waned. Gawain had hoped for a swift return to Camelot, but Arthur did not make the decision to move the court, and after a few days snow set in, closing the roads. Gawain suspected that they were to remain immured in Carlisle for the winter.

When he thought about Arthur's reasons for being so indecisive, his uneasiness increased. The king had never really thrown off his grief, though now he had stopped speaking of Loholt, as if he tried to cut out of his life the few brief weeks when he had a son. Gawain had never heard him mention Kay at all.

He wondered if Arthur felt that returning to Camelot would be the final acknowledgement that all was over and he must take up his life again. If so, Gawain could understand the delay. But he was afraid that there was another reason, that Arthur remained in Carlisle because Briant could not leave, and where Briant was, there also was Brisane.

Gawain did not imagine that Arthur loved the lady. Nothing so crude. But with her he lost his abstraction; she could charm him into smiling. By the time that Briant was well enough to get around the court on crutches, his status as prisoner had drifted imperceptibly into that of guest.

Christmas came and brought more snow, piling in the courtyards and against the gates and shutters. Now it was impossible to leave the castle, even to ride or to hunt, let alone travel for any distance. Lamps burned throughout the day.

Because of the weather there were no guests for the festivals of Christmas and New Year. The castle was quiet. Gawain could not help remembering that these were the first great courts without Kay. Although the seneschal had professed impatience, his attention to detail meant that everything ran smoothly. The Carlisle steward did his best, but he did not have Kay's genius for timing, or for unfolding small surprises and a variety of entertainments during the days of festival.

On New Year's Day, Gawain went looking for Gareth in his rooms, and found him with the shutters flung wide and the room icy; he stared out at the eddying snow.

"Gareth," Gawain said gently.

Gareth did not turn or look at him. "I want to go home," he said, his voice stifled. "I want Lionors. I'm worried about her—

about our child. I can't even send word." He swung round fiercely on Gawain; tears glittered on his face. "I want Kay back! I want everything as it used to be!"

Gawain went to him and embraced him. "I know."

After a moment Gareth pulled away from him, scrubbing at his eyes with his sleeve as if he were still a small boy. "I'm sorry," he said. "I'm sorry to be such a fool."

Gawain closed the shutters. "You're not," he said. "I want all that, too. I pray to God for it. But I can't see how it can ever be."

Briskly, trying to smile, he turned back into the room. "Lancelot sent me to look for you. He's arranging an archery contest in the Long Gallery. I thought I might risk a bet on you."

Gareth shook his head. "No. What's the point of pretending?"

Gawain put an arm round his shoulders. "Please. It will help the king." He listened to Gareth's long sigh, and took it for acquiescence. "Go and wash your face," he said. "I'll wait for you."

At one end of the Long Gallery, Lancelot had set up a target. A small group of the knights—Gaheris and Griflet and Bedivere among them—clustered at the other end with bows in their hands. Gawain saw with surprise that Briant des Isles was with them.

The Breton lord had abandoned his crutches some days before, and now needed only a stick for support. He was well enough to ride; he could have left but for the snow. None of that was news to Gawain, but he was still disturbed to see Briant taking his place among Arthur's knights.

In an alcove about half the way along the gallery, Arthur was seated with Brisane. Since her arrival she had abandoned her penitent's gown; now she wore a robe of warm red velvet, trimmed with sables. Jewels glittered on her hands and at her throat. She leant close to the king, smiling, gesturing towards the knights at the bottom of the hall.

Gawain approached and bowed, with Gareth, still reluctant, a pace behind.

"My lord Gawain!" Brisane stretched out her hand welcomingly; Gawain bent over it and touched it with his lips. "Have you come to take part in this contest?"

Gawain shrugged slightly. "If it please you, lady. But I've never pretended to skill with a bow. Gareth here would tell you that I can't hit a barn from the inside."

He glanced at Gareth as he spoke. His brother gave him no help; his sombre features showed no sign of saying anything even faintly amusing. He nodded curtly to Brisane, and strode down the gallery to join the others.

Brisane's eyebrows went up, a delicate motion, halfway to being insulted.

Gawain said, "Forgive my brother, lady. He is anxious about his lady, in Camelot. She is with child."

Brisane relaxed, her lips curving into a smile. "A devoted husband," she murmured. "But no doubt his lady will be well cared for, in Camelot?"

The question was aimed at Arthur, who had been listening, but with that abstracted air that suggested most of his attention was somewhere else. He was turning a golden wine cup in his fingers; Brisane reached out and took it from him.

"See, Sir Gawain," she said. "This is to be the prize for the archery contest."

"Most generous, my lord," Gawain said.

"And yet there might be a greater prize still."

"Oh? And what might that be, lady?"

For a moment Gawain wondered if Brisane meant a prize that she would give. If so, it would be almost as if she took on the role of queen. He must have let some of his disquiet show in his face, for her eyes flashed at him, and there was an edge in her voice as she said, "Why, Sir Gawain, the king's favour, of course. What prize could be greater than that?"

Lancelot had begun to organise his contestants. He would not take part, but had appointed himself as judge. Gawain was pleased to be herded down the gallery to take his place with the others; it was a relief not to have to make courtly conversation with the lady Brisane. He did not like her, evil or not. She took too much on herself. In Camelot she would have had to defer to the queen; her beauty and her brilliance might have paled beside the other noble ladies. Here, she was without a rival.

Deep in these thoughts, Gawain was almost startled to have a bow thrust into his hands by Lancelot.

"Wake up," his friend said. "Three arrows into the target, if you please. You follow Gareth."

Gawain was just in time to see his brother send three arrows one after the other into the gold with the air of not even thinking about it, and turn moodily away, ignoring the murmur of applause that broke out. His own score was respectable and no more, and he was not surprised to be eliminated at the end of the round.

He withdrew to another alcove—keeping his distance from Brisane—to watch the end of the contest, which had developed into a struggle between Gareth, Griflet, and Briant des Isles.

Bedivere came and stood next to him, resting one booted foot on the stone seat. "Care for a small bet?"

Gawain smiled. "On Gareth, yes."

Bedivere let out a disgusted grunt. "The lad's not concentrating. Ten gold crowns says that Briant wins this bout. He's a fine archer. Well shot!" he said, as Briant sent the last of his three arrows neatly into the gold. "You know, Arthur could do worse than make peace with Briant. Make him one of us."

"A Knight of the Round Table?" Gawain said, startled.

"He's knight already. And better fitted to sit at the Table than some I could name."

Kay, Gawain wondered silently. "He made war against Arthur," he said.

"And so did many others, who became his friends after. Your father, Gawain, for one. In God's name, do you want Briant's heart cut out? What better way of dealing with your enemy than to make him your friend?"

Again in silence, Gawain thought, Yes. If it is true friendship. He applauded with the rest as Griflet dropped out and left the final contest between Gareth and Briant.

To Bedivere he said, "If he proved worthy, I would rejoice."

He went on watching. Gareth seemed to be recovering himself, or perhaps the tension of the contest had sharpened his concentration. His last flight of arrows bunched tightly together in the very centre of the target, the third arrow even splitting the second.

Even before Briant shot, Bedivere growled, "I'll pay you at supper."

Briant's last arrows all hit the edge of the gold. He handed the bow to Lancelot; he was smiling, at ease, and clasped Gareth's hand readily. He lost well, Gawain thought.

"You're growing tired," Gareth said. "Is your leg paining you?"

"It is," Briant said, "but I'll not make that my excuse. You shot well."

Gareth bowed to him.

Behind him, the lady Brisane said, "Sir Gareth, you must come and take your prize."

Gawain had half expected she would be furious to see Briant defeated, but she was all graciousness, and looked on with a smile as Arthur presented the gold cup to Gareth.

When Gareth had thanked him, she said, "Since you're in a giving mood, my lord, perhaps you might care to remember what we talked of this morning?"

Gawain was aware of a sharpening in the king's expression. Arthur started up from his seat, and then sank back into it.

Slowly, his voice very tired, Arthur said, "As you will."

Lady Brisane looked around her. All the knights who had taken part in the contest were listening to her.

"My lords," she said, "I know that you will rejoice to hear that peace has been agreed between King Arthur and my lord Briant des Isles. My lord Briant will swear to serve the king, and King Arthur will take my lord Briant into his household." She paused, and laid a slender hand on the king's arm. "My lord?"

Arthur brushed a hand over his eyes. Very slowly now, almost reluctantly, like a child repeating a lesson not perfectly learned, he said, "It is my will that my lord Briant should serve me, and in token of my trust in him I offer him the post of High Seneschal of Britain."

Utter silence. Into the silence came one voice—Gareth's—strong in outrage. "No!"

At the protest Arthur gathered himself together, and something of kingliness came back into his bearing. "You tell me no? May I not do what I will with my own?"

"My lord, the seneschal's office—that was Kay's."

Gareth's voice was thick, as if he could hardly form the words. Gawain got up, left the alcove, and went to stand at his side.

"Kay forfeited his office," Arthur said. "Is Britain to have no seneschal?"

"You swore an oath to Kay's father," Gareth said. "You swore that no one but Kay should have the seneschal's office while you both lived. Are you breaking that oath?"

Arthur got to his feet. Brusquely, he said, "Sir Gareth, you forget yourself."

"And you forget yourself, my lord!"

Gawain stepped forward and put a hand on Gareth's arm. He could see Brisane, still seated, her eyes sparkling with a joyful malice.

To Arthur, he said, "My lord, we should at least discuss this in council. It's true that Britain needs a seneschal, but to break an oath—"

"It was Kay who first broke his oath—his oath of loyalty to me. Shall I honour a murderer and a traitor, and slight a good man who offers me his service?"

"It is your oath we speak of, my lord." That was Gareth again, shaking off Gawain's restraining hand and pushing forward, closer to the king. "And you will find, my lord, that no good knights will serve you, if they cannot trust your word!"

A half-sob broke from him. He hurled the golden cup to the floor at Arthur's feet, turned, and slammed out of the gallery. As the echoes died, a long sigh rippled through the knights who remained, the relaxation of tension. Gawain heard Bedivere mutter a curse.

"Knights have been banished for less defiance than Sir Gareth has given me here," the king said bleakly. "But I will be merciful. He is young, and hot-headed, and I know he . . . cared for Kay. Gawain, I shall expect you to lesson him to discretion."

Gawain could do nothing but murmur agreement. Arthur turned to Briant, and the Breton lord, stiffly because of his injured leg, knelt before him and placed his hands between

Arthur's. While the lady Brisane smiled, and the knights looked on, Arthur swore Briant des Isles to his service as Knight of the Round Table and High Seneschal of Britain.

Chapter Twenty-six

A sleet-laden wind whipped across Carlisle. A raw, damp wind; the thaw was setting in. Sir Gawain, letting himself out onto the battlements, closed his eyes against the sting of it, and then cautiously edged them open to make out the figure of his brother a few yards farther along, round the curve of the turret.

He moved closer, one hand against the wall, half fearful of being blown off. "Gareth."

His brother, elbows on the parapet, hunched deeper into his cloak, the gesture almost a rebuff. Gawain stopped himself from putting words to his anxiety; he was not sure he knew how to approach Gareth any more. To look for him and find him up here alone made Gawain even more uneasy. He captured the flapping edges of his own cloak, and leant on the parapet next to him.

"We've been walled in too long," Gawain said.

Gareth shrugged and grunted agreement, seeming to lose a little of his tension. "I came to look at the road," he said. "How soon, do you think, before it's fit to travel?"

"A week, if the thaw keeps on. If it freezes again, who knows?"

"I want to go."

"Where?"

Gawain was not sure if he should have asked that question. He was even less sure if Gareth was going to answer it.

There was silence for a minute, followed by, "To Camelot, to my lady. And then, perhaps, to her manor. I don't know."

"It wouldn't be wise to ask Lionors to travel at this season. When should the child be born?"

Gareth frowned, as if he was calculating. "Easter—no, closer to Pentecost."

"She will have the best care, at Camelot. Gareth, she might need it." After last time. He did not speak the words, not wanting to remind Gareth of that tiny, dead child.

Gareth did not need reminding. "I know." His voice was doggedly steady. "That's one of the few things that's stopping me from throwing my service to Arthur in his teeth, and riding out of here. To anywhere."

"And what are the other things?"

"I swore an oath. I haven't forgotten!" Flame sprang up in his voice and died again. "And you. And Lancelot. And something—just a hope that one morning I'll wake up and find that this whole hideous mess is no more than a dream."

Gawain rested a hand on his arm, and stole a look at him, while Gareth still stared out across the snow-streaked fells. Gareth had begun to look older, he thought, in the three weeks since Briant had been named seneschal, the once-amiable features set. You grow formidable, little brother. . . .

"You know," Gareth said, "the steward came to me this morning. He's starting to think about the Candlemas Court. He'd been to Briant to ask him for orders, and Briant—Briant implied that he was incompetent for needing to ask. Gawain, Briant thinks the seneschal's office is—is a kind of favour to wear on his helmet. Kay worked!"

In his indignation he was starting to sound more like the Gareth Gawain knew.

Faintly encouraged, Gawain said, "So what did you tell the steward?"

"To do everything as Sir Kay would have liked it. And to come to me if he had any real problems. I sent him away quite happy."

Gawain smiled. Striving for a lighter tone, he said, "Yes, you're the only one of us who has any real idea of what the seneschal's job entails. Perhaps Arthur should have given it to you."

It had been the wrong thing to say. Gareth straightened, and stared down at his brother, his face implacable with anger. Gawain had a sudden vision of what Gareth's enemies would face. Formidable indeed. . . .

"Do you think I would take it?" Gareth snapped.

His mouth closed like a trap. He did not wait for Gawain to reply, but shouldered past him and disappeared through the door to the stairs.

Gawain waited a little to let him go. Gareth was in no mood for comfort, or jokes. Shivering, he leant against the parapet again and looked out.

Though snow still blanketed the high fells, on the lower slopes patches of brown, and even of green, showed. The south road itself was visible as a darker line, not clear yet. Gawain let his eyes follow it, the road he longed to travel almost as much as Gareth, and then leant forward, blinking against the sleet.

He could just make out, where the road disappeared round the shoulder of a hill, a moving speck. Straining to see, he distinguished at last a horse and rider, making for the castle. Gawain stood there, oblivious of the cold now, hands gripping the rough stone, until the rider came closer.

There was not much to gather from his appearance: a hunched figure in a hooded cloak, his horse a stocky chestnut, its head down from fatigue. He had come far, then, this rider, and in conditions like this his mission must be urgent or he would not have come at all. Suddenly anxious, Gawain made for the turret door and the stairs, slipping a little in his haste, and then along the passage that brought him out into the main courtyard.

One of the gates was dragged open to admit the rider. He urged his horse to the centre of the courtyard and then dismounted, clinging to the bridle as if that was all that kept him on his feet.

Gawain went to him. "Yes? Have you brought news?"

The man turned to him, clutching at his arm. "Sir Gawain! Thank God!"

Gawain did not recognise the man. His face under the hood showed broad, blunt features, burnt by cold. He peered at Gawain through reddened eyes, no more than slits. As the movement swung back his cloak, Gawain saw that he wore the livery of one of Arthur's men-at-arms.

"Have you ridden from Camelot?" he said.

"Aye. Take me to the king."

He staggered as he handed his horse over to the groom who had come out to receive it. Gawain put a hand under his elbow and guided him towards the door; he was in the last stages of exhaustion. Gawain's amazement gave way to fear as he asked himself the reason for urgency like this.

Arthur was in his private room, hunched over the fire. Opposite him sat Briant, sprawled at his ease, a wine cup in his hand. Firelight splashed over him, catching in his golden hair and the gold mountings on his belt. Beside him was his lady, fingering a scrap of bright embroidery. All three looked up as Arthur's servant announced the messenger.

The man-at-arms stumbled into the room and went down on his knees before Arthur. "My lord, I bring news. A letter from the queen."

As he fumbled in the front of his tunic, Briant said, "What news, fellow? Tell us what you know."

The messenger glanced at him, startled; clearly he did not know who Briant was. His eyes went to Arthur, who nodded, and he said, "War, my lord. That's the news. Claudas of Brittany is preparing for war."

He extracted the letter at last, and gave it to Arthur. Arthur stared down at it, turning it in his fingers, making no attempt to open the seal.

"War with Claudas?" he said, sounding almost stupefied.

Now the messenger's eyes, in a look of alarm, went to Gawain where he stood by the door.

Gawain beckoned to him. "With your leave, my lord," he said to Arthur, "I'll find this man lodging. He needs rest. Later you can question him."

Arthur did not reply, still gazing down at the letter, but he moved his hand dismissively.

Gawain drew the messenger into the outer room, and called the servant. "See that this man is warmly lodged and fed. Tell Sir Gareth of his coming—no doubt the messenger can give him news of his lady. And ask Sir Lancelot to attend the king."

When the servant and the messenger had gone, Gawain went back into the inner room. Arthur had opened the letter and was reading it; when he had finished, he handed it across to Briant. Brisane leant over so that she could read it, too. Gawain felt a stir of uneasiness. Though at Camelot Guenevere had often advised the king and had a part in his decisions, she had never assumed a right as Brisane did now.

"What does the queen tell you, my lord?" Gawain asked.

Arthur turned to look at him, rubbing a hand across his eyes. Gawain thought how tired he looked, almost as exhausted as the messenger who had just gone out. His features looked grey and hollow, more than the weeks of inactivity could account for. His hair was dry and dull. Anxiety touched Gawain like a cold hand; was Arthur ill, yet told him nothing?

"She says that Claudas is preparing for war," the king replied slowly. "He masses troops and ships on the Breton coast. When he can be assured of crossing safely, he will attack."

"But why?" Gawain asked.

"The queen says he has made no formal declaration of war. But my ambassador in his court writes to her that Claudas seeks revenge for the murder of Sir Meliant de Lis." He shook his head irritably, and gestured as if batting away a wasp. "Who is this Meliant? Who murdered him?"

Briant sat up and handed the letter over wholly to Brisane. "Meliant de Lis was Claudas' sister's son," he said. "A very promising lad. He fought on my side in these late wars."

"I killed him in the last battle." A new voice from the doorway: Lancelot. He touched Gawain on the shoulder and came into the room, closing the door behind him. "My lord, you sent for me?"

"No," Arthur said. "But it's as well you're here. You say you killed this . . . Meliant?"

Lancelot took a step nearer to the king. His sombre face was drawn, the bony structure very prominent. "He sought me out on the battlefield. I had no wish to kill him. I am sorry for it."

"To kill in battle is no murder," Arthur said. "Does Claudas look for a quarrel against me?"

Gawain's fears intensified as he saw the look that passed between Briant and Brisane: he, almost questioning; she, arrow-bright, triumphant. Gawain almost wanted to stand in front of Lancelot as if to shield him from a weapon.

"Come, Sir Lancelot," Briant said. "There's more to the story than that, and you know it. Why did the young fool seek you out? Why don't you tell the king that?"

Lancelot shrugged. Gawain wanted to scream a warning at him. Though Lancelot was regretful, he clearly had no concept of the trap that was about to spring shut on him.

"Two years ago," he said, "at a tournament at Lonazep, I killed Sir Meliant's father. It was no will of mine, my lord. I unhorsed him, and in the fall he broke his neck. Such things happen. No one was more sorry than I."

Arthur murmured understanding. "Go on."

"Then Meliant vowed revenge on me. He—"

"He came to me," Briant said. "And I made him knight. I thought he was a young hot-head, but I could see the honour of his cause."

"He challenged me," Lancelot went on; the interruption had shaken him, Gawain could see. "I met him at Roche Dure, when I went there with Sir Gareth on your embassy. I offered him penance, but he would not take it. Nothing would do but he should fight with me. My lord . . ." He spread his hands. "I did not want to kill him. I refused his challenge."

Briant snorted. "Refused it! You were ready enough to take him on when he called you 'coward.' If I hadn't dragged him out of the room and packed him off to his manor with Kay, you would have fought with him then."

Remembering what Gareth had told him about this affair, Gawain thought Briant might well be right. There were limits to the insult that Lancelot could be expected to take.

"I didn't want his death," Lancelot said. "If I had fought with him, I could have defeated him, yet let him live. His honour would have been satisfied."

"But then he sought you out in the battle?" Arthur said. His wandering gaze grew suddenly fixed; he looked more like himself. "This is the young man you killed at the end of the battle?"

"Yes, my lord," Briant said. "And I'd like to know—and I'm sure Claudas would like to know—why Lancelot went on fighting after I had surrendered. When you killed Meliant, Sir Lancelot—" he spat the title "—the battle was over. By my way of thinking, that's murder."

Lancelot turned to him, genuinely bewildered. "Surrendered? I didn't know that."

Gawain knew he was speaking the truth, but knew too, despairingly, that he would never be able to prove it. He himself had taken word to Lancelot, but Lancelot, caught up in the stress of battle, had not heard him.

"Then write to Claudas, my lord," Briant said, his voice heavy with sarcasm, "and tell him that Sir Lancelot killed his nephew Meliant because he was not aware that the battle was over. I'm sure Claudas will be entirely satisfied and trouble you no longer."

Anger lit in Lancelot's eyes. "You call me to account, my lord

Briant. But what of yourself? If you were so careful of this young man's safety, why did you let him fight at all? You knew very well what he wanted."

"True." Briant looked honestly regretful. "But I did not wish to dishonour him."

Gawain thought he could detect an inconsistency. If Briant was so careful of Meliant's honour, why had he stopped the duel at Roche Dure? His thoughts raced. Briant had stopped the duel, where a skilled fighter like Lancelot could have defeated Meliant yet let him live, but had allowed Meliant to fight in the battle, where his death was much more certain. But that would mean that Briant had deliberately supplied the cause for Claudas' invasion. Briant was a Breton, holding lands from Claudas. . . . Gawain opened his mouth to speak, not knowing what he meant to say, but Lancelot forestalled him.

"Meliant died with all honour," he said to Briant. "I regret his death, but I do not take the blame for it. Death in battle is no murder."

"He died after the battle," Briant insisted.

"And how does Claudas know that, my lord?" Lancelot's anger rose now; he had moved into the stance of the fighting man. "Unless you sent him word?"

Briant touched the stick that he still used, propped up against his chair. "If I were whole, Sir Lancelot, I'd challenge you myself for that. I'm Arthur's man now, and he knows it, even if you don't. But what you should know is that since the battle I've had no men at my command, no messenger I could send, and Carlisle has been cut off by the snow." He made a disgusted noise. "Use your wits, Lancelot. Most of my men who fled the battlefield were Bretons. Some of them must have made their way home. Why would they not tell a story that touches their overlord so nearly?"

Goaded, Lancelot turned to the king. "My lord, do you believe these charges? Why should I want the death of Meliant de Lis?"

Gawain looked at the lady Brisane. She glowed now, exultant. As far as he could see, she had yet to set stitch in the flimsy scrap of embroidery she held.

Briant's voice was very soft as he replied. "My lord Arthur, ask yourself what Meliant's death has achieved. An invasion of your lands by Claudas of Brittany, in a righteous cause. Now ask yourself why Lancelot killed him?"

Lancelot was not wearing a sword, but his hand flew to where the hilt would have been. "You call me traitor!"

He was beginning to lose control of himself, he who was always so rigidly controlled. He might have flown at Briant even without a weapon if Arthur himself had not motioned him back. The king half rose, and then sank back in his chair. He looked

Exiled From Camelot

troubled, confused. His hands shook with the tremor of an old man. What frightened Gawain more than anything was that Arthur was not in command.

"Sir Lancelot is no traitor," the king said, but his voice had lost its firmness. "What could he gain from this war with Claudas, except for an honourable death in battle?"

It was Brisane who answered. She leant forward; Gawain thought she looked like a snake, glittering, about to strike. She whispered the words, "Your death."

Lancelot broke into an angry protest, but let it die away as he saw that Arthur was quite unaware of him, his eyes locked onto Brisane's as if they were beads on the same thread.

"You know well, my lord," she said, in the same sibilant tone, "what Sir Lancelot has to gain if you were to die."

In the room was utter silence except for the crackling of the fire. There was no need for more accusation; it was true that Lancelot's only route to the queen lay through Arthur's death. There was nothing that Lancelot could say in his own defence, for his love for Guenevere was never mentioned; for all official purposes it did not exist. Gawain knew of it, as everyone knew, but if it was brought into the open and Lancelot broke with Arthur, enough knights would follow him to shatter forever the fellowship of the Table.

The king slowly turned his eyes on Lancelot, and Gawain could see how his knowledge, that he had never revealed before, was haunting him.

"My lord," Lancelot said, "you know I have never sought for your death."

Arthur's gaze shifted and fell away from him. His disquiet growing, Gawain came towards him, beside Lancelot.

"My lord," he said, "you know that Lancelot has served you faithfully, and fought at your side for years. If he had wished to kill you, he has had a thousand chances."

He thought he had reached Arthur, but before the king could reply, Brisane spoke.

"But not, perhaps, to kill you without blame to himself, to let your enemy strike the blow that brings you down."

"I was there when Meliant died," Gawain said. "I took the word of Briant's surrender to Lancelot. It was already too late to save Meliant."

A hard, tinkling laugh came from the lady Brisane, cutting off any reply that Arthur might have made.

"Do you listen to this, my lord? A man who is Lancelot's friend, a man who still plots, with his brother, to restore the murderer Kay to his office? A man who would be if you were dead?"

For a moment Gawain was silent, overwhelmed by her audacity. This was what Kay had meant, then, that she would destroy Arthur by striking at his chief men: Kay, and Lancelot, and now himself. Lancelot had refused to believe Kay; was he changing his mind now?

"My lord Arthur," Lancelot said, "put this to the test. Let us ride to Camelot, and send our forces into the field against Claudas. You will see whether my lord Gawain and I are faithful to you or not."

Briant let out another disgusted snort. "You would be mad, my lord, to ride into battle with either of them. Once you were dead, it would matter little to you whether you were struck down from in front or behind."

Arthur sighed. Since Brisane had brought the charge against Lancelot into the open, he had not spoken. Now he said, "Sir Lancelot, you have a case to answer, for it seems to me that this young man's death could have been avoided." Arthur was trying to speak with his old judicial authority, yet Gawain had the sensation that he was groping for words. "You will remain here, and for your own honour as much as my safety, you will remain under guard in your own quarters. When we have countered the threat from Claudas, I will return here and we will discuss more fully the matter of Sir Meliant de Lis."

Gawain stood amazed. For all the change in Arthur, he had never expected that the king could be brought to turn against the man who was perhaps his closest friend. Was it all Briant's plotting? Or was Brisane truly the enchantress Kay had accused her of being, using her arts to ensnare Arthur?

While Gawain was struck to silence, Lancelot once more began to protest, only to bite the words back. Gawain could see him forcing down anger, reasserting self-control by a painful effort of will, until his face became an impassive mask. He bowed his head and murmured acquiescence.

Arthur ignored Lancelot, the protest and the submission, and said, "Sir Gawain, I believe you are guilty of nothing but too much zeal on behalf of your friends, and Gareth of not knowing when to guard his tongue. You will both ride with me. As for you, my lord Briant—"

"I shall stay here, my lord, and hold Carlisle on your behalf, as my duty bids me."

The king gave him a faint, feral smile; Gawain caught at the expression as the only thread of hope that Arthur was not quite enmeshed by Briant and his lady. He was comforted still more to see Brisane, a cold venom invading her eyes, triumph driven out by uncertainty.

"Your predecessor—" it was a moment before Gawain realised Arthur spoke of Kay "—often resented being left behind to guard empty walls while other men sought honour on the battlefield. Perhaps he was right. I shall not make the same mistake with you, my lord Briant. My constable will guard Carlisle. You shall ride with me to Camelot, and then into battle against Claudas, and all the honour in the world will be yours for the winning. Serve me well, and you will see I can be grateful. Betray me, and—" He shrugged. "If I die on the battlefield, my lords, I will at least die knowing whom I could trust."

CHAPTER TWENTY-SEVEN

"My brother and I came into the world at one birth," said Lady Alienor. "I always knew what he was thinking. I knew when he let this thing into his mind."

It was evening. She and Kay sat one on each side of the fire in her solar, while at the other side of the room her waiting woman stitched at an embroidered shift. Her father now lay buried on a spit of land that overlooked the lake, and Kay trusted that his soul was finally at peace. Since her seizure in the chapel that morning, Alienor had been completely rational.

"You speak of the Lady?" he said.

Alienor nodded. She twisted a strand of her pale hair, twining it around her fingers.

"Meliant called her so. He allowed her to possess him because she offered him revenge for our father's death. I could feel her there, in his mind." She shivered. "I know she wanted to possess me, too."

"But you never consented."

"No. But it was hard. . . . I know that Meliant thought me mad with grief for our father, but it was the struggle against the Lady. It left me with little strength to live from day to day. And now, it all seems—shifting light and darkness." She looked into the fire, her gaze growing abstracted.

Kay ventured to say, "You have a brave spirit, lady." Alienor smiled but did not look at him. He added urgently, "Put it out of your mind. Forget."

She paused, frowning, and then said, "I remember little enough. You, my lord—you were here before. . . ." She rubbed at her forehead, as if she could force memory back.

Cautiously, Kay asked, "Do you remember Loholt?"

At the name she started, stared at him, and said, "Loholt! I remember him at Claudas' court. We grew up together—of course, he was younger than Meliant and I. He was a horrible child." She hesitated, swallowed, and went on, "I had a kitten once. Loholt . . . no, I won't say what Loholt did to it. Meliant killed it in the end, out of pity."

Several things suddenly began to make sense to Kay. He assumed that Arthur had made inquiries about where Loholt had grown up, but Loholt must have had some convincing tale to tell that made no mention of Claudas. Surely Arthur would have questioned his son's upbringing in the court of his enemy.

"I didn't know," he said, "that Loholt grew up in Claudas' court. None of us did."

"His mother, the lady Lisanor, was there, under Claudas' protection," Alienor told him. Her voice grew dry. "She seemed to need a lot of protection."

Then Claudas could have been part of the plot from the beginning, Kay realised. Send Loholt to Arthur's court, use him to destroy Arthur, and then set him up as a puppet king, with Briant as seneschal, to bring all Britain under the effective rule of Claudas. Kay could not help admiring such a simple and elegant structure, with the advantage from Claudas' point of view that he would not need to expose himself until his victory was certain.

But that plot had gone wrong. With a sudden catching of the breath Kay realised that he had averted it himself when he killed Loholt. With the boy dead, Claudas had to move more directly, if he was not to give up everything. He had sent troops to Briant, Kay was sure, for the battle against Arthur that had been fought that morning. Kay shifted restlessly in his chair, frustrated that there was no way to find out the result of that fight.

"Sir?" Alienor said. "Does something trouble you?"

Kay made himself smile. "Many things, lady. And there's little enough I can do about any of them. Tell me," he went on, "were you ever aware that Loholt was enslaved to the Lady, too?"

Alienor's eyes widened again. "When? In Claudas' court?"

"That I don't know. But when he was here, certainly. You remember that he was here?"

Slowly she shook her head. "I think . . . I can't be sure." Shivering again, she said, "I remember his body, carried into the hall. And then one of Briant's men rowed it out into the lake and sunk it there. But by then the body had no head. Was that not just an evil dream?"

"No. I think it truly happened. Brisane took the head and bore it to Arthur in Carlisle."

Understanding crept into Alienor's face. Slowly she said, "I do not like Brisane."

Kay leant forward and reached across the hearth so that he could take her hand. "Has Brisane ever told you that she is the Lady?"

Convulsively Alienor tightened her fingers around his. "No."

"She told me so. And I believed her." He shuddered, remembering Roche Dure. "Even so, she may be no more than a vessel for this hellish thing that possessed Loholt and your brother. There may still be hope, even for Brisane."

Kay was not sure why he said that, unless it was for comfort, for tears gathered in Alienor's eyes.

"I pray there may be hope for my brother." She leant towards him, folding both her hands round his. "This morning, in the chapel, I felt her power again—battering at me, at my mind, my will, demanding entrance. Kay, do you think that she might have been seeking refuge because Meliant had driven her out, at the last?"

"It may be so."

Kay's throat was suddenly dry, his mind whirling. He was not sure if he believed what he said, only that Alienor desperately needed to believe it. She was so close to him, all that questioning beauty, her hands warm around his. . . . Kay moved back and drew his hand away, and so that he should not seem to be rejecting her he got up and went to the table, where a jug of mead and cups had been set, and poured for both of them. Alienor's waiting woman still bent over her stitchery, as if unaware of what they said or did.

Kay handed Alienor her cup and sipped from his own, but he did not take his seat again. Instead he paced, from hearth to table and back again, the movement in itself a kind of release.

"So, lady," he said, striving to sound efficient. "What of the future? Who owns your brother's lands now?"

Alienor watched him with a sudden alertness, but she did not question his change of subject.

"Meliant had no heir. He held lands in Brittany from my mother, who was Claudas' sister. But this manor was my father's. I don't know who it might belong to now."

"By Arthur's law, lady, there is nothing to stop you inheriting from your brother. If Briant won this battle, then law is dead in Britain, but Briant has made me certain promises, and if he intends to keep them, I can confirm you in your rights. I will remain here as your steward for as long as I can be useful."

Alienor looked puzzled. "You don't mean to leave us, Kay?"

"I don't wish to. But if Arthur has won, you may find my presence . . ." His lips twisted as he sought for a word. "Disadvantageous." Realising that she might not understand why, he asked, "Do you know that Arthur stripped me of my knighthood and my office, and sent me into exile?"

Alienor nodded gravely. "They spoke of it—the villagers." Her gravity dissolved into a smile, so sweet that it almost brought him to his knees. "They do not seem to think it matters."

"And you, lady?"

"I? Are you telling me I should send you away so that I might have favour from Arthur?"

Kay spread his hands. "You would have good reason."

Her smile sharpened; her eyes grew brighter. Kay recognised all the strength and courage and intelligence that had been thrown into battle against the Lady, and felt his breath grow short.

"I will not base my life on such reason," Alienor said. "I will do what I think best, and if Arthur questions me, I know how to answer him." She gestured to the chair Kay had left. "Come, Master Steward, sit down, and let us take counsel together."

Kay sat on a bench beneath the window of the room above the manor gate. The shutter was open a crack; through it he could see the causeway and the place where the road disappeared into the forest. It was the morning after the battle, and so far there had been no sign of anyone, friend or enemy, trying to approach the manor.

Beside Kay, a bow and a quiver of arrows leant against the wall. Kay had buried himself deep in his cloak; in this icy room, he was afraid that his hands might be too cold even to handle the bow.

He had done his best with the manor's defences, and there were others on watch in other places, but this was the key position because an enemy was more likely to come across the causeway. There was a shortage of skilled bowmen. Apart from himself, there was the fowler and the eldest of Ursula's tribe of children, a lad so tall Kay was surprised he had not been claimed for the war.

The day before, Kay had asked him, "Where were you, lad, when Briant was looking for men?"

"In the forest, sir," the boy had replied, straight-faced. "Chasing the pigs. They take a terrible lot of catching, pigs."

Kay had set up a sack of straw in the hall as a target, and left the boy to teach his skill to some of the other children.

Now he shifted uneasily on the bench; he grew stiff with cold. There was still no movement from the edge of the forest. Kay wished he knew who or what was likely to appear, wished he had some way of knowing who had won the battle. Arthur . . . surely Briant could never prevail over Arthur? Kay prayed for Arthur's victory, but he did not know what that would mean for him. He was afraid that what he had said the night before to Alienor was true, that his presence here would do her no good with Arthur. He shrank from the logical conclusion, that he might be forced to move on.

Pulling his mind away from that, he went over what still needed to be done. For the time being the villagers were safe, the manor defences in place, but there were still a hundred other problems. Kay focused his worries on sheep. By this time they should be down off the fells and in shelter; Thomas had begun the repair of the sheepfolds, but had stopped when everyone retreated to the manor. And was there enough fodder? And what if the shepherds, bringing the sheep down, ran into a pack of Briant's men? Kay wished it was the season to milk sheep, or to shear them, for they could have used both the milk and the wool, but at this time of year all they could hope for was the meat—and not too much of that, or they would deplete the flock for next year.

His musings were interrupted by the door opening. He glanced round to see Gisela, Estrildis' elder daughter, letting herself into the room with a cup in her hand.

"Mistress Avice sent you this, sir," she said. "It's her cordial. It'll warm you, sir."

Kay thanked her absently, half his mind still on sheep, and folded his hands gratefully round the cup. The cordial gave off an aromatic steam; mostly mead, Kay guessed, with some kind of herbs.

"Thank Mistress Avice for me," he said.

Gisela dropped him a little curtsey. "Has anyone come, sir?" she said.

Kay shook his head. "Not yet. If we get through today . . ." He realised that Gisela was Yann's girl, and must be anxious about him. Skirting around the topic, he said, "Maybe some of our own people will be back."

He thought she looked very faintly encouraged, but frightened too. "Sir—you won't just shoot first?"

"No." He half smiled. "Do I look so fierce?"

Nervously, she returned the smile. "You're—you were—a knight, sir. A warrior."

"Not a very good one." He sighed. "They would tell you, at Camelot, that Kay is more at home in the kitchens than on the battlefield. Better at counting swords than using them. Nothing on his mind but ceremony. Or sheep."

"Sheep, sir?" A small gurgle of laughter was startled out of Gisela. "I never knew knights thought about sheep."

"They don't." Kay could not help wondering sardonically if Sir Lancelot had ever visualised a sheep, alive and on four feet, as distinct from wool and milk and the meat on his plate. "True knights think of honour, and glorious deeds."

"Then it's as well for us you're different, sir," Gisela said, startling Kay in his turn.

Hiding a slight feeling of awkwardness, he turned away to look out of the window again, and thought that he saw movement in the undergrowth on the edge of the trees. He let out a breath, releasing the tension that clutched at him.

"Sir?" Gisela said.

Without replying, keeping his eyes fixed on the forest, Kay held out the cup to her; she took it, and replaced it with the bow. Kay groped for an arrow, fitted it to the string, while Gisela swung the shutter a little wider. For a few seconds Kay thought he had been mistaken, or the movement had been no more than a forest animal, but then it came again, and he thought he caught a glimpse of a face, peering out from cover. He raised the bow.

"Sir," Gisela breathed, anguished.

"It's all right," Kay said. "Just a warning shot."

He released the arrow; it went winging across the causeway and buried itself in the trunk of an outlying tree. Kay grunted approvingly. Let them decide what to do about that.

What happened was not what he had expected. The bushes shook wildly, and then a man appeared, stooping, and ran out onto the causeway. Kay readied another arrow, but before he could shoot the man had straightened up and was waving his arms over his head.

"It's Yann!" Gisela cried. "Yann's back!"

Kay relaxed, and put the bow to one side. The girl's face was alive with happiness; Kay smiled up at her.

"Go down and let him in," he said.

Still cautious, Kay followed her down the stairs, his hand on his sword, though he did not expect any trouble. Thomas the carpenter was on watch by the archway, a long knife laid across his knees. He and Kay raised the bar and pulled back one of the gates.

When they looked out, the causeway was empty again; Kay started to draw his sword, only to sheathe it again as he saw Yann reappear from the forest with two other men, one of them supporting the other, who was slumped over the neck of a tired horse. Slowly they approached across the causeway.

"Simon, too!" Gisela said.

"Simon?"

"Clemence's man. She'll be so happy!"

Gisela seemed inclined to run into the house with the news, but ended by staying where she was. Kay watched the advancing group. He assumed that Simon was the other man on foot, since the mounted man had his head down, unidentifiable. Simon was tall, dark, a good, open face, Kay thought, and he seemed unhurt.

By this time, the group was coming through the gate. Yann looked filthy and exhausted but he grinned widely. He held out his free hand to Gisela, and kissed the hand she gave him, but most of his attention was on his friend, the horseman, who was wounded. Kay could see the man's clothes down one side were stiff with dried blood; his face was grey. Kay might almost have thought he was dead already, but for the others' care of him.

"This is Yves, sir," Yann explained. "We came from Brittany together, and fought together. When he was hurt, I promised I'd get him to safety. Sir?"

He looked a little uncertain, as if he wondered whether Kay would take in another of Briant's men.

Kay nodded. "You're welcome, all of you. Get him inside."

"I'll go and tell Mother, sir," Gisela said. "She'll know what to do."

She ran on ahead. Yann and Simon helped their companion to dismount, while Thomas closed the gate and barred it again.

"Who won the battle?" Kay asked as they began to cross the courtyard. Yves was half carried, his arms across the shoulders of the other two.

"What does it look like?" Yann said. "Arthur won the battle."

When they reached the hall, Gisela was even then coming with Estrildis to meet them. She worked as the manor's healer, and she had already made her preparations, expecting some of their own people to be wounded if they had to fight to defend themselves. She took one look at Yves, gave a disapproving sniff, and beckoned Yann and Simon to follow her, calling for her other daughter Sibella as she led them away.

Kay found the fowler, crouching over the hall fire with a cup of mead in his hands, and sent him to take over the watch on the causeway. He despatched a couple of the children to unsaddle and stable Yann's horse. Then he went to the kitchens and asked Avice for food for Yann and Simon.

By the time he returned to the hall the news had spread and more of the villagers were pouring in. Yann appeared with Gisela, their hands clasped together, she questioning him eagerly. Close by were Simon and Clemence and the baby, who buried her face in the curve of her mother's neck, not sure whether she trusted this tall, dark stranger.

When Simon had coaxed her into his arms, Clemence came over to Kay and dropped him a curtsey. She looked incandescent with happiness. If the coarse remark Briant des Isles had made about her had any foundation in fact, Kay thought, it was all forgotten now, and she had done nothing she need regret.

"Thank you, sir," she said.

Kay felt a tightness in his throat. "Thank me? Why? I didn't bring him back."

"No, sir, but—that night, with Briant's man. Without you, sir, what would I be able to tell Simon now?"

Kay shook his head, still disclaiming her thanks. "I wish you all joy," he said.

He himself felt a great peace, and a great exhaustion. Arthur had won the battle. He must still be alive. Later, when Yann and Simon were ready, he could ask them for more news. But surely this time Briant des Isles, if he still lived, must be rooted out of Britain for good and all, along with his lady. Surely this time Arthur would be able to return to Camelot in peace.

Chapter Twenty-eight

The expected attack on the manor never took place. Later on the same day that Yann and Simon returned, a group of about half a dozen men appeared at the other end of the causeway and looked as if they were about to cross; a couple of well-placed arrows from the fowler changed their minds rapidly. After supper the old man told a long and rambling story about how he had beaten off the invasion single-handed. Although Kay kept up the watch for a few days longer, there was no other disturbance.

Two days later, Yann and Gisela were wedded in the manor chapel by Father Paulinus, with Kay assisting. Already Gisela's sister Sibella was laying siege to the rapidly recovering Yves, who seemed likely to surrender without firing a shot.

Kay at last succeeded in having the sheep brought down from the fells and folded at the other side of the village. He met the shepherd for the first time, a dour, elderly man who seemed to prefer sheep to people. The shepherd refused to join the rest of the villagers in the manor house, and spent his nights, like his days, with his flock.

By the time the sheep were folded, Kay was beginning to think it might be safe for the villagers to return to their homes, but then the snow came. No one wanted to go back; they were warmer and more comfortable where they were. So they stayed, and day slipped into day with little to distinguish one from the next. The lake froze over. Snow drifted against the walls and over the causeway and hung heavy on the forest trees. The year turned.

Kay's mind was on the dwindling food supplies. Avice was now operating a strict system of rationing, but even so, their stores would not last the winter. They would be driven to eating the pigs and the sheep, and if they survived they would be utterly destitute by spring. And Kay had not forgotten his pledge to provide seed corn for the spring planting.

He could see no way of keeping his word. Even when the roads were open again, and there might be markets at Carlisle and Roche Dure, they had nothing to sell. Alienor had offered him her jewels, which Meliant had not taken from her, and Kay would have sold them quite cheerfully if he had thought he could get a price. But here, in the North, there was no market for such things. What would sell was what was scarce: milk, cheese, eggs, wool, corn. And these were the things they needed to buy.

By the time the thaw set in he was no nearer to a solution. His anxiety bit more sharply because everyone else trusted him, and looked forward to better times ahead. Kay went to confession again, feeling the weight of past pride. Though Father Paulinus absolved him and blessed him, he had no suggestions to scratch on his wax tablets.

On an afternoon towards the end of January, Kay had been through the deserted village, taking bread and other supplies to the shepherd. He found the old man playing quietly on a reed pipe, the sheep huddled together, their breath warm, their bleating soft and muted. Sunlight slanted red across the shoulder of the fell.

On his way back to the manor house, Kay had almost reached the causeway when he heard the sound of a horseman approaching up the road behind him. He stopped and waited at the edge of the trees, his hand on his sword hilt.

A moment later the rider appeared: a man-at-arms with the dragon on his surcoat. "Sir Kay!" he said.

Kay stiffened at the use of his old title. He did not recognise the man, but he guessed he was one of the Carlisle garrison. The man had obviously not expected to see him, and was already looking acutely embarrassed, realising the mistake he had made.

"I—I have a letter here for the steward of this manor." He choked over the words as if it was hard to get them out.

Kay gave him an icy smile. "I am he." He held out a hand for the letter. The man fished it out from the front of his tunic and gave it to him—a single sheet, sealed with Arthur's dragon. Kay immediately lost any desire to play games with the man; all he wanted to do was go somewhere to read the letter in private, and hide from anyone who might see that his hands trembled. "Come with me," he managed to say. "I'll find you lodging."

Back at the manor, Kay handed the messenger over to Avice, and made for the steward's room. Sitting at the table, he eased up the seal and unfolded the sheet. The letter was a short one. It informed him that King Arthur, with his retinue of knights and a company of men-at-arms, would be their guests on the road to Camelot in three days' time. It instructed Kay to make sure that suitable lodging was ready. It was signed by Briant des Isles, High Seneschal of Britain.

Kay sat for a long time with the letter spread on the table in front of him. He wanted to be sick, or weep, but he did neither. He was very cold. He did not know why he should feel betrayed.

After a while he took pen and paper and began to write, another letter, much longer than the one he had received. It took a long time, and when he had finished the light of the short winter day was already dying. Kay went to find the lady Alienor.

She sat on the floor in front of the fire in the hall, playing with

Clemence's baby. As Kay approached she took one look at him and handed the little girl to her waiting woman, with a murmured instruction to return her to her mother.

When they had gone, she jumped up and took Kay's hand. "What is it? Are you ill? Come to the fire—you're ice cold."

Kay let her sit him down on the bench beside the fire, not troubling now to hide his shivering. He pressed both letters into her hands. She unfolded the shorter first, scanning it earnestly; then she looked up, eyes hot with indignation.

"Arthur has given your office to that—vermin!"

Kay could not reply; he made a helpless gesture towards the letter.

"I'll not have him or any of his men on my land," Alienor continued. "Call the messenger—I'll write a reply myself."

Kay started up and caught her by the hand, forcing himself to speak. "No, lady. You must not. Arthur is your liege lord. You must ask him to confirm you as owner of this manor, and then to give you the supplies you need to get your people through the winter."

"I'll die first!" Alienor snapped.

"No, lady—think of your people."

Frowning still, she gestured to him to sit down again, and she took her place on the bench at his side.

"Read the other letter," Kay said.

Alienor glanced down at the direction. "This is your writing, Kay—to Sir Gawain of Orkney?"

She unfolded the letter and began to read. Kay had begun by asking for Gawain's forgiveness, and Gareth's, and bidding them farewell. He went on to explain the problems on the manor, and begged Gawain to see that the people's needs were supplied from Carlisle. When Alienor had finished, she looked up at Kay, holding his eyes, her own wide with dismay.

"But Kay, you'll be here to tell Sir Gawain all this."

"No. I must leave here tonight."

He cut off her protests with another helpless, passionate gesture. "Lady, I was exiled from Britain. If I'm found here, my life is forfeit. I don't think Arthur or any of his knights would carry out the sentence, but . . . besides, that isn't the reason. I cannot—lady, I cannot—bear to see Arthur again like this. I cannot meet him, and know—and see Briant in his company, in his favour. . . ." He was growing incoherent, and made himself stop, a hand pressed to his lips.

"You love Arthur very much," Alienor said.

"He is the air I breathe, my life's blood—" He broke off, horrified. He had never admitted so much, even to Gawain. He took a shuddering breath. "When he sent me away, I thought I would die."

Alienor reached out and covered his hand with her own. "Kay—my friend—have we not made you happy here? You've done so much for us."

"Yes—yes, a little, beyond hope. I would stay, lady; it tears my heart to leave. But I cannot stand here and face Arthur. I have not the courage."

Alienor sighed. "We need you," she said. "What shall we do without you?"

"You will do very well. Better now, without me. You have your strength again. The time of your need is over."

Alienor shook her head, reluctant still, but Kay could see that she understood and would, in the end, give way to him.

"Must it be now?" she said. "It's almost night."

"I cannot stay." It was irrational, he knew, but until he had left the manor behind, until he had managed to lose himself, he would not be able to shake off the terror of turning the corner of a passage, or stepping through a door, and finding himself face to face with Arthur.

"Lady, you must give that letter to Sir Gawain of Orkney," he said. "Or if he does not come, to his brother Sir Gareth. They will understand. You can trust them. Arthur, too—he will not let you and your people suffer because of his quarrel with me."

Alienor eyed the letter dubiously; Kay was afraid she was going to throw both documents into the fire.

"Lady, I promised your people I would provide seed corn for the spring planting. They—they believe in me. This is the only way I can keep my word, by leaving now and commending you to Arthur's mercy."

"I'll ask nothing of Arthur."

"Gawain, then. He was my friend."

"Perhaps." She turned the letter over and over between her fingers. "Where will you go?"

"I don't know."

"Then what—"

Kay shrugged. "I can sell my sword, perhaps. Or perhaps there's some lord somewhere who could make use of a competent steward, and isn't too fussy about his reputation. I'll survive, lady." He drew her hand, very briefly, to his lips, tentatively, giving her every chance to pull away. Then he rose to his feet. "I must get ready."

He went back to his bedroom and thrust spare clothes into his saddlebag. There was very little to pack, just the few possessions he had brought from Roche Dure. He added one blanket, for he thought he would need to sleep out. He struggled briefly with himself, wondering if he ought to leave Gareth's sword behind with the letter, but in the end he kept it. He would need a weapon, and Gareth would understand.

From there he went to the kitchens. He had intended to beg some food from Avice, but the kitchens, for some reason, were deserted. It looked as if something had interrupted the preparations for the evening meal. A pot on the fire was boiling over, and he drew it to one side. Then he gathered up bread and cheese, and a couple of apples, enough for the first day or so of his journey. He stowed the food in his bag, and went to the stables.

The air was warm, and heavy with the smell of pigs; they had already been brought in. The animals shifted uneasily on his entrance, rustling the straw. Enough light still came in through the open door for Kay to saddle Morial, and he made sure it was closed securely before he led his horse round the side of the house to the main gate.

They were waiting for him in the courtyard. Alienor and Father Paulinus stood together in the midst, with all the villagers silently grouped around them. Red light and shadow moved over their faces, from a single torch that flared over the gate.

Kay stood still. They should not have come. He could not bear it. He did not know how to move across the courtyard to the gate. As he stood, paralysed, Father Paulinus darted forward and grabbed him by the arm. He was frantically shaking his head.

Kay found that he could move after all. He covered Father Paulinus' hand; he shook his own head regretfully. "I must go, Father."

There was a murmur of dismay from the crowd. Kay straightened, and raised his voice.

"I commend you to your lady's protection," he said, "and to Arthur's mercy. It will be ready, poured out for you, if I am not here. My work is done."

With the priest by his side, he led Morial forward. Alienor fell into step beside them. Kay was conscious of eyes, pleading, accusing, or simply stunned. He saw Clemence weeping. No one spoke.

Kay was terrified that when he came to the gate someone would try to hold it against him; he did not know if he had the strength, in body or mind, for a struggle like that. But as he drew nearer he saw Thomas the carpenter raise the bar, and Yann dragging open the gate.

When it was wide enough, Yann stepped forward and clasped his hand. "You'll come again, sir," he said.

It was not a question. If it had been, Kay had no words to answer it. He looked back at his people; they had closed in around him, still in the same silence. He tried to speak, but his voice failed utterly. Alienor hugged him, and he could not even put his own arms round her in return.

He mounted Morial and set the horse in motion, the hooves ringing sharply on the stones of the causeway. Halfway across he reined in and looked back. Alienor and Father Paulinus stood in the gateway, the others behind. Kay raised a hand in farewell, and Father Paulinus echoed the gesture, a sign of blessing. Kay urged Morial on again, and turned his face to the forest.

At first he let Morial take his own pace. All winter the war horse had been under-exercised, and even in the near darkness beneath the trees, he settled to a fast trot. They left the deserted village behind, and soon were climbing past the sheepfold and across the unploughed fields, and on to the bare fell.

The moorland was empty, except for where patches of snow still gleamed white in the hollows. To Kay's left, pale streaks still showed in the sky where the sun had gone down. To his right, a few early stars glittered.

The track snaked ahead of him along the ridge. He leant forward, and Morial's trot shifted imperceptibly into a fast gallop. Kay fled, not knowing what pursued him. The moorland whirled around him, and the wind of his own passing shrieked at him.

As darkness deepened, he slowed Morial into a walk. This was madness, he knew, to set such a headlong pace in the dark. If nothing else, he risked injuring Morial. He patted the horse's neck in a mute apology.

Looking around him, Kay was not sure how far he had come. The track still led onwards, almost due north. North was Carlisle; Kay did not want to go that way. The road he had travelled with Meliant from Roche Dure had crossed the ridge, Kay remembered; somewhere in that wild gallop he had missed the turning. He pulled Morial's head round, intending to go back, but now he knew he risked losing his way in the dark.

Soon he came to a fork in the track. Left was the way he had come; to the right a path zigzagged downwards into night. It was not the road he was looking for, but it led in roughly the right direction, and he turned into it. Soon the slope grew so steep that he dismounted and led Morial, slipping on the tussocky grass, groping now in almost total darkness.

Before long he realised—not from sight so much as the sharp, resinous smell and the faint soughing of the wind—that he was in a pine forest. The track levelled out, so that he mounted again. On his right, he could hear running water, a stream that lived again after the frost.

Farther, into the impenetrable dark. He grew tired, his senses blurred, and common sense told him to stop and make camp until morning. But something drove him, something within him that wanted nothing except to be far away from Arthur, far away from the village, far from anyone who would remember him as Kay. He kept on.

Gradually, he realised that the darkness was lifting. The trees thinned out and overhead the waxing moon, still no more than a thin crescent, shed a faint light over the track. Almost without realising it, he urged Morial on, into a trot first, and then a smooth canter. Kay had never travelled this road before, but he knew that he was going south.

The trees gave way altogether on his left. He could see nothing in that direction but a sweep of scintillating darkness. At the same moment that his senses told his mind he was looking at the faint reflection of the night sky in a partly frozen lake, Morial stumbled.

In a flash of understanding, Kay realised that he had been riding too close to the edge of a bluff overhanging the water. The ground gave way. Morial plunged, fighting for a foothold, his haunches heaving over a black drop.

Kay tried to throw his weight forward, only to slide sideways into emptiness as the horse struggled. The reins snapped and the trailing end lashed though Kay's hand. He fell into splintering black and silver. A sharp pain lanced through his head, and then everything was swallowed up in a soft tide of darkness.

Chapter Twenty-nine

In council at Carlisle, the knights raged around Arthur. Gawain alone sat in frozen silence. Even the day before, when Briant had accused Lancelot of treachery, he had not believed this could happen. He thought he might be witnessing the irrevocable splitting of the fellowship.

Arthur looked grey and shrunken, ageing almost visibly as he sat in a high seat that suddenly seemed too big for him. Briant, in contrast, had expanded to dominate the room, his golden hair glistening, almost writhing, in the cold daylight. At Arthur's other side, Brisane, too, sat in council. Face flushed, eyes bright, scarlet lips parted, she seemed to have taken on all the colour that was drained from Arthur.

Out of the clamour one voice, determined, made itself heard at last: Ector de Maris, Lancelot's half-brother.

"Do you think, my lord," he said to Arthur, "that any of us will follow you when you accuse the best of us of treason?"

Arthur glanced up at him, a shifting glance that slid away.

It was Briant who replied. "Sir Lancelot has brought Claudas of Brittany down on our heads in a rightful quarrel."

Ector ignored him. Still speaking to Arthur, he said, "Do you believe this?"

Arthur gathered himself, a desperate grasping at authority that Gawain found chilling in the man whose authority had always been effortless.

"Lancelot killed Meliant de Lis," he said hesitantly. "When the battle was over, when—"

"Lancelot did not know that," Ector said. "Meliant sought him out on the battlefield."

"The boy drew on his own death." Bors added his measured contribution. "He was valiant, but rash, and he had no true quarrel with Lancelot."

"Not the death of his father?" Briant said.

"An accident—"

The wrangling began again. Gawain watched the king, who seemed almost like a captive between the two who held his will in thrall. He began to believe what Kay had said to Gareth in Roche Dure, that the lady Brisane was an enchantress, and now she had Arthur ensnared in her webs. If that were true, then no arguments, nothing rational, was going to penetrate the king's clouded mind.

"What of the oaths you swore?" Briant made himself heard again. "Have you forgotten them? Now, when an enemy stands at our gates?"

Quietly Gawain got to his feet and went to the door of the council chamber. To one of the guards he said, "Go to Sir Lancelot's rooms, and have him brought here."

The guard gave him a dubious look; he could not have avoided hearing the quarrel that was going on.

"On my authority," Gawain said.

Still looking unhappy, the guard went. Gawain returned to his place. Briant was still speaking, trying to give orders for the mustering of troops against Claudas, but very few of the knights were prepared to listen to him or to take his orders. When Kay had been seneschal, he had left all the military dispositions to Lancelot; now Briant was trying to take the place of both men. And Arthur let him talk.

At last Ector lost patience again, springing to his feet. "Why should I send men to be killed, for a king who calls my brother traitor? Better I should bring troops to Carlisle to free him—"

"Treason, my lord?" It was Brisane who spoke, with a smile of pure delight. "Plain treason, heard by all of us."

"Woman, you should not sit in council, much less speak—" Bors began, but Briant cut him off.

"My lord king, you see how little trust you can put in this man. Perhaps Sir Ector has conspired with his brother to bring Claudas into your kingdom."

Ector's hand went to where his sword hilt would have been, if he had not been unarmed for the council. "I'll meet you for that, Briant," he said.

"No."

The voice, Lancelot's, was quiet, but it cut the noise of the council chamber like a sword blade. He stood in the doorway, flanked by his guards. An uneasy silence fell.

"I thank you, Brother, for your loyalty," Lancelot said. "Bors, Lionel." He nodded to his kinsmen. "It grieves me that my lord Arthur cannot trust me, but it would grieve me more if I was the cause of quarrel between him and any other of his followers. Especially when we stand in such grave danger. If I may not draw sword for my king, then—"

"Who brought you here?" Briant, blustering, tried to take back control, but it had slipped away from him. "Who gave a traitor leave to speak in council?"

Gawain rose. "I did." He went to stand by Lancelot's side. "Do you call me in question, my lord Briant?"

He was not sure how Briant would have replied, for at that moment the king raised his head. He said painfully, "I will hear Sir Lancelot."

Lancelot bowed to him. "My lord, I would ask nothing better than to fight at your side against Claudas. But if that may not be, I will not take from you other noble men who will fight in your quarrel—a just quarrel, for I swear as I have sworn before that I bore no enmity towards Meliant de Lis. I would have given him penance for his father's death. I had no desire to kill him." He paused, but now no one would have dreamed of interrupting him. "Ector," he went on, "by any love and loyalty you feel for me, I charge you to hold by your oath to Arthur. And any others of you who would take up my defence. Drive out Claudas; the rest I leave to God."

As Lancelot spoke, Arthur watched him with a fierce intensity. He leaned forward, gathering himself to rise. Gawain thought that he wanted to get up and embrace Lancelot, and welcome him back into fellowship. But the first to move was Brisane, closing her hand over the king's.

"Words are easy, my lord," she said, "but think of this man's deeds."

Arthur subsided into his chair; he looked ill.

Lancelot bowed gravely. "I have no more to say, my lord. My prayers will go with you."

He went out, his guards following. Gawain returned to his seat. There was no more argument. Briant proceeded to the swift disposition of their troops; he planned to ride on the following day. The rest of the knights listened, grudging their attention, but unprotesting.

Gareth leant across to Gawain and spoke softly. "Briant isn't pleased with you."

Gawain shrugged slightly. "It was the only thing to do. No one but Lancelot would have calmed them."

"All the same, Briant didn't like it." Gareth bared his teeth in a fierce smile. "First Kay, then Lancelot. If Kay was right, Brother, then you're the next."

"Where is Briant taking us?" Gareth muttered. "This place looks deserted."

"Except for the sheep," Gawain said.

It was the day after the disastrous council. Arthur and his men had left Carlisle that morning—a larger troop and better equipped than those who had ridden to relieve the siege so many months before, but Gawain felt even less hope of victory. How could anyone go on defending what they no longer loved?

Gawain and Gareth rode near the head of the column, just behind Arthur, Briant, and the lady Brisane. The rest of the knights and men-at-arms were strung out behind them, straggling with tiredness at the end of the day.

They had passed a sheepfold at the entrance to the village,

and heard the subdued movement of the animals enclosed there, but the houses themselves looked derelict. Ahead, the road disappeared again into forest.

"Briant said the king could have lodging here," Gareth went on. His voice was heavy with suspicion. "Is he leading us into a trap?"

"With Arthur surrounded by his knights?" Gawain said. "It would have to be a good one."

All the same, he reached for the hilt of his sword, and loosened the blade in its sheath. He did not like this desolate place any more than his brother did; he would have preferred to stay on the main south road, and make camp beside it, rather than look for shelter here.

The belt of woodland was narrow; the path emerged on to the shore of a lake; a causeway led across to the gate of a walled manor house. Gawain still did not feel reassured. There were no lights showing, not even a torch burning at the gate. Only a wisp of smoke rising into the sky showed that the place was inhabited at all.

Arthur reined in at the end of the causeway. "What place is this, Briant?"

Briant gestured expansively towards the gate. "A humble manor where I have entry, my lord. You'll be well entertained, I promise you. You'll find friends here unlooked for."

For some reason, as Briant spoke, Gawain found himself looking at the lady Brisane. Her lips were curved in a cruel smile, scarcely a smile at all, but radiating satisfaction. Gawain exchanged a glance with Gareth; the idea of a trap suddenly did not seem so absurd.

"Sir Gawain," Briant said to him, "have the knights and men-at-arms make camp for the night in the village. My lady and I will escort the king."

Gawain was startled at the peremptory order. Mildly, he said, "It is not fitting, my lord Briant, for the king to lodge anywhere without his knights to attend him."

He was prepared for an argument, but Briant merely shrugged and set his horse in motion, leading the way across the causeway. Gawain relayed the order for the men-at-arms to fall out and make camp, but chose an escort from the knights and formed them up in a tight column with himself and Gareth at its head, before following the king to the gateway.

By the time Gawain came up with them, Briant was pounding on the gate and shouting for admittance. At first there was no reply.

"Perhaps everyone is out?" Gareth suggested in a bright tone with an edge to it.

Briant ignored him and renewed his pounding. After a

minute's pause, there came the scraping sound of a bar being lifted, and then one gate was pulled back. Briant pressed through the gap as soon as it was wide enough to admit his horse.

"What's this insolence, fellow?" Gawain heard him ask. "How dare you keep your lord waiting?"

"No lord of mine," the reply came.

By this time Gawain had ridden through the gate behind Brisane and the king, and saw the man Briant spoke to: a tall, grizzled fellow with one arm. He was staring up at Briant with a look of truculent hostility.

Briant slashed the flat of his sword across the man's shoulder; he stood rock-solid under the blow.

"Do you disclaim the king?" Briant asked.

The man's gaze travelled indifferently over Arthur and the knights who were filing into the courtyard. "I know naught of kings," he said. "I serve my lady."

He certainly did not mean Brisane. Gawain started to be interested. He manoeuvred his horse forward, meaning to talk to the man, but before he could speak, Briant said, "And where is your lady? Why is she not here to greet us?"

"She waits for you in the hall," the man said.

Briant started to say something else, another rebuke for insolence, and then broke off with a curse. He dismounted, and flung the horse's reins at the man.

"My lord," he said to Arthur, "I ask your pardon for this poor welcome. The steward should be brought to account for it."

There was a flash of savage enjoyment in Briant's face as he said that; Gawain could not understand it. The king dismounted, too; there were no grooms to see to the horses, so Gawain asked Bedivere if he would take one or two men and find the stables, while he himself collected the rest of the escort. He did not mean to let Arthur out of his sight until there was some explanation for this uncanny place.

Briant led the way across the courtyard and through a door that led into a short passage and then to a pillared hall. Tables were set up there, but not yet laid for supper. The high table had been pushed to the back of the dais, and at the front of it was a single chair. A woman sat there, in the light of the only torch that burned, on the nearest pillar. She wore a plain linen gown. Her pale hair was braided around her head; she seemed to gather the light to her, as if it were she, and not the torch, that shed the pool of radiance where she sat. Gawain drew a breath in wonder. Pure beauty; pure simplicity. She might have been a queen.

She did not rise as Briant, with Brisane and Arthur, advanced down the length of the hall. Gawain led the rest of the knights, a few paces behind. To his surprise, Briant did not kneel to her, or even address her as a knight should speak to a lady.

Instead, he said roughly, "Where's the steward, girl?" To Arthur he added, "She's a poor, mad thing, my lord. She plays at rule, but she doesn't understand what's going on."

The lady lifted her head. Her voice, when she spoke, had a biting clarity. "I am the lady Alienor de Lis, chatelaine of this manor. I do not recollect, my lord, that I invited you to visit."

"Strange madness," Gareth murmured.

Briant looked slightly disconcerted but ploughed on. "Do you know who this is, girl?"

"You will not address me as 'girl,'" Lady Alienor said. "For I have found courtesy where you never thought to look for it, and nothing less will content me now. As to your question, my lord; yes, I know who you are. You are Briant des Isles, who led my brother to his death, along with many other good men of this manor. And your lady Brisane, who entrapped my brother with her sorcery, and would have entrapped me, too. And this—" her gaze went to the king; her voice flashed scorn "—this is King Arthur, whom I should ask to do me right. King Arthur who holds the justice of this realm in his hands. King Arthur who drove his truest friend away from him, and would not leave him even this poor refuge."

There was utter silence. Brisane's lips were tight with fury; Briant looked as if he would explode.

But it was Arthur who broke the silence, his voice quiet. "Lady, what do you mean? Who do you speak of?"

"I speak of Kay." Lady Alienor flung the name at Arthur as if it were a weapon, and he flinched from it. "Sir Kay, for I will give him the title he deserves, that it was not your right to take from him."

Arthur's face was working. "Kay was here?"

"Is he here now?" Gareth said, his voice hoarse. He had pressed up to Gawain's side, and was listening with a painful intensity.

"No." Alienor flicked him a glance, but most of her attention was for the king. "He was here, but his heart would not sustain him to stand before you, and see another bear his office, and know that he had lost your trust and your goodwill. He rode from here three nights ago, and you can be sure, my lord king, that he will never trouble you again." She paused, the force of her attack wavering. Her voice dropped suddenly. "Kay is dead."

Gawain heard a soft sound from Gareth, low in his throat, and unobtrusively closed a hand round his brother's arm. "Lady," he said, "if Kay rode away from here as you say, how can you be sure he is dead?"

Lady Alienor turned to Gawain; clearly she had no idea who he was, and just as clearly she did not care.

"The day after," she said, "his horse came back here, with the reins broken. I sent men out to search, as many as could be spared. They came to a place where the road led by the side of a lake. The bank was freshly broken away. There were a few scraps from Kay's cloak on a thorn bush by the water, and his cloak brooch, half buried in the mud. My men searched, but they found nothing more. He is dead." She gave Gawain her evidence in a calm voice, but it had begun to quiver by the end.

"Was he your lover?" Brisane suggested, malice flickering through her voice like a serpent's tongue.

Alienor did not trouble to reply; her contempt seared across Brisane in silence.

"My lords, I will not say you are welcome," Alienor said, after a time. "But you may stay here tonight. In the morning I will very gladly bid you farewell."

Ever since Alienor had told him Kay was dead, Arthur had stood in silence, staring at her. Gawain had a sudden vision of how the king would look when he was old. When Arthur next spoke, it was not to Alienor; it was not to anyone.

"Kay was a murderer." His voice was the scraping of a blade over stone. "He was a traitor. He is justly punished." He fell silent, and then spoke again. "He cannot be dead."

Disturbed, Gawain started towards the king, but the lady Brisane was before him, gathering both the king's hands into her own.

"Kay was unworthy, my lord," she said. "He had earned your displeasure many times before. You are tired; in the morning you will understand more clearly." To Arthur her manner was all graciousness, but it became icy cold as she turned back to Alienor. "Is it too much to ask for a room where your king may rest?"

Alienor clapped her hands, and from a door at the side of the hall an old woman appeared, so promptly that Gawain guessed she had been listening outside.

"Avice, show these . . . noble lords where they may lodge."

The old woman invited them to follow her with no more courtesy than a jerk of the head. The rest of the knights followed Briant and his lady, who escorted the king, but Gareth had sunk down on a bench by the nearest table and Gawain stayed with him. He had no fear for Arthur now; the king's only enemies were the ones he had brought with him. Gareth had his head sunk into his hands; Gawain did not know if he wept.

When everyone else had gone, Alienor got up and came to them.

"Lady," Gawain said to her, "I grieve for Kay, and I rejoice that he had such a friend as you."

The look she gave him suggested that she considered believing him; when she looked at Gareth there was even the beginning of sympathy.

"Is one of you Gawain of Orkney?" she asked.

"I am," Gawain said. "This is my brother, Gareth."

"Then I have a letter for you. A letter from Kay. Come to my solar and I will give it to you."

Gawain urged Gareth to his feet, and guided him out of the hall, following Alienor. His brother did not weep, but he had a white, stunned look. When Alienor ushered them into her solar, Gareth slid into a seat by the wall and shadowed his eyes with one hand.

The solar was a pleasant room, even though the cushions and hangings were worn and mended. A bright fire burnt on the hearth, and on the table was a lamp. By its light, a small man in priest's habit was reading a breviary. At the other side of the table a woman—Alienor's waiting woman, Gawain guessed—had her head bent over some embroidery.

As they entered, the little priest got up and stood with a questioning look.

"Father Paulinus," Alienor said, "this is Sir Gawain of Orkney, and his brother Sir Gareth. Kay's friends."

Father Paulinus nodded; he was trying to smile, but the crumpled face looked nearer to tears. He caught at a pair of wax tablets that hung from his girdle, scratched something with the stylus, and held the message out to Gawain. Startled, Gawain read what he had written: *We have said Mass for him.*

"My lady Brisane cut out Father Paulinus' tongue," Alienor said. "He displeased her. But thanks to Kay he is still our priest."

"Thank you, Father," Gawain said gravely.

Alienor showed Gawain to a seat by the fire and gave him the letter. He opened it and read. In bare, uncomplicated phrases, Kay explained himself, explained the difficulties that the manor still faced, and begged Gawain for his help. When he had finished, Gawain handed the letter across to Gareth, who took it and held it, but did not read.

"What do you think, Sir Gawain?" Lady Alienor said. "Are you able to help us? For Kay's sake?"

"For your own sake, lady. And certainly for him. I will send a message to Carlisle in the morning. You shall have provisions, seed, tools, and men to do the work. And when I come to Camelot I shall see that your title to the manor is ratified."

"That will not please my lord Briant," Alienor said dryly.

"Then my lord Briant will have to bear it. Seneschal or not, he can't overturn the law. I think my authority will stretch so far."

For the first time since Gawain had seen her, Alienor smiled at him. The knight wished he could have known her at a happier time. She would have graced any of the glittering courts of Camelot, instead of being buried here at the back of nowhere, with some taint of madness clinging around her.

He could not help asking, "What did Briant mean, lady, when he called you mad?"

"For a while I was." Alienor seemed not to mind that he had asked the question. "By the sorcery of my lady Brisane. She sought to possess me through my brother Meliant."

"Meliant was your brother?"

"Yes. Did you know him, my lord?"

"No. But I was with him when he died. I remember now—his last word was 'Alienor.' He thought of you, lady."

Alienor raised her hands to her face briefly. "Sir Gawain," she said, her voice hushed, "did he cast her off at the last—that fearful thing—the Lady?"

"Truly, I believe he did."

Alienor let out a long sigh of thankfulness. Father Paulinus, listening intently, crossed himself.

"Lady Alienor," Gawain said, "when we journeyed from Camelot to Carlisle, Kay was taken prisoner. He came to Carlisle, very ill, and I cared for him. He would not say what had happened to him, but someone had tortured him, and he cried out in his sleep about the Lady. Do you know anything about this? Did he speak of it?"

Alienor shook her head. "Kay said nothing of it. But it was here he was held prisoner. That was when I fought the madness, and I do not remember what happened." She paused, and then added, "But Meliant would not have tortured him. He would not!"

Gawain reached out and took her hand reassuringly. "You know him best, lady."

"He was wild—and carried away by his will to revenge our father. But he was not cruel, not evil. That was the presence in him. Sir Gawain, take care. Do you know that Brisane is the Lady?"

"I suspected it."

"You must get Arthur away from her," Alienor said. "What will become of Britain—of us all—if Brisane's evil can possess the land's king?"

Gawain felt a creeping terror threatening to overwhelm him. He had guessed so much of this, but it had been in shadow, until Alienor poured in her light. Not long ago he would have thought it unimaginable, that Arthur could be brought down by a woman's sorcery, but now he could see it happening. It had already begun. Brisane had weakened Arthur, shamed him, separated him from two of his chief councillors. His knights were losing their trust in him. Gawain could not be sure that Arthur still had the strength to go on resisting her.

He wondered if it would do any good to go to Arthur and tell him what he had discovered; yet, so much was still in doubt, and so much rested on the word of Alienor, whom Briant had accused of madness. It was too early yet, Gawain thought. He needed proof. Something tangible. Something Arthur would be unable to ignore. He sighed.

"Do you want to go to your rest, sir?" Alienor said. "And your brother?"

She motioned towards Gareth, who still sat with head bowed, the letter loosely in his fingers.

"He cared deeply for Kay," Gawain said in a voice he hoped would not carry. "They knew each other very well."

Gareth had evidently heard. His head jerked up; his eyes were brilliant.

"I want Kay." His lips twisted into a smile. "I want him to come in through that door, and look—you know how he used to look, Gawain. As if he couldn't quite understand why the good God permitted you to exist." He stifled unsteady laughter. "I don't think any of you understood Kay, not even you, Gawain. When I first came to Camelot—" He turned to Lady Alienor, aware of her presence enough to realise he would have to explain. "When I first came, at the Pentecost Court, I didn't tell anyone who I was. I was tired of being Gawain's little brother, you see. I asked Arthur if I might serve in the court for a year. I think I saw myself doing something decorative with a wine cup."

Now it was Gawain's turn to stifle laughter.

Gareth shot him that brilliant gaze, and went on, "Arthur handed me over to Kay. After the meal, he took me down to the kitchens, and just looked at me. You know, I was taller than he was, even then, and I couldn't work out how he managed to look down at me. He said, 'Well, boy, are you just playing at humility, or do you want to work?' He took my breath away! He was absolutely right—I had been playing, until then. I was thinking about the stories they would tell about me afterwards, as if I could cheat my way to a reputation. No—not even that. I hadn't thought at all. But with Kay standing there waiting, I had to think fast. I said, 'I want to work, sir.' And he made sure I did!"

"I was worried about you," Gawain said. "In those days, of course, I didn't know Kay as well as I do now."

Gareth shrugged impatiently. "There was no need. Lancelot was kind, too. He gave me money, and clothes, and he used to help me with training when I had some spare time. But he still didn't get the point. Kay was the only person who did. I'd made my decision, and he saw I stuck to it." Now he was deeply serious. "I learnt more about knighthood in Kay's kitchens than on the practice ground with Lancelot." His voice choked suddenly. "I wish I'd told him that."

"He knew," Gawain said, touching his shoulder. "He took such pride in you. Even if he would have died rather than admit it!"

"He hid everything," Gareth said. "No one understood him. And now they never will."

He bent his head into his hands and let the tears come at last.

CHAPTER THIRTY

Sir Gawain felt no joy in his return to Camelot. Too much had changed. Kay's absence hurt now even more than Lancelot's, for Lancelot was often away, while Kay had been at home in Camelot as a fish is at home in the sea. The loss of that brisk, irascible presence made the court seem strangely empty.

War was washing up against the city walls. Preparations were already in train, organised by Guenevere before ever the king returned. Gawain had no stomach for watching Briant take responsibility into his own hands.

He spent the first day of his return in the city, talking to the country people who had come for refuge, fearful of Claudas and his troops. They had all seen something, or spoken to someone who had seen something, and the patient knitting up of scraps of evidence, the sifting of fact from rumour and speculation, was a job Briant had no patience for.

When Gawain had made his report, and had little thanks for it, he went to the muniments room and set one of the scribes looking for the deeds to Lady Alienor's manor. Then he let himself out into the garden. Daylight was dying; the winter trees, still bare, seemed shrouded in sadness. But beneath the trees sharp green shoots thrust upwards, a promise of spring to come. Gawain could find no answering spring of hope in his heart.

Snowdrops shivered in the grass at his feet; he stooped and picked a handful, for Lionors. Her reunion with Gareth had been a bright flame in the midst of desolation. The thought of it, and the expectation of their child, warmed Gawain now.

He was returning along a different path when he saw someone coming to meet him: the lady Brisane, resplendent in scarlet and sables. The colours she painted on the shadowy garden seemed crude and incongruous; Gawain glanced aside to see if there was a way of avoiding her, but she had already seen him.

"So beautiful!"

Her fingers closed around the flowers in his hand, claiming them. Gawain surrendered them with a half-bow; he found her touch faintly repellent.

"I have wished to speak with you, Sir Gawain," she said.

There was a confidential air about her. She bent her head close to him; he breathed in her aromatic perfume.

"If I can serve you, lady. . . ."

Brisane smiled. "I wished to consult you about my lord

Briant. He finds his new office . . . difficult. So many of Arthur's knights scorn his authority." She sighed. "It is natural enough, I suppose, that they should be slow to welcome new ways. But you, Sir Gawain, gave us your help in Carlisle. . . ."

Gawain felt uneasy. What help he had given at that disastrous council had been for Arthur, no one else. And perhaps for Britain, which could not be defended if Arthur's knights quarrelled with their king.

"If you could speak to some of the other knights," Brisane suggested. "Sir Ector, Sir Bors. You could remind them of their loyalty. After all, you are the king's heir. You have authority."

Gawain shook his head. In the hope of shortening this interview, he took Brisane's arm and guided her along the path.

"As Knights of the Round Table, lady," he said, "we are all equal. None of us has authority over another. My lord Briant would do well to remember that. And if I tried to lesson Sir Ector or Sir Bors, they would rightly find it an impertinence."

Brisane stopped and faced him again. "But you are Arthur's heir. Should they not respect you, against the day when you are king?"

"Lady, you mistake." Gawain felt more uneasy with every second that passed. He wanted to be rid of her, and yet he did not see how he could do it with courtesy. "I am little younger than Arthur. I do not expect to inherit."

"But in battle, my lord, even a king may die." She looked speculative now. She passed her tongue over those red lips. "Even in this next battle against Claudas."

"I might die myself," Gawain said.

Soft laughter came from Brisane. She lifted one hand to touch Gawain's hair; it was all he could do not to flinch away from her. Her perfume was hot in his throat.

"If Arthur died, Gawain, you would be king. You would need a queen."

Gawain's breath was taken away. Had she just suggested that he assassinate Arthur and take her to wife? Was she not in truth wedded to Briant? Or was he starting to panic, reading absurdities into an innocent remark?

Badly thrown off balance, he managed to say, "I have no such thoughts, lady."

The soft laughter again. "I can scarcely believe," Brisane said, "that this is Sir Gawain who speaks. When the most beautiful of all ladies in Britain would vie for the honour of being your lady?"

Gawain shook his head, disclaiming.

"You force me to immodesty, sir, to confess that I myself . . . were it not for my lord Briant—"

"But he is your lord." Gawain was thankful to remind her.

"And my brother in this fellowship. It would be dishonour to all three of us if I should look on his lady."

Brisane laughed softly. "Honour is a word, sir. A word for men. I am a woman, and I know what is more than honour. You are human, sir, are you not, and not an angel out of heaven?"

He was human, and her nearness was having its human effect on him, but warring with it was that curious sense of repulsion that he had felt at first.

Stiffly, he said, "I cannot see the profit in talk like this, lady."

"Only that you should grasp what is yours for the taking, Sir Gawain. Do I not please you? Am I not beautiful?"

"Yes, lady, you are very beautiful."

"Then may we not . . . comfort each other a little? War is very near, and all of us must one day die."

Somehow, now that she had grown more direct, Gawain found that he could cope with her better. He took a step back, bowing to her, feeling stupidly formal.

"My lady, you must forgive me. I am not free." Loosing pain from the depths of himself, putting words to what he never spoke of, he said, "I have a lady. She . . . left me. But I am hers in honour, while my life lasts."

He watched the emotions flickering over Brisane's face: disappointment, disbelief, calculation. He realised, if he had not known it before, that seducing him had been only a move in her game. Her heart was not touched, perhaps not even her senses. She dropped him a deep reverence; there was a glittering smile on her face.

"Such faithfulness!" she said. "And the lady does not appreciate it? She's a fool, then. Others, Sir Gawain, would value you more highly." She rose again, stretching out a hand to him. "Think of what I have said. With me or another, Britain is in your grasp."

Abruptly she turned and vanished up the path in a rustle of silks. Gawain followed more slowly, but as he passed one of the stone seats at the side of the path he sank down on it, to calm his whirling thoughts before he had to meet anyone else.

Brisane had offered herself, but it was not simple pleasure she had in mind. Had she truly meant to abandon Briant and play for the rank of queen as Gawain's consort? Or had she a plan deeper still?

Gawain remembered the warning Kay had sent. Briant and Brisane together meant to destroy Arthur, and first to weaken him by destroying his closest councillors. Kay was gone now, and Lancelot threatened. Gawain felt the chill of his own danger.

He could not help wondering what would have happened if he had responded to Brisane. Would she have arranged for someone to find them together, to set more quarrels among Arthur's men in this crisis? Gawain could have found himself banished. At the very least, he would have lost Arthur's trust.

He thanked God that he had escaped, but he knew there would be another attack. He was not sure if he had the strength to meet it. Sitting in the garden, with darkness gathering around him, Gawain felt very much alone.

On the following morning, Gawain had just finished dressing, ready to attend the council that Briant had called. A tap sounded on his door; Gareth came in with Lionors.

Gawain went to her, and kissed her hand, and then her cheek. "You look well this morning, Sister."

It was true. Although Lionors' slender figure had filled out with her pregnancy, her step was springy and there was a glow of health about her.

"Much better now," she said, with an affectionate look at Gareth. "Last time I was sick from morning to night; now I think I could ride to Cornwall and back again, and never notice it."

"Don't you dare try," Gareth said.

Lionors smiled at him, but there was a sadness behind her eyes that made Gawain ask, "Has Gareth told you about Kay?"

"Yes." She frowned. "I cannot believe Kay was a traitor."

"I know," Gawain said. "We don't believe it either. I had hoped we might clear his name, but now I think the truth, whatever it was, died with him."

There was a little silence, which Gareth broke. "Gawain, I came to ask you something." He hesitated, and then went on with difficulty. "This council . . . we must go into the council chamber, and see Kay's name gone from the Table, and Briant's in its place. I don't know if I can bear it. I don't want to make a fool of myself in front of everyone. Will you go with me now, early, and see—and then perhaps . . ."

His voice stumbled into silence. He caught at Lionors' hand, and clasped it hard.

"Yes, of course," Gawain said.

Most of the court were still rousing, and they met few people on the stairs or in the passages. The anteroom to the council chamber was empty except for the guards at the door. Gawain went in, followed by Gareth with Lionors.

The room was shadowed. Beneath the grey tracery of roof and walls, the Table stood, a golden ellipse with a thicker diapering of gold around the edge, where the knights' names were inscribed. It was silence, light, the visible affirmation of God's hand on Arthur's kingdom. Would it withstand evil, Gawain wondered, or would it dissipate into golden dust motes and be lost like the dust when the sun goes down?

He waited by the door while Gareth, after a moment's hesitation, strode round the Table to the place that had been Kay's. He stood for a long time, leaning forward a little, his hands flat on each side of the name written there.

He was so still that Gawain caught Lionors glancing anxiously at him, and began to feel anxious himself. "Gareth—" he began.

His brother raised his head. He was white; his eyes blazed. "Look."

Gawain went round the Table to him. Between Gareth's hands against the silky golden surface, the lettering of deeper gold burnt into the wood: *Sir Kay.* Gawain drew in his breath. Like Gareth, he could not drag his eyes away. *Sir Kay.* Nothing more; no change. Yet it was a vindication cried out from heaven itself.

Very slowly, Gareth said, "He is not dead." He was beginning to smile a little. "He is not dead. He is not disgraced. He is still knight. No one can deny it now. No one would dare!"

He sank into Kay's seat and covered his face with his hands.

Lionors went to him and stooped over, putting her arms around his shoulders. Gawain was still uncertain of what to do next when the sound of footsteps came into the silent room, from the stair that led to Arthur's private quarters. The door opened; Arthur stood there, with Briant des Isles at his shoulder. To Gawain's relief, there was no sign of the lady Brisane.

"What is this?" the king said.

Gawain made no answer in words, but indicated Kay's name on the Table. Arthur crossed the room, and stood transfixed, staring. In wonder, Gawain saw the king's face, that had been grey and haggard for so long, quicken into something like himself, as if he drank in the golden name as a man dying of thirst drinks the water that will save him. Only the shadow of the old Arthur as yet, but Gawain could not suppress a quivering hope that perhaps he had returned.

"My lord?" Gawain prompted.

Arthur rubbed a hand across his eyes; it was Gareth who spoke, straightening and reaching up a hand to Lionors. He was quite calm.

"I am going to find him. He may be hurt, or ill, or in danger. My lord, do not forbid this, because I do not want to disobey you, and yet I will go." To Lionors, he said, "I'm sorry."

She smiled, gripping his hand. "Don't be. I'll do very well here, while you're away."

Gawain's attention was still on the king; so far Arthur had not spoken. When he did, he sounded quite natural, and more in command of himself than he had been for weeks. "Your lady shall have all care, Gareth. I would ride north myself, if Claudas did not threaten us here. Perhaps Gawain will go with you? I will write—"

He was interrupted by Briant, who still stood by the door; Gawain could see that he had no idea what was happening.

"What is this?" Briant said. "Why are you sending men north when they're needed to fight here?"

Arthur turned to look at him, almost startled, as if he had forgotten that Briant was there. "Kay's name is still on the Table."

"While I don't see yours at all, my lord Briant," Gareth said, with a flash of malice that was quite unlike him.

Briant shrugged. "What else could you expect when we came to Camelot only two days ago. There will be time now to get it changed."

Gareth gave way to unsteady laughter.

"My lord Briant," Gawain said, "you don't get the Table changed. The Table changes of itself."

Briant gave him a stare, and a snort of contempt. "What are you talking about? Do you expect me to believe rubbish like that?"

Arthur had begun to look at Briant as if he had never seen him before, the sort of look that Gawain might have prayed for, if he had been able to imagine that slowly dawning realisation of the truth. Briant himself was still no more than irritated, still not understanding that his dominance of the king slipped farther away with every second that passed.

"My lord Briant," Gawain said, "the Table was made for Arthur's father, King Uther Pendragon, through the wisdom of his councillor Merlin. Merlin made the Table as an . . . an echo in this world of the table where our Lord Christ sat with his disciples, and our fellowship, with the Lord's help, exists as a memory of that. The names appear on the Table through the will of God, not the craft of any mortal."

Briant was frowning. "Are you telling me that this is sorcery?"

"No, my lord. Just the opposite. The Table is a holy mystery."

Growing uncertain, Briant approached the Table, peering down at the names and running his hand along the edge. He snorted again, but Gawain thought that he could see fear behind his eyes.

"Absurd! I am High Seneschal of Britain; I have the right to sit here."

"No man has the right," Gawain said flatly. "The privilege, perhaps."

Briant ignored the quiet correction. He turned to Arthur. "Is this right, my lord, that the name of a murderer, a traitor—and a man by all reports dead—stays on the Table, while I am your faithful servant and yet have no place? Is this the will of God?"

"Clearly it is," Arthur said dryly.

Gareth, quietly forceful, formidable as Gawain had seen him in Carlisle, leant forward across the Table towards Briant.

"My lord, when a knight dies, his name fades from the Table. Kay's has not faded, so clearly he is not dead. So far as I know, it has never happened that a knight has been so disgraced that his name disappeared, but truly, I believe if Kay had done what he was accused of, his name would have faded, for he would have been dead to this fellowship. But it has not!" Growing excited, he brought his hand down flat on the surface above Kay's name. "It shows he is innocent, my lord. The voice of God himself proclaims it!"

Briant took a step or two farther round the Table, until he was close enough to see Kay's name for himself. His face was highly coloured, anger struggling against a superstitious fear.

Sneeringly, he said, "So you tell me, my lord Arthur, that you have no voice in choosing your own knights? That you must obey this Table like a snivelling priest poring over his mass-book? Is this what it means to be a king?"

"Under God, yes," Arthur said. "Briant, until you understand that, you won't understand what we're trying to do in Britain. Serve me faithfully, and there will be a place for you in time."

"In time!" Briant's anger was conquering his fear. "My lord, you yourself accepted my service at Carlisle, and named me Knight of the Round Table."

Arthur spread his hands. "For that, I ask your pardon. It may be that I did what I had no right to do. I have been . . . confused, by many different griefs." More quietly, speaking to himself and not to Briant, he said, "It is the first time that I have made a choice that the Table has not accepted. Truly I have moved far from the will of God. But yet I believe there is grace and mercy. This Table shows it to me now."

"Grace and mercy?" Briant echoed furiously. "For a murderer and a traitor? For Kay?"

Arthur nodded. "Even for Kay," he said, "and even for me. For my brother is not dead, but alive, and I may yet find him and heal the hurt between us. Gawain—"

Arthur broke off as Briant took the few steps that brought him close. The seneschal grabbed the king by the shoulder.

Brutally, Briant said, "Kay killed your son."

Arthur's face convulsed with pain.

"Briant," said Gawain, "there you speak the truth, for Kay never denied that he killed Loholt. But what he would never tell anyone was the reason he did it. I do not believe this tale of Kay stabbing Loholt so that he could make his own escape. That is not Kay as I knew him."

Gawain took a breath; he had his proof now, and he knew how to use it. He knew the course that was laid out for him, even if he did not know whether his strength would sustain him to the end of it. He felt a dizzying sensation, as if he were suspended above the earth, instead of on it. "Not all killing is murder, my lord Briant. Many times you have called Kay a murderer. Do you stand here now, with the Table as witness, and repeat that charge?"

"Yes." Briant spoke without hesitation. "A murderer and a traitor to his king."

"Then, my lord, I must ask you to prove it with your sword."

Gareth sat up, his face a blaze of delight, and Lionors, though she shook her head, betrayed an admiration Gawain could not be unaware of. But Arthur looked startled, and Briant was frankly disbelieving.

"You're challenging me? You?"

Gawain had a sudden insight into how Kay must have felt under the continual contempt of those who called him no fighter, as if that meant he was no true man. He experienced himself a stab of angry defensiveness, but he made himself reply quietly.

"Yes, my lord. Just because I love peace does not mean that I fear to take up my sword if the cause is good. I challenge you to prove your accusations, for I say that Kay is innocent, and God will so ordain that his innocence is made plain to everyone."

While he spoke there came the sound of voices in the anteroom, as the first of the knights gathered for the council. Two or three—Sir Ector among them—appeared at the door, and stood silent in the face of Gawain's affirmation of trust in Kay.

Briant, too, was silent. Gawain thought that he could see a return of the man's uncertainty, a superstitious terror of what the Table meant.

"Well, my lord?" Arthur said.

Blustering, Briant replied, "No honourable man would use sorcery in a fight."

"True, my lord," Gawain said, "and that is something you would do well to remember, for there was sorcery on the battlefield the day Meliant de Lis fought with Lancelot."

For a moment Briant looked utterly baffled. Gawain had a sudden flash of certainty: *He does not know all that his lady does!* He might have felt sympathy for Briant if there had been time to feel anything except the need to defend Kay.

Arthur repeated, "Well, my lord Briant? Will you accept this challenge? There will be no sorcery on our side, I promise you."

Gawain did not miss that revealing phrase: "our side." Briant understood it, too.

"You turn from me now, my lord, in your craven fear of this Table," Briant said. "But you will see who has your good most truly at heart. Myself, or Sir Gawain who risks weakening you when you need all your strength to fight Claudas. Gawain who is a traitor and a friend of traitors. Yes, I accept the challenge."

Chapter Thirty-one

Very early the next morning, while the city was still rousing, Gawain left the citadel for the tournament field and his fight with Briant des Isles.

Although the land stood on the brink of spring, it was a raw, grey day, with a sweep of cloud fanning across the sky. A cold light spread reluctantly from the east. The horses' hooves clinked on the cobbled streets. Gawain shrank deeper into his cloak and shivered.

He did not look forward to fighting with Briant. He was less sure than he had been that his challenge had been the right decision. True, Kay must be defended and Briant thrust from the court before he had the opportunity to do more damage. And Gawain had not lost his faith in Kay's innocence; he had been sure of that even before the Table had confirmed it. What he was not sure of was whether he would win.

He had long lost his faith in trial by combat. He had seen too many fights won by strength and not by right. He felt it was presumptuous to demand a miracle, to expect God to give the victory to the weaker or the less skilful. Gawain had never pitted himself against Briant, had never had the opportunity to assess the Breton's skill or his style. He did not know what he had to face; to himself, he admitted he was afraid.

The king, at the head of the column of riders, reached the gate of the city and ordered it to be opened. As he rode through, Gawain caught a glimpse of the gate guard, staring in undisguised curiosity. The king led the way along the twisting road to the tournament field.

As they left the city behind, Gareth, riding beside his brother, began to whistle, a pure sound in the still air.

Sourly, Gawain said, "You sound cheerful."

Gareth grinned at him. "Why not? We're about to get rid of Briant. And then you and I will ride north and find Kay, and—"

"You're very sure. I don't know that I can beat him."

Gareth's grin became a smile of real affection. "Sir Gawain, this modesty becomes you well," he said with mock courtliness, and added more informally, "You're going to mince Briant into little pieces."

The road dipped and climbed again, back and forth across the slope until it came to the tournament field. Wind swept across it, bending and silvering the grass. It seemed desolate to

Gawain when he remembered the last tournament. Then the field had been thronged with knights and servants and townspeople, and edged with bright pavilions like enormous, exotic flowers. Where Briant had just drawn up his horse had been the stand for the ladies of the court. There had been music and laughter. Now his enemy waited for him in grey silence.

By now the whole of Camelot knew about the combat, but Arthur had limited the number of his escort. Of his knights there were Gawain's brothers, Gaheris and Agravaine, besides Gareth, who had insisted on acting as Gawain's squire. Along with them were Ector, Bors, and Lionel, Lancelot's kinsmen, their presence confirming what no one doubted, that Gawain's defence of Kay was a defence of Lancelot as well. Briant had a couple of men attending him. All these Gawain had expected to see on the field. He had not expected Queen Guenevere herself, with Lionors and Brisane.

Servants had erected some makeshift seating, with a canvas awning to keep off the wind. Guenevere led the other two women to take their places. Even at a distance, Gawain could see that Brisane was in a towering temper. Her stance, the carriage of her head, shrieked it at him, though he could not see her face clearly. He was encouraged to realise that she did not want this fight.

Gareth dismounted, drove the end of one of Gawain's lances into the ground, and came to hand him the other one. Gawain unfastened his cloak and let it slip into his brother's grasp.

"Remember," he said, "whatever happens, you must not interfere. If I'm to beat Briant, I have to do it fairly, so that not even he can complain about treachery."

Gareth sighed regretfully. "I know. I was never a squire, Gawain, but I know the duties. Even if I'd like nothing better than to get my hands on Briant. You were too quick for me yesterday," he said. "Another half-minute, and I would have challenged him myself."

Perhaps you should have, Gawain thought silently. He was convinced his brother was a better fighter than he was himself. He tried not to think about what would happen if he lost now. Briant would kill him if he could. If he survived, he, too, would be marked as a traitor, along with Kay. He wondered if Arthur would be forced to send him into exile. . . .

Determinedly, Gawain cut off that train of thought. Briant, at the far side of the field, looked ready, and Arthur took up his position to signal for the combat to start.

Gareth grinned up at his brother. "Good luck," he said.

He moved away, with a farewell pat on the horse's neck. Gawain slid his shield into place, gathered up the reins, and levelled his lance. Across the field, Briant had done the same.

Arthur raised his arm and brought it down. Gawain urged his horse into motion.

At first he felt as if he had an infinite amount of time to plan his manoeuvre. Briant's approach seemed slow, like a wave lazily scrolling up to the shore. Then the rush and thunder of the horses was all around him, as the wave batters a rock. He caught the glitter of Briant's lance point.

Gawain's body had been doing the right things while his mind drifted. He crouched low over his horse's neck, swerving slightly so that Briant's lance glanced off his shield. At the same time his own lance took Briant full in the centre of his shield, and shattered. Briant rocked with the impact, his horse skittered sideways, but he kept his seat.

Gawain slowed his horse to a trot and brought it round in a wide circle, back to where Gareth waited. He had begun to get Briant's measure now. Little finesse; leap in with both feet and hack his way to victory. Gawain let out a long breath. Briant had the advantage of height and weight, and probably physical strength as well; Gawain was not sure if he had the skill to overcome him.

Back at Gawain's starting point, Gareth handed him the second lance. His face was alive with excitement. "You have him—like that!" he said, clenching a fist.

Gawain shrugged. "Maybe."

Briant had already turned and was charging down on him. Gawain spurred towards him. This time he was completely in control. Briant was ready for his swerve; Gawain swerved the other way, inside his lance thrust, and brought his own weapon forward with a twist that sent Briant off balance. The Breton lost his grip on the reins and slid sideways, crashing to the ground, while his horse galloped off, careering around the edge of the field.

Gawain dismounted. Briant tried to get up, thrusting himself to his knees, half stunned. Gawain knew he should attack, knew very well that if their positions had been reversed Briant would have been on him already. He drew his sword and waited.

Briant had managed to get to his feet, and stood head down, shaking it. His hand groped for his sword. Gawain wondered if the fall had injured him. He lowered his shield and took a pace forward. "My lord Briant—"

Briant snapped into movement. His sword was out; he leapt for Gawain, bearing him down. Gawain was forced to one knee. He got his shield up in time to block the downstroke of Briant's sword, and brought his own weapon round in a scything movement that Briant had to parry. The weapons locked; Gawain knew if he let Briant pin him to the ground, he would be dead within seconds. He could see Briant's face under the helmet, teeth set, lips snarling, eyes aflame.

Gathering his strength, Gawain thrust upwards. Briant staggered back; Gawain scrambled to his feet. With no thought at all now for letting his opponent recover, he followed him, raining blows on his shield. It had to be now; he could not let Briant's strength wear him down. He had to get inside that guard.

He feinted to the left, drawing Briant's defence, and then slid in a stroke to the right, low and travelling upwards. He felt his sword bite into Briant's thigh. Blood spurted. Briant lurched sideways, cursing, swung his sword round in one last wild stroke, and fell.

The wound was not serious. Gawain did not expect it to stop the fight, but he saw it was in the leg that had been broken and weakened in the battle near Carlisle. Briant floundered to his feet, tried to put weight on the injured leg, and went down again.

Gawain waited briefly, sword poised, and then stepped forward. "My lord Briant, do you acknowledge Sir Kay's innocence now?"

Briant gazed up at him, his face twisted with hatred. "No."

Gawain looked at his own sword, with Briant's blood petalling along the edge of the blade. He knew what the rules of the combat would have him do now. He looked up at Arthur, who had come to stand on the other side of Briant.

"My lord, I can't kill him," Gawain said.

Arthur met his eyes for a moment and then motioned him back. Gawain let his sword fall, and stood with bowed head, breathing hard.

To Briant the king said, "You do not admit Kay's innocence?"

This time Briant made no reply but a savage shake of the head.

"Your life is Gawain's," Arthur said, "or mine. But I grant it to you before you ask." Gawain could see that the king knew very well Briant would not ask; the Breton had courage, at least. "You will go back to the court, where my healers will bind your wound. Then you will collect your lady and your men-at-arms and what belongs to you, and be gone out of my kingdom. Go to Claudas, for all I care. Warn him to think again about invading Britain."

Briant had struggled up onto one elbow while the king spoke. He said, "My lord, it was Lancelot, not I, who brought Claudas to—"

"That lie won't serve you now. I don't believe it, any more than I believe the other lies you fed me with, when grief made me fool enough to listen to you. What did he offer you—the crown of Britain as a vassal state to Brittany? No—don't answer. Get up and be gone, before my patience runs out."

Arthur stepped back, gesturing to Briant's men, who had come up, leading his horse. Once they were helping their lord to mount, the king turned away, and walked across the field to where Guenevere still watched with Lionors and the rest of the knights. He did not look at Briant again.

While Arthur had been speaking, Brisane had left her seat and drawn closer. She did not spare Briant a look or a word. Her gaze, vibrant with malice, was fixed on Gawain.

"Fool!" she said. "You could have had everything. Now you will never be a king."

The beautiful face, framed in her sables, twisted in contempt. Without waiting for him to reply, she swept away, back to her horse.

Gawain stood shivering, watching her go, grateful for the cloak that Gareth folded round his shoulders once again. Gareth retrieved the sword that he had dropped, tore up a handful of grass, and began to clean the blade.

"Your famous courtesy is going to get you killed one day," he said.

Gawain tried to smile, could not trust his voice to speak, and took refuge in silence.

"You see, I was right," Gareth said tranquilly. "We're rid of Briant. And tomorrow, when Arthur has written his letters, we can ride north and start to look for Kay."

Later on the same day, Arthur sent for Gawain to his private room. He was seated at the table when Gawain arrived, sealing the letters he had promised. "I can ill spare you or Gareth," the king said, "but I have tried your brother's loyalty too far already. He must go where his heart leads him, and it's not good for him to go alone. Truly, I wish that I—" He broke off. Gathering up the letters, he gave them to Gawain.

"One for Kay, when he is found. And one for the Constable of Carlisle. I've ordered him to release Lancelot and provide you with men to search. You will take command in the North until I come myself."

"I?" Gawain said, startled. "I had thought Lancelot . . ."

He let the protest die away. Arthur did not explain himself, and Gawain did not feel he could ask for reasons. Feeling slightly awkward, he was bowing, ready to withdraw, when the king said, "Gawain."

He beckoned for Gawain to come close to him again. When Gawain stood beside his chair, the king reached out and took his hand, where he wore Kay's carnelian. The stone smouldered in the lamplight.

"Kay's ring," Arthur said.

"I promised to keep it for him, until he comes again."

Arthur sighed, and passed his hands over his face and into the tawny hair. "You were always so sure. Sure enough to offer your life." His eyes were bleak. "I grew up with Kay. But I was not sure." He paused, and then said abruptly, "Will you give me the ring?"

Gawain hesitated, not unwilling, but taken aback by the request and the king's manner of making it.

"That's not a command, Gawain," Arthur said. "I would not command you in this. But I should like to . . . to speak to Kay, to give back what I took away, to make my peace with him, if I can. Many things were wrong between us, before ever Loholt came to court. Perhaps they can be put right, if Kay will wear my ring again."

Gawain drew off the ring, and dropped it into Arthur's outstretched palm.

"Kay loves you," he said. "Nothing in this world or the next can ever change that."

Arthur accepted the words with a wry half-smile. Gawain left the king holding the ring in his fingers, watching it gather the lamplight as if it held the splendour of a long-forgotten sun.

Chapter Thirty-two

Gawain had intended to ride straight for Carlisle and send out search parties and messengers in the hunt for Kay, but once they crossed the bridge upstream of Roche Dure Gareth persuaded him into making long casts on either side of the road, in the hope of picking up news. For five days they searched, and found nothing.

On the morning of the sixth day they returned to the road, after another vain detour into the hills. The trees stood in a mist of green. The sun shone. Birdsong blended with the soft murmur of a thousand streams. For all his disappointment, Gareth enjoyed the warm breeze on his face and whistled softly.

"We'll make for Lady Alienor's manor," Gawain said. "We can be there by nightfall. She'll be glad of the news that Kay is still alive."

"And Kay might have gone back there." Gareth's optimism instantly revived. "Or they may have word of where he is."

Gawain looked sceptical. "If not," he said, "we ride for Carlisle. We're wasting time, trying to do it alone."

They spent the rest of the morning climbing, at first through hazel brakes and bracken, and then, leaving the trees behind, across open moorland, sometimes dismounting to lead the horses when the upward slope grew steep, splashing through small streams and skirting thickets of gorse and bramble.

Just after midday they came to a shoulder of the fell, and looked down on a long and narrow lake lying like a spearhead between two crags. Though the sky was blue, the water looked grey and forbidding.

Gareth peered out into the distance. "Is that a village at the other end?"

Gawain looked in the direction he pointed. "I'm not sure. Your eyesight is better than mine. It might just be the shape of the rocks."

"We'll stop for something to eat," Gareth decided, quite certain in his own mind, "and then go down and look."

Gawain did not protest. As they dismounted and turned the horses off to graze, he said slowly, "If I remember what Lady Alienor told us, this is the lake where her men found traces of Kay."

"Then the people down there might have seen him!" Gareth said.

Gawain smiled faintly, and cautioned, "If there really are people down there."

While they ate, Gawain explained where he thought they were, scratching his map on a stone that jutted up from the turf. Gareth's spirits rose. After the briefest possible stop, he looked for the way down.

There was no real path. Gareth found the descent to the lakeside agonisingly slow. They had to search for footholds on the hillside, coaxing the horses down and hoping every moment that they would not find their way barred by a sheer drop.

At last they reached the waterside, not far from the nearer end, the base of the spear. The village, if it existed, was close to the point. Mounting again, they rode beside the lake. On their right, walls of tumbled rock rose to the beginnings of another stretch of woodland, with a few straggling thorn bushes growing in cracks, and a few yards of turf and shale between the rock and the water. Everything was very quiet, except for the movement of the horses and the liquid song of a lark, high and distant.

After a few minutes Gareth paused, pointing ahead once more. "Look!"

This time he knew he was not imagining it: a thin column of smoke, rising unwaveringly into the still air.

"Too close for your village," Gawain murmured.

They pressed on, rounding a spur of the hillside that jutted out into their path. Beyond the spur, they could see a fire burning by the lake shore. A dark figure, one man alone, was crouched over it, feeding it with wood. Gareth drew in a breath, but dared not speak.

As the two knights drew closer the man looked up, as if startled by the sound of the horses, and then sprang to his feet. He raised one hand to his throat in a gesture that was heart-wrenchingly familiar. Gareth gave a glad cry, and flung himself from his horse. The man standing by the fire was Kay.

His face was pale, his eyes sunken as if someone had flung gouts of hot pitch onto snow. He held the tatters of his black cloak tight around himself like a shield. There was something in the way he looked that made Gareth come to a halt a yard or two away from him.

In a shaken voice, Kay said, "I have seen you before, but never so clearly. My mind gives way. . . . You cannot truly be here."

Terrified, Gareth shot a look at his brother. Gawain dismounted and approached more slowly, going right up to Kay and taking his hand between both his own. Kay's eyes devoured him, but he never moved, except for the shudder that ran through him at Gawain's touch.

Gawain said, "Dear Kay, it is true. We are here. We've found you at last. There's nothing more to—"

He broke off as Kay sagged against him. Gawain caught him in his arms and lowered him, unconscious, to the ground.

Gareth crouched down beside them. "Gawain, he's not dead—"

"Fainted." Gawain's voice was blessedly calm. "Fetch some blankets."

Thankful to do something, Gareth brought his bedding roll, unfastened it, and wrapped the blankets around Kay. Anxiety made him clumsy.

"He's so cold," he said. "He looks ill."

Gawain was bent over Kay, his face intent, one hand laid lightly on the pulse in Kay's throat.

"You would look ill," he murmured, "if you'd lived like this for—what? Two months, almost."

"Living here?" Gareth said, staring round him wildly, almost expecting to see shelter spring up out of the ground.

"Near here, I expect. I don't suppose he built this fire for fun. Bring me a water skin."

Gareth went back to his horse. A few yards along the shore he could see what looked like a cave opening; just beyond it a spring trickled from the rock face and ran across the strip of shore to the lake. Nearby, two fish, neatly gutted, broiled over the fire on an arrangement of sticks; a belt knife glittered on the stones beside it.

"Rescue Kay's supper." Gawain nodded towards the fire as Gareth handed him the water skin. "He won't want to eat it just yet."

Gareth moved the fish out of the flames, cursing over burnt fingers, while Gawain splashed water onto a handkerchief and touched it to Kay's temples. Kay stirred and muttered something almost inaudible. Gawain raised his head gently and held the water skin to his lips. Kay drank, choked a little, and opened his eyes.

"Gawain," he whispered at last.

"Yes."

As Gareth came back and crouched beside Kay and his brother again, he saw the bewilderment in Kay's face change to wariness.

"The Lady—is she here? Has she not done enough?"

Gareth was not sure what he meant. He glanced uncertainly at Gawain, and saw that he was almost equally at a loss.

"No, Kay, she is far away, I promise you," Gawain said.

Kay struggled to free himself from the confining blankets, and managed to sit up, bowing his head into his hands.

"I dare not believe you," he said. "Once, she showed me Arthur. If I believe you now, my mind will fail."

Gareth still could not understand what he meant. He reached

out and touched Kay's shoulder. At the touch, Kay glanced briefly at him, and hid his face again. Gareth knew what he had to say.

"Kay, forgive me. The way I behaved in Roche Dure was . . . unspeakable."

Until now he had not quite realised how the burden of that night still weighed on him, and what a relief it would be to rid himself of it at last.

Kay raised his head again, looking at him fully, a sharp, mistrustful look. It pierced Gareth like a spear; somehow he had never really believed that Kay would not forgive him. He felt tears starting. Through refracted light he saw Kay reach out to him; he wanted to embrace him but he dared not. On Kay's other side, Gawain sat still as a rock.

"This I cannot bear," Kay said softly. "If she plays with me now then she has won." He let out a long, shaken breath. "You have never done me wrong, Sir Gareth."

Gareth still wanted to embrace him, to laugh or weep, but he contented himself with clasping Kay's hand.

"I've missed you," he said. "But all's well now. We've found you, and it's all over."

Kay's bewildered look returned. "No. I'm still disgraced. I can't . . . how can I believe you?"

Gareth held his hand tightly. "Arthur has sent for you." He could not stop his voice from shaking. "Your name is still on the Table. Kay, we've come to take you home."

Kay stared at him, and then turned his gaze, desperately questioning, to Gawain.

"Yes, it's true," Gawain said. "Gareth, you are an idiot, spilling it all out like that. It's all true. Rest a little, and we'll explain it to you."

Kay still kept his eyes fixed on Gawain, as if he could read the story in his face. "Arthur . . . wants me?"

Excitedly Gareth started fumbling in the front of his tunic.

"He wrote you a letter." He pulled out the crumpled page, straightened it, and offered it to Kay. "Here. Read it."

Kay gazed at it, extended a hand hesitantly, and then drew back. "I can't. Read it for me, please."

Glancing at Gawain, who nodded agreement, Gareth broke the seal and unfolded the sheet.

"'Kay, your name still stands on the Table.'" As he read, he felt something of the king's urgency invading his voice. "'God knows I have treated you unjustly. We must talk, and this time you must tell me all the truth. Go to Carlisle, and wait for me there. I will ride north again when I have dealt with Claudas. Until then, obey Gawain's commands as you would obey mine. Arthur.'"

All the while Gareth had been reading, Kay had kept silence, drinking in the king's words, his face wiped clear of all expression, except for the revealing depths of his eyes. Gareth could not bear it any longer; when he had finished the letter, he got up abruptly and went to see to the horses, unsaddling them and finding a spot on the lake shore where they could graze.

By the time he returned, Kay and Gawain had moved to sit by the fire, and Gawain was telling Kay what had happened in Camelot. Gareth squatted beside Kay and launched enthusiastically into the end of the story, how he had found Kay's name still on the Table, and how Gawain had fought with Briant to prove Kay's innocence.

"You challenged Briant?" Kay said, with a wondering look at Gawain.

"I don't know why everyone sounds so surprised." Gawain's smile softened the irritation of his words. "Someone had to stop him. Besides, after you and Lancelot, I was his next target. If he'd won the fight, I would be dead or exiled now."

"Oh, I wish you'd been there to see—" Gareth said.

Kay interrupted him. "Lancelot? What do you mean?"

"Of course, you don't know," Gawain said. "Lancelot is under arrest in Carlisle. Briant accused him of deliberately murdering Meliant de Lis to give Claudas of Brittany a rightful excuse to invade."

Kay drew a long breath, sudden enlightenment in his face. "It was Briant who brought in Claudas. Claudas sent troops to him, to Roche Dure. I think he means to put Briant on the throne of Britain and then rule as his overlord."

"That's what I thought," Gawain said. "And when we left Camelot, Arthur was preparing to fight them both. It may all be over now," he added, as fear leapt into Kay's eyes. "Don't worry. Arthur is Arthur again. Claudas isn't going to defeat him."

"I should be there, with him," Kay said.

Gareth leant forward, trying to distract him. "We have letters for the Constable of Carlisle, and for Lancelot. Lancelot is to be released. Gawain's orders are to secure the North, until Arthur comes. There'll be work for you to do, Kay."

Kay shrugged, a little uneasily.

"Kay, you're still knight," Gareth said. "Your name is on the Table. And you'll be seneschal again—"

Kay stopped him by reaching out to grip his wrist. "You don't know that. I killed Loholt, that much is true. I can't—I can't expect everything to be as it was. Arthur may have to accept the word of the Table, and still not wish to look upon me." His voice caught on the last few words, and he sat with head bowed, a hand pressed to his lips. After a moment he controlled himself and went on, every word painfully forced out. "I should like to tell you—if it would not offend you to listen—what happened, and how it was Loholt died."

"It doesn't matter—" Gareth said.

Gawain shook his head at his brother. "Tell us anything you want to, Kay."

Hesitantly at first, and then with more confidence, Kay told them what had happened after he left Arthur's camp on the fells, how he had been held prisoner at Meliant's manor, and how, at last, he had escaped. By the time he had finished, he was exhausted, white and trembling. The sun had gone down behind the crag, and long shadows stretched across the lake towards them. Gareth thought that what he had heard would tear his heart in two.

"So it was Loholt who tortured you?" Gawain said, his voice hushed.

Kay nodded. He looked bitterly ashamed still, as if the evil he had uncovered was somehow his fault.

"He deserved to die!" Gareth said.

"Perhaps." Kay sighed. "But he was young—and trained to evil. I wish I could have saved him." Voice quivering, he said, "I wish with all my heart he had truly been the son Arthur wanted."

He sat huddled in on himself, gazing out blindly across the lake.

Gawain respected his silence for a moment, and then touched his shoulder. "Dear Kay," he said, "why did you not tell all this to Arthur before?"

Kay looked at him again. In the gathering shadows the firelight threw into cruel relief the haggard lines of his face.

"I dared not," he said. "I was afraid that Arthur might not believe me. I could not face his hatred, if he thought I had slandered his son. And if he had believed me—I would have stolen his right to grieve."

Gareth found it hard to understand the depths of this self-loathing, but he found it all too believable that Kay would sacrifice himself to save his king from pain. It would never have occurred to Kay that Arthur might value him, that his loss would be grief in itself.

He did not know what to say, so he made himself busy instead, replacing the fish over the fire and bringing their own provisions to add to the meal. They would have to spend the night by the lake; it was already too late to go any farther, and Kay would need to rest before he was fit to travel. Meanwhile Gawain gave Kay the news he had of Lady Alienor's manor, particularly the orders he had sent to Carlisle for supplies and men.

"We'll ride there tomorrow," he said. "Lady Alienor will be glad to see you. She and her people thought you were dead."

Kay looked dismayed. "Dead?"

Gareth sat down again on Kay's other side and laid out oatcakes, cheese, and dried fruit on a napkin.

"Your horse came back without you," he explained, and went on to tell Kay about the search Lady Alienor's men had made. "Kay, what happened? How did you come here?"

"I was riding by night," Kay said. "There was a kind of madness on me—a terror of having to face Arthur again. Morial missed the edge of the bluff, up there." He pointed towards the head of the lake. "I hit my head going down. When I woke up, it was already getting light. I was caught up in a thorn tree growing out over the water. But for that, I think I would have drowned. Just there, the water runs deep, up to the edge of the crag. I managed to free myself from the tree, but I couldn't climb up, so I let myself down into the lake and swam, looking for somewhere to come out." His face tensed at the memory. "I got to shore just a little way along from here, but I collapsed, and I must have lain there for the best part of the day.

"Some fishermen found me. Without them, I would have died, I think. It was too far to carry me to their village, so they sheltered me in the cave there. That's where I woke up. I was ill for several days, and they cared for me. After that—oh, it seemed easier to stay than to go on. I'd nowhere to go, and I was so very tired. . . ."

"The fishermen visit me occasionally, and bring me food." He summoned the ghost of his old sardonic smile. "They think I'm mad, or holy, or perhaps both. They've been very good to me."

When supper was over, Kay covered the fire with turf. Taking a single glowing twig, he led the way into the cave. A narrow opening gave onto a wider space. The floor was beaten earth, the walls damp grey rock sloping inwards and arching into a roof just above Kay's head; Gareth had to stoop.

The twig Kay used to kindle a rushlight on a ledge at the far side; beneath it was Gareth's sword, set hilt uppermost in the form of a cross. Against the cave wall was a heap of bracken and heather. Apart from that, the cave was empty.

Gareth took one look, and said disgustedly, "I'm surprised you didn't freeze to death."

"You'd better sleep," Gawain said to Kay. "Then you'll be fit to ride tomorrow."

Kay sank down on the heap of bracken. Not looking at either of them, he said, "I—I'm afraid to sleep. I'm afraid to wake and find you gone, or realise you were never truly here. I'm sorry. I think I am not entirely in my right mind."

Gawain sat beside him. "Lie down," he said quietly. "We won't leave you."

This time Kay obeyed him, giving him one glance of bitter self-reproach before he hid his face. Then he sought for Gawain's hand and kept a feverish grip on it.

Thankful for an excuse to get out, Gareth went to fetch the

bedding. By the time he returned, Kay had begun to sink into unconsciousness, but he shifted restlessly, muttering disjointed words.

"This isn't Kay," Gareth said. Anguish made his voice thick. "His spirit is . . . broken. Gawain, what are we going to do?"

"Nothing," Gawain let his free hand rest lightly on Kay's hair. "Nothing but be with him, as long as he needs us."

"Is that all?" He dropped a blanket beside Gawain and stooped to cover Kay with another. Then he took his own blanket and retired to the cave mouth, preparing to stretch himself out across the opening. There was so little he could do, except guard against danger from outside.

"He needs healing," Gawain said, "but we may not be the ones to give it. Kay's true healing will have to come from Arthur."

When they were ready to leave the next morning, Gareth took Kay up in front of him on his horse. Kay was languid, almost drowsy, as though the revelations of the previous day had been too much for him. Leaning back against Gareth's shoulder, he seemed at peace with himself, but even more remote from the Kay Gareth had known.

Gareth felt sick at heart. He wanted his Kay back—difficult, irascible, challenging, with that unexpected streak of mischievous humour. This passive shadow in Kay's body was not the friend he loved. Gareth could do nothing except care for him, hope, and pray.

Especially now that Kay was with them, it was impossible to think of climbing the hill by the same precarious track they had come down. Instead they rode around the lake shore; at the head of the lake they forded a shallow river and came upon the fishermen's village, no more than a group of a few tumbledown huts.

Two or three women beat clothes on stones at the river's edge. When they saw the horsemen, one of them called out, and a man appeared from the nearest hut, blinking in the sunlight. He was squat, balding, dressed in tunic and breeches of ragged sacking, with a wolf's pelt across his shoulders, fastened with teeth.

Kay roused a little at the sight of him, and Gareth reined in.

The man shambled over to the horse, and squinted up at Kay. "You're leaving us, sir?"

He spoke so thickly that Gareth could scarcely understand him. Kay reached a hand down to him, and the man reached up and clasped it.

"My friends came for me." Kay's voice was low, shaken. "I must go, but I will not forget you."

The man stepped back, and raised his hand in a clumsy

salute. Gareth urged his horse on again; in a few minutes the village had fallen behind as the track wound up the hill towards the forest.

"We could help them," Gawain suggested. "Better houses, livestock, seed and tools to plant crops. . . ."

He was rewarded by a flickering smile from Kay.

"I should like that," he said.

By midday they had come out onto the ridge. When they stopped for food Kay sat in silence, running his fingers through the thick, springy grass, gazing fascinated at small, creeping plants, or the pattern of acid yellow lichen on a stone. He reminded Gareth of men he had seen who emerge into life again after a bad wound or a long illness.

They came to Alienor's manor in the afternoon. The first sign of life was sheep on the fell-side, some of them with lambs. As the road descended, they passed into ploughed land, the young green shoots of corn already showing.

Kay sat up, suddenly alert. "The spring planting. . . . Gawain, this is your doing."

Gawain, who had been riding slightly ahead, slowed to let his brother come up with him. "Yours, too," he said.

Kay shook his head slightly, but his attention was not really on Gawain. Gareth could feel his tension as he gazed ahead to the houses of the village.

The first building they passed was a smithy; the sound of rhythmic hammering came from it. The next house along had its roof beams stripped bare, and a man was crawling around up there, renewing the thatch.

Kay called out, "Simon!"

The thatcher's head whipped round. Gareth had a hideous vision of him losing his balance and crashing to the ground, breaking his neck, but after a minute's utter stillness he slid to the edge of the roof and swarmed down a ladder, crying out as he came, "Yann! Gisela!"

The sound of hammering stopped. The smith put his head out of the door. From round the back of the smithy a girl appeared, carrying a basket. Abruptly she dropped it, and ran towards the horsemen. Kay slid from the horse to meet her, clasping her hands.

"Sir—you've come back!" she said.

The thatcher and the smith came up a moment later, pressing forward to shake Kay by the hand, and the girl Gisela ran off up the street, to reappear a moment later, dragging an older woman along with her. Suddenly the village was alive with people hurrying to greet Kay, surrounding him as they reached to take his hand, or just to touch him, as if to reassure themselves that he was real.

Gareth remained on horseback. Surprise kept him still at first, then he wondered if he ought to be trying to protect Kay in case he was overwhelmed by the force of his welcome, but at last he saw that Kay, although shaken, was in no need of help. He was listening eagerly to the news the villagers poured out.

"Sir, Yves and Sibella want to wed."

"The pigs got out, sir, and ate two sheets Mistress Estrildis had laid on the hedge to dry."

"I'm with child, sir, and Yann says . . ."

"Arthur's men brought six cows from Carlisle, sir, and six plough oxen."

"Mistress Avice said you weren't dead, sir. 'Too cursed stubborn to die,' she said."

The whole crowd began to move along the street towards the manor house, drawing Kay with them. Gareth glanced at his brother, whose face was lit with affectionate amusement.

"They might notice us at last," Gawain said. "Say, some time tomorrow morning."

Gareth laughed, and put his horse into motion at the tail end of the procession.

Someone must have run ahead with the news, because by the time the crowd crossed the causeway and poured into the courtyard, Lady Alienor was waiting. The villagers dropped back. Kay, who had ended up carrying a small, red-haired child—Kay? Gareth thought, amazed—handed her back to her mother and went forward to kneel at Alienor's feet.

"Lady," he said, "it is . . . great joy, to see you again."

The effect of his courtesy was ruined by Lady Alienor, who bent over him, tugging at his shoulders.

"Get up, idiot. We all thought you were dead. How dare you go off like that and never send us word?" By this time Kay was on his feet again and she was hugging him. "Kay, we've all missed you so much."

She still kept hold of Kay's hand as she turned to Gawain and Gareth, who had dismounted and drawn closer. She was smiling and weeping at the same time; Kay, too, had tears on his face, but to Gareth's relief he looked more like himself again, the unnatural peacefulness broken up.

"You're welcome, sirs," Lady Alienor said. "And doubly welcome for the help you sent us from Carlisle. Now the manor is prosperous again."

"And so is all Britain, lady," Gawain responded. "For Briant des Isles has been driven out, and soon Arthur will hold all his lands in peace."

Lady Alienor's face changed. "Briant? Driven out?"

"Gawain fought him and defeated him," Gareth said. "Arthur saw what he was, and sent him from Camelot. He went to

Claudas of Brittany, and I hope they have much joy in each other."

As he spoke, Alienor released Kay's hand and moved towards them, anxiously searching their faces.

"Here we knew nothing of this," she said. "But we know more than you, it seems. For three days ago Briant passed through here, and said he had orders to secure the North for Arthur. My lords, Briant holds Carlisle."

Chapter Thirty-three

Kay bathed and shaved and changed into fresh clothes. His few possessions were still in his room, brought back, he supposed, when Morial returned to the manor. When he was ready, he went to Alienor's solar.

The others, with Father Paulinus, waited for him there, seated around the fire. Their faces turned towards him as he went in, so that he paused by the door, self-conscious in the light of their welcome.

Then Gareth sprang up and led Kay to his own seat, carefully adjusting its position close to the fire, until Kay said, "Stop fussing, lad; I won't break apart," just to see the inexplicable delight flood into Gareth's eyes. Gareth brought a stool and folded himself up at Kay's feet.

Gawain said, "We're discussing what to do about Carlisle."

"About Briant?"

Gawain murmured agreement. "By this time," he said, "Arthur must have brought Claudas to battle. I can't believe that Claudas would prevail, now that Arthur is himself again. Now that his knights can follow him gladly."

He paused, staring into the fire as if he could call that battle into being in front of his eyes.

"That means Arthur must already be riding north," Gareth said, prompting him.

Kay could see how hard it was for Gawain to pull himself back to present reality, as he said, "Yes. At least, we must act on that. And if Arthur finds Carlisle closed against him, he will have two choices: to lay siege to it, or to withdraw to Camelot and fortify himself there. Either would give Claudas time to recover and try again."

"That's why Briant has gone there," Gareth said.

Gawain frowned thoughtfully, his eyes still on the dancing flames. Kay traced the gentle, well-loved features, the golden hair burnished by the firelight, and wondered how many of the people who saw Gawain only as a courtier, at best a healer, skilled only in the arts of peace, were aware of the core of strength in him, the fighting man, the strategist, who would reveal himself only at the time of greatest need. Different from himself, Kay thought ruefully, flailing around at random in his efforts to prove himself.

Gawain roused from his meditation as Gareth said restlessly, "Carlisle is full of Arthur's men. What can Briant do there?"

"Not full," Gawain said. "Arthur took as many men as he could when he went south to fight Claudas. Besides, as far as anyone knows in Carlisle, Briant is High Seneschal of Britain." He flicked an apologetic glance at Kay, as if acknowledging that his friend might be sensitive about that. "They'll obey Briant until someone tells them different."

"They wouldn't obey Briant if Arthur came and laid siege to them," Gareth said.

"No," Gawain said. "If you were Briant, what would you do?"

"Kill them?" Gareth had a sudden sick look on his face.

"Not unless he wanted to reveal himself as Arthur's enemy. From what my lady Alienor tells us, he doesn't want that, or not yet. Kay, you were seneschal. What would you do if you were Briant, and you wanted to remove Arthur's men and put your own in their place?"

Directly appealed to, Kay shrank briefly from replying. Even to imagine himself into the situation seemed too close to resuming his old authority.

"I can't . . ." he began, only to realise that he knew exactly what he would have done. "Send out patrols," he said. "North, to see what the Scots are doing. Half a dozen of Arthur's men, with one of Briant's as their officer. Keep them busy, and too far away to know what's happening. Write some vitally important letters to very distant kings, and send out couriers. Imprison a few. Soldiers are always infringing regulations. Strictly speaking, that should be the constable's job, but the seneschal outranks him. No one would blame Briant for anything except maybe excess of zeal. Or—"

"All right!" Gawain stopped him, half laughing. "Providing Briant shares your devious mind, Kay, we can assume that not many of Arthur's men are free to fight for him any more."

"How many men has Briant there?" Gareth asked.

It was Alienor who replied. "We fed twenty when he passed through here."

"He could have brought in more from Roche Dure," Gawain said. "And Claudas could have sent troops by sea, though I doubt it. He would need all his men for the battle against Arthur."

"All this is a waste of time," Kay said, provoked in spite of himself. "What does it matter how many men in Carlisle would follow Arthur, if they still trust Briant? We could sit here guessing until the walls crumble. What's amusing you, lad?"

The last, irritable question was drawn out of him by Gareth, who was grinning up at him; he reached up a hand and closed it, warm, around Kay's.

"We have Kay back again," he said.

Kay dismissed him with an impatient shake of the head, though he did not withdraw his hand.

"What you haven't thought of, Gawain," Kay said, "is that if Arthur's men are imprisoned, they become hostages. And if what you told me is true, then Briant has one very important hostage that no one has mentioned yet."

"Lancelot!" Gareth breathed out.

"Sir Lancelot is a prisoner?" Alienor asked.

"For the death of your brother, lady," Gawain said. "Which Briant called deliberate murder, to give Claudas the right to invade. He called Lancelot traitor, and so when Arthur rode south he left Lancelot in Carlisle under guard."

"Arthur was much troubled," Gareth said, as if imprisoning Lancelot needed some excuse.

"And while Lancelot believes he is imprisoned under Arthur's orders," Kay said, "he will make no move to escape. But if he were free, he could lead Arthur's men to victory."

Gawain leant forward and said earnestly, "Kay, what are you thinking?"

"It should be obvious," Kay said. His voice was tart, his only defence against the terror and exaltation that were invading him as the plan formed itself in his mind. "Someone must go to Carlisle and speak with Lancelot. Someone whom Briant will not suspect of bringing word from Arthur. He will not suspect me. I will go."

He was prepared for the chorus of protest, including Father Paulinus, who scratched furiously on his wax tablets. The only person who did not join in was Gawain; he sat watching Kay with a light in his eyes until the voices finally died.

"Your reasons, Kay?" he said quietly.

"I swore faith to Briant." Kay's voice shook as he remembered. "Arthur exiled me, and I thought never to see him again."

"But Briant knows your name is still on the Table," Gareth objected.

"But Briant does not know that I know." He reached out a hand to Gawain, pleading. "I could say that I returned to him out of fear of Arthur. I could beg him to intercede for me. Once he seemed to find my service useful. He may do so again."

As Gawain listened, his face became filled with doubt and pain. "I don't like to think of the use he may put you to," he said. "I fear for you. And—forgive me—when you speak to Lancelot, are you sure that he will believe what you tell him?"

"We have letters, for him and the constable," Gareth said. "You could take those."

"No," Kay said. "I must carry nothing that would tell Briant, if he found it, that I have had any contact with Arthur or his knights. That would ruin all. As for Lancelot—" He sighed and rubbed a hand across his brow, fearful that growing weariness would not let him put his case clearly. "As for Lancelot, if I offer him a way of retaking Carlisle for Arthur, what he thinks of me will not matter at all."

He watched Gawain, aware of his friend's indecisiveness, terrified that his plan would be rejected for his own safety. "Sir Gawain," he said, needing the little touch of formality, "by Arthur's command I must obey you. I beg of you, give me your leave to do this. The time is coming when I must kneel before Arthur again, and abide his judgement. If there were something—even a little thing—to set against all the pain I have caused him, if I could have some part in giving him Carlisle . . ."

His voice shook; his vision blurred through tears. He felt Gareth's clasp on his hand tighten.

"Kay," Gawain said gently, "if this is truly what you want—yes, I think it is worth the risk."

"I wish we could go with you," Gareth said.

Kay was fighting not to let the tears fall out of sheer relief. "You can't," he said. "Briant would—"

"Perhaps we can," Gawain interrupted. He had a sudden, brilliant look, as if he had become more alive. "Not with you, but following you, a small support force? There are men here. If we could arrange a signal, you and Lancelot could open the gates—"

"Yes!" Gareth said. He was sitting upright, energy in every line of his face and his body. "How many men can we raise?"

"Wait," Kay said. "The men of this manor have been taken to the slaughter once already, by Briant. Are we going to do the same for Arthur?"

Gawain turned to Lady Alienor. "What do you think, lady?"

"I . . . do not know." She was hesitant, coiling a strand of hair around her fingers. Her look was inward. "The people of this manor have already suffered in this war. I will not order any of my men to fight again, and leave their wives and children. But if they will go with you of their own free will, Sir Gawain, then they have my leave." She turned to Kay. "They will go if you ask them."

Kay raised a hand in protest. "I do not wish to ask anyone to take such a risk. Or to bring such grief on their women again. Lady, we have rebuilt here from almost nothing. I do not want to be the one to throw all down again."

"Not for Arthur?" Alienor said.

Kay was silent.

After waiting a little for the reply that never came, Alienor went on, "Kay, these people are not children. They have the right to make their own decisions. It's almost time for supper. We still keep your custom of eating our evening meal together. We'll go to the hall and join them, all of us, and we'll tell them what is happening. We will ask nothing. But when they know as much as we know, then they may do as they please."

Gawain smiled slightly. Swayed by his approval, Kay agreed,

though he was still reluctant. He followed Alienor and Gawain along the passage and down the stairs to the hall, where the villagers already gathered. Between weariness and shrinking from what he had to say, Kay did not know how he was going to get through the meal.

He took his place at the high table, between Alienor and Gareth. The hall was warmly lit by torches. The villagers looked happy and alert; there was an excited buzz of conversation. When Kay was served, he could scarcely manage to eat, although Clemence's mead tasted better to him than the finest wines of Camelot.

After a little while, Alienor laid a hand on his arm. "Speak now and have it over." She smiled, with a hint of mischief. "Before you fall asleep."

Kay stood, and looked around the hall. Talk died almost at once, as faces were turned towards him. It was the men Kay picked out, those who had returned home beyond hope, and those who had been strangers but had made a place for themselves. Not fighting men, to be deployed at their commander's whim, but men with a job to do—husbands, fathers, sons. His heart recoiled still more from what he was going to do.

He cleared his throat. The silence grew more intense, as if his listeners knew that he was not simply preparing a few platitudes about how pleased he was to be back.

"You know," he said, "that Briant des Isles holds Carlisle. What you do not know is that he does not hold it in Arthur's name. He has broken with Arthur. All he has done, he did to bring Britain under the rule of Claudas of Brittany, with himself on the throne."

A faint murmur sprang up in the hall, only to die away almost at once.

Kay went on: "My lord Gawain of Orkney wishes to lead an assault on Carlisle, to retake it for Arthur and drive out Briant. To do that, he needs men. I know what the men of this manor have already suffered, and the women who waited for them, too. So I do not ask anyone to join Sir Gawain. But I ask you to go home tonight and talk of this among yourselves, and then to speak to Sir Gawain tomorrow, after chapel, if you are willing to help him. No one need fear to refuse, for no one will lose honour or my lady's favour, if he does not go."

That was all he wanted to say; he was going to sit down again, but Simon, Clemence's man, was on his feet, down in the body of the hall.

"Sir, we're told that Arthur banished you. You came to us as the Breton's man. Why are you speaking for Arthur now?"

Kay straightened again. That was the question he had hoped no one would ask.

Exiled From Camelot

"I speak for Arthur because I know what Britain will be under the rule of Briant des Isles. It's true, I served him—" His voice broke. He flung out a hand towards Simon. "I'm Arthur's man. Now and always. I cannot change."

Again Simon stopped him from sitting, although he was not quite sure how he managed to stay on his feet.

"Will you lead us, sir?"

"No," Kay said. "Sir Gawain will lead you, with his brother Sir Gareth. Both of them are better knights than I could ever hope to be."

He sat then, and raised a hand to cover his eyes. Beside him, he was aware of Gareth rising to his feet, and felt his friend's hand on his shoulder.

"Kay doesn't tell you why he will not lead you," Gareth said, the young voice ringing vigorously through the hall. "Kay is going back into Carlisle, alone, to deceive Briant. When we attack, he will open the gates for us."

Chapter Thirty-four

Towards sunset on a warm, spring day, Kay drew near to Carlisle. Mounted on Morial again, he had not found the day's ride from the manor a hard one, but he felt tangled in webs of weariness. He had lost strength, he knew, in the weeks spent by the lake; he hoped only that what was left would sustain him to the end.

The westering sun threw his shadow out, huge and attenuated, rippling over the uneven ground. The road had begun to wind across the slope of the hill where the castle stood, and his shadow swung back and forth with it, as if a dark hand reached out to entrap him. Kay blinked in the changing light, his eyes aching, and forced down rising fear.

The castle squatted at the end of his road. From a distance, Camelot might almost be spun out of air and silver, a castle in a tale, not earthbound at all, while Carlisle, grey and uncompromising, weighed heavy on the ground it covered. Kay would not have been surprised to see it start to sink into the hill.

He knew that his imagination betrayed him, prising open an entrance for fear to invade his mind. He was not afraid of dying; that might even be welcome, if it was a clean death, in Arthur's service. What Kay feared was the unclean torment that would not release him into death. For the thousandth time he wondered if the lady Brisane was at Carlisle.

While they made their plans at the manor, no one had said much about Brisane. Gawain had told Kay that she had been angry when Briant had accepted the challenge to fight, as if it did not suit her own plans, but she had left Camelot with Briant, and Kay thought it unlikely that she had broken with the Breton altogether. He had not discussed her with Gawain, in case his friend changed his mind about allowing him to go.

He had left the manor that morning in a bustle of planning and preparation. Every one of the fighting men, from Thomas the carpenter to Ursula's tall son, had presented themselves to Gawain after chapel. There were the workmen from Carlisle, as well, who had come with tools and provisions and stayed to help. A small force, with no hope at all of taking Carlisle if they tried to storm the gates, but with help from within it was not impossible.

They had decided that the attack would take place in seven days. A little time for Gawain to train his men, and for Kay to establish himself and speak to Lancelot; not long enough for

Briant to progress much further in turning the North against Arthur. On the seventh night, if Kay managed to recruit Lancelot, he would place a lamp in a window high in the west tower, where the guest rooms would be empty now. That would be Gawain's signal to attack, to retake the fortress for Arthur.

Arthur. . . . Kay wondered where he was. Like Gawain, he could not believe that Claudas could defeat him now, but it might be some time yet before the king could ride north. Kay found himself trying to imagine how it would be when he faced Arthur once again, but the images he called up shook him with such terror and hope and longing that he had to thrust them away. There was no room in his mind for anything but the next task that he had to do.

He approached the castle gates. They were closed. Kay brought Morial to a halt and called out with all the authority he could gather. From somewhere above, a voice asked him to identify himself.

"I am Kay, servant of Lord Briant," he said.

A long silence. Kay had time to wonder whether he would be left standing outside all night before he heard the bars being lifted and the gate inched open.

He guided Morial through the gap, dismounted, and tossed the reins to a waiting groom. "Inform my lord Briant that I am here," he said.

The command had been given to the gate guards as a group; after a pause one of them detached himself and disappeared through the archway at the other side of the courtyard. Kay waited, schooling his features into impassivity. He was acutely conscious of eyes like darts, glancing at him and sliding away again, as if no one dared to look at him directly. He let his own eyes rest on the grey walls; he did not know the Carlisle garrison well enough to guess whether the guards were Briant's men or Arthur's.

Soon the guard returned with one of the indoor servants. This man Kay recognised as one of Arthur's; he looked shocked and uncomfortable at the same time.

He approached Kay with a half-bow, indicated the archway and the passage beyond, and said, "If you will kindly come with me, sir. . . ."

The "sir" had slipped out; the man looked embarrassed and hurried off, leaving Kay to follow. After no more than a minute he realised that they were on their way to the suite of rooms he had occupied himself when he was seneschal. Kay knew he should have expected it, but he had not, and the discovery broke up his calm so that he was shaking when the servant opened the familiar door and showed him into Briant's presence.

Briant lounged in a chair beside the hearth where another

servant kindled the fire. He poked the servant with one foot and said, "Out." The servant grabbed the log basket and fled, leaving Kay alone with Briant.

The Breton had not changed from when Kay had last seen him. The fleshy, high-coloured face was folded into good humour with a glint of malice as his eyes travelled over Kay. He wore a green velvet bedgown, as if he had been interrupted in dressing for supper, and turned a jewelled cup in his thick fingers.

"Well, Kay," he said. "What are you doing here?"

Faced with him, launching into the part he was to play, Kay found terror threatening to stifle him. All that sustained him was the thought that the man he was pretending to be would be very much afraid.

He took a pace forward, and fell on his knees at Briant's feet. "My lord, I beg you, shelter me."

Briant looked down at him. His eyes were quite cold, Kay thought, not good-humoured at all.

"You left my service when you fled from the manor."

Kay fought for breath, a hand at his throat. "My lord, it was Arthur—I could not face him, dared not. . . ."

So much of the part he was playing was the truth, it was scarcely necessary to pretend at all.

"So where have you been all this time?" Briant said. "And why have you come back?"

"I was lost—ill. I thought I would die." Kay forced desperation into his voice. "I've nowhere to go. No one will take me in. Please, my lord, I beg you. . . ."

His voice cracked. He felt so unstrung it would have been easy to break down into sobbing.

"What do you want of me?" Briant said.

"Let me serve you, my lord. Speak for me to Arthur."

The mention of Arthur had Briant's attention coldly focused on him. Struggling to separate what he knew from what he was supposed to know, Kay shrank in on himself, and covered his face with his hands. Seconds later he felt Briant's hand fasten in his hair, forcing his head back so that he had to look up.

Briant was leaning over, the glittering eyes close to Kay's. "Do you serve me, or Arthur?"

"Arthur drove me away. But you are high seneschal—it is the same. . . . My lord, if you asked him, he would let me live—"

Briant interrupted him by thrusting him aside, so that Kay fell sideways onto the sheepskins before the fire. Whimpering, Kay raised himself. He reached out a hand towards Briant, trembling as if he dared not touch him, but fastening his fingers on the furred edge of the bedgown. "You can protect me," he said.

Briant gave a cold smile. "If I choose."

Kay tightened his grip on Briant's robe. Shuddering, he

bowed his head, feeling the tears start, knowing how close he had been in truth to the thing he feigned to be.

He felt Briant twitch the robe out of his grasp, and then heard him say, "Get up, Kay. Dear God, do you call yourself a man? Get up and stop snivelling."

His voice had changed, the malice gone, leaving nothing but a weary distaste, with even a hint of laughter. Kay drew a deep breath, knowing that the first hurdle was passed. Before he could obey Briant, he heard the sound of the inner door open. He raised his head and turned. His eyes widened; this time nothing of his fear was dissembled. On the threshold was Brisane, robed in silk, a queen's jewels in her hair.

She swept past him, her silks hissing an inch from his face, and stopped at Briant's side. "What is this?" she said coldly.

"You can see what it is."

Briant sounded sulky, unresponsive to her, the indulgent manner he had used at Roche Dure completely changed. It was true, then. Briant had mismanaged things at Camelot, fought and lost and been driven out when he should have consolidated his power over Arthur. Brisane was displeased with him, and he was less besotted with her than he had been.

All these thoughts fled through Kay's mind as the two of them looked down at him. They shared the same venomous expression; even if they were no longer lovers, they were allies still. Kay recoiled, feeling the fire hot at his back. His heart turned to water when he thought what they might do to him.

But when Brisane spoke, it was to say indifferently, "You will be late for supper, my lord, if you do not dress."

For answer, Briant clapped his hands, and a servant edged his way into the room. Scarcely looking at him, Briant said, "Send the steward to me."

When the man had gone, he said to Kay, "Well, Kay, what shall I do with you? What place among my followers would please you?"

Kay swallowed, trying not to look at Brisane, aware of her speculative gaze. "Anything, my lord," he gasped out, "so long as you let me live."

"Anything? Really?" Briant was smiling now. "To carry logs or water, or scrape dishes, or clean out the castle privies? The man who was once High Seneschal of Britain?"

In the midst of this baiting, Brisane made an impatient sound and stalked out again, back to the inner room.

Kay relaxed a little at her going. "I will do as you command, my lord," he said.

Briant snorted. "Then for a start, I command you to get up. Dear God, I can't bear to see a man grovelling. Get on your feet, and try to look as if you're going to stay there."

Kay stood, feeling a little more sure of himself now, ready to abandon the coward's part he had played. He straightened his clothes and dabbed at the traces of his tears with a handkerchief.

Briant jerked his head towards a table in the corner. "Drink, if it will stiffen your spine," he said.

The last thing Kay wanted was to cloud his mind with wine, but he dared not disobey. There was a jug of water, so he poured some of that, and stood sipping it.

A few moments later there was a tap on the door and the steward came in. "My lord, you sent—" He broke off, staring at Kay in blank astonishment.

Briant gave a short laugh. "Don't stand there gawping. I've found you an addition to your staff, Master Steward. Don't waste time in thanking me, but take him away. Find him somewhere to sleep, and put him to work. You'll think of some suitable task for him, I've no doubt."

There was a hint of enjoyment in the final words, as if he assumed that the steward had hated Kay and would take pleasure in the chance to humiliate him now. But the good humour faded as, for a moment, neither Kay nor the steward moved, and he snapped, "Get out, the pair of you."

The steward took a step towards the door, with a hand held out to Kay, half commanding, half deferential.

Kay followed, and when they were out in the passage, he said, "I'm sorry, Master Steward. This is difficult for you." He managed a faint smile. "Try to pretend you never saw me before."

"Try to pretend—" the older man broke out fretfully. "My lord, this is—this isn't fitting! What does he think I'm going to do with you?"

"Set me to combing the dogs for fleas, perhaps," Kay hazarded, striving for a lightness of tone as much for his own dignity as to save the steward from embarrassment.

The steward made a disgusted noise. He led Kay rapidly along passages and down stairs, towards the part of the castle where the servants lodged.

"I'll find you a room near mine, sir," he said. "Though it's not what's right for you." He came to a sudden stop, and turned towards Kay, wringing his hands in agitation. "My lord, I've prayed daily for your return—but not like this!"

Infinitely touched and grateful, Kay took a step towards him and grasped his shoulders.

"I thank you," he said. "But if you would serve me now, the best thing you can do is to obey my lord Briant. Find me a task to do, and forget what I once was."

"Never!" the steward said vehemently, but he turned and went on, more calmly now. After a few paces, he said, "Obey my lord Briant! He's ready enough to give orders, but he has no more idea of the seneschal's office than—than my granddaughter! Who is a fine child, sir, but no more than three weeks old."

"Congratulations," Kay said, a genuine smile tugging at his mouth. "But you know the work, Master Steward. You have no need to let my lord Briant worry you."

The steward sniffed. "Sir Gareth said to me, before he left, 'Do everything as Sir Kay would have wanted it,' he said. And that's what I've tried to do, sir." He stopped, and pushed open a door. "In here, sir."

The room Kay entered was small, with bare walls and floor. In it was a narrow bed, a table and chair, and a clothes chest.

"It's not what's right for you, sir!" the steward exclaimed, growing distressed again.

"It will do very well," Kay said.

"I'll have the bed made up, sir, and the fire lit. And I'll send someone with supper, when it's ready. You needn't come down to the hall, sir."

He bowed, and would have left, but Kay stopped him.

"You must find me a task to do. I won't draw Briant's anger down on you."

The steward lifted his hands and let them fall helplessly. "Task—what task? If I put you in the kitchens, I'll have half the lads slicing their fingers off, staring at you instead of their work."

"Have you no accounts?" Kay said. "Or letters to be written? I could—"

"Yes," the steward interrupted. "Of course, sir, that's the answer! You can work on them here, and no one will trouble you. But tomorrow is soon enough for that. Tonight you can eat and rest. You look ill, sir, and that's a fact."

Kay gave a tiny shrug, the man's concern closing his throat.

"I'll see to it now, sir," the steward said, his hand on the door latch. "And I'll find you plenty of work for tomorrow." A gleam of humour crept into his face for the first time. "And I'll tell my grandchildren I once gave orders to Sir Kay!"

When the steward had gone, Kay crossed the room and leant against the edge of the narrow window, gazing out. He could see nothing but sky, and a jumble of rooftops, and the tears in his eyes blurred even that. The steward's kindness, and his last words with their hint of hope for the future, came close to breaking him down, but by the time a knock came on his door he was in control of himself again.

Two serving lads were there, one with an armful of bedding, the other with logs and kindling. The steward must have told them not to stare, because their elaborate efforts to avoid noticing Kay were in truth more embarrassing than any open display of curiosity. Kay solved the difficulty by pretending great interest in the uninteresting view from the window.

Before long the fire was blazing up, and the bed prepared with fine linen and fur that had certainly never graced its humble frame before. More comings and goings produced a change of clothes and a furred bedgown, and hot water to wash. Kay stripped off his stained clothes thankfully, and was relaxing in the bedgown by the time the servants made their last visit, with his supper.

As he sat down to his meal, Kay felt more like an honoured guest than the lowest of the servants. He had no doubt that was what the steward had intended. His heart eased, and he began to feel that after all he might be able to carry out his task.

Briant had not told him that he had broken with Arthur. He did not trust him, then, in himself, or because he might talk to others in the castle. Kay had a mad impulse to confide in the steward, and ask his help and advice. It was as well he was alone, because the impulse soon ebbed and he realised how it would involve his friend in danger. But he began to explore how he could make use of his present position while keeping all the risk to himself.

While he thought, he examined the meal that had been set in front of him. After his weeks of near starvation by the lake, the array of dishes seemed bewildering. A basket of rolls, crusty and still warm from the oven. A dish of chicken—the cook had a new way with spices, it seemed—enough for three or four. A heap of veal pasties. Apples and nuts and little candied sweetmeats. A jug of wine. When Kay tasted it, his brows shot up; it was the vintage he himself reserved for the king's table. The steward had given him the best he had.

He was going to be offended, for Kay had no idea how he was going to eat enough to do the feast justice. He considered a few austere remarks about what was suitable for the season of Lent, and discarded them. In the end he did the best he could, and shared the remains of the pasties and the fruit with the lad who came to fetch the tray; shedding his embarrassment, the boy gave him a conspiratorial grin and wolfed the lot down happily. Later, Kay slept, comforted.

For the next two days, Kay worked diligently at the castle accounts. He was almost happy. He liked numbers; they were predictable, and they stayed where they were put. But he had not forgotten why he was really there.

He needed to reach Lancelot, but he let a little time elapse blamelessly in case Briant watched him. Briant, however, seemed to have lost interest. Kay never even spoke to him and saw him only at the evening meal, when he sat demurely among the castle clerks at the bottom of the lowest table. Brisane, too, ignored him, for which Kay was profoundly thankful. She might have other ways of watching him, he knew, but he made himself put that possibility out of his mind. If he started to fear enchantment crouching around every corner, he would not dare to do anything.

His first move was to steal a kitchen knife, a long, vicious-looking thing that he honed meticulously on the edge of his window opening late at night when he was unlikely to be disturbed. The next step would be to speak to Lancelot, and he gave some thought to how he could best bring that about. Gossiping to the boy who cleaned his room and made up his fire, he discovered that Lancelot was still guarded in his own apartments.

"Says he submits to Arthur's will, my lord." The boy looked indignant; of course, they all idolised Lancelot. "He bears it all patiently." He added another log to the fire and said, "There's them that say Arthur must be mad, or under a spell. How else would he think his best knight was a traitor?"

Catching Kay's eye, the boy seemed to realise that his last remark had been less than tactful. He caught up the empty log basket and stammered his way out of the room. Kay was satisfied.

When the steward appeared, at the end of the day's work—his fourth now, in Carlisle—Kay said, "Master Steward, I need to speak to Sir Lancelot."

The steward hesitated, giving Kay a very intent look. Kay wondered if he had been too direct; the man was not stupid. But all he said was, "Sir Lancelot sees no one, sir, by his own wish. Only the servant who looks after him, and sometimes my lord Briant."

"Always the same servant?" Kay asked.

"Yes, sir." The steward paused again, and then his face broke into a slow smile. "But we're serving figs tonight, sir, and figs always disagree with him, something terrible. I'm sure I'll have to find someone else to do his work. Will tomorrow suit you, sir?"

"Yes," Kay said, returning the smile. "Tomorrow will do very well."

Chapter Thirty-Five

With the tray in one hand, Kay manoeuvred the door open and went inside. Two bored guards—Briant's men—ignored him, but he was glad when he had closed the door on them.

The room inside was bare to the point of austerity. Even in Camelot, where Lancelot spent most of his time when he was not wandering, he had accumulated few possessions around him; here in Carlisle, his quarters looked almost unoccupied.

Lancelot himself was seated in the window alcove, leaning forward as if he strained towards the very sight of freedom. How long had he been here, Kay wondered. Two months? He himself had at least been able to move around; penned up like this, he might have gone mad.

Lancelot stirred at the sound of the door, but did not look round. "Put the tray on the table," he said.

Kay obeyed, setting out the dishes and pouring a cup of wine. It was a good meal, selected from Lord Briant's table. No one was treating Lancelot as a criminal. Not yet.

Kay stole another look at him. Though Lancelot's face was partly turned away, Kay could still see that the gaunt features had hollowed even more; the taut body had grown slack, like a bow unstrung or a blade rusty from disuse.

Kay took a step towards him, and Lancelot suddenly turned.

"Get out; stop creeping around as if—" he began, and broke off, staring.

Kay met the gaze. Never taking his eyes off him, Lancelot unfolded himself from the window seat. He said nothing. Kay drew himself up. Lancelot had the way of some tall men, of making him acutely conscious of his own lack of height. Arthur never did so, nor Gareth.

Lancelot's look was austere and unfriendly. "What are you doing here?" he said.

Kay was reminded of their last meeting at Roche Dure, and of Lancelot's withering contempt. It showed now in his face and his voice, as he went on without giving Kay the chance to form a reply.

"Briant's servant—of course. But I did not see you fighting at his side. Carrying trays is about what you're fit for, but tell your lord not to send you to carry mine in future. Now get out."

Though it was difficult, in the face of that cold gaze, Kay stood his ground.

Exiled From Camelot

"My lord Lancelot," he said quietly, "you must listen to me. I have important news for you."

"News? From where? From Briant? Go and tell him to do his own deceiving." He turned away and walked back to the window as if the conversation was over.

Kay said, "My lord, what I have to say comes from Arthur."

Lancelot whipped round to face him again. The look on his face terrified Kay, the ferocity all the more daunting because it was still kept under control.

"Arthur? You have not seen Arthur. You would not dare to look on him."

Kay smiled faintly, sadly. "True. But all the same, my lord, I have word from him. I beg you to listen to it." When Lancelot did not move or speak, he went on, "Briant is no longer high seneschal. He has broken with Arthur. Arthur has driven him from Camelot."

As Kay spoke, a flicker of hope sprang up in Lancelot's face, only to be quenched again in the same icy hostility. "Why should I believe you? I saw at Roche Dure that there is no truth in you."

Kay wanted to fling himself at Lancelot's feet and plead with him, or perhaps to lose his temper and batter against that invincible incredulity, but he recognised that the only chance he had of convincing Lancelot was to remain calm.

"In Roche Dure, my lord, you rebuked me when I spoke against Briant's lady. Have you not good reason now for believing what I told you then?"

Lancelot stirred uneasily, and let himself down again on the stone seat in the window. "She may have been mistaken. . . ."

Pressing his advantage, Kay said, "She wove her plots against you, my lord, as she wove them against me. I fell into her net and she thought to destroy me. You too, my lord, sit here now because of the lies that she and Briant told against you. Sir Gawain was the third. In Camelot the lady Brisane did what she could to work against him. But in Camelot Briant made a mistake. He fought Gawain and lost."

Lancelot jerked his head up; he was truly listening now. "Gawain defeated Briant?"

Kay nodded, with a gleam of pride that Gawain called him friend. "Arthur knows now that you and I had no thought of treachery towards him. He has already fought with Claudas, and we believe he must have taken the victory. He will ride north, my lord, and—"

Kay realised as he was speaking that somehow he had said the wrong thing, that he had lost Lancelot again, as the other man's face regained its look of cold distaste. He understood why as Lancelot interrupted him.

"You and I? The saints in heaven know that I intended no

treachery to Arthur. I killed Meliant de Lis in fair combat. But you? You killed Arthur's son. You took service with his enemy. Are you really still clinging to the hope that he can forgive you?"

His voice no more than a whisper, Kay said, "My name still stands on the Table in Camelot."

In two strides, Lancelot was across the room again, gripping his shoulders, his fingers digging in cruelly. "That is most foul blasphemy."

"Yes, my lord," Kay said. "Blasphemy, and a lie that would defile the gates of heaven. Or it is the truth. Which, my lord? It's not my reputation alone that stands on your answer."

At first he did not know what Lancelot would do: go on listening, or strangle him. After what seemed like an hour of apprehension, staring up into that bony, implacable face, he felt Lancelot's hands relax as he stepped back.

Guardedly, he said, "If it is true, how do you know it?"

"I have seen Gawain."

Rapidly, while he had Lancelot's attention, he began to explain in more detail what Gawain had told him about the events in Camelot, and how Arthur had at last realised that Briant meant him no good. Lancelot listened, but he still gave no hint of what he thought.

"And if this is true," Lancelot said, as Kay fell silent, "why do you come and tell me now?"

"No word has come from Arthur yet," Kay said. "Here in Carlisle, they still believe Briant is Arthur's man. Briant plans to hold the North against him, while Claudas still works in the South. If Arthur comes to Carlisle, the gates will be closed against him. He will have to besiege it. What do you think Briant will do with you then, my lord?"

Slowly, almost reluctantly, Lancelot said, "I would be a hostage."

Kay felt like cheering; he had got there at last.

Lancelot spread his hands. "What can I do?"

"In two nights, my lord, Gawain will lead an assault. I will help you to break out of here, and you must lead the loyal men to open the gates."

As Kay spoke, he realised that he had lost Lancelot again. His eyes glittered; his mouth moved in a cold smile.

"Oh, now I see, Kay. When Arthur left Carlisle, he ordered me to stay here under guard until he returned. I pledged myself; I have kept that pledge. Now, if I set foot outside that door—suppose I found Briant and a band of his men? Killed while trying to escape. Killed while breaking faith with Arthur. Oh, that's clever, Kay. Very clever. For a minute you almost had me believing you."

Kay wanted to scream with frustration. He wondered if his

imprisonment was turning Lancelot's wits, though there was a crazy logic about his suspicions. It would be too easy for him to sit here, in fancied obedience to Arthur, until the siege was set and he became Briant's most powerful bargaining piece. By then it would be too late to change his mind.

"You won't risk it, then?" Kay said, letting a taunting note creep into his voice. "You prefer to do nothing? To sit and wait for Arthur's leave to save yourself and destroy Briant, and hand Arthur's fortress back to him. As if you're afraid of any force Briant could send against you. As if Lancelot of the Lake couldn't defeat them all single-handed!"

By the end Kay felt his breath coming short, and he began stumbling over the words. Urgency was pressing hard on him now; he was not sure how much longer they would have alone.

"I have no weapon," Lancelot said.

"When has that ever stopped you? But I have thought of that, my lord."

All this while, Kay had been carrying the kitchen knife concealed under his tunic. He could feel the cold length of it against his side. Now he began to draw it out. Lancelot's eyes dilated. The change in his expression gave Kay a second's warning as he sprang, bearing Kay backwards and wresting the knife away from him. Kay found himself flat on the floor, with Lancelot pinning him down, the knife at his throat.

To Kay's shame, a cry was torn out of him. He had seen his throat sliced through, the blood spurting. Lancelot's eyes, close to his, were dark flame.

"Are you mad?" Kay panted. "Would I dare come anywhere near you, in malice, with a weapon? If Briant wanted an assassin, would he send Kay? Why would he want you dead when you're so much more use alive? Start thinking, Lancelot, instead of nursing that damnable pride!"

To his amazement Lancelot relaxed his hold on him a little. One corner of his mouth curled into a smile. "That sounds like Kay," he said.

Kay was still not sure what he was going to do, but at that moment there came the sound of footsteps outside, voices, and the door opening. Swiftly, Lancelot rolled off Kay and sprang to his feet. Kay raised himself on one elbow, and looked up to see Briant, standing in the doorway flanked by his guards.

"Sweet saints, Kay!" Briant said irritably. "Wherever I go, I trip over you. Get up."

Kay sat up, but stayed on the floor; it seemed the safest place to be. Lancelot had moved away to the window again. Somehow the knife had disappeared.

"Take your creature away, Lord Briant," Lancelot said. "He wearies me."

Briant grunted. "They told me he was here. What did you want?" he asked Kay.

Kay clasped his hands together. They were shaking; this time there was no need to pretend. "I came to ask Sir Lancelot to speak for me to my lord Arthur when he comes."

"A coward's plea, Kay," Lancelot said.

Briant's eyes narrowed into a look of suspicion, flicking from one of them to the other. "Lancelot is an accused traitor."

"Accused, yes, but not proven," Kay said. "Who can doubt that Arthur will believe him and receive him again? His friend, his best knight—" His heart was wrung as he made the admissions; his voice shook with the pain of it. "Sir Lancelot, I beg you—"

Briant cut off his pleading by grabbing him and hauling him to his feet. "Get out," he said, propelling Kay towards the door. "Get back to wherever the steward has hidden you. Whatever Lancelot has done, he's ten times the man you are. Go!"

Kay went, closing the door behind him, stumbling down the passage under the eyes of the guards, until he turned the corner and could straighten up and try to regain command of himself. He was breathing hard. That last display had come too close to the truth.

He was still not sure if he had convinced Lancelot. He had no proof to show that he was not lying. But Lancelot had hidden the knife. And he had not betrayed Kay to Briant; instead he had picked up the cue Kay had given him. There was hope. Kay could only go on, and pray that when Gawain launched his attack, Lancelot would be ready.

Two nights later, Kay was still praying, and even less sure that Lancelot trusted him. A sick fear weighed on him, but he knew that he had to go on, to set the plan in motion as if certain that Lancelot would help.

When the evening meal was over and the castle had settled down for the night, he took a lamp and set it in the window of the room in the west tower that he had chosen for the signal to Gawain. He did not light it yet. If he failed to free Lancelot, there would be no signal, and Gawain would be warned. Kay expected that he himself would be dead, but at least he would not have drawn others into his own danger.

Leaving the lamp in position, he retreated softly down the stairs and along the passages towards Lancelot's quarters. His heart beat uncomfortably fast; he tried to breathe evenly, but the breath seemed to stop in his throat.

He let his hand rest on the hilt of Gareth's sword, feeling the rough-cut jewel cold against his damp palm. This would be the first time he drew the sword in battle; he prayed to bear the weapon honourably.

Outside Lancelot's door was a pair of guards, as there had been before. Kay walked up to them. Trying to sound cool, indifferent, he said, "I wish to speak with Sir Lancelot."

The guards eyed him, unfriendly. "No one speaks with Lancelot. Not without my lord Briant's orders."

Kay did not waste time in arguing. He stepped forward, between the two men, hammered on the door, and called out, "Lancelot!"

At once, both men grabbed him and flung him backwards, so that he staggered across the passage and fetched up with his back against the opposite wall. He managed to get his sword out before they were on him.

"Lancelot!" he shouted again.

He brought the sword round; it jarred against both his enemies' blades at once. Kay thought he had less than a minute to go on living. Without the wall at his back they could have cut him down already. He warded off another blow and felt the other guard's sword bite into his thigh, cold as a spear of ice.

"Lancelot!"

Merciful God, was the man asleep? Then the door opened; Lancelot stood on the threshold, the knife in his hand. Kay saw his expression quicken, and realised that Lancelot had not entirely believed him, not until now, when he saw him fighting for his life.

One of the guards arched backwards, dropping his sword, as Lancelot slid the knife into his back. Almost casually, he jerked it out, grabbed the second man and spun him round as his sword was beating down Kay's wavering defence, and drove the knife into his stomach. The man doubled over, clutching at the hilt, and fell.

Kay sagged back against the wall. "You're late," he said.

Lancelot shrugged slightly. "I'm sorry for your hurt, Kay."

He looked down at his adversaries. The first was dead; the second still writhed feebly for a few seconds, until blood gushed from his mouth and he lay still. Lancelot bent and picked up one of their discarded swords.

As he straightened up again the sound of running footsteps came from farther down the passage. Two more men-at-arms appeared, their swords in their hands. Kay struggled to gather himself again, but as the men came closer they halted, glancing uncertainly from the bodies to Lancelot and back again.

Lancelot raised his sword. "Are you for Arthur or Briant?"

A light sprang up in the men's faces. "For Arthur!" they cried.

Lancelot smiled, and pointed his sword at the first man. "You. Go to the constable and tell him to muster all Arthur's loyal men, arm them and send them to the gates." The man sped off. To the other, Lancelot said, "You, come with me." At last he turned to Kay. "You've done well. Can you get to the infirmary and have the wound bound?"

Kay felt a sudden spurt of anger at being so coolly dismissed, but he fought it down. "I must light the signal," he said. "Sir Gawain will be waiting for it."

Lancelot hesitated and then nodded, as if he thought that might be just about within Kay's capacity. Beckoning to his follower, he ran off towards the stairs.

Kay sheathed Gareth's sword—it had not drawn blood after all—and began to limp slowly after them. He felt dizzy, and had to steady himself with one hand against the wall. The wound was not serious, but he was losing blood; he might faint if he did not bind it soon, but he thought that he could last long enough to light the lamp. Then, whatever Lancelot thought, he would try to join the fighting at the gates, if it was still going on.

He had brought tapers with him, and at the bottom of the stairs that led to the tower room he lit one of them from a torch that guttered in its bracket. The tiny flame danced and flickered in the draughts from the windows as he climbed. He had to shield it with his other hand. Every step was a struggle. He became aware of pain for the first time, pain like a suffocating blanket. His eyes were blurring, so that all around him was darkness, except for the leaping flame. He wanted to lie down and sleep, but he knew he could not.

He came to the tower room at last. It was shadowed, silent. His breath sobbing, Kay stumbled across the room. He had reached the window before he realised that the lamp was not on the sill where he had left it.

Behind him was a faint shiver of movement. Kay turned. The lady Brisane stood between him and the door. The lamp, unlit, was in her hands.

"I think not, Kay," she said.

Chapter Thirty-six

Kay's hand dropped to his sword hilt, and instantly the flame of the taper dipped and sank to a bluish grain of light. He cupped his hand round it again, and breathed more easily as the flame strengthened.

Even so, the taper itself was too weak to carry across the castle walls to wherever Gawain waited in the darkness of the hills. Kay needed to light the lamp, and he knew Brisane would stop him.

Mockingly, she said, "Did you think we wouldn't watch you? Did you believe we trusted you—especially once we knew you had spoken with Lancelot? Did you really think us as stupid as all that? Throw your taper away; it's no use to you."

Kay still went on guarding the tiny flame. Soon the taper would be burnt out, but until then a shred of hope remained. If nothing else, it lit the room with a pool of golden light; the thought of being in the dark with Brisane terrified Kay.

"What have you done?" he said.

She smiled, a cruel look, with something of anticipation in it. "My lord Briant waits in the courtyard by the gates, with enough men to slaughter Lancelot and the few he will be able to gather. Briant is not . . . subtle, but that task should be well within his powers. There will be no help from outside. Afterwards, Lancelot and most of Arthur's men will be dead, and we can give up this tedious pretence of loyalty. Kay, you have given us Carlisle."

Kay could see it all happening as she said, unless somehow he could give the signal. Gawain would not come, and Lancelot would die believing that he had been betrayed.

Playing for time, while his thoughts scurried around frantically, he said, "And . . . what will you do with me?"

The cruelty in her face was open now. "Oh, we shall let you live," she said. "Until you scream for a clean death. Do you really need to ask?"

Kay caught his breath in a gasp of hope that might well have been fear. He took a step forward and reached out as if he wanted to clutch at a fold of her robe.

"No, I beg you—" he began, but there was no need to go on. In her enjoyment of his cowardice Brisane had let him get too close, and he dashed the lamp out of her hands.

It shattered on the stone floor. The oil splashed out in a great star, and Kay tossed down the last of the taper into the middle of the pool. Light flared up; Kay darted aside so that nothing hid the flames from someone watching the window. He could not keep back a cry of triumph. After all, he had sent the signal.

Brisane had flinched back, drawing her flowing silks away from the flames, and was caught briefly off balance. In those few seconds, Kay drew his sword, and slipped between her and the door.

He had meant to lock her in with him, but the key was missing from the door and the only bar was on the inside. He turned and faced her. He knew as if he could see into her mind what she would do now, if he could not prevent her: go down to the gate, and add her powers of illusion to Briant's fighting strength. Carlisle might still be lost.

As the flames died, the room was filled with a sluggish smoke and the reek of burning oil. Brisane, recovering herself in the near darkness, turned to the door, but stopped when she saw Kay. Her lips curled back in a feral snarl. "Let me pass."

"No," Kay said.

"You fool! Do you know what I can do to you?"

Kay took a breath. He became aware once again of his pain and loss of blood, but he fought for mastery of his failing body. He must hold her here; it would not be for long. Once the gates were open and Gawain's troops were in the castle, what happened next would not matter.

"While I hold this sword," he said, "I don't believe there is very much you can do to me." Talking helped to clear his head, and he could see that it infuriated Brisane. "You can reach my mind, of course, but while I stand here that won't do you much good. I think I can bear your illusions, for a while at least. You see, lady—" he allowed himself a smile "—I may be a poor warrior, but I am not quite the coward you think me."

He gripped the sword two-handed and faced her. Brisane swooped towards him, a flashing movement, but when she saw that the sword did not waver she stopped before she came within its reach.

Her eyes glittered. "You think you can bear my illusions?" she said. "Shall we see?"

Kay's fear surged up, but he had expected this, and he was ready. He tightened his grip on the sword. For a moment nothing happened, and then he felt a crawling sensation at the edges of the wound on his thigh. He looked down, and saw maggots slithering out of it, as if his own body spawned them. Within seconds they were all over him, sliding between his clothes and his skin, burrowing between his clamped lips and digging into his eyes. All his instincts told him to scream, to drop the sword, and to claw at the vile things. He remained still, and abruptly they were gone.

"Is that the best you can do?" he said.

His voice was unsteady, showing Brisane just how much the illusion had shaken him, but Kay did not care. He did not need to prove himself; all he needed to do was stand fast.

Brisane did not reply, or not in words. Instead a darkness fell on Kay's eyes. The room vanished. The floor gave way under his feet. When his vision cleared he found himself up to his waist and sinking in thick, black mud.

His body spasmed. The sword was heavy, dragging him down. He wanted to let it go, and struggle and grasp at anything that might help him keep his head above the surface. The mire sucked at him. Panic told him to free his hands, to flail at it and try to thrust it away. He flung his head back as the soft ooze touched his chin; a gasping cry was forced out of him and sank to a stifled choking as mud filled his mouth. The black tide flowed over his eyes.

In the same breath the room flicked back into being. Kay had gone down on one knee, but he still held the sword. Brisane had drawn closer, almost stooping over him, but still out of range of the blade.

Gasping, Kay said, "Your arts fail you, lady. No more than games, after all."

Brisane looked murderous. She made no response, not even by throwing him into another ordeal, and in the brief respite Kay got to his feet again. He had been afraid she might be a shape-changer, able to slide past him in serpent form or even to take on bird's shape and fly out of the window, but all the changes she had shown him in Roche Dure had been phantoms called up in his own mind, not any true change of her own body. If she had been able to escape, she would have done so.

As he stood, still breathing deeply, his gaze was drawn past her to the tapestry that hung on the wall by the window. A flame crept up it, casting a red light into the room and silhouetting Brisane so that her shadow fell across Kay.

At first Kay braced himself, thinking it was the beginning of another illusion, but then Brisane half turned to find out what he was watching. He saw from her face that she had not expected it. He realised what must have happened; a little of the spilt oil had trickled as far as the bottom edge of the tapestry, carrying the flame with it, and in the uncountable moments while Kay had struggled with Brisane's illusions the tapestry had caught fire. Now it was burning well; as Kay watched, flame spurted up the whole length of it and licked at the wooden roof beams.

Brisane stared at it and then spun to face Kay. "Let me out!" she said. "I shall burn!"

Kay assumed that she was tricking him, grasping at the fire as an excuse to pass the door when her illusions had failed to move him. "No," he said.

Brisane glanced from side to side. She had a trapped look; Kay asked himself if her fear might be real. He went on standing in the doorway, the sword still raised, but he wondered how long this exchange had been going on, what was happening in the fight round the gates, and whether it might be safe to let Brisane go. He shrank from seeing her burnt before his eyes.

The tapestry blazed all along one wall. Kay could feel the heat of it. The roof beams had caught and carried the fire across the ceiling. A scrap of burning wood had fallen and set light to the mattress of the bed.

In the midst of the flame Brisane stood, clutching her silks around her with one hand, while with the other she batted frantically at floating sparks in the air. Kay saw that she was afraid.

"Sir Kay, let me out!" she begged. "I shall burn—my body will burn here, and my soul will burn in hell."

"Then it will feel at home there," Kay said, but his heart was not in the taunt. He grew uncertain. He did not want to let a woman burn, even Brisane. It would be more fitting, he thought, to give her up to Arthur's justice.

Still keeping the sword raised, he took a step back. "Come then," he said.

With a gasp of relief, Brisane darted for the door. She pushed past Kay; behind her it looked as if the whole room had formed itself into a ball of flame, blasting outwards. Kay grabbed Brisane's arm and dragged her onto the stairs, thrusting her against the wall and shielding her against the flame that roared out of the door and engulfed the landing where they had stood seconds before.

Exhausted and weak, Kay stared upwards. The door blazed. Smoke and flame poured out into the stairwell. Fire already attacked the beams and the wooden stair rail.

Not looking at Brisane, Kay said, "Get down, or we'll be cut off. Quickly."

Brisane did not move. Kay could feel her hands grasping his arms, her nails digging into him. They felt like talons. In the welter of heat, his heart froze. He turned his head. Brisane's eyes had sunk, grown paler, colder. The skin was stretched tightly over the bones of her skull. The lips smiled.

"Fool," Brisane's mouth said in the voice of the Lady.

Kay still held his sword. He fought in Brisane's grasp, trying to get enough space to bring it into play. The body was vulnerable, whatever demonic thing inhabited it; he had proved that when he killed Loholt. But he was weakened by the wound, and he could not bring the sword round.

The sunken eyes were locked on to his own. The mouth was a rictus, but he thought it spoke, or perhaps the words were a soft whisper in his own brain.

"Serve me. Follow me. I will give you everything."

His eyes closed briefly as he thought what "everything" might mean. "No," he said.

Snarling, Brisane threw him off, so that he staggered back against the stair rail. It was blazing, and gave under his weight. Kay clutched at the splintering framework, hung poised for a second over the drop to the flagstones below, and managed to regain his balance. By then, Brisane was fleeing down the stairs.

Kay stumbled after her. His mind was free, but he thought at every step that his injured leg would not support him. He had no hope of catching her, until he saw that for some reason she had halted, staring down.

Smoke filled the stairwell as the fire spread. Kay came up to Brisane and peered into it, his eyes stinging, following her gaze. Below, a single figure climbed towards them, a tall warrior, weaponed and cloaked, an arm over his face to shield it from the flames as he fought his way upwards. Kay did not recognise him, until the figure halted, a few steps down, and lowered the protective arm. He found that he was staring down into the face of Arthur.

Kay swayed; in his ear he heard the bone-flute laughter of the Lady.

"Fool!" she said. "Do you think this is truly Arthur? Or is it a demon that takes his shape? Remember Roche Dure, Kay! Strike, and kill!"

Somewhere in Kay's foundering mind a last vestige of logic asked him why Brisane would tell him to kill a demon. But that did not matter. His fingers loosened from their grip on the hilt of the sword and it fell clattering to the stairs. Gareth's sword; he would not raise it against Arthur, not even against the appearance of Arthur, not even if the thing tore him apart in the next moment.

"I will not strike my king."

He forced the words out, but his voice wavered and died. He sank to the ground, trying awkwardly to kneel on the narrow stair. Beside him, Brisane spat out a curse. She stared from him to Arthur. The king did not speak, but he took one more step that brought him within a sword's length of her, and raised Excalibur. Flame rippled along the blade, bright as morning.

Brisane turned and sped back up the stairs, hesitated for no more than a breath as she reached the landing, and flung herself back into the blazing room. Kay let out a half-sob of terror. From the room above came a shriek, drawn out, pain and terror and defeat given a voice, and then a roaring as the roof fell in. Kay bowed his head and hid his eyes.

Seconds later he felt hands grasping his shoulders. A voice said, "Kay?" Incredulous, he looked up into the amber eyes of his king. Brisane was gone, and Arthur was still Arthur.

"You're hurt," the king said. "Can you walk?"

Kay tried to get up, but whatever it was that knitted his will to his body had given way. He shook his head, and scrubbed a hand across his eyes. With the fire hungry around them, Arthur sheathed Excalibur, which he had laid down on the stairs at his side, and then picked up Gareth's sword and fitted it into Kay's scabbard for him. Gently he raised Kay to his feet and kept an arm around him for support.

Kay tried feebly to thrust him away. "No—the fire. . . ." he said.

"It's all right. There's time."

The roof blazed, raining down flakes of fire. Flames licked all along the stair rail. The only way to safety was a narrow tunnel, close to the inner wall. Arthur guided Kay downwards, step by painful step. Choked by smoke and fumes, Kay held on to him. Heat and pain and loss of blood were driving him down into a torrent of darkness, but he knew he could not be swept away if Arthur did not wish it.

They came at last to the bottom of the stairs and out into a wide, paved hallway, where the Carlisle steward was already organising a chain of people with buckets of water to put out the fire. Arthur let Kay sink to the floor again, and sat beside him, pulling Kay back against his shoulder.

"Rest for a minute," he said. "I think no one is ready to receive me, I came so unexpectedly." Kay felt a warm pulse of laughter. "There'll be time soon to have that wound seen to."

Kay could not look at Arthur's face, but he found a voice for what he wanted to say.

"Take me back, lord. I'll be your servant. I'll do anything. But don't send me away again. I shall die. I cannot bear it."

Arthur did not reply in words, but the arm he held around Kay's shoulders tightened a little. Kay found that response quite satisfactory.

A little later, the steward, smudged and disordered from the fire, came and stood before the king. "There's a woman in there, my lord," he said, agitatedly. "Or she was a woman. Trapped under the beams."

"Brisane," Kay murmured.

The steward looked startled. "No, sir. It's not my lady Brisane. It's no one I've ever seen before, sir."

"Have her brought out," Arthur said.

The steward looked uneasy, and went. Shortly afterwards Kay saw him giving orders to two of his men as they manoeuvred a litter up the stairs. After a longer interval, they manoeuvred it down again, with more difficulty this time, and paused with their burden before the king.

Kay made himself look. On the litter, seeming very tiny in

death, lay a woman. Her limbs were curled up as if she had tried to hide herself from the fire, and her skin was cracked and blackened and shrivelled away. But enough of her was left for Kay to recognise her. She was the insignificant brown sparrow of a woman who had served the lady Elaine of Corbenic.

Chapter Thirty-seven

Kay woke, and opened his eyes on blurred light and darkness. He did not know where he was. He felt warm. The light was warm, the flickering of a fire somewhere out of the range of his vision, and perhaps the fringes of a golden circle of lamplight.

He reached out a hand, exploring. He was not in bed; he lay on cushions on a wooden settle, and he was wrapped in furs. Under the furs he was naked, except for a bandage round the wound in his thigh. The filth and reek of the fire had been bathed away.

A murmur of voices came from the other side of the room. Kay shifted, trying to raise himself, and at once the murmuring stopped. Kay heard Arthur's voice, loud enough for him to distinguish the words.

"That will do for now. I'll send for you again later."

Movement, and a door opening and closing. And then Arthur was standing over him.

Kay gazed up at him, beyond words. Arthur was smiling, though he looked a little uncertain.

"Forgive me for this," he said, with a gesture towards the settle and the furs. "I wanted you with me. I wanted to be there when you woke. But I haven't had time to sit at your bedside."

Kay was not sure how he was expected to respond. "I don't remember . . . how I came here," he said.

"You fainted when the healers came to search your wound. No—don't be ashamed. It was a miracle you held out as long as you did. Long enough."

"Is all well now?"

Arthur nodded. For a moment Kay thought he was going to sit beside him on the settle, but he remained standing.

"Yes. I came north three days ago and found Gawain at Lady Alienor's manor. He told me what you had planned—and that you had walked back in here alone. A plan worthy of Kay!" His voice took on an edge. "Immeasurably rash and stupid—and valiant."

At his praise, Kay felt tears stinging his eyes. He blinked them away. He could not speak.

"With my men added to Gawain's," Arthur said, "we had no trouble storming the gates. Besides, Lancelot had almost finished the job before he let us in. We lost few men. And all your manor people are safe, Kay. Some of them are in the infirmary, but they'll all live to go home."

Exiled From Camelot

Kay was glad to hear that, but he could not help thinking that Arthur was talking for the sake of talking, or trying to find a way of saying something else altogether. At last he managed to ask, "How did you find me?"

Arthur let out a short spurt of laughter. "Where else was I supposed to look for you? Who else would respond to the crisis by trying to burn the castle down?"

The laughter died. Arthur went on looking at Kay for a moment, a gaze of daunting intensity, and then moved away. Kay tried to sit up, his muscles shrieking protest, his cushions scattering. He did not want Arthur to go.

The king was back a moment later, turning some small object in his fingers, his eyes fixed on it. Then he held it out, and Kay recognised the ring, his own carnelian.

"Gawain gave me this," Arthur said. "Will you wear it again?"

Kay could do nothing but hold out his hand, shaking. Arthur captured it; his own hands felt warm. He slid the ring back on to Kay's finger, where he had worn it for half a lifetime. The gold winked in the firelight, and the flames woke a glow in the depths of the carnelian.

"It feels loose. Be careful with it." Arthur turned Kay's hand to the light, so that the falcon's head was outlined in all its fierce beauty. His voice unsteady, he said, "He still looks exactly like you. My falcon."

Still holding Kay's hand, he sat beside him on the settle. "Tell me, Kay. Tell me the truth. Why did you kill Loholt?"

Kay's eyes dilated. His fingers gripped convulsively at Arthur's hand. "My lord, I thought you knew!" Arthur shook his head. "I thought Gawain had told you."

"No. He offered to, but I wanted to hear it from you."

"But—you came for me, in the fire."

Arthur looked down at the hand he held, and touched the ring. "That was little enough, after I had driven you out. The Table justified you, Kay, but it accused me. I have never stepped so far outside the will of God." He broke off and shook his head impatiently. "You're my brother. Was I supposed to leave you to burn?"

Kay was beyond speaking again. He could only look at their clasped hands, and the lambent flame of the ring.

"It's over, Kay." Arthur's voice was half stifled, too. "All's well between us. But I must hear the truth, and hear it from you."

Painfully, every word dredged out of the depths of him, Kay told the story. By the time he had finished, he trembled with exhaustion, and his face was streaked with tears.

Arthur said, "Loholt had . . . given himself to evil."

His gaze was dark and abstracted. Kay could not bear to see the sorrow in his face.

"At the end, my lord," he said, "I think he wished to go back. I think he wanted to renounce the devilish thing that possessed him. He may not be truly lost."

"I pray you're right." Arthur sighed. "I misjudged him. I saw what I wanted to see. I let my need for a son blind me, and from then on everything I set my hand to went wrong." He focused his gaze on Kay again; Kay could scarcely bear what he saw in Arthur's face. "I drove you so far away from me that you could not trust me any longer. You could not bring your trouble to me."

"I should have—"

"No." Arthur's voice had grown harsh. "If you had told me this at All Hallows, would I have believed you, or forgiven you? We were so far apart that we could not reach out to each other, and the fault for that was mine."

"My lord," Kay said, "you are the king. You cannot—"

"The king should be a man, too, or he is nothing. That's my curse, Kay, that I look out at my kingdom and miss what is close to me. I've taken you for granted. You're lodged so deep in my heart that I came close to forgetting you were there. How long since you came to me without being sent for? How long since you called me Arthur?"

The questions did not ask for a reply; in any case, Kay could not have made one.

Arthur said, "I was grieved, and angry, but I should have remembered what I've always known." His voice quivered as if he was on the verge of laughter, or tears. "I've never met anyone with such a . . . fatal capacity for running into trouble. Or anyone so—so passionately loyal to me. I forgot that, and I almost destroyed you."

To Kay it sounded almost as if Arthur was about to ask his forgiveness. He did not think he could bear that. He kept his eyes fixed on their clasped hands. "My lord . . . Arthur," he whispered. "I wanted to win such honour for you, but I've failed in everything. I've tried so hard to be different—"

Arthur released his hands, only to clasp him by the shoulders. "Oh, no, Kay, don't ever change." His voice was suddenly joyous. "Be Kay still—as difficult and cross-grained and obstinate as you always have been. Be the critic of our courtliness. Be the voice that divides honour from hypocrisy. Go on making a nuisance of yourself and stop us from becoming smug. Go on needling us and irritating us and snapping at us, in case we ever forget that nothing in this world can reach perfection. Be yourself, Kay. Be what we need."

Gazing up into the blazing golden eyes, Kay felt that it might almost be possible.

✥ ✥ ✥

Exiled From Camelot

Gawain paused at the foot of the stairs that led to Arthur's rooms. The late afternoon sun laid a bar of light across the stone-flagged passage; the stairs led up into shadow.

He was tired; he had not slept since he had led the assault on Carlisle. He had still not recovered from the surprise of being left in command, even after Arthur had joined him with his men, more than doubling the numbers of the little band he had mustered from the manor. He was still more surprised to find himself in charge now, with the king and Lancelot under the same roof. The greater part of him would have been quite content to be left to his usual work, with the healers.

Now he had to report that Carlisle was secure. Briant des Isles, and his men who still lived, were under guard. Arthur's own troops had taken their places at the gates and in the watch towers. The dead—thankfully few on either side—were ready for burial and the wounded were being cared for. The fire was out, and repairs were already under way. The steward was preparing a feast in celebration and had come to Gawain anxiously asking if Sir Kay would be fit to preside over it.

Gawain could not answer that question. He had seen Kay twice since his troops had broken into the castle—once lying on the floor at the foot of the west tower, his head in Arthur's lap while one of the healers bandaged a wound in his leg, once bundled up in furs on the settle in Arthur's room. Both times he had looked like a warmed-up corpse. As well as reporting to Arthur, Gawain was anxious to find out how Kay was now.

As he started up the stairs, rapid footsteps overtook him: Gareth. He carried Kay's sword in its sheath.

"All secure?" Gareth said, and without waiting for a reply went on enthusiastically, "I've never seen a man look more relieved than the constable! Kay was right—Briant had taken over his authority and started imprisoning Arthur's men with next to no excuse. The constable thought it was Arthur's wish, and couldn't imagine what he thought he was doing. I told him that—"

He broke off as they reached Arthur's door and Gawain tapped on it. Arthur's voice told them to come in. The king sat at the table, writing; on the other side of the room Kay sat in a chair by the fire, drowsing, his head supported by the carving at the side. He was wearing a velvet bedgown too big for him, that obviously belonged to Arthur. He looked ill and exhausted; he also looked tranquil, cared-for, at rest.

Kay roused at the sound of the door, and smiled at his friends as they came in. Gareth went over and sat before the fire, at his feet, the sword laid at his side.

"Get up, Gareth, you idiot," Kay said. His voice held laughter, not rebuke. "You should be kneeling to the king."

Gareth gave him the look of a mischievous but obedient child, and stayed where he was.

Arthur watched them with a tolerant expression, and then turned to Gawain. "Well?"

"All is well, my lord. Carlisle is yours again." He reported rapidly on the various arrangements he had made. "And the steward is organising an exceptionally splendid meal to celebrate."

Arthur ran his hands through his hair. "I had thought to have supper here—just the four of us, and Lancelot." He sighed. "But I suppose we must make the gesture. Kay, will you be well enough? I want you to fill my cup for me."

Kay started up, hands on the arms of his chair. Gawain saw, with a stab of joy, that he wore Arthur's ring again. Burning spots of colour had sprung up in his cheeks. "My lord—you still wish me to be seneschal?"

Arthur went to him and gathered Kay's hand into his own. "I thought all that was understood. Of course I want you to be seneschal. Who else can do the job? Who else can I give it to? Gareth? God forbid! The court would starve in a fortnight!"

At his feet, Gareth let out a small explosion of laughter. Kay looked down at him, eyes glinting, but his voice was affectionate as he said, "Gareth is most skilful with a pot-scourer."

"There, Sir Gareth," Arthur said. "Praise any knight should be proud of." More seriously, he added, "Truly, we should honour all skills, if they are offered in true service." He relinquished Kay's hand, and went back to the table where he began to pour wine, shaking his head at Gawain when he offered to do it for him.

"So we shall feast tonight," Arthur said. "Kay, you had better send for the steward, and have him find you something fit to wear."

As the king handed round the wine cups, Gawain remembered something he had not said.

"My lord, I think you should speak to Lancelot." Arthur looked at him inquiringly, but said nothing. "When the fighting was over, he went back to his own apartments. He says that he still thinks of himself as your prisoner, and will not presume to come into your presence until you send for him."

Arthur frowned, and let out another faint sigh. "Unnecessary. But I understand how he feels. I will go and speak with him. He must feast with us, too."

"And you must decide what to do about Briant," Gawain said.

"He will certainly not feast with us!"

"Briant lives?" Kay said, startled.

"Tediously, yes. It would be easier for everyone, including Briant, if he had had the decency to get himself killed in the assault. As it is, I must sit in judgement on him." Arthur made an impatient sound, and took a gulp of wine. "How can I sentence him to death? Half of what he did was done with my leave—almost at my command."

Kay began to protest, but the king waved his words away.

Gawain said, "Send him home."

"Yes, back to Brittany," Arthur said. "Though we'll let him wait, and wonder for a while. I have a mind to take him back to Camelot, and judge him there." Thoughtfully, he added, "The true evil, I think, was with the lady Brisane, and not with Briant at all."

To Gawain's surprise, Kay was unable to repress a murmur of disagreement, and then flushed as Arthur looked at him.

"Explain yourself," the king said.

"My lord, truly I believe that Briant did not know the depths of his lady's evil." Kay sounded awkward as he began, but rapidly grew more fluent. "He would have defeated you, if he could, by force of arms. There's a kind of honesty about that. And he treated me well, as he understood it. Loholt threatened that he meant to torture me, but Briant never tried to do it. He thought he could buy my service, but he was prepared to pay for it." He gave a painful little shrug. "Now Brisane—"

"Brisane had taken evil into herself," Gawain said.

"Yes. And I feared her. I was repelled by her. And yet . . ." Kay paused, his eyes deep and dark, looking down into the wine that so far he had not touched. Gareth reached up and rested a hand on his arm, comforting. "When I saw Brisane dead," Kay went on, "I think I understood. The true Brisane, the root of all her changes and enchantments, was the waiting woman of Elaine of Corbenic. A small, insignificant woman, a woman you would never look at twice. And what is a woman's power? Beauty, and wealth, and high estate. Brisane had none of these. If she turned to evil to gain all three, was it perhaps because no man would want her or respect her without them?"

He stopped, looking almost too weary to continue, but not one of the three men in the room with him would have dreamed of interrupting.

"She took Briant as her lover," Kay went on at last. "She made a plan to put him on the throne of Britain. She sent out the demon within her into two others—at least two—into Loholt and Meliant de Lis. Together they planned to weaken you, my lord, by entrapping three of your followers—myself, and Lancelot, and you, Gawain, would have been next. She placed Briant in the court, and then how would she have undermined the throne—an assassin's knife, or poison?"

Arthur made a sound of disgust. "Or playing on me to make one wrong choice after another until my people themselves rose up and cast me out? And I was too stupid to see it!"

Kay reached out a hand to him, but Arthur had turned away.

"Brisane's plan crossed Briant's," Kay said, sounding more subdued now. "Briant had a use for Loholt alive, but for Brisane he was better dead. With Loholt as a puppet king, she would never have been queen. I believe it was Brisane's spirit within Loholt that drove him out to challenge me, alone, on the causeway. She used me as the instrument of his death. I wish it had not been so."

He bowed his head. Not looking at him, Arthur said, "Go on."

"Briant did not understand what his lady was about. He desired her, but he had no respect for her. He laughed at her powers. 'Women's magic,' he said. He let her work, but he never truly confided in her or trusted her. If he had, he might be sitting on the throne of Britain now."

Arthur turned back to him. "And for that you pity her?"

"She was tempted, and she fell," Kay said. "She sold her soul for what she wanted, and she was cheated of it at the last. Beauty, wealth, power, love, and respect. . . . If Briant saw himself as another Arthur, why should Brisane not have wished to be Guenevere? But she died the little waiting woman. Lost, all of it.

"She . . . tempted me," he went on, his voice shaking. "I could see how I might fall. At the time I could feel nothing but fear. But now—yes, I pity her. And I understand."

Arthur went over to him and laid a hand on his head, a gesture of infinite gentleness.

"Kay, we all have choices to make. Brisane made the wrong ones. Your pity honours her, and I doubt she deserves it. I must still pardon Briant."

Kay murmured a few words of acquiescence. He said nothing more. Gawain could see that his defence of Brisane had drained out of him perhaps more than he had to give.

As Arthur moved away, it was Gareth who broke the silence, his voice strong and deliberately cheerful. "I've almost forgotten what I came for."

He rose to his knees, and drew Kay's sword from its sheath. He held it out to Kay, the cross-guards balanced on his palms. "Yours, my lord. I bore it when we stormed the gates."

Kay looked at it, but made no move to take it. The blade was fire.

"Go on," Arthur said. "You'll need a sword in my service."

Kay reached out and touched the hilt, and then raised the hand to his forehead, bewildered.

"Gareth, forgive me," he said. "I've lost yours. I had it in the fire, but I don't know—"

"It's here." Arthur crossed the room and retrieved Gareth's sword from where it stood against the wall. "It comes back to you with a noble history, Gareth. Last night it held back Brisane."

Exiled From Camelot

Kay looked embarrassed as Gareth sheathed his sword and laid it across his knees, before he took his own from Arthur.

"I've been thinking," Gareth said to the king, "with your leave, my lord—"

"Surely you don't need my leave to think?" Arthur inquired gently.

Gareth flushed, and ploughed on. "My lord, since Kay's knighthood was taken from him in public, don't you think there should be some kind of ceremony when you receive him again?" He ignored the look of white terror Kay turned on him. "Everyone ought to know that he is not dishonoured."

Arthur was smiling; Gawain could see that he had caught Kay's reaction, and understood it perfectly.

"Kay's knighthood was never taken from him," Arthur said. "The Table made that clear. To try to give it back would be perilously close to blasphemy. But, yes, Gareth—" the king's eyes laughed at Kay "—the story must be told, and everyone assured that I have no more loyal follower."

Kay leant forward, almost spilling his wine. "My lord, you cannot do this!"

"I will have you honoured, Kay. Come, you can bear it. You're no shrinking maiden."

Even the warmth of Arthur's affection could not dissipate Kay's urgency. "My lord, you must not tell this story." He took a breath, gathering himself, and Arthur's laughter died as he realised that this was more than Kay's reserve. "Everyone knows that you accepted Loholt and would have made him your heir. What will they think of you if they know what he truly was?"

Arthur began to reply, and broke off, sudden doubt in his face.

"He's right, my lord," Gawain said, regretfully. "Forgive me, my lord, but your followers' trust in you has been cruelly shaken. You can't give them more reason to doubt your judgement."

"Then they will think Kay is a murderer still," Arthur objected. "Kay, after all the rest, how can I ask that of you?"

Kay had drawn himself up in the chair, with the old, arrogant tilt of the head, his hawk's face alive. His eyes shone.

"It's little enough, my lord. Not much worse than some of the other things they have said of Kay over the years. They may complain about your clemency, but what of that? I can bear it." He sniffed disdainfully. "Truly, there are but a few whose opinions I respect. Most of them know the truth already. For the rest—" he shrugged "—let it go."

Arthur spread his hands. He had begun to smile slowly. "Kay, you give me . . . inestimable gifts," he said.

Chapter Thirty-eight

Arthur spent Easter at Carlisle. The Court was quiet, a thanksgiving for perils past. A few days later, the company set out for Camelot, along with the men from Lady Alienor's manor who had joined Gawain in the assault and now were going home. Even though Arthur intended to be back in Camelot for the Pentecost Court, there was time to break the journey there.

Kay brought a young man from the steward's staff at Carlisle to take over the work of supervising the manor. For the first two days of their stay, Gawain scarcely saw Kay, as he instructed the new steward in his duties. But on the second evening, he ran Kay to earth in the steward's room, where he was writing a letter.

"Have you finished? It's almost time for supper," Gawain said.

"So late?" Kay was abstracted. "I'm writing to the bishop," he explained. "Father Paulinus must have a deacon to help him."

He went on writing, more rapidly, only to put down his pen as a knock sounded at the door. It opened and a woman came in. Gawain remembered her from his brief stay at the manor before the assault on Carlisle. She dropped Kay a curtsey.

"Mistress Estrildis," Kay said, clasping his hands on the table in front of him. "How may I serve you?"

"I would speak with you, sir," Estrildis said abruptly.

She gave Gawain a sidelong look, as if what she had to say would be better said without anyone else to hear, but when Kay made no response except for an encouraging murmur, she went on, "They sent me, sir, the rest of the people. They asked me to speak to you."

"Yes?"

Estrildis reddened a little. "We're all agreed, sir. We think you should marry our lady, and stay here, and be good lord to us."

Kay was utterly still. His clasped hands tightened. Quietly, he said, "Your pardon, mistress. That cannot be."

Estrildis frowned. She looked a good deal less embarrassed now that she was able to be argumentative. "Our lady must marry, sir, and get an heir. And who knows her better, or her people?"

Gawain saw that Kay's stillness was breaking up, was becoming something like uncertainty, as if he woke suddenly to a prospect he had never contemplated. Before all this, in Camelot, Gawain had observed more than one court lady cast glances at Kay, attracted by his high position or his stormy good looks, and he had always thought Kay had been unnecessarily severe in the way he ignored every one of them. Now Gawain began to realise that Kay had never even noticed.

"I honour your lady," the seneschal was saying, more slowly now, as if he groped towards a meaning. "I love her for the noble spirit within her. But I cannot love her as a knight should love his lady, and I am sure she has no such thoughts of me."

Estrildis snorted. "She's no giddy girl, sir, with a head full of silliness." She spoke with all the force of a woman who has two daughters well married. "If you ask her, she'll see what's best."

Kay shook his head—reluctantly, Gawain thought. "My lady Alienor deserves all joy," he said. "And one day she will find her knight—younger, more worthy, and not tied to the court as I am. Someone who will make his life here with her."

"He won't be you, sir," Estrildis said. When Kay did not reply she curtsied again, withdrew towards the door, and added, "Think on it, sir," before she let herself out.

When she had gone, Kay took up the pen again, but instead of writing he turned it between his fingers.

"Kay, are you sure?" Gawain said gently.

Kay started, and shot him an embarrassed look, as if he had forgotten that Gawain was there. "No," he said. "I'm not sure. But I am . . . right. Lady Alienor and I are not for each other."

With a touch of regret, Gawain could not help agreeing. He had seen Kay and Alienor together. She was open and free with Kay, joyful in his presence, as she might have been with a beloved older brother. Gawain was as certain as anyone could be that she had never thought of Kay as a lover.

But he found, as Kay shook his head impatiently and bent over his letter again, that he was almost certain of something else, too. Somewhere, still in Kay's future, was a lady who, although she might never know it, would have reason to be grateful to Lady Alienor.

Kay never mentioned the subject again, and Gawain was reminded of it only once more, when Kay was taking his leave of Alienor before going to bed that same night. Bending over her hand, he said to her, "Lady, do you remember that once I promised to bring you to Camelot?"

Laughing, Alienor shook her head. "Was that when I fought the madness?" she said. "Truly, Kay, that was kind of you. And one day I might claim your promise, for everyone tells me how splendid Camelot is. But for now, I have work to do here."

Kay kissed her hand, and bade her goodnight.

On the eve of Pentecost the road brought Arthur's company to the crest of a hill. Arthur drew rein and they saw rising across the valley the towers of Camelot, imprinted on a pale sky streaked with cloud. Lights showed in the windows, and in the city below, secure within its walls. Unconsciously, Kay let out a sigh. He had never thought to come here again, at least, not with any right of entry.

Gawain, riding beside him, reached across and laid a hand on his arm. "Home," he said.

Kay nodded. Suddenly, he was afraid.

"So beautiful," Gawain breathed out. "Untouched. . . ."

"Untouched?" The word was repeated by Agravaine, with a braying laugh that shattered Kay's mood and brought him swivelling round in the saddle. "Untouched? When the king harbours murderers and traitors? Brother, you should choose your words better."

"Untouched by the war, is what I meant," Gawain said mildly. His hand on Kay's arm tightened before he released him. "It would be pride to claim that even Camelot is untouched by sin."

Gawain followed as Arthur set his horse into motion again and led the company down into the valley.

"As for you," Agravaine sneered at Kay, "I wonder you dare set foot here."

I wonder it too, Kay thought. He made himself smile, made himself speak amiably, without even an edge to his voice. "Agravaine, how could I deny myself the sight of your ugly face every day?"

Agravaine snorted and dropped back. Kay turned away from him, but he could not push the words out of his mind: "I wonder you dare. . . ." He had told Arthur that he did not care what people thought of him, and deep down that was true, but there would be pinpricks, from Agravaine and his like, every day while the affair of Loholt was remembered. And it would not be easily forgotten.

As the company rode through the city, among crowds who came out into the darkening streets to cheer and shout their welcomes, Kay's apprehension grew. He had been ready to die for his king. He was not at all sure that he knew how to live for him.

He slept uneasily that night, but on the morning of Pentecost itself he found there was no time to be worried. He had too much to do, if the Pentecost Court was to run smoothly.

When Kay woke, his servant was ready to help him arm for the ceremony that took place in the cathedral before Mass. He thought that he might have time to visit the kitchens first, but Gareth intercepted him on the stairs and took his arm. "Come here. I want you," he said.

Kay let himself be towed into Gareth's apartments. At the door of the bedroom he checked. Lionors was in bed, sitting up against pillows. A tiny, swathed form was in her arms, a dark head burrowing between her breasts. Kay took breath, and found no words.

"A daughter," Gareth said. "Three days ago."

He was grinning as if he thought he had done something exceptionally clever. Gareth, a father! Kay marvelled. Gareth, whom he still thought of as the impudent kitchen boy he had been not all that long ago.

Lionors beckoned, and Kay drew nearer to the bed, hesitant, afraid of his own clumsiness. The baby slept.

"She lives, Kay," Lionors said. "She's warm."

Still terrified, Kay dared for a moment to cup his hand round the silky curve of the head. Lionors' happiness pierced him, the more so as she let him share it.

"Have you . . . all you need, lady?" he said.

"Of course." Lionors laughed softly. Her eyes met Gareth's. "What more could I ask for, now?"

In the end it was Lionors who had to banish Gareth, warning him that he and Kay would be late for the ceremony. The bell for terce was already ringing as they hurried across the cathedral square and through the open doors.

In the Cathedral of St. Stephen pillars sprang upwards and fanned out into a tracery half hidden in shadows. Below, a myriad tapers burned, as Arthur's knights waited for the beginning of the Mass of Pentecost and the renewal of their vows.

Kay, dropping to his knees on the stone floor, felt giddy, as if he floated in light. His hands were clasped against the crisp linen of his surcoat, his black and silver, that he had thought never to wear again.

Gawain and Gareth knelt one on each side of him. Without saying anything, they gave him their support. Kay was not sure that he could come through this without it.

A faint sighing swept through the assembled knights as Arthur appeared and stood on the steps that led from the nave to the choir. He waited for silence to return, then spoke.

"This Feast of Pentecost is the crown of our year. And more so today, for we have come through great danger. For that especially I am glad that so many of you can be here today to renew your vows, not just to me as your king, but in the sight of God to preserve your honour as knights. But before you take that oath, there is something I must tell you." He paused and then said, "Sir Kay."

Kay grew tense. Iron bands clamped themselves around his chest. He did not know what was going to happen. Arthur had promised him there would be no ceremony. But the king was gesturing for him to join him on the steps.

Gawain, at Kay's side, smiled faintly, as if he knew what all this was about. "Go on," he murmured.

Unsteadily, Kay got to his feet and walked across the vast reaches of the nave until he stood at the foot of the steps. Arthur stopped him there, and turned him to face the assembled company, keeping his hands lightly resting on Kay's shoulders.

"All of you know," he said, "that Sir Kay killed my son Loholt. And for that I exiled him. What you must know now is that since then Sir Kay has done me sufficient penance, and I have forgiven him. Today I receive him again into this company. From now on, this matter will not be spoken of, and no man will hold this death against him."

Kay could not look at the faces of the knights turned on him as the king spoke. He kept his eyes fixed on distance, on soaring branches of stone. Arthur had feared for him, feared that the burden of secrecy would be too hard for him to bear. And he had taken thought. Now, although Loholt's evil would be forever hidden, Kay would not be branded murderer. And after all, what the king said was true. He had done penance.

When Arthur stopped speaking, he turned Kay to face him once again. His face was grave, but his eyes promised warmth. "Kneel, Kay," he said.

Kay was thankful to obey; he was not sure how much longer he could stay on his feet. And suddenly it was all easy, right and inevitable. The familiar words rose readily to his lips. In the presence of all the company, Kay renewed his oath with his hands between his king's.

When Mass was over, the knights filed out of the cathedral. Kay, following Gawain and Gareth, felt a hand on his shoulder. He stopped, and turned. Standing before him was Sir Lancelot.

"Sir Kay," he said. His grave features dissolved into a faint smile. "I rejoice at your return. Camelot would not be the same without Sir Kay."

Kay could not speak for a moment. He could not help remembering Lancelot's contempt in Carlisle, or the moment when he had pinned him down with a knife at his throat. But it would have been churlish to mention it. "I thank you," he said abruptly.

Sir Lancelot paused, as if he meant to say more, or expected more from Kay, but then bowed and passed on. Kay was left staring after him, the other knights eddying round him, until he remembered where he was.

After that, Kay was caught up in preparations for the Pentecost feast. Nothing difficult there, except to chivvy the kitchen staff into some semblance of a proper routine, and wonder as he did so why everyone seemed so inexplicably pleased to have him back.

When he returned to his own rooms with a little time to bathe and change before the feast, he found his servant shaking out the folds of a robe Kay had never seen before.

"A gift from the king," the man said, holding it up.

It was grey velvet, laced with silver at wrists and neck, and clasped with silver brooches in the shape of falcons' wings.

Kay swallowed a treacherous tightness in his throat. "That will do very well," he said crisply.

At the beginning of the feast he filled the golden cup for Arthur. As he handed it to the king, he said, "Have you forgotten your custom, my lord, of waiting to hear of some marvel before you sit down to dine?"

Arthur smiled at him. "Is it not marvel enough, Kay, that we all sit here together in friendship?" He drank, and passed the cup to Lancelot.

His duties taken care of, Kay was free to take his own seat beside Gawain. Back where he belonged, in Gawain's circle of warmth, he could efface himself, and if there were still stares and whispering he could ignore them.

As the knights and ladies withdrew at the end of the meal, Kay lingered to supervise the clearing of the tables. He turned as he felt a hand on his shoulder: Gawain.

"Will you attend the queen?" his friend said.

Kay took a step back. "No, I . . . I have duties."

He glanced from side to side; the servants and pages were removing the dishes and table linen with swift efficiency. Gawain could see it too.

"Would you have it said that Sir Kay failed in courtesy?" Gawain's tone was affectionate, teasing.

Kay could not suppress a tiny spurt of laughter. "Would you have it said that Sir Kay has changed?"

Gawain gripped his shoulders. He was laughing too, but there was a seriousness behind his eyes. "I would have everyone know," he said, "what Kay has been all along."

He took Kay's arm and led him out of the hall in the direction of the queen's apartments.

Before they reached Guenevere's door, Kay could hear the music. Sunlight spilled out into the shadowed passage. As he stood on the threshold of the solar, his vision blurred on the shifting glitter of silks and jewels. Panic seized him; this was a mistake.

Gawain urged him into the room. Suddenly Guenevere herself was in front of him, golden, warm, her hands held out to him.

"Sir Kay, you're welcome," she said, and added in a lower voice, "My lord Arthur told me all."

He took her hands, bent over them, let his lips touch her fingers. What Kay wanted to do was cling to her and fall on his knees in front of her, but he knew that he would make himself and the queen utterly ridiculous if he gave in to such an impulse. He was frozen, unable to move. He fought for breath.

"Kay, you're the very man I've wanted," Guenevere said. She led him farther into the room. He looked in vain for Gawain. Then the queen seated the seneschal at a small table in an alcove, where a board and chessmen were set out.

"I've had no game all winter," she said. "I tried to teach my page, but such a feather-headed boy, Kay, you wouldn't believe! A moment."

She turned away. Kay drew an easier breath. Seated here, with the chessmen in front of him, he might fancy himself invisible. A page set wine beside him, then the queen returned and took the seat opposite him. Carefully she advanced a pawn.

Kay countered the move. His mind reviewed the possible developments of the game, branching out in all their delicious complexity. He took a sip of wine. The light and shimmer of the room, the lilt of courtly conversation, were at a safe distance. With luck, Kay thought, he should survive.

As the game drew to an end, with Kay resigning to forestall an inevitable defeat, the other knights approached to take their leave. It was time for the council. Kay walked down to the council chamber beside Gawain. Since his return, he had not been there, had not seen for himself the miracle of his name still in its place on the Table. Now he saw the Table as a golden blur, the letters splintered. Kay slid into his seat, avoiding anyone's eye until he had taken a few calming breaths and could look up as Arthur entered down his private stair.

When all the knights were seated, Arthur signed to the guards, who brought in Briant des Isles. They led him around the Table until he stood before the king.

Kay could see the change in him. His pose of bluff good humour was wiped away. The highly coloured complexion was grey, the skin of his face pouched like old leather. He looked cold. Though he faced the king steadily, Kay could sense his fear.

"My lord Briant," Arthur said, "I do not mean to bring you to trial."

"Is that your way?" Briant retorted. "To make an end of me without a trial? Is that Arthur's famous justice?"

Arthur glanced down at the Table, and then back at his enemy. His voice was quiet.

"If I were you, my lord Briant, I should not ask for justice. For if you came to trial I cannot think of any judge who would not condemn you to death."

"No judge in Britain," Briant said. "And if we talk about justice, what about your creature there, who swore oath to me and then broke faith? Put no trust in Kay. If he had kept his word, you would never have taken Carlisle. There is no loyalty in him."

Kay stiffened. In silence, he came to his feet, but at a gesture from Arthur he sat down again. The king was smiling quietly.

"Kay's loyalty lies where it always did," he said. "And a forced oath is no oath at all. But if he stands in need of mercy, then so do you, my lord Briant. And you shall have it."

Arthur waited, but now there was no response from Briant, though he had gathered himself as if he suspected trickery behind the king's words.

"Tomorrow you shall have an escort to the coast," Arthur continued, "and take the next ship to Brittany. I shall give you letters for King Claudas. And may you and he take great joy in each other, for truly you weary me."

There was a moment in which Briant might have spoken—in protest, thanks, or more defiance, Kay could not tell—and then Arthur motioned to the guards. They drew close to Briant once again and led him away. Arthur was already drawing the meeting to an end before the doors of the council chamber closed behind him.

Later that evening, after supper, Kay let himself into his workroom. He had a taper in his hand, which he used to light the oil lamp. Yellow light flowed over the huge work table, over the mounds of unanswered letters, untotalled accounts, out-of-date inventories, and all the other pieces of paper that no one else had felt like dealing with. Kay let out a faint sigh. For the first time he knew he had come home.

All this was for tomorrow, but Kay could not resist picking up the nearest letter and blowing the dust off it. Peering at it, he identified the seal of King Mark of Cornwall. What did *he* want? What new way had he found of making an unmitigated nuisance of himself? Tentatively, Kay eased up the seal.

Some time later he stopped writing and looked up as the door opened. Arthur stood in the doorway.

Kay rose. "My lord—Arthur," he said. "What can I—"

"It's late to be working," the king said. "Gawain told me I might find you here."

"I just thought—" Kay gestured towards the piles of paper.

"Yes, yes, I know."

Arthur looked restless. He crossed the room, investigated the wine jug on the table by the window and found it empty.

"Shall I call one of the pages?" Kay asked.

Arthur shook his head. He leant back against the table, his hands flat on it. "Gawain has done well," he said. "Perhaps there's more to him than I thought. Perhaps he has the makings of a king." His lips twisted wryly. "If I have any right to judge."

Kay went to him. Daringly, he put his hands on Arthur's shoulders and looked up into the face of the man he loved and honoured above all others. He could still trace there the memory of the eager boy he had believed was his true brother. Overlying that was the man's experience, the uncertainty, the compromise, the struggle to be a king and still keep alight the flame of those first ideals.

"You are the Pendragon, the greatest king who ever was, or will be," Kay said.

Arthur shook his head regretfully. "Rubbish, Kay. When I almost let my kingdom slip away from me." He blinked, as if his eyes stung. "Brisane . . . skewed my sight. But there—easy enough to blame someone else. The real fault was mine."

He drew Kay into a brief embrace, and then held him away at arm's length. Kay thought his breath would fail.

With an immense effort he drew himself up, head arrogantly tilted. "If you honestly think that, Arthur, your wits have gone blackberrying."

Arthur's eyes widened and he laughed. "Oh, Kay, welcome home." He tightened his grasp on Kay's shoulders and then released him. "Come on, take me down to the kitchens. Show me where you keep the best wine."

He strode over to the door and flung it open, looking back over his shoulder. His heart quiet at last, Sir Kay blew out the lamp and followed his king.

About the Author

Cherith Baldry was born in Lancaster, England, and studied at the University of Manchester and St. Anne's College, Oxford. She was a teacher for some years, including a spell as lecturer at the University of Sierra Leone, West Africa. Cherith is now a full-time writer, mostly of children's books. Her main interests are fantasy and science fiction, and she is currently working on a children's fantasy, The Eaglesmount Trilogy, which should appear in spring 2001. She has a special interest in Arthurian legend, and has published several short stories in which she explores the character of Sir Kay.

More PENDRAGON™ Books from
GREEN KNIGHT PUBLISHING

IN BOOKSTORES JANUARY 2001

The Arthurian Companion Second Edition
by Phyllis Ann Karr

Written in a warm and entertaining style, *The Arthurian Companion* contains over one thousand entries, cross-referenced and annotated. It is an alphabetical guide to the "who's who" of Arthurian legend, a "what's what" of famous Arthurian weapons and artifacts, and a "where's where" of geographical locations appearing in Arthurian literature. An extensive chronology of Arthur's reign is included. Revised and corrected, this new edition of *The Arthurian Companion* is a valuable reference for fantasy fans, researchers, and lovers of medieval romance.

PRAISE FOR THE FIRST EDITION:

"*The Arthurian Companion* is one of those rarely found reference books that one wants to read from cover to cover."
— American Reference Books Annual

GK6208. ISBN 1-928999-13-1. 592 pages.
$17.95 US; $25.95 CAN; £12.99 UK

More PENDRAGON™ Books from
GREEN KNIGHT PUBLISHING

IN BOOKSTORES MARCH 2001

The Pagan King
by Edison Marshall

The mysterious Song of Camlon tells of a mighty warrior who will win the crown of Cambria. This is Arthur's great destiny—or so prophesies Merdin the seer.

To claim his birthright, the simple Welsh rustic must overcome the tyrant Vortigern, his brilliant son Modred, and the other formidable foes arrayed against him. Is Fate the architect of Arthur's success, or is his rise to power determined by the strength of his sword arm and the shrewdness of his advisors? The naive young warrior must learn much about his enemies, both open and secret, and the prophecies that so rule his life before he can step from the pages of dark history into glorious legend.

The Pagan King, first published in 1959 and long out of print, is one of the first modern novels to rediscover the Arthurian legend's Welsh roots. In Edison Marshall's splendid retelling, readers will share the agonizing losses and thrilling victories of one of the world's greatest heroes.

GK6209 ISBN 1-928999-17-4. 336 pages.
$14.95 US; $21.95 CAN

More PENDRAGON™ Books from
GREEN KNIGHT PUBLISHING

IN BOOKSTORES MAY 2001

The Merriest Knight:
The Collected Arthurian Tales of Theodore Goodridge Roberts
edited by Mike Ashley

Noted Canadian author and poet Theodore Goodridge Roberts was fascinated with Sir Dinadan, perhaps the most practical of the Knights of the Round Table. Roberts expressed his affection for the character Malory dubbed "the merriest knight" through a cycle of bright and witty tales published throughout the 1950s in the popular magazine *Blue Book*.

Under the guidance of editor Mike Ashley, *The Merriest Knight* gathers for the first time all of Roberts' tales of Sir Dinadan—including the previously unpublished "Quest's End"—and several other long lost Arthurian works by this master of the stylish adventure yarn and the historical romance. Within these pages, readers will find a collection of tales that are sometimes poignant, often humorous, and always ingenious, as well as a Camelot made fresh by the wry and often scathing eye of Sir Dinadan, who never rushes into battle without first being certain of the need to fight at all.

GK6210. ISBN 1-928999-18-2. 528 pages.
$17.95 US; $25.95 CAN; £12.99 UK

More PENDRAGON™ Books from
GREEN KNIGHT PUBLISHING

IN BOOKSTORES AUGUST 2001

Legends of the Pendragon
edited by James Lowder

Green Knight Publishing's latest original anthology is a collection of stories exploring the earliest days of Arthur's realm. What made Britain ready for the coming of Camelot? How were the Round Table's victories and failures foreshadowed in the tragedy of Vortigern, the tyrant who welcomed the treacherous Saxons as trusted allies; the prophecies and magical acts of the ever-mysterious Merlin; the deeds of Uther Pendragon, father to the future king; or the training and earliest adventures of the young Arthur himself?

Legends of the Pendragon presents stories with a wide range of tones and styles, with works from such notable authors as Phyllis Ann Karr, Cherith Baldry, Nancy Varian Berberick, Darrell Schweitzer, Keith Taylor, and others.

GK6211. ISBN 1-928999-19-0. 320 pages.
$14.95 US; $21.95 CAN; £10.99 UK

All Green Knight titles are available through your local bookstore or by mail from Wizard's Attic, 900 Murmansk Street, Suite 7, Oakland, CA 94607. You can also see Wizard's Attic on the World Wide Web at http://www.wizards-attic.com